FORGE BOOKS BY ELMER KELTON

LONG WAY TO TEXAS

THREE NOVELS

BY ELMER KELTON

FORGE®

A TOM DOHERTY ASSOCIATES BOOK

NEW YORK

LONG WAY TO TEXAS: THREE NOVELS BY ELMER KELTON

This is an omnibus edition comprising the novels *Joe Pepper,* copyright © 1975 by the Estate of Elmer Kelton; *Long Way to Texas,* copyright © 1976 by the Estate of Elmer Kelton; and *Eyes of the Hawk,* copyright © 1981 by the Estate of Elmer Kelton.

Introduction © 2011 by Dale L. Walker

A Forge Book
Published by Tom Doherty Associates, LLC
175 Fifth Avenue
New York, NY 10010

www.tor-forge.com

Forge® is a registered trademark of Tom Doherty Associates, LLC.

Library of Congress Cataloging-in-Publication Data

Kelton, Elmer.
    Long way to Texas : three novels / by Elmer Kelton. — 1st ed.
        p. cm.
    "A Tom Doherty Associates book."
    ISBN 978-0-7653-2976-9
    1. Texas Rangers—Fiction. 2. Texas—Fiction. I. Title.
PS3561.E3975L66 2011
813'.54—dc22

                                                                2011021562

First Edition: October 2011

Printed in the United States of America

0 9 8 7 6 5 4 3 2 1

CONTENTS

INTRODUCTION

BY DALE L. WALKER

There came a time, about forty years into his sixty-year career as a Western writer, that Elmer Kelton reached the attention of literary critics and began being mentioned in college courses and graduate theses on Texas literature. Asked if these developments made him nervous he said, "They tend to make me more self-conscious than I used to be. I have more of a feeling that people are looking over my shoulder and sometimes reading more into my work than I intended to put there, finding hidden meanings where I had not hidden any."

He remembered a story about the great silent-screen comic actor Buster Keaton. After a long period of obscurity, Keaton was "discovered" by critics who began writing about his genius and the deep messages he placed in his films. His reaction to this was to laugh and insist, "All I ever tried to do was make a funny picture."

"I know what he meant," Kelton said. "All I've ever tried to do is write an honest and interesting story that says something about our West, past or present, and about life."

From writing stories for *Ranch Romances* in the 1950s through authorship of sixty-three books (forty-seven of them novels) he remained true to this seemingly simple recipe, and the three novels in *Long Way to Texas* are each representative of his idea: an honest, interesting story about "our West" (by which he almost always meant his beloved home state of Texas) and about life.

<hr />

Elmer Kelton had a model upbringing for a Western writer. He was born at a place called Horse Camp on the Scharbauer Cattle Company's

Five Wells Ranch, near the town of Andrews, in West Texas, in 1926. His father was a cowboy there, his grandfather the ranch foreman, his mother a rural schoolteacher. As was natural for such a lad, young Elmer was taught the trade that at least three generations of Keltons had made their life's work. However, in Elmer's case a gap opened between the teaching and the learning. One story said that when he was sent out as a jingler (horse wrangler) to watch the herd, he had one eye cocked on the horses, the other on a Zane Grey novel; another, which he admitted "had the stamp of truth," occurred when the family lived close to the town of Crane and father R. W. Kelton, called "Buck," was foreman of the nearby McElroy Ranch. Elmer, after graduating from Crane High School, had the nerve-wracking duty of telling his father that he aspired to be a journalist and not a cowhand. Buck Kelton absorbed this news stoically and fixed his son, Elmer said, with a "look that could have killed Johnson grass," and said, "That's the way with you kids nowadays. You all want to make a living without having to work for it!"

Elmer entered the University of Texas at Austin in 1942, his studies interrupted by World War II, in which he served as an army infantryman in Europe. He returned to the university in 1946 and earned his journalism degree in 1948, a year after he married Anna Lipp, with whom he fell in love in Austria. Ann, as she is known, and Elmer were married sixty-two years.

After a couple dozen rejections, he made his first professional fiction appearance in 1947 with a light cowboy tale titled "There's Always a Second Chance" in *Ranch Romances,* a Chicago-based magazine that had among its devoted fans Beatrice "Bea" Kelton, Elmer's mother. Fanny Ellsworth, editor of the fifteen-cent monthly pulp, paid Elmer fifty dollars for his story and seems to have taken the Texan under her wing as he became a regular contributor to the popular magazine. He also sold stories to other pulps, such as *Leading Western, Western Romances, Thrilling Ranch Stories,* and *Texas Ranger Maga-*

zine, and in 1955, with his first novel, *Hot Iron,* he began a long association with Ballantine Books of New York.

For all these successes, Kelton abided by the time-honored warning to newly published writers: Don't quit your day job! In fact he abided by the warning for over forty years, working as a livestock journalist for the *San Angelo Standard-Times,* serving as editor of the *Sheep and Goat Raiser Magazine,* and as associate editor of the *Livestock Weekly,* all based in Kelton's hometown of San Angelo, Texas. He retired from newspaper work in 1992 to devote full time to book writing.

Joe Pepper was published in 1975 under the byline "Lee McElroy," the name deriving from two Texas cattle ranches, the McElroy and the Lea, where Kelton's father worked as a cowhand and where Elmer grew up. He had used a pen name once before, in 1969 when his novel *Shotgun Settlement* appeared as "by Alex Hawk." That year three of his novels were released and his publisher, Ballantine Books, must have advised he invent a name for one of them.

By 1975, after twenty novels in the nineteen years since *Hot Iron* appeared in 1956, Kelton was on a well-earned roll. His *The Day the Cowboys Quit* (1971) and *The Time It Never Rained* (1973) had each earned prestigious literary awards, and now he was at work on a book that would be among the beloved cowboy stories of American literature, *The Good Old Boys.* And he had an idea simmering about a confrontation on the Texas plains between a Comanche warrior and a buffalo soldier of the 10th Cavalry. This would become the 1980 masterpiece titled *The Wolf and the Buffalo.*

Among its distinctions, *Joe Pepper* is one of only a handful of Kelton novels—*Shadow of a Star, Horsehead Crossing,* and *Manhunters* are others—dealing with outlaws and deadly gunplay. Early in the book, Pepper, while he awaits the hangman, reveals his capacity for violence to a preacher and tells of shooting dead a *pistolero* named Threadgill. Without ever taking his six-shooter from his belt, he "caught him at about the second button on his shirt," Joe says. And as to letting another enemy, an evil cattleman named Ordway, live, he states, "It taught me a lesson I didn't forget as the years went by: when in doubt, *kill* the son of a bitch." (Later on, seeking revenge, he confronts this old nemesis, saying, "You know what hate tastes like?" then shows Ordway what it tastes like.)

One other thing about Joe Pepper. For a man who is on the wrong side of the law most of the time, he has a keen sense of justice. It is up to the reader to decide whether he's a good guy, or bad, or something between.

In *Long Way to Texas,* originally published in 1976, Kelton returns to a favorite historical era, the Civil War, for the story's backdrop. The book also returns to the saga of the Buckalew family of Texas, which he began in 1965 with *Massacre at Goliad* and continued with *After the Bugles* in 1967 and *Bowie's Mine* in 1971.

The year is 1862 and the "long way from Texas" is actually the 350 miles separating Glorieta Pass, in northern New Mexico Territory, from El Paso. An obscure but decisive battle—so important it became known as the "Gettysburg of the West"—took place at Glorieta Pass in March 1862, in which Confederate soldiers attempted to rout a Union Army force from a strategic area southeast of Santa Fe. After two days of fighting, the Confederates retreated.

In Kelton's story of the aftermath of the battle, Lieutenant David Buckalew and the men of the Second Texas Mounted Rifles, the remnant of the Confederate force, are under siege by Indians and low on rations and water. To make matters worse, young Buckalew is having a personal crisis, worried about his leadership abilities and considering himself a failure and a faint shadow of his renowned father.

He desperately needs to prove he is his own man, a genuine soldier and leader, and at a desolate Comanchero trading post finds a fateful key to his self-doubt.

Buckalew and Joe Pepper are standout examples of the kind of characters Kelton loved to create, people who are "strong yet vulnerable enough that the reader can be concerned about what happens to them," he said. "I like my main characters to have values and to abide by those values against whatever comes, even though in a physical sense they may be defeated."

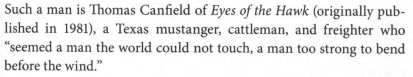

Such a man is Thomas Canfield of *Eyes of the Hawk* (originally published in 1981), a Texas mustanger, cattleman, and freighter who "seemed a man the world could not touch, a man too strong to bend before the wind."

His story is told by seventeen-year-old Reed Sawyer, a sailor who landed at Indianola on the Gulf of Mexico in the winter of 1854–55, was hired by Canfield, and joined a freight cart caravan of Mexican folks and goods to Stonehill, the caravan harried along the route by thugs hired by a ranchman named Branch Isom.

Canfield's forebears were among the earliest Texas pioneers, and he inherited their courage and fortitude. To the Mexican citizens of his town of Stonehill, Texas, he is "El Gavilán"—the Hawk—so called for the fire in his eyes, especially when confronted by the likes of Isom. This insolent newcomer to Stonehill intends to build his fortune at Canfield's expense but seriously underestimates his opponent. Canfield is a man so consumed with hatred and a lust for revenge, he regards Isom as a minor problem compared to his ambition of killing the entire town of Stonehill.

"Elmer Kelton does not write Westerns. He writes fine novels set in the West." So said Dee Brown, author of many books on Western history, including the monumental bestseller *Bury My Heart at Wounded Knee*. In Kelton's novels, Brown added, "a reader meets flesh-and-blood people of an earlier time, in a story that will grab you and hold you from the first to the last page."

Prolific Western novelist Jory Sherman said, "Elmer Kelton is to

Texas what Mark Twain was to the Mississippi River," Texas Governor Rick Perry called Kelton "a Texas treasure," and the six-hundred-member Western Writers of America recently voted him "the greatest Western writer of all time."

He earned seven Spur Awards from Western Writers of America, four Western Heritage Wrangler Awards from the National Cowboy Hall of Fame, honorary doctoral degrees from Hardin-Simmons University and Texas Tech University, a lifetime achievement award from the National Cowboy Symposium in Lubbock, Texas, plus other honors from the Western Literature Association and the Texas Institute of Letters.

Texas novelist Judy Alter, author of the standard critical work *Elmer Kelton and West Texas: A Literary Relationship* (1989), described the author as "very gentlemanly, soft-spoken, self-demeaning, and without a trace of author-ego, unfailingly polite with a lot of West Texas cowboy courtliness and a wry West Texas sense of humor. He is a thoroughly nice man."

Elmer Kelton died in San Angelo at age eighty-three on August 22, 2009.

He summed up his work in saying, "A good novel of the West is just as valid as a novel set anywhere as long as it is honest and reflects reality. My real subject is the human condition, and this is universal."

JOE PEPPER

CHAPTER 1

Well, preacher, if you've come to pray over me in my last hours, I'm afraid it's too late. I've seen a few of them last-minute conversions, and I never put much stock in them. I doubt as the Lord does, either. But I'm grateful for your company anyway. Looks like they're going to hammer on that scaffold out there all night, so I won't be getting no sleep. Far as I'm concerned they could put it off a day or two and not work so hard.

Don't be bashful. If you want to hear my story, all you got to do is ask for it. It can't be used against me now. I've seen what they said was my story lots of times, written up in the newspapers and penny-dreadfuls. Lies, most of them. Some reporter listens to a few wild rumors, gets him a pencil, some paper and a jug, and he writes the *whole true story* of Joe Pepper, big bad gunfighter of the wild West. Damn liars, most of them newspaper people. Tell one of them the time of day and he'll set his watch wrong.

I think I know what you're after . . . you'd like to have the story straight so you can tell it to your congregation. Maybe it'll scare some of them twisty boys and turn them aside from the paths of iniquity. It might at that, though I can't say I've wasted much time regretting the things I've done. My main regret has been over some men I didn't shoot when I had the chance.

Don't expect me to give you the dates, and maybe I'll disremember a name or two. I figure a man's head can just hold so much information, and he'd better not fill it up with a lot of unnecessaries.

I've always liked to tell people I was born in Texas, but since you're a preacher I won't lie to you. I always wished *I was* born in Texas. The truth is that I was born just across the line in Louisiana. My daddy and mama, they could look across the river and *see* Texas; they was of that old-time Texian breed, and it was just an accident of war that I wasn't born where I was supposed to be. You've heard of the great Runaway Scrape? That was after Santa Anna and them Mexicans wiped out the Alamo and massacred all of them soldiers at Goliad. The settlers, they lit out in a wild run for the Sabine River to get across into the United States before Santa Anna could overtake them.

Now, my daddy was in Sam Houston's army for a while, leaving my mama with some neighbors on the land he had claimed in Austin's colony. But when the Scrape started, he got to fretting about her, knowing she was nigh to term. Didn't look then like Sam Houston intended to fight anyway; he just kept backing off, letting Santa Anna come on and on. So my daddy deserted and rushed my mama across into Louisiana where she would be safe. While he was there, Sam Houston and his bunch whipped the britches off of Santa Anna at San Jacinto. Daddy missed out on that. He also missed out on the league and *labor* of land that the Republic of Texas granted to all the San Jacinto soldiers. If he'd of been in on that, we'd of been a lot more prosperous than we ever was.

The rest of his life he always told people he had been a soldier under Sam Houston. He didn't tell them about the deserting, and the Runaway Scrape.

When the war was over my folks went back to the farm, and of course I was with them by then. You'll hear people who don't know no better bragging about what a wonderful grand thing it was, the Republic of Texas. Either they don't know or they're so old and senile that they've forgot. It was a cruel, hard time. There wasn't no money to be had, hardly, and most people had to grub deep just to hold body and soul together. Seems to me like the first thing I can remember is following my mama and daddy down the rows of a cotton field. Time I was old enough to take hold of a hoehandle, they had one ready for me. Only time I ever laid it down in the daylight was to take hold of something heavier. I remember watching my folks grow old before their time, trying their best not to lose that little old place.

I was grown and hiring out for plowman's wages when the War between the States come on. I was a good marksman like everybody else in that country then; most of the meat we ever had on the table was wild game that I went out and shot. There was people that used to run hogs loose along the rivers and creeks, living off of the acorns and such. Every once in a while I would shoot me one of those and tell the folks it was a wild one. They wouldn't of eaten it no other way. Religious folks they was; they'd of taken a liking to you, preacher. But I always felt like the Lord helped them that helped theirselves, and I helped myself any time it come handy.

Well, like I say, the war started. Right off, I volunteered. My old daddy, he joined up too. It had always gnawed at him, I reckon, that he wasn't there when Sam Houston won that other war. He wanted to be in on this one. So he left Mama and the kids to take care of the place, and him and me went off to war. He never did get there, though. We hadn't been gone from home three weeks till he was taken down with the fever and died without ever seeing a Yankee. We gave him a Christian burial three hundred miles from home. I always wanted to go back someday and put up a stone, but I never could find the place, not within five miles. Probably fenced into somebody's cow pasture now.

The war wasn't nothing I like to talk about. My part in it wasn't much different from most any other soldier's. I taken three bullet wounds, one time and another. I killed a few men that had never done nothing against me except shoot at me. Maybe that sounds funny to you, but it's true. There wasn't nothing personal in it; they was shooting at *everybody* that wore a uniform the color of mine. They didn't know me from Robert E. Lee. It was our job to kill more of them than they killed of us.

Everybody seemed to feel like it was all right for me to shoot strangers in the war, but in later years they got awful self-righteous. Some wanted to hang me when I'd shot a man that *did* have a personal fight with me, men that wanted to kill Joe Pepper, only Joe Pepper beat them to it. Folks would say I'd forgotten the war was over. Well, it never *was* over for me. Seems like I've been in one war or another most of my life. I never could get it straight, them changing the rules on me all the time.

I was way over in Pennsylvania when the war was over and they told us to go home. I had taken a good sorrel horse off of a dead Yankee, but that chicken-brained captain of ours led us into an ambush that a blind mule could've seen, and the horse got shot out from under me. The best officers we had got killed off in the first years of the war, seemed like, and mostly what we had left in the last part was the scrubs and the cutbacks. The night after they told us to go home, I slipped along the picket line and taken a good big gray horse of the captain's. I figured he owed me that for getting my sorrel shot. I knowed he wouldn't take the same view on it, though, so I was thirty miles toward Texas by daylight.

That horse was the making of my first fortune, in a manner of speaking. Big stout horse he was, about fifteen hands high, Tennessee stock. Once I had schooled him, I could rope a full-grown range bull on him and he'd bust that bull over backwards. But that was later on, of course. That was when I was still known as Joe Peeler. The Joe Pepper name came later.

When I got back to the old homeplace I found out Mama had died, and the kids was taking care of the farm themselves. Couple of the boys was grown and plenty able. They didn't have no need of me, and one thing they *didn't* need was an extra mouth to feed. So I taken off and headed south with an old army friend of mine, Arlee Thompson. He had come from below San Antonio in the Nueces Strip country. That was a rough territory them days, Mexican outlaws coming across the line to see what they could take and run with, American outlaws settling there so if they was pressed they could always run for Mexico. The honest people—what there was of them—had a hard time. Even the honest ones fought amongst theirselves a right smart, *Americanos* against Mexicans and vice versa. You'd of thought they had trouble enough without that, but they didn't seem to think so.

The ranches had let a lot of their cattle go unbranded through the war because there just wasn't enough men to do the job. There was grown cattle there—bulls three and four years old that had never felt knife or iron—cows with their second or third calf at their side, their ears and hides as slick as the calves' were. Cattle wasn't worth much in them first times after the war, hardly worth anybody fighting over. People fought anyway, of course. Men'll fight when they can't even *eat*. Me and Arlee, we figured there'd be money in cattle again. We set out to claim as many as we could. *Mavericking* is what we called it them days, after a man named Maverick who said all the branded cattle belonged to the man who registered the brand, and all the unbranded cattle belonged to *him*.

Now, there was some people who didn't take kindly to what we done. You ever hear of Jesse Ordway? He was a power in that lower country. He didn't go to war himself, so he was sitting down there putting things together while most of the men was off fighting Yankees. He gobbled up a lot of that country, taking it away from the Mexicans, buying out war widows for a sack of cornmeal and such like. He didn't object to people branding mavericks as long as they was working for him and burning *his* brand on them, but it sure did put the gravel under his skin to see other people doing it. He thought he had him a nice private little hunting preserve. The rest of us was poachers.

But damn good poachers we was. Inside of a year me and Arlee had us a pretty good-sized herd of cattle apiece. We didn't own an acre of ground, either one of us, but half the people down there didn't. Jesse Ordway didn't actually own a fraction of what he claimed. Most of it he just squatted on and used because he was bigger and stronger than anybody else and had the gall to hold it.

I didn't tell you yet about Arlee's sister. Millie was her name. Arlee wasn't much to look at, tall and thin and bent over a little, and had a short scar over one cheek where a Yankee bullet kind of winked at him as it went by. But Millie, she must've took after her mother's side of the family. I've got a picture of her here in the back of my watch. See, wasn't she the prettiest thing ever you laid your eyes on? Picture's faded a little, but take my word for it. She wasn't much bigger than a minute, and had light-colored hair that reminded me a little of corn silk. And eyes? The bluest eyes that ever melted a miser's heart.

She was living with her old daddy on the place he had claimed as his share from the revolution. It was a league and a *labor* just like they'd of given *my* daddy if he had stayed with Sam Houston. But the old man Thompson had had his share of hard luck and had lost most of his country one way and another. He was down to just a little hard-scrabble outfit about big enough to chunk rocks at a dog on. Time me and Arlee got there, he was most blind, and it was up to Millie and a Mexican hand named Felipe Rios to take care of the work. Jesse Ordway had branded up a lot of the old man's calves for himself, and there wasn't much the old man or that Mexican boy could do about it. The old man prayed a good deal, asking the Lord to forgive Ordway because he knowed not what he done.

You'll have to pardon me, preacher, but that's one thing I never could accept about these religious people, always asking forgiveness for their enemies. Ordway knew what he was doing, and he didn't need forgiveness; what he needed was a damn good killing.

First time I seen Millie I couldn't believe she was Arlee's sister. But there was a resemblance; they both had the same big blue innocent eyes. You could've told either one of them that the sun would come up out of the west tomorrow and they'd believe you. I told Millie a good many lies at first, till my conscience got to hurting. People will tell you I never had a conscience, but they don't know me. It always plagued me when I done something I thought was wrong. So most of my life I've tried not to do them things. Other people might've thought I done wrong, but I don't have to listen to *their* conscience, just *mine*.

The old man died a little while after I got there. I reckon he had been ready to go before but had waited till Arlee was at home to take care of Millie. Old folks are like that sometimes, you know; they just keep the door locked against death till they're ready to go, then they seem to walk out and meet it of their own free will. I've seen some that greeted it like a friend.

The day came when we got news that the railroad had built west into Kansas, and people in South Texas began to round up a lot of them cattle and drive them north to turn into Yankee dollars. Me and Arlee had us close to two hundred steers apiece over and above the maverick heifers we had put our brands on. The heifers had to stay—they was seed stock for the future. But them steers was excess, a liquid asset like the bankers always say. During our mavericking time we would split them fifty-fifty. We worked together, me and Arlee. We would put his brand on one and mine on the next. Felipe Rios helped us, but he didn't get no cattle. He was working for wages, when we had any money to pay him. Anyway, he was a Mexican. They let Mexicans maverick cattle for other people, but they was stealing if they maver-icked for theirselves. They would get their necks lengthened. Sounds rough, but that's the way it was, them days.

Four hundred steers wasn't enough to make up a good trail herd, so we throwed in with some more smaller operators and put together something like thirteen hundred head of cattle.

Jesse Ordway tried to crowd us. He brought in a couple of Rangers and claimed we had stolen a lot of the cattle—me and Arlee and some of the others. He bluffed and blustered, and I reckon he thought he had them Rangers in his pocket, but he didn't. They listened to him real polite, then started asking him to show the proof. That was one thing he couldn't do. The Rangers cussed him out for wasting their time and rode off and left him.

Then he tried to bluff us. He brought a gunfighter he had used to run some of the Mexicans off of their country, a *pistolero* name of Threadgill. He was before your time; you probably never heard of him. He was just a cheap four-flusher anyway. He got by on bluff, not on guts. The only thing game about him was his smell.

Ordway brought Threadgill and some others up to stop us the morning we throwed our herd onto the trail. Threadgill was the man out front. The way they had it made up, he was supposed to kill one or two of us and the rest would turn tail and run.

I used to carry my pistol stuck into my belt them days. I never did fancy a holster much. I watched Threadgill's face. Just before he reached for his gun, I could see it coming in his eyes. I didn't try to draw my gun; that would've taken too long. I just left it in the belt and twisted the muzzle up at Threadgill and pulled the trigger. Bullet caught him at about the second button on his shirt. One of them other toughs tried to draw his gun, but a shot come from behind me, and he was already falling before I could get my pistol pointed in his direction.

It was over in about the time it takes a chewing man to spit. There was that big Texas gunfighter Threadgill laying on the ground at Ordway's feet, dead enough to skin. The other one was laying there coughing, going the same way only taking a little longer. I looked around and seen smoke curling up from Felipe Rios's pistol. He had one of them old-fashioned cap-and-ball relics that must of weighed forty pounds.

It would've shamed that hired tough considerable to have knowed he was killed by a Mexican.

I kept my pistol pointed at Ordway's left eye, where he couldn't hardly overlook it. I hoped he would do something foolish, so we could adjourn court right then and there. But he decided not to press the case. He taken the rest of his men and went home, looking like a scalded dog.

The story got noised around, and nobody else in that part of the country gave us any argument. If anything, them old boys came out to help us push our cattle along. A lot of them was glad to see anybody get the best of Jesse Ordway.

I could of shot him right then and there, and later on I wished I had. It would've saved me and lots of people a right smart of trouble. It taught me a lesson that I didn't forget as the years went by: when in doubt, *kill* the son of a bitch.

We had a pretty easy drive, as cattle drives went; there wasn't none of them real easy. We caught the Red River in flood and lost one of the cowboys there. The average cowboy couldn't swim a lick.

We could've easy had some Indian trouble up in the Nations, but as it turned out we didn't. We run onto a bunch of Indians that thought we ought to give them some of the beeves just for trailing cattle over their land. Arrogant bunch, they was. The only reason they had that land in the first place was that the government gave it to them; they didn't have any business charging taxpaying citizens for traveling across it. Couple of the boys gave them a steer apiece, but they didn't get any of mine.

Nearest we ever come to a real fight was amongst ourselves. There was a fat boy with us who owned something like four hundred head—

more than any of the rest of us. Name was Lathrop Nettleton, and he
figured that as the biggest owner he ought to ramrod the outfit. None of
us paid him much mind. We each of us went about and did what we
could see needed to be done, and we mostly just ignored him. He got to
mouthing at me one time, and I had to knock him down. I invited him
to pull his gun if he was a mind to, but he wasn't. Time we got to Kansas
we was all mighty sick of him. I'm proud to say he was just as sick of me.

We pulled into Abilene and got the cattle sold and split up the
money according to the cattle count. You ever see one of them trail's
end celebrations, preacher? No? Well, that's probably a good thing. I'm
here to tell you it's no place for a man of the Gospel. There was other
cow outfits in there besides ours, so the whole place was overrun with
Texas cowboys trying to wash three months of dust out of their throats
with the most damnable whiskey you've ever drunk—begging your
pardon again, preacher. And then there was the girls over there on the
tracks. I didn't go for none of that, you understand; by that time I had
made up my mind I was going to marry Millie Thompson even if I had
to carry her off like some Mexican bandit. Her brother Arlee was with
me, and I sure didn't want him telling her no tales out of school. So I
stayed with the whiskey and played a little cards.

There was a small saloon over next to the railroad that seemed kind
of comfortable. It was run by an old-time Union soldier who had lost
an arm in the war. I kind of taken a liking to him; I reckon he was the
first damnyankee I had ever seen that was cut up enough to suit me.
There was one of them Eastern gamblers, too, the kind that always
wore a swallowtail coat and a silk hat. I figured he had to be crooked; I
never did trust a man that had slick hands and wore a coat in the summertime.

I ought to tell you that I wasn't just the average run-of-the-mill cowboy when it came to cards. In the army I'd spent some time amongst a
bunch of Mississippi River boys who could make a deck of cards do
just about anything but sing "Dixie." I had learned a right smart from
them, at no small expense to myself. Still, I didn't think I wanted to
try that Eastern gambler on for size. I never could understand them
cowboys that knew they was outclassed but still would go up against

one of them sharps. Playing for matches on a saddle blanket is a lot different from playing for blood on one of them slick tables.

Some of the boys from our drive wanted to play him. Normally I'd of tried to talk them out of it, but Lathrop Nettleton was amongst them, and I figured it would do me good to see him nailed to the wall. So I just sat there and watched them play. I knowed sooner or later that gambler was going to suck them boys under and drown them like a coon drowns a hunting dog.

He was smooth about it. He taken his time before he set the hook. He'd win a hand and then let one of the other boys win one. Seemed like for a while he was losing more chips than he was taking in, so pretty soon some extra hands from other outfits sat in on the game. Gradually he got to winning. Along about midnight he was taking all the chips. Some of the boys had sense enough to draw out before they lost it all, but Lathrop Nettleton just hung and rattled to the bitter end. Before that gambler got through with him Nettleton had lost everything those four hundred steers had brought him. He was lucky to have a saddlehorse to ride home on. The gambler gave him back twenty dollars' worth of chips. "For seed," he says. "I want to see you back here again next year."

I might've felt sorry for Nettleton then if he hadn't started to beg. That was one thing I never could stand to see a man do. The one-armed barkeep finally had to put him out of there; told him if he couldn't afford to lose, he couldn't afford to play.

I didn't interfere. I could of told Nettleton if I'd wanted to that I had been watching the gambler palm cards all night.

The boys was pretty well whipped down. The gambler set them all up to a drink at the bar before they went back to their wagons. Nettleton was already gone. I just sat there at the table by myself, glad Arlee hadn't been in the game. When the boys finished their drink and started for the door they asked me if I was coming with them, I told them no, I wasn't quite ready for the bedroll yet.

That gambler knowed I had money on me. When there was just him and me and the barkeep left in the place, he says to me, "The night's still in her youth. Like to play a few hands, just me and you?"

I slipped that pistol out of my belt and pointed it up in the general direction of his Adam's apple. It got to working up and down. "So that's it," he says. "You're going to rob me."

I says to him, "No, the robbery has already taken place. If I'd of told them boys they'd of tore you to pieces and fed you to the dogs. I thought the best thing was to stay here till they was gone and give you a chance to square things up without throwing your life into forfeit."

He blustered and bluffed about not being a cheater, but I had him cold, and he knowed it. He finally caved in. I told him the only fair thing was for him to give back all the money he had won from the boys. I said it might help their feelings if he throwed in a little extra for interest. He turned kind of clabber-colored, but he shoved all the chips across the table. I got the barkeep to cash them.

I told that gambler if I was him I wouldn't wait around for daylight. "Getting their money back won't be enough for the boys," I says. "They're liable to come hunting for you. Smart thing would be to get you a horse and leave now. You could be a long ways up the track before sunup, and I'd be a few days coming back if I was you."

That one-armed saloonkeeper seen it pretty much the way I did and seconded all my advice. He said they was good people, them Texas cowboys, when they was on your side. But they was woolly boogers when they was against you. That gambler walked out of there with nothing much besides his silk hat and that swallowtail coat and whatever cards was still up his sleeve. I had all his money.

You couldn't say I lied to him, exactly. I didn't exactly tell him I *was* going to give the boys their money back. I just sort of let him believe that was the way it was going to be. But the way I seen it, it wouldn't be fair to give the money back to the rest of the boys if I didn't give it to Nettleton too. I didn't want to be dishonest about the thing, so I just kept all the money for myself.

I never told Arlee Thompson the whole truth. I told him I'd had me a set-to with the gambler after the rest of the boys got through, and that I had better luck than they did. I didn't let on to Arlee how much money I really had till we got back to South Texas. I had all my share of the cattle money, minus the little bit I had spent on whiskey and new clothes, and I had all the money off of that poker table. It was a pretty good road stake for them days.

I was a little afraid some of the boys would go back over there the next day and find out from that Yankee barkeep what had happened. Things could of got a little unpleasant. But none of them seemed like they wanted to ever see the place again. They didn't have the money to be going back there anyway, most of them. They'd had their plow cleaned.

We passed Jesse Ordway's trail herd heading north as we went south, going home. We had got out on the trail a long ways ahead of him and sold our cattle early in the season when the price was at about its peak. First ones there generally lapped the cream, and the late ones taken the skim milk. I know Ordway wasn't none too pleased to see us. Them days it was custom to invite passing strangers to stop for a meal or two—even the night—at your wagon. But Ordway didn't give us any invite. I didn't let it worry me. I was already way ahead of him because some of the mavericks I had branded had been his once upon a time; he was so busy branding other people's that he hadn't got around to all of his own. It was the quick that won the marbles them days, and the slow just wasn't in it at all.

Naturally we got home several weeks ahead of Ordway, and I didn't let no grass grow under my feet. I had done a lot of thinking about Millie Thompson. I'd lay awake at night and imagine I could hear her talking to me, laughing with me. She had a voice that kind of lifted sometimes and broke and sounded like a hundred little silver bells tinkling. It doesn't take much of that to set a young man to making all kinds of dreams and plans. I wanted to build her a home and live in it with her for a thousand years.

I had kept that money a secret. When we got back to South Texas I went to listening and looking, and pretty soon through Felipe Rios I found out there was three-four Mexican families wanting to sell out. Felipe was telling them they ought to stay and fight, but he was just a bachelor, and they was family men. Jesse Ordway had been pushing on them pretty hard, running off their cattle, burning their hay, scaring their womenfolk. Not himself, understand, but people he hired for that kind of thing. They knew when he got back off of his trail drive that they was fixing to catch hell. They couldn't look to the law for help. Them lawmen wouldn't take two steps out of their way to help a Mexican.

Without acting too interested I managed to find out what Ordway had been offering them. When I figured out the places I wanted and could afford, I went and bought them. Them Mexicans thought I was one *crazy gringo*, but they was tickled to take my money and run. One of them told me Jesse Ordway would be shoveling dirt in my face before the first cold norther of the winter. But I reckon he figured it was better mine than his, because he was sure glad to take what I offered him.

I oughtn't to've been, but I was some surprised to find out that Millie Thompson wanted to marry me as much as I wanted to marry her. I had thought I might have to argue with her. You wouldn't think so to see me like I am now, an old man, but there was some folks—women anyway—who used to say I was handsome them days. I never was one to argue much with a woman.

We had us a church wedding with all the trimmings. Surprise you, preacher? Bet from all the things you heard about me, you thought I was never in church in my life. But I was, once or twice before that and at least once since that I can remember. There was a time long years ago when I climbed up into a church loft to get away from a bunch of angry old boys that was after me, but there wasn't no praying done that time, not that I recall.

We took us a short wedding trip to San Antonio . . . stayed in the best suite of rooms we could get in the Menger Hotel, just down the hall from where Captain Richard King himself was holding forth. The *King Ranch* King, you know. Looking at him, I even taken a notion that if I worked extra hard and played my cards right, I might get to be as big a man in the cattle business someday as he was.

You a married man? Then I suppose you know how sweet things was for me and Millie for a while. That picture I showed you in the back of my watch . . . she had that made in San Antonio. You can see the sparkle in her eyes if you look close. Oh, that was a happy time.

I never completely put Jesse Ordway out of my mind, though. I kind of kept track of where I thought he would be, one day to the next. I had us a crew of carpenters camping out and building us a house before Ordway ever got home. Naturally he taken the Lord's name in vain when he found out what I had done. The places I picked was all on the river. The Mexicans had been doing a little irrigation, and there was a lot more good land that a man could have put into farms if he had the inclination and the strong back to do it. Ordway had figured on taking that land dirt cheap and growing a lot of feed on it so he could run even more cows than he already had. And I had come along and set myself square down in the middle of his road.

Couple days after he got home he came over to the place where I had the carpenters working. It was like he didn't even see that house, like all he could see was me, and he sure didn't appreciate the view. He told me I had as much as stolen the land from him, and I told him I had bought it free and clear from the previous rightful owners, and now I had all the papers to show that I was the present rightful owner, and he could go soak his head in a muddy tank.

He says to me, "You know what I mean. You'll have no luck here. You'd do a lot better to move far away and start over." He offered to buy the land from me at seventy-five cents on the dollar. The other twenty-five percent I could mark down on the books as a fee for education.

By this time he had hired him another gunhand, a beady-eyed *pistolero* named Sorrells. You probably never heard of him. He had a right smart of a local reputation, but that was a long time ago. This Sorrells sat on his horse alongside Ordway. Dun horse it was, best I can recollect; I remember thinking to myself that if anybody was to shoot Sorrells—which was more than likely—maybe I could buy that horse off of the sheriff. Sorrells didn't say nothing, just sat there and tried to look mean. I taken him to be of about the same caliber as Threadgill, the other one Ordway had sicced onto me, and I had salted him away without no sweat on my part.

I told Ordway I'd buy *him* out at fifty cents on the dollar, which would've been a good deal on his part because he didn't own half of what he claimed. I'd of had to steal the money someplace if he had taken me up, but I was satisfied I could do it. Ordway just stared at me, hard. Sorrells kept looking from me to Ordway and back to me again, waiting for Ordway to tell him to go ahead and kill me. He was awful anxious to earn his wages; I reckon he liked to see that a man got his money's worth. But Ordway had a pretty good memory, and maybe he thought I'd of shot him as well as Sorrells if he'd of given me the excuse. He was right; I sure as hell would.

Felipe Rios was there too, a few steps off to one side of me.

Ordway caved. He backed his horse up a little and told me I'd better chew on it and be awful careful of my luck. I could tell when they rode away that Sorrells was disappointed. Some people just naturally enjoy their work more than others do.

Me and Millie had been sleeping in one of the old Mexican houses while we waited for our new one to be finished. Fresh married like we was, it didn't make a particle of difference where we slept. The days was way too long anyhow, seemed like, and the nights too short.

Well, that night turned out to be long enough. The Mexican house was maybe two hundred yards from where the new one was going up. Sometime about midnight I heard shooting. I jumped out of bed and grabbed my britches. The shooting stopped before I could get my pants and boots on and run outside. I could see the new house was afire. I could see people running around down there, and I could hear horses. I couldn't shoot because I was apt to hit the carpenters or Felipe; he was camped down there with them. I heard the horses loping away in the dark and men hollering in Mexican. But they wasn't Mexicans, I could tell. A man don't need much of an ear to tell when it's some *gringo* trying to *talk* Mexican.

There wasn't nothing we could do to save the house. It was plumb gone. So was one of the carpenters; they had put so much lead in him that it taken two extra pallbearers to carry him. Felipe wanted to chase after them, but Millie was scared for me to leave her alone.

Next day I called out the law. They said it was Mexican bandits. I knowed they knowed better, and I cussed them for a bunch of chicken-livered cowards. But they was local, and they was afraid of Jesse Ordway.

I thought once that I was going to get even. Ordway was married; had him a thin, shivery little woman he had found over in San Antonio teaching in a church school. Reminded me of a scared rabbit locked up in a cage. She was as afraid of Jesse Ordway as she would've been of a rattlesnake. They had a boy about seven or eight years old, and it seemed to me like he took after his mama more than his daddy. Didn't seem like there was any fight in her or in the boy either. His daddy would say something, and that boy would cringe like a pup that's had the whip put to him.

Anyhow, Ordway was on a kind of house-building spree of his own. His was going to be a lot bigger than mine would've been. For a while I had a notion of going over there and burning it down some night, but that wouldn't of paid me back anything. And after what he had done to me I knowed he would have it guarded like a vault full of gold bars. There was an easier way of getting him.

I found out he was having the lumber hauled down from San Antonio. Me and Felipe went out on the road one day and got the drop on them freighters and persuaded them to haul one whole shipment over to my place. I figured Ordway owed me that, and I also figured if he came to get it back it might give me a good excuse to kill him.

He didn't even try. He didn't have to, because that lumber never done me no good. I couldn't hire a carpenter anywhere in the country to start building that house back. The word had gotten around. I'd of built it myself, but a saw and a hammer just never did fit my hands. Millie had to keep living in that old Mexican house. She never once complained about it. That nice frame house had been my idea in the first place, not hers.

Things was quiet till into the fall of the year. I had about decided Ordway had given up on me till one day he rode up with three or four hands, and the gunfighter Sorrells at his side. He taken a look at the pile of his lumber laying out there, but he didn't say anything about it. He taken a lot longer look at the rifle I had in my hands, pointed about six inches below his collar-button. He told me that sure wasn't any polite way to treat company, and I told him I never treated *company* that way. He offered to buy me out for the money I had invested in my place. That was a twenty-five percent better offer than his first one, but I told him that wouldn't allow me any pay for the time and labor I had already put in.

He didn't seem inclined to raise the ante. He just told me what he had said the last time, that I'd better be careful of my luck.

I knowed he would have a hell of a time burning down the Mexican house because it was of adobe, and the roof had a covering of dried mud on it. He might *melt* it down, if he could make that much water, but he would never burn it down.

They hit us that same night. I can't say it was by surprise, because we sort of expected them. The surprise was that there was so many of them. I found out later that he didn't use his regular hands because he didn't want any of them talking when it was over. He went down to the border and hired him a bunch of renegades from the other side that he knowed wouldn't come back and incriminate him. So the ones that hit us that night was him and Sorrells and them renegades.

All I had was myself and Felipe and a couple of hands that I had hired to work cattle, not fight. They didn't do much fighting; they turned and ran. Felipe got shot in the leg in the first charge; he was sleeping out under an open arbor and couldn't get to the house in time. They swarmed over him and clubbed him and left him for dead. So then it was just me, with Millie loading my guns.

They tried first to set the place afire, but there wasn't much that would burn. Every time one of them would come charging up with a torch I would either hit him or come so close that he would drop the thing and run. They gave it up directly and set in to trying to cut the house to pieces. They shot out all the windows in the first few minutes—they was of wood, not glass—but them thick adobe walls stopped most of the bullets. Now and then one would bust through, but most of them either glanced off or stuck in the mud blocks.

There wasn't but one door to the place, and we had it barred. The only way they could come in was through that door or one of the front windows. They might've made it if they had had the nerve to gang up and all rush us at one time. But I reckon they knowed a bunch of them would die in the trying. They sat out there and potshotted at the windows, and I knowed we had them beat.

Then it happened. One of them slugs came right through the wall. The wall was of a double thickness of mud blocks, but I reckon there was a few places where the mud mortar on two blocks was on the same level. It was soft enough that the bullet came through.

Millie screamed. God, preacher, you never heard such a scream in your life. It hit her just under the heart. I had just time to catch her before she fell. All I could do was lay her out on the dirt floor and straighten her legs. She clutched at my shirt and cried out one more time; it must've hurt her something terrible. Then she was gone.

My Millie—my pretty Millie—was dead.

The shooting had stopped. They had all heard the scream. I heard a voice I knowed was Ordway's, telling them to rush the house. They just stayed put. Way I heard it later, that scream froze their blood, most of them, and the few others didn't want to try to swarm the house by theirselves. Ordway was out there in the dark, cussing a blue streak at them in Spanish and English both, because some was white and some was Mexican. Finally a couple of them made a run for the door. I dropped one of them six feet from the house; the other turned and ran. It was too dark to be sure, but I thought it was probably Sorrells.

After that I heard them pulling out. Ordway was telling them they wouldn't be paid a cent if they didn't go through with their bargain, but they rode off and left him. Directly everything out there got quiet. I sat myself down on the floor and taken Millie's hand and just held it for the longest time. I'm not ashamed to tell you, preacher, I cried like a baby. And when I was done crying, I sat there and talked to her like if she could of heard me, telling her what all plans I had had, and how much I loved her.

A long time after, I heard a noise and thought maybe they had come back. I got my rifle and eased the door open and waited, hoping they would try another rush so I could see just how many of them I could kill.

It was Felipe Rios crawling along, pulling himself a few inches at a time.

I helped him inside, and he saw Millie, and he crossed himself the way all them Catholics do, and he said something that sounded a little like Spanish but wasn't. I got him wrapped up the best I could in the dark; it was too risky to light a lamp. Then we waited for morning to come. It was one of the longest nights I ever spent in my life.

The two hands who had run away from us had done one decent thing, at least; they went to town and fetched the law. They didn't figure to find me alive, or they wouldn't of ever come back. I cussed them up one side and down the other and told them if I ever seen either one of them again I'd kill him like a dog. At the time, I meant it.

Word got to Arlee Thompson somehow, and he came over in a hard lope. He taken it pretty hard about Millie.

The law was no more help to me that time than they had been before. They declared the whole thing was the work of Mexican bandits who had surely gotten back across the river by now. I told them it was Ordway, that I'd heard his voice, but they told me I was mistaken. The last thing they wanted to do was to tangle up with Jesse Ordway. He could of stolen the county courthouse piece by piece and they'd of fetched him a wagon.

It taken me a while to figure out what to do about Ordway. What I really wanted was to go over there and just shoot him down. But I would never of been allowed to live that long.

We buried Millie on her old family homeplace. Arlee thought that was kind of strange, but I told him I wouldn't be keeping my land, and I wanted her to rest in her own ground where maybe there would be kin around through the times to come.

I sent word to Ordway that if he still wanted to buy me out, I'd sell to him on the terms of his last offer. I wanted cold hard cash because I figured on leaving the country. I didn't want no check, draft, or bank order. He sent me word what day to meet him in town at the bank with the deeds ready to sign over.

Felipe Rios was still weak. He had to have a crutch to walk, and he had to be helped onto a horse. But in the saddle he could handle himself pretty good. After all the help he had been, I hated to just leave him flat. I arranged with Arlee to give him a job. The morning I left for town I told Felipe to go to Arlee's. He wanted to go to town with me, but I told him he didn't have no business there, and he'd better do what I said. When I headed down the town road, I looked back once and seen him heading out in the direction of Arlee's.

I seen half a dozen O Bar horses tied at racks along the street. In front of the bank was a rig with Ordway's brand painted on it. Ordway's little boy sat up there all by himself. I figured he had been told to stay out of the bank, and he was way too young to wait in one of the saloons or Mexican *cantinas*. I rode straight up to the rack nearest to the bank door. I stopped and looked at the boy. He seemed to be a little afraid of me, because he kind of shrunk up on the seat of that rig. I asks him, "You a pretty good cowhand, son?"

He shook his head without saying anything, and I told him it was a thing a man could learn if he had to. I unfastened my saddlebags.

In the bank, Jesse Ordway was waiting for me. He had Sorrells there with him, maybe figuring I might come in shooting. But I didn't, and I could see in Sorrells's eyes that he was laughing at me. They had beaten me, and he was enjoying it. Maybe Ordway was enjoying it too, in his way, but he was more interested in business. With him it wasn't the principle of the thing; it was the money. He didn't try to shake hands with me; I wouldn't of done it noway. He says to me, "We have everything ready for you to sign. And I have the money all counted out for you. Sorry about your wife."

That was the order he ranked everything in. The money first.

I looked around the bank. Over to one side I seen Ordway's wife sitting near the bank president's desk. She was the same as every time I had ever seen her, scared. I had wondered a time or two how come she ever married such a man in the first place, because it was plain there wasn't no love lost for either one of them. I figured maybe she was too scared of him to say *no*. I wondered what she was in the bank for, and then I remembered that as the wife she was probably expected to sign papers.

Seeing her there kind of brought things back to me in a rush. Ordway's wife was alive, but mine was dead. And he had been responsible for killing her.

I tipped my hat to Mrs. Ordway and bowed a little, the way we was all taught to do, them days. I says, "Sorry my wife's not here to visit with you." I suppose I meant a little malice, because she must of known what her husband had done. She looked down and mumbled something I couldn't hear.

Ordway says, "Something's got to be done to stop those Mexican bandits."

I knowed he was a liar, and he knowed I knowed it. I seen a hard smile come across Sorrells's face.

Ordway says, "Too bad you didn't sell out earlier. All that misfortune would not have befallen you."

You know what hate tastes like? It's got a flavor all its own, not like salt, not like pepper, not like gall. It's not like anything else I know. I tasted it then like I've never tasted it another time in my life.

I laid out what papers I had, and he laid out some legal agreements he had had a lawyer draw up. I never could figure out lawyer talk; I always suspected it was just a code they make up to rob the rest of us with. It didn't matter; the money stacked on that table did all the talking I needed to finish the deal. Ordway says, "It's all counted out."

I told him I'd count it myself, just to be sure. They had it in big denominations, twenty- and fifty-dollar bills. I doubted that this little cowtown bank had had all those bills on hand; they had probably had to send to San Antonio after them. It came out to about the same amount of money I had had when I first got home from that trail drive to Abilene, plus fifteen dollars a head for about two hundred cows I had mavericked or run a new brand on. There was probably more cattle than that, but the deal didn't call for a physical count, just range delivery.

I says, "This don't take into account the improvements." There hadn't been many, really. I had just fixed up some old pens and trap fences that was there to begin with but was run down some.

Ordway didn't seem too inclined to argue. He says, "All right, I'll add a thousand dollars."

It was too easy. I'd always found that when a man just up and gives you something, you'd better watch him because he's probably figuring to give you something *else* you didn't bargain on. I looked into Ordway's eyes, and I knew. It didn't matter what he paid me; he didn't intend to let me get out of this country alive. Once we finished this deal, I was as good as dead, and he would get most of his money back . . . maybe all of it.

I decided I had just as well take all I could get. I didn't really have any extra horses, but I didn't see where a little lie right there could hurt anything. I told him I had twenty head that hadn't been counted into the deal. He could have them for fifty dollars apiece or I would drive them to San Antonio and sell them. He motioned to the banker, and they counted me out another thousand dollars.

I put all the money into the saddlebags and then buckled the flaps down tight. I seen Ordway looking at them bags the way a hungry cat looks at a bird. I started to take them, and Ordway laid his hands across one of them. "The papers first," he says. "You got to sign the papers."

The deeds was all spread out there on the table. I wrote my name everywhere the banker told me, then blew on the ink to make it dry.

Ordway taken his hand off of the bag then. He had a look like a cat which had just got the bird in his mouth.

I says, "Jesse Ordway, you're a greedy man. Just what makes you want all this land so bad?"

He looked at his wife, then looked out the door toward where his son was still sitting in the rig. He says, "I got a family. I'm trying to build something worthwhile that I can leave to my son."

You ever notice that's what all them old land-hogs used to say? They was never building anything for theirselves, if you heard them tell it. They was always doing it for somebody else. The milk of human kindness was bubbling up and overflowing out of their hearts. Charity to the core. But they'd kill you for that charity if you got in their way.

I pushed my chair back away from the table and stood up. I says, "Ordway, I hope you're ready."

"Ready for what?" he asks me.

I says, "Ready to leave it to your son." I pulled my pistol out of my belt and shoved it up almost against his forehead. You never seen such a surprised look in a man's face. His mouth dropped open, and his eyes went as big as hen eggs. He made a reach for his gun, but he never touched it. I pulled the trigger. He fell back like he had been hit with a sledgehammer.

I had caught them all by surprise, but I could see Sorrells reaching for his gun. I swung around and caught him just as he cleared leather. I watched him fall on his face in the middle of the room.

The whole place was filled with powder smoke; it was hard to see across to the far wall. But nobody else in there was any threat to me. Surely not the banker, because he raised his hands like he thought it was a holdup. Mrs. Ordway had her mouth wide open like she wanted to scream, but nothing would come out.

I says to her, "You don't have to be scared anymore. You're shed of him. What's more, you're a rich woman."

I picked up the saddlebags, swung them across my shoulder and walked out the door.

From up the street came four of Jesse Ordway's hands, walking along like they had been sent for. I was the last person they expected to see come out after the shooting. Later, when I had time to think about it, I figured they was coming down to be Ordway's "eyewitnesses" after him and Sorrells killed me.

They pulled their guns and spread out. I was about to take a shot at one of them when somebody else done it for me. I seen one of them go down and grab his leg and scream like he had gone into a fire. The others stopped in their tracks, dropped their guns and raised their hands.

There was Felipe Rios across the street, sitting on his horse. His gun was smoking like he had been burning greasewood.

I taken a look at Ordway's boy, who was trying to hold the team and keep it from running away. I says, "Boy, you better go in yonder. I think your mama needs you." Then I got on my horse, laid the saddlebags across my lap and rode over to where Felipe was.

I couldn't decide whether to thank him or raise hell with him. I says, "Thought you was going to Arlee's."

"Later," he says. "I thought you might need help."

"You can't go to Arlee's now," I tells him. "I just killed Jesse Ordway and Sorrells. They'll figure you was part of it."

He nodded like it wasn't no surprise to him. He says, "It was in your face."

"I got to leave here now," I tells him. "You feel like you can keep up with me?"

"I don't see where I have any choice," he says. "These people will hang me if I stay."

Them days when a man got in trouble he went south. A day and a half of hard riding would take us to the Rio Grande. On the other side of the river they didn't care how many *gringos* you had killed; the more the better. Felipe wasn't in very good shape for a long ride like that, but I decided he would make it if I had to tie him in the saddle.

Good sense told me we ought to ride out of that town as fast as we could make those horses go. But that was Jesse Ordway's town, and I didn't want to run. I wanted us to take our time and let them all have a good long look at our backside. We rode slow and easy down the street, past them O Bar men. One of them was still holding on to his leg and trying to make the blood stop running. I says to him, says I, "You-all are working for a widow-lady now. You better go down to the bank and see what she wants you to do."

We just walked our horses till we got past the first bend in the road, to where the brush hid us from town. I says then, "Let's ride, Felipe."

And we rode.

CHAPTER 2

I've come to many a fork in the road during my life, and a time or two I've took the wrong direction. One thing I've finally learned is that you never know what a woman is going to do. If I'd known more about Jesse Ordway's quiet, timid little wife, my life might of turned out a lot different. I naturally figured she would scream murder, and I didn't stay around to listen to her.

A long time later, way too late for it to do me any good, I found out she figured I'd done her a sizable favor. She told them I had killed her husband and Sorrells in self-defense. Naturally I can't exactly blame her for not telling me right then. I got away in kind of a hurry, and it taken her some time to get her thinking sorted out too, I expect. The banker, of course, told the story some different the first time, but he changed it later when he saw how the wind blew. He wasn't going to argue with a widow . . . not a *rich* widow.

Not knowing all this, and figuring they would keep the telegraph wires hot all the way to the Rio Grande, me and Felipe kind of abused our horses in getting there. We didn't stop to rest till we was on the south side of the Bravo, drying the water out of our ears.

A man crossing the river for a day or a night's entertainment these days, he don't rightly appreciate how it was then. Going into Mexico wasn't something you done lightly or without good cause. Most of the *gringos* you found then was there because it was healthier than being someplace else, and not just because they chose it of their own free will. It was a nervous feeling to be in an alien country where they spoke a whole different language and where a man didn't know what the law was. You'll likely think that's funny, Joe Pepper worrying about obeying the law, but I always tried to. I never did hold with a man breaking the law without he had a good reason for it. I always had a good reason, or at least thought I did at the time. Once or twice, maybe, I might've erred a mite in my judgment. I was always in favor of the law as long as it didn't harm anybody.

I had a right smart of money in my saddlebags, and that was enough in itself to make a man nervous. You never know when you'll come across somebody dishonest. Some ways from the river we struck a road which Felipe said would lead us to a village ten or fifteen miles to the west. I got to thinking of all the things I'd heard about Mexican bandits and such, and of course I knowed there was many a Texas outlaw hanging out south of the Rio Grande. Them kind of people are apt to do a man harm for a lot less money than I had with me.

Along the way I kept looking around for landmarks that I would be able to remember. We came up finally to a place where the road made a bend around a motte of trees, and I thought I ought to be able to find it again. I rode on a little ways to where I didn't think Felipe would figure out the spot I had in mind, then I sent him on ahead while I doubled back. I paced out a spot due west of a certain forked tree and buried most of that money wrapped up in a slicker.

I didn't distrust Felipe, exactly, it was just that I didn't completely trust him, either. I never trusted *nobody* when it came to money, except maybe my mama and Millie Thompson. Probably that came from a time when I was a boy that my uncle gave me a silver dollar for helping him chop his cotton for four days, and my daddy taken and spent it on flour for the whole family. That was *my* dollar, not the family's.

I kept out a little traveling money so we wouldn't have no need to get lank or dry. After a while we came to this village Felipe knew about. I had a few minutes' worry as we met a bunch of soldiers guarding the road. They stopped us and asked questions about who we was and what we was doing there. Felipe answered for us—told the damnedest pack of lies you ever heard. He said later a man never wanted to tell the truth to a bunch of soldiers because they'll hold it against you.

It was a bigger town than I had expected from what Felipe had told me. It had growed a right smart since he had been there as a boy. The thing I noticed right off about it was the soldiers. You would of thought they was fixing to have a parade, they was so many. I never had paid any particular attention before to what was going on in Mexico. I didn't know they had their own war going on at the same time we was having that unpleasantness of ours between the states. It was a mixed-up deal. A bunch of Frenchmen had been in there muddying up the waters, but by this time they was out, and the Mexicans was fighting amongst theirselves over just who was supposed to be *in*. I never could get it straight in my mind just who was against who, because one time there would be a bunch who was friends, and the next time the same people was enemies and the people who had been their enemies was their friends, and . . . well, you know how complicated life gets sometimes.

I tried not to get involved with it. I never did rightly understand what *our* war was about, so I sure didn't figure to mix into somebody else's. The longer I stayed there, though, the more I learned how hard it was to keep out of it. You couldn't stay on the fence. Somebody always had ahold of your leg, pulling to get you down.

People didn't seem to pay much attention to us when we rode in. They was used to *gringos* coming and going, and they didn't seem to get concerned about them as long as they brought money and didn't kill any of the local folks. During our War between the States there had been a good many Union sympathizers in Texas who found the climate kind of unhealthy at home and hightailed it across the river. After the war the traffic changed over . . . there was Unionists going north and a lot of un-reconstructed rebels going south, swapping places with one another. The ones that went south didn't know they was just leaving one war and wading up to their necks into another one.

And besides those that was in and out of Mexico on account of the war, there was always the plain-out fugitives, looking for a place where the long arm of the law was a little short in the reach. Some of them was outlaws and killers. Some was men like me . . . good men, you know, just a little down on their luck. For all I knew, every Ranger and sheriff and two-bit *pilón* constable in Texas was out hunting for me.

I had some little advantage in knowing the language. I had been around Mexicans a fair bit over the years and could understand the lingo if they didn't take to throwing any of that educated stuff at me. I could even talk back to them in pretty good fashion, enough that I wasn't going to starve to death because I didn't know how to say "beans." First thing a man learns in another language, if he's around the people that use it, is the cusswords. Give a man a fair vocabulary of cusswords and he'll get along.

We was tired and hungry and dry to the gizzard. We sure wasn't looking for no trouble. For once, trouble wasn't looking for us, either. We hitched in front of an adobe place where we could hear a guitar player and a fiddler, and some people laughing. We knowed we wasn't getting into no church, but it sounded friendly. We ordered us a bottle of *tequila* and some supper. Barman brought us the bottle; I had to ask him for glasses. Good thing you never seen what them glasses looked like, preacher, because you'd of never drank a drop. But them days I wasn't fussy, and besides, that Mexican *tequila* was strong enough to kill anything it touched that wasn't human. Anything human too, if taken in quantity.

We ordered up something to eat. I disremember exactly what it was; I just remember that they forgot to leave the fire at the stove. That Mexican cooking took a right smart of getting used to.

Afterwards, when we was working on the second bottle, I got to noticing how many *gringo* faces was coming in and going out. First thought I had was that some was probably spies for the Rangers and the other laws, but then I decided the hell with them, let them spy. As long as I didn't cross that river, I doubted they would come and get me. After I had studied on it awhile, I decided most of the people was like me, they couldn't go back. Or wouldn't.

As Mexican towns went, it was a comfortable sort of a place. They didn't ask questions as long as you paid cash. Me and Felipe, we decided it was a good place to stay and rest awhile. His leg was still causing him a right smart of trouble. I hadn't made any plans as to what to do with myself. I had always thought I would enjoy just laying around someplace with nothing to do but play cards and drink whiskey and eat. I did, too, for the first few days. After that the days got to running forty-eight hours long. I was still young then. I hadn't learned patience.

In the back of my mind I had thought I would just sort of kill time there till I figured the law had put my case back in the warming oven, then I would dig up my money, cross the river and make my way west, maybe to Arizona or California. I sure didn't figure on setting down roots in Mexico. So we just laid around days, and nights we'd work our way from one *cantina* to another, trying to find one that had better liquor. None of them did, but the hunting gave us something to do.

I got to noticing how many *gringos* had taken up business of one sort or another, like *cantinas* and mercantile and that kind of thing. It began crossing my mind that maybe I ought to do the same. But I didn't know nothing about the mercantile trade, and all I knowed then about the saloon business was what I had learned from the front side of the bar, which is a damn bad place to learn anything.

Gradually I came to know that some of the boys wasn't completely idle. One time there was half a dozen *gringos* whose acquaintance I had made that disappeared from sight for several days. They showed up again, finally, spending money like it was seawater and they was drunken sailors, scooping it out with both hands. Word filtered down about a big bank robbery in one of the Texas towns a ways up from the border. I played poker with some of them boys and won a fair part of their take and noticed a little bloodstain on some of the bills. Didn't seem to have no trouble cashing them at the bar, though. They was all negotiable.

I could've went with them boys on their little "trips" if I had of wanted to, but that wasn't my style of work. Being handy with the pasteboards, I could always get a good part of their money anyway without having to travel any farther than the gaming tables. That was safer than comparing marksmanship with some sharp-eyed Ranger, too.

By and by I got to feeling real restless, cooped up in town like I was, and sometimes I would take my good gray Tennessee horse and ride out over the country, just looking at it. Seemed to me like it ought to be good for ranching. There was some Mexican outfits, mostly owned by the big old rich *hacendados*, and some few that was owned by *gringos*.

The way I was told, the best way for a *gringo* to operate was to take in some local Mexican as a partner. That made the deal set better with the other Mexicans, and they wasn't so apt to steal him blind. I had noticed a lot the same in regard to *gringos* who was in business in town. The most successful was the ones that had Mexican partners.

Looking at that land and the cattle on it made me start feeling a little homesick, which is a dangerous thing for a man on the dodge. It gets to giving him foolish notions about going back. I must of said something to somebody, when I was feeling the *tequila* a little, though I never could remember it afterwards. If I hadn't, that Orville Jackson never would of latched onto me.

Later on I figured it wasn't just chance that put Jackson into a poker game with me. But at the time it seemed like a natural thing that we sort of fell together. I figured from the first that he was on the up-and-up because his last name wasn't Smith, and his first name wasn't Bill or Jim. I figured nobody would just make up a name like Orville.

The way Jackson told it, he had been in business in Texas before the war, and his favor kind of stayed attached to the Union. After the war broke out, there was some people who felt so strong about it that they made it their business to roam around the countryside hanging Unionists, or people they thought might even have any inclinations toward the Union. Them same people are the kind that take prisoners out of the jail at night and lynch them but never have the guts to join a posse that goes out and catches them in the first place. They get real righteous, but they only kill when there ain't no danger in it.

Anyway, this Orville Jackson sold his property in something of a hurry and lit out for Mexico between two days.

Some of the Unionists who went to Mexico found ways to get to the North and fight us rebel boys, but Jackson didn't have that strong a feeling about the war. He looked around awhile and bought him some land in Mexico and built himself a ranch. He taken in a Mexican partner, naturally, and all in all he done right well for a *gringo*. But lately the partner had died and there was a lot the partner's widow didn't understand about the ranch business. With the war long since over, Jackson was kind of thinking he would like to sell his ranch and go back to

Texas. He figured by now them old hanging parties was probably busy licking the boots of the Yankee occupation soldiers and selling them hay and oats and horses and whiskey and getting rich off of the Union. Which was correct, of course; that was exactly what they was doing. Them kind of people was always changeable in their politics.

Jackson didn't proposition me right off to buy the place. I hadn't given him no reason that I remembered to think I had the money to buy it with. But he had figured from looking at me that I knowed cows. Once a man gets cow manure stuck to the bottom of his boots, it don't ever all come off. We talked about cattle a right smart, and I told him about me going up the trail to Kansas. So he asked me if I would like to go out and spend a few days at the ranch with him and help him with the branding. He said he would pay me for my time.

I figured I would make a lot more money at the gaming tables, but I was hungry to get back out in the country for a change. I told him I would go if we could take Felipe with us. He didn't see nothing wrong with that.

The morning we started out, things got a little excited in town for a while. We run into an agitated bunch of the local citizens, running up toward the local *calabozo*. They sort of swept us along. We got there in time to see the soldiers bring out a bunch of men—maybe seven or eight, including a couple that couldn't of been more than just boys— and stand them up against an adobe wall. The people was yelling and cursing and begging, but the officer in charge seemed like a man who enjoyed his work. He lined up a firing squad and raised his sword and called off the signals.

Now, I've seen men die in battle more times than once, and I've seen them die other places. But I had never seen a firing squad before. Most everybody I had ever seen fall had a gun in his hand. Watching the soldiers stand them poor devils up there helpless and shoot them down like cattle at the slaughter . . . well, I tell you, my blood ran cold. It took half a bottle of *tequila* to burn the chill out of me.

Jackson didn't enjoy it either, but he said it was something a man had to pretend like he didn't see. Happened down there all the time, and a *gringo* just had to keep from taking sides or getting himself involved.

Pretty soon he was talking about cattle again, but I kept seeing them people slammed back against that adobe wall with their blood leaking out.

We was half the day getting there. It wasn't nothing fancy, Jackson's place, just a kind of adobe headquarters and brush pens and the like. His wife that he had brought from Texas had died on him a good while back, and he was living with a good-looking Mexican woman. At this time he still hadn't made any move toward selling me the ranch, but I had already begun thinking about it. I got to wondering if he would throw that woman in on the deal if a man was to buy him out.

Don't look so shocked, preacher. My wife Millie had been dead for quite a while by that time. I had got to where I was watching them girls around the *cantinas* some, and they was looking better to me all the time. I don't suppose a man in your line of work ever gets them feelings, but a man in mine is subject to a lapse now and again, like the fever and the ague. I've found that the best cure for temptation is generally to give in to it, get it over with, and then you can turn your mind to other things. Long as you resist, it keeps coming back at you and getting in the way of your thinking.

As you get up toward the age where I'm at now, of course, it don't bother you much. You get a lot more of the fever and the ague.

Later on, remembering back, I come to realize that Jackson must of sniffed it out somehow that I had money, the same way he recognized that I knowed the cow. He didn't really need no help from me for the branding; he had more good Mexican *vaqueros* than he needed. Mostly he just kept me with him and showed me the good points about the place. He had that good-looking woman bringing us something to drink every time we was in the house. He didn't have to be very smart to figure out that I enjoyed watching her go by.

I had been there three days before he throwed the question at me. We was sitting in the house that night, sipping at some good American whiskey. "What do you think of it?" he asks me. The woman was walking away from us at the time. I told him I thought she looked mighty good. He let me know he was talking about the ranch, not about the woman. And he let me know the whole deal was for sale. Including the woman.

I remembered about his Mexican partner, and that there was a widow. He said the partner was a partner on paper only, just for the satisfaction of local politics, and that the widow didn't own but a token share.

Not knowing the widow, I had my doubts. I was afraid she might not be happy with the deal. She could get me crossways with her countrymen and give me hell.

"But you *know* the widow," Jackson says, "and what's more, she likes you." He pointed with his chin toward the kitchen. "María there, she's my partner's widow."

After that he didn't have too hard a job selling me on the notion. His proposition sounded real good. Too good, in fact. I was suspicious of it at first. Nobody ever gives you anything in this life without they're trying to take something even bigger away from you. Bad as I wanted to, I couldn't see my way clear; the deal just sounded too good. But by and by I caught him lying about his calf crop. I had already seen enough of his tally books to know he couldn't have as many calves as he claimed.

Once I caught him trying to cheat me I felt better. If you can't find out where a man is trying to best you on a trade, you'd better steer clear of it.

The upshot was that we finally made a deal. I slipped off by myself, rode to where I had buried that money and dug it up.

I reckon I kind of expected Jackson to be a little sentimental about leaving the place after all of them years, but he must not of been. Or else it hurt him so much that he didn't want to stretch things out. We signed the papers in front of a magistrate in town, and he lit right out for the Rio Grande.

Felipe was my *majordomo*, sort of, though at first we had to leave things to the regular *vaqueros*, pretty much. They knowed the country, whereas me and Felipe had a lot to learn.

I hadn't been there more than two weeks before I learned why

Orville Jackson had wanted to sell. There was some four-legged wolves killing on the baby calves and some two-legged ones stealing on the grown cattle. A man could poison the four-legged ones, but the two-legged variety was a whole different proposition. I found out they was mainly of two varieties—the government soldiers on the one side and the local rebels on the other.

The one thing Orville Jackson had neglected to tell me was that he was serving as a sort of free commissary to both sides of the war.

In Texas there was always one quick and final remedy in a situation like this. If you caught a man stealing off of you, and you got the drop on him, you reformed him real quick. That way he didn't ever come back and trouble you again unless you was subject to bad dreams, which I never was. But this here was a lot more ticklish proposition. María pointed out to me that if I was to kill any soldiers they'd have me in front of that same adobe wall where I seen them citizens lined up. If I was to kill any of the citizens . . . well, all the adobe walls wasn't in town.

She said the best thing for me to do was to just accept that which couldn't be changed and go on the best I could. Keep the cows happy by putting out plenty of bulls on the range, she said, and hope they kept the calves coming faster than the thieves could steal them. I could pretty soon see it wasn't that easy. I was always a slow reader, but I'm apt with figures. I could tell without counting on my fingers that they was getting way ahead of me. Orville Jackson had left Mexico just in time.

Things really started closing in on me one day when I was up on the part of the ranch that fronted along the river. In a way that was my favorite part, and in another I hated it. I would go up to that river and look across and get to wanting so bad to go back to Texas that I couldn't hardly keep from spurring out into the water. But sometimes I could see people over there. I was satisfied in my own mind that they was all Rangers and sheriffs, camping over there waiting for me to do something foolish.

That particular day me and Felipe heard a sudden lot of shooting a mile or so upriver. Felipe's inclination was to head off in the opposite direction, which would of been smart, but I thought it was somebody killing my cattle. I told Felipe in a sharp way to come on and go with me. I didn't know exactly what I was going to do about it when I got there, but I figured it would come to me in due course. I generally found that when the time came, the idea came, too.

Felipe sure wasn't keen on it, which led me to wonder if maybe he didn't know more of what was going on than I did. We loped over a hill and seen a big clearing down there leading away from the river. There was maybe half a dozen men, dead and dying, scattered over that clearing, and some horses and packmules with them. We seen one man still laying down behind a packmule, firing a shot now and again at somebody over in the brush. By and by he ran out of ammunition. I seen some soldiers get up from that brush and walk out toward him. They was evidently hollering at each other, but me and Felipe was too far away to hear any of it. The man stood up with his hands in the air, and some more soldiers came out of the brush. There was one with them wearing a bright-colored uniform, and I knew right off he was an officer of some kind. He was giving orders. The soldiers scattered out, checking all the dead and wounded men and animals. The officer walked up to that prisoner, talked to him a minute, then pulled out a pistol and shot him in the head.

He hollered something at the soldiers, and they shot two more men that was only wounded, so that they wasn't just wounded anymore.

"Let's go," says Felipe. "It isn't healthy here."

Right about then they spotted us. I began to feel like Felipe was smarter than I used to give him credit for. I wished he had been a better persuader. The officer pointed in our direction, and I knowed it was too late to run. Some of the soldiers spurred up to us.

The only thing left for us to do was to stand our ground and try to talk ourselves out of trouble, seeing as it wasn't none of our business to start with. It wasn't none of mine, anyway, but I could tell right off that Felipe considered it his. While he waited he cussed the soldiers and called them a lot of things that didn't fit comfortable on the ear. I had taken great pains not to choose up sides, but being of the blood, I reckon Felipe couldn't help it. He might as easy of taken the other side, but he didn't.

I don't suppose you ever had occasion to look at the business end of a dozen rifles, preacher, I tell you, the muzzle looks as big around as a number-four washtub. Them soldiers invited us to go down with them for a conference with the *capitán*, and we accepted the invitation.

When we got down into the clearing I could tell real easy what the excitement was about. They had taken the packs off of them dead mules, and they was full of rifles and ammunition. Them citizens they had ambushed had just swum across the river from the Texas side with a bunch of U.S. Army goods for the rebels. Now, I'm sure the U.S. Army hadn't *given* them all that weaponry. There was a bunch of them unreconstructed Confederates on the Texas side, though, that would cheerfully burglarize an armory and sell for gold to any and all comers.

I couldn't figure out at first why they had tried to cross the Rio Grande in the daylight instead of in the dark. Then I noticed one civilian amongst the soldiers and seen the *capitán* give him a handful of silver. It didn't take even a *gringo* long to figure out that these boys had been betrayed. The betrayer didn't wait around to count his money; he acted like he had a whole hive of bees in his britches.

I seen the way Felipe looked at him. I figured if we got out of this mess with our skin still on tight, and Felipe ever crossed trails with that Judas, there was going to be a little knifework done.

The *capitán* taken his slow, sweet time in getting around to us. He was like a cat playing with a mouse that ain't ever really going to go nowhere. He just gave Felipe a glance, but he stared at me a long time like a man who enjoys his work. "A *gringo*," he says, real pleased with himself. "I am Captain Tiburcio Santos. You would be, I believe, the Señor Peeler."

I told him he sure was right, that I was Joe Peeler. That was my real name, you remember.

He had a grin wider than the wave on a slop jar, only it wasn't at all funny. "And what reason, Señor Peeler, can you think of why we should not shoot you right here and leave you lying dead among your friends?"

Well, sir, I could think of a hundred good reasons, and ninety-nine of them was that I was too young to die: I didn't think that would impress him much, so I told him the other one. "Because these was no friends of mine. I never seen them in my whole life till just now."

He says, "I find that hard to believe. Convince me."

I didn't waste no time in the telling, how come me and Felipe to be here, how we had heard the shooting and had come to investigate because this was my ranch, and because I figured anything which happened on it was of more than just passing interest to me. I told him these citizens—whoever they was—was trespassers on private land.

Pretty soon I got to feeling like he knowed it all the time, that he was just playing with me because he liked to watch me sweat. And I was doing plenty of that. There was a sergeant sitting on his horse beside the captain, and he had his pistol pointed straight at me, and his finger was twitching. All he was waiting for was the word.

The captain said he thought it would be natural for me—being the owner of the land—to take a bribe or a *mordida* to let these louse-ridden, dirty rebels smuggle arms across it to fight against the freedom-loving, legally constituted authorities. I had to keep telling him that I wasn't in no way mixed up in their Mexican politics, that I was a peaceful, law-abiding man who had just bought this place and was trying in my own awkward way to make a decent living out of it.

It gradually soaked in on me that if I had really been part of the smuggling setup, he'd of known it through the Judas. He was just fishing around for a payoff. The *mordida* is a kind of a hidden tax that everybody pays. A little man pays a little *mordida* to a little official for little favors. A big man pays a big *mordida* to a big official for big favors. For me and Felipe to ride away from here without any surplus holes in us was going to be considered a big favor.

It never was in my nature to bow and scrape and make myself little, not unless it was for a good cause. This was for a good cause.

I tells that captain, "I'm sorry if you or any of your men have come to any danger or harm on my land. And although I am in no way responsible for this, I would be glad to have you-all take a few steers back to town with you for the benefit of all your company."

The captain said he could take *all* the cattle and leave me and Felipe dead, if that was his inclination. I told him I realized he could but hoped he would see fit to take the gift as my guest . . . my *honored* guest. I damn near gagged.

The captain sprung his trap then. He says, "I had some conversations with the previous owner of this ranch and thought I had completed an arrangement with him. Now I must start over with you. It appears to me that what you need is a Mexican partner."

I told him I already had a Mexican partner.

"A woman." He kind of snickered. "I know all about that. What you need is a *strong* partner, one who has influence in the right places. One who has power at his command. One who someday will perhaps even be governor, *quién sabe*? In the right hands this property of yours could become a highway of commerce with those on the other side of the river."

I knowed what he meant by that. It would be a handy place to bring cattle stolen from the Texas side of the Rio Grande. That thought had already occurred to me.

I knowed then why he hadn't already shot me.

I says, "I'll have to think about it some." The longer he gave me to think about it, the longer my health would hold up.

He says, "You think, but be sure you think right. A partner in the right position could make you a wealthy man. An enemy in the right position could bring you ruin . . . and death. So think about it, Señor Peeler, until we meet each other again."

I couldn't decide right then who I was the maddest at, him or Orville Jackson. That was why Jackson had wanted to unload this place on me; he was fixing to get himself a new Mexican partner that wouldn't fit in his bed. Now Jackson was on the right side of the river, singing happy songs to himself and counting my money, and here I sat face to face with a brazen thief who was about to clean my plow.

The soldiers gathered up all the arms and ammunition including me and Felipe's guns. After they was out of earshot, Felipe commenced calling them bloody butchers and swine and such other endearments. I told him none of this was our fight and we'd better stay out of it. Didn't seem like he heard me, and anyway, we *was* mixed up in it already. I told him finally that it might be a cagy move on our part if we was to put the spurs to our horses and leave this locality. If any of them rebel citizens was to come along and find us here amongst their dead friends and kin, they might get the wrong idea and do us bodily harm.

Felipe understood those citizens pretty good. We left there in a lope, him taking the lead.

María was some upset when we told her that night. She seemed to be more sorely afflicted by the fact that the packtrain got ambushed than she was over me and Felipe having ourselves a narrow escape. By and by I found myself sitting at the table all alone. I got up and went to the kitchen for a cup of coffee and found María and Felipe in a real serious discussion. I pulled back so they wouldn't see me. My first thought was that Felipe was getting some partnership rights that I hadn't intended to give him. Directly I seen him and her go out together to one of the brush *jacales* where the *vaqueros* stayed. They talked to the *vaqueros* awhile. Finally one of them went to the barn, saddled a horse and rode off in the night.

It gradually came to me that there was a lot more to María than Jackson had told me. Probably more than he knowed.

I can't say I ever entertained any real hopes of getting to be a big cowman in Mexico, but in my idle moments I sometimes let myself dream a little. It was the kind of dream some of them Mexican boys get from smoking that funny weed in their cigarettes. But it's a hard go being a cowman. Even when everything goes right, it's hard to make ends meet. And when you're trying to operate in a country where they're fighting a war across your land, and the only time they ever stop is to go fill up their bellies on your beef, well sir, you *have* got complications. They didn't just pick the big steers to butcher. Times I'd come across a calf bawling for milk and would find its mammy laying there with both of her hind quarters gone. A man can afford to lose the steers sometimes, but the cow is the factory.

I'd come in at night cussing about it, and María would always take the rebels' part.

"They are fighting for what is good and just," she would always say.

They probably thought they was. But I've watched them kinds of fights off and on for a good many years, and it always seems like somebody gets at the head of it sooner or later and turns everybody else's dying into a personal gain for himself. You show me a hero, preacher, and I'll show you a damn fool who is being used for somebody else's profit.

I would get so mad at María that I would almost put her out of the house. But never quite. I had a notion that she would find all the sympathy she needed from Felipe.

I quit going to town unless I was forced to it, and then I would try to go in at night, do whatever I had to and get out. Sooner or later I knowed I was going to have to face that Captain Santos again, and I wanted to put it off as long as I could. If he made up his mind to declare himself in as my partner, I knowed I would have a hard time stopping him. He had the whole local military contingent to back him up, and all I had was a little bunch of *vaqueros* that didn't really owe me anything.

Of course I could do what I had done to Jesse Ordway; I could just shoot him. But I wouldn't live to see the sunrise.

I wasn't sure this Mexico ranch was worth dying for. Not *me* dying for, anyway.

Did you ever get yourself into a mess of fleas, to where you didn't know which spot to scratch first? Where you itched in a dozen places and had only two hands to scratch with?

That was the shape they had me in. I'd find out somebody was running off cattle on the south end of the place, and I'd ride down there as fast as I could go. While I was gone, some more would hit the north end. Sometimes it was the rebels, sometimes the soldiers from town. I can't say they was overgreedy; they just taken a few here and a few there. But you can finally empty a well with a teacup if you dip fast enough.

The whole thing come to a head one day just by pure luck . . . *bad* luck, as it turned out. I heard some cows bawling and rode up on a bunch of them rebel citizens driving off twelve or fifteen head. They was taking the cows and trying to leave the calves behind so they could travel faster. If you know anything about cattle you know it ain't in an old cow's nature to go off and leave her calf behind without she puts up a devil of a struggle over it.

I don't know what I figured I could do about it, seeing as they had me pretty badly outnumbered, but I was so mad I rode down there anyway. I wasn't so mad as to be stupid, though. I didn't put my gun on them. A couple or three had their guns on *me*. There was seven or eight of them, a lot of people for such a small bunch of cattle.

I picked out the one I figured was the leader. I told him in the nicest way I knowed how that I considered him a lowdown sneak thief and a cross between a rattlesnake and a coyote. He was a fiery-eyed young gent of about Felipe's general size and age. I never thought about it then, but later I got to wondering if they might of been kin, seeing as Felipe had taken to such strong feelings about the rebels. That *hombre* just sat there and looked at me while I talked to him. His eyes crackled like dry brush on fire. When I had run down a little, he set in on me.

"These cattle are of Mexico," he says, "and you are a *gringo*. By what right do you claim cattle in Mexico?"

"By right of money," I says. "I bought these cattle and this ranch fair and square with good old American green-back money." I've never been noplace in my life where money didn't talk louder than the law, if there was enough of it.

"Stolen money, no doubt," says he. "Or money made from the sweat and blood of poor Mexicans you *Tejanos* have enslaved."

Me, I never had enslaved nobody, black, white or brown, and I damn well told him so. But you ought to know how them fanatic types are, preacher, since the worst fanatics in the world are in the field of religion. They don't hear nothing except their own voices, and they think it's the voice of God.

He gave me a lecture on heaven and hell and the rights of the downtrodden and the greed of the rich, and all that. Later on, when I was in a better mood to ponder on it, I almost laughed. Why, he considered me *rich*. I reckon a man with a patched shirt looks rich to the one that's got no shirt atall.

Since he seen fit to bring religion into it, I tried to give him a lecture about that commandment which says "Thou shalt not steal." He acted like he thought I was trying to change the subject on him. He didn't see it as stealing to take something off of a rich *gringo*, especially when it was going to feed the poor and the rebellious.

It was pretty much of a standoff. I wasn't going to convince him, and it would've been suicidal to of tried to shoot him. I should of gone off and left them in possession, but that went against all my training. So I stayed and argued with them whilst they kept on driving my cattle away. I was just wasting my time. I wasn't any more to them than a gnat buzzing around a horse's rump.

Turned out that I stayed a little too long. All of a sudden there was the biggest bunch of shooting you ever heard, and bullets flying around and horses squealing and pitching. For a minute I thought maybe it was a bunch of my *vaqueros* come to my rescue, but I disabused myself of that notion when I seen the uniforms. It was the soldiers, ambushing this bunch of cow-stealing rebels.

I can't say a lot for their marksmanship, because most of the rebels got clean away. They rode like they was all married men, getting back to the bosom of their families. I decided it might be smart if I went home too. But I didn't get very far. One of them soldiers got off a lucky shot, and that was the end of my good old Tennessee gray horse that I had brought home from the big war. I ate a bucketful of pure old Mexican dirt and had a little trouble getting my breath started again. Time I was able to get on my feet, there didn't seem to be much use in it. A bunch of them soldiers had me surrounded, and it was like it had been that day me and Felipe stumbled onto the ambush of the gun-runners.

Captain Santos wasn't with them this time, which I thought at first was some improvement. But his sergeant was there, the one with the itchy trigger finger. I figured I'd try to put the best face on a bad situation. I thanked him for rescuing me from that bunch of cattle thieves.

You know something? He didn't believe a bit of that.

One of the men tickled me in the ribs with the muzzle of his rifle. The sergeant motioned for me to get to my feet, *pronto*. I didn't see where it would help my situation to argue with him. They searched me and taken away the pistol I had on. That was the second time they had taken guns away from me. Seemed like they was determined not only to make me feed their army but to equip it with artillery. One of the men taken my pocketwatch, the one with Millie's picture in the back. I grabbed at it and got a gun butt up beside my head. I ate another bucketful of dirt.

When my eyes cleared to where I could see, that sergeant had my watch open, listening to the little tune it played and looking at Millie's picture. He made some comment about her that I'd of been pleased to kill a man for if the circumstances had been more favorable. But I was at a considerable disadvantage at the time. I could feel the blood running down the side of my face, hot and sticky. I had a headache that would of set a mule on its haunches.

"This time," the sergeant says, "we have caught you redhanded, *gringo*, working with those damned rebels."

I had already argued myself out, trying to make that rebel see my side of it. I didn't have it left in me to argue with this sergeant. I expected them to shoot me right where I sat. I hurt so bad that it would of been merciful. But mercy didn't have no part in his thinking.

"*El capitán* will be most pleased to see you, *gringo*," says he. "Especially when I tell him the company you keep."

I don't suppose you ever had your head cracked with a gun butt? It makes it awful hard to concentrate. Just getting on the horse was a chore. Mine was dead, but they brought up one which a rebel wasn't going to need anymore. I couldn't tell what color it was, hardly. I fell off once. The sergeant tied a short piece of rope around my neck and the other end to the saddlehorn, and told me that the next time I fell off I would hang myself. That helped my concentration some.

It was way after dark when we finally got into town. The fiddles and the guitars was playing in the *cantinas*, but I didn't enjoy the music. They drug me through some big tall wooden doors into a *patio* of some kind, and across to a cell which had a wooden door that must of weighed five hundred pounds. They throwed me in there and locked the door and left.

I laid there a long time waiting for my head to quit hurting, but it never did. It was too dark to see anything, so I asked if there was anybody with me, and I found out I had the whole thing to myself. I felt around and found a goatskin, which was all the bed they provided. The way I felt right then, a feather tick wouldn't of helped. I can't say I slept much. My head hurt like thunder, and I found out I wasn't as alone in that cell as I thought I was. Little crawling and running things was in there with me. They must of liked the place because they didn't seem to be making any great effort to get out. They was just trying to be friendly, especially the lice.

There wasn't no window in the cell, but come morning I could see light start to seep around the edges of that heavy wooden door. The walls was of adobe. It appeared to me I could probably cut my way through them if I had plenty of time and something to scratch with. But that could turn into a lifetime proposition. Walls like that was often three feet thick. And when a man got through one, chances was he would find himself in another cell like the one he had crawled out of. I doubted they figured on keeping me around long enough for me to find out.

They didn't seem to figure I needed any breakfast; leastways they neglected to bring it. My head hurt me a lot worse than my stomach did, anyway. I'd been looking at the daylight around that door for a long time before finally I heard somebody thumping around out there, fiddling with the bolt. The light hurt my eyes when they swung the door in, but I got used to it in a minute. There stood that sergeant with a mean black whip in his hand, and right behind him was Captain Santos.

"Señor Peeler," Santos says, kind of smug and satisfied with himself, "I hope you slept well."

Now, that rankled me a little because I knowed he didn't care whether I'd got any sleep or not. I changed the subject considerable and tried to give him some idea what kind of a son of a bitch—pardon me, preacher—I thought he really was. The sergeant commenced a little persuasion with the whip.

It was the first time anybody had taken a whip to me in my life, if you don't count the times my daddy taken a quirt to my rosy little cheeks when I was a button. This wasn't no quirt, it was one of them old blacksnakes like they use down there to drive bulls into the ring. It had a bite like something out of hell. I rolled over to get away from it, bumped my sore head on the hard dirt floor and come near fainting.

I heard the captain say, "Enough, Sergeant. I think he understands you."

I understood *both* of them. I had very little hope right then that I would ever get out of that place alive.

The captain says, "So this time you were caught, Señor Peeler, helping those people drive away cattle to feed their accursed rebel camps."

I thought I ought to tell him once, whether he believed me or not, so I says, "I caught them taking my cattle. I was trying to stop them." I was wasting my breath, and there wasn't much of it to spare.

The captain says, "Why weren't they dead, then, some of them? And why aren't *you* dead? If you had really tried to stop them you would have killed some of them, and they would have killed you. You lie, *gringo*. Sergeant, show him what we think of *gringos* who lie to us."

There was nothing I could do but curl up in a ball and take it, and try to think up all the slow and brutal ways I could kill them both, if ever I got the chance. With all due respect to your profession, preacher, these sky pilots that get up and preach against hate don't know what they're talking about. They don't know how good it can make a man feel to hate under the right circumstances. I've knowed times when hate was all that kept a man alive.

The sergeant finally quit whipping me. Santos says, "Are you ready to admit your guilt?"

I gave him some advice, which he didn't take, and the sergeant whipped me again. Then he left, and it was just me and the captain in there by ourselves. I figured up my chances of killing him before the rest of them could kill me. They wasn't much good. I was so weak I probably couldn't of made his nose bleed. He must of read my mind, because he reminded me that he had a whole squad of men just outside the door, and they would leave me looking like a milk strainer if I made one wrong move.

"I am sorry about this," says he. "I looked forward to being a partner with you."

"Go to hell," says I.

That didn't seem to bother him much this time. The shape he had me in, I can see why he was getting more tolerant. He says, "No, we can't be partners anymore. I am going to buy you out."

That sounded a little strange to me, him talking about *buying*. Looked to me like all he had to do was *take*.

I told him I wasn't selling, but he told me I would; it was just a question of *when*. He asked me if I was hungry. I told him I was. He said that sure was too bad, because I wouldn't get nothing to eat until I decided to sell out, or until there was snow three feet deep out there in the *patio*. And that wasn't no snow country.

The steel bolt sounded like a gunshot when they locked that door shut on me again and left me in there with the rats and the cockroaches and the lice. Off and on all day I could hear people shuffling around outside, but that door never opened again. Finally I watched the light fade from around it and knowed it was nighttime. That goatskin felt a little better; I slept a right smart. My head quit hurting, but my stomach got to raising Cain with me. I had done without anything to eat a good many times before, but I never had got to where I could get along without noticing it like some people seem to. I'd rather face up to a posse of deputy sheriffs than to put up with an empty stomach.

The light gradually come around the door again, so I knowed it was daytime. I got to listening for them to come, but they didn't. I drawed up my belt as tight as I could. People tell you that'll help, but I'm here to inform you otherwise. There's no substitute for a square meal.

I judged it was along about the middle of the day before finally I heard them working that bolt. I shut my eyes, because the light was going to hurt. The captain came in, him and the sergeant. The sergeant was carrying his old friend the blacksnake. My back was all sore and welted from the treatment he had already given me. I could feel my flesh crawl when I looked at that whip.

Santos had some papers in his hand. Says he, "I have been to a lawyer, and he has drawn up these papers for me." He handed me something all written out in a nice hand, and punched with a fancy seal. It was all in Mexican. I could talk Mexican fair to middling and understand it when they talked, but I couldn't read their writing much. I handed it back to him and told him I didn't know what it was. He said it was a deed to the ranch. He reached in his shirt and pulled out a little leather bag with a puckerstring drawed up tight. He shook it so I could hear the rattle of coin.

"Gold," says he. "This gold and your freedom when you sign this deed."

For a minute I was sore tempted. I says, "And how about something to eat?"

"When you sign," says he.

I had no way to know how much gold he had in that sack. It probably wasn't nowhere near what I had paid Orville Jackson, but right then I was a whole lot more concerned with getting away than I was with the money. I was on the point of telling him yes when my thinking got to running a little straighter. All of a sudden it come to me that once he had my name on that paper, he could do anything he wanted to with me. He could kill me and take that gold back. If I was in his place, that's what I would of done.

If I signed that paper I was a dead man.

I never was one to beat around the bush, so I told him just the way my mind was running. It made him mad that I could see through him, I reckon, because he said something sharp to the sergeant and walked out. The sergeant went to work on me with that whip to where I quit worrying about my empty stomach.

That was the last I seen of them that day. Night come, and I sat there all huddled up on the goatskin doing a lot of thinking. Two whole days and a bit of another they had had me in there without a thing to eat. You can't imagine how one of them tight little cells gets to smelling, either, especially when nature calls and you got noplace else to go. I tell you, I was sure down in my thinking.

I didn't know how things went by Mexican law, but I knowed by American law I didn't have no legal right to sign away the whole ranch, just my own share in the partnership. Exactly how much of a share María owned had never been straight in my mind; it was maybe ten percent, or something like that—whatever her husband had to make it look right to the Mexicans. That was a technicality, and I never was no hand at technicalities.

One thing bothered me. If all they needed was my signature, why didn't they just forge it? Then they could shoot me and drag me off to the buzzards. I sure wasn't going to raise up from the dead and contest them. I wondered, but I had sense enough not to ask them; maybe they just hadn't thought of it.

Gradually I realized that in the end Santos was going to get my signature. But the longer I could hold it away from him the more chance I had to see another sunrise. When you're that close to the taw line, you realize that even living in a dark smelly cell is better than dying.

They didn't wait till noon the next time; they was there early, Santos and the sergeant, and a detail of men that stayed outside.

Under ordinary circumstances when you get into a negotiation in Mexico you'll find it takes a long time. They'll visit and talk about everything but the business at hand. When it finally comes into the conversation it's real casual, like something that just popped into their minds that minute and ain't important anyway.

Santos wasn't like that. Right off he says, "You ready to sign?"

I asks him, "How much gold you got in that sack?"

He says it don't matter, it's more than I deserve. I says, "I want more, a lot more." The sergeant moved up with his whip, but the captain says, "*Bueno*, you can have more."

Says I, "You fill that sack to where you can't cram no more into it and still draw the string tight."

The captain said all right, he would. No argument. Right then I knowed all my suspicions was right. He would pay me anything he had to because he was going to take it back off of my dead body anyway. Same as Jesse Ordway had figured. From his standpoint a man couldn't hardly beat a deal like that.

Santos waved the deed at me.

My hand was shaking, I was so weak from not having anything to eat. I told him I couldn't write my name in that kind of shape, that I was in bad need of nourishment. And I told him I couldn't eat it here in this place because it smelled so bad.

He thought he had me beat, so all of a sudden there wasn't nothing too good for me. He says to come on, he'll take me to his quarters and have some food brought to me. He led me out of that cell, and I made up my mind right then and there that I wasn't ever going back into it. I still held a few cards in my hand. I was going to play them out one at a time and as careful as I could.

Walking was a chore at first. I had been sitting or laying down in that cell for most of three days and hadn't gotten to exercise my legs.

I doubt that they fed their other condemned men as well as they fed me, but of course they wasn't trying to get as much from them. I had me some *tortillas* and some eggs and *cabrito* and black coffee, and I topped it all off with a long drink of *tequila*, which was of a pretty fair grade. He was a captain and could afford better than most of the *peons* and the convict soldiers. I had eaten till I had filled out every wrinkle in my belly and even hurt a little bit.

I always agreed with the Indians on one point: when you can eat, *eat!* You can't ever be sure when your next meal is coming.

A couple of good-looking young women cleared off the table. The captain pinched one of them twice, fore and aft. He was feeling pretty good about then. He had had a little snort of *tequila* himself. She slapped his hand, kind of gentle. I figured she was one woman whose work was never done.

The captain brought out the deed again, and he says, "Is your hand steady enough now to sign?"

I had played one card and got my belly filled. Now I played me another. I says, "In my own good time, Captain. You promised to fill up that sack with gold."

He walked over to the bed and got down on his knees and pulled out a strongbox. It had a Texas bank name on it, and I could well imagine how he come into possession. It had a padlock that could of been used for a leg iron. When he swung the lid open, he taken a big canvas bag out and opened it to get some more coins. Soon as I seen their gold color my natural ambition came to the front. I says, "That's all right, just let me have the whole bag."

He chided me some about the sin of greed, but I didn't figure he qualified as no preacher. Finally he brought that whole canvas bag over and laid it on the table. Oh, but it had a fine solid sound to it. The ring of gold and silver pieces was always my favorite kind of music.

"Now," he says, "sign."

I picked up the bags one at a time, the little leather one first and then the big canvas sack. I had no way of knowing how much real money they held, but I sure liked the heft of them. The liking must of showed, and he thought he had set the hook for sure. He pushed the deed in my face.

Says I, "*Capitán*, it occurs to me that when I sign this deed you'll have all you want from me. You could take me out to that adobe wall and be shed of me good and proper. You'd have all this gold back and my ranch besides. I wouldn't be very smart to get into that shape."

The sergeant stepped up and volunteered to wear a little more shine off of that blacksnake. For a minute it looked like the captain was fixing to let him; his face went as dark as old shoe leather. Him and the sergeant went off in a corner and had theirselves a whispering conference. Directly the captain came back. He says in a hard voice, "Just what is it you want?"

I told him I wanted to go to the Rio Grande.

He drawed his pistol and cocked it and shoved it in my face. "*Gringo*," says he, "I would not have to take you to the wall. I could shoot you right here and splatter your brains all over this floor. I could have your carcass dragged off to the brush like a mongrel dog."

He didn't have to tell me that; I already knowed it. Says I, "That's why I want to be safe at the river before I sign."

He cussed me for a double-crossing hound who had eaten his food and drunk his *tequila*, then refused to honor my word. I told him he still had my word. I would sign the deed. But I would do it when I was safe at the river. Signing it now, I says, I'd be dead in ten minutes.

Him and the sergeant had another conference over in the corner, a little louder this time. I could hear most of it. I heard the sergeant suggesting what I had already thought of, that they just shoot me and forge my name. But the captain said they had to handle this so that dog of a magistrate would accept it. The magistrate was a man with a gavel where his heart should be. He had no woman, and he slept with his lawbooks instead. He was a stickler for observing the last fine point of the law and was rich enough that he did not need to take the *mordida*. Worse, he was kin of the governor, so they didn't dare force him. Worst of all, he knowed my face and he knowed my signature. I had signed it in front of him when I bought the ranch.

The captain never would of made a poker player. I could read his face when he came back. He had decided to give me what I asked for. They probably figured they could still kill me at the river and get the gold back after I had signed the paper. But he had to try one more time.

He says, "*Gringo*, you ask for too much."

"It ain't much of a ride from here to the river," says I. "You want the ranch, and I want a sporting chance to live."

He gave in finally, like I knowed he would, though it killed his soul to bend so much for a lousy *gringo*. He sent the sergeant out, and in a little while he was back and said everything was ready. They had a detail of half a dozen men waiting outside of the office on horseback. They had throwed my saddle on a sorry plug that couldn't of outrun the rest of them if they had all had one leg broke.

I told the captain there was one more thing I wanted, my watch with Millie's picture in it. The sergeant had it, and it tore him plumb up to give it to me. He opened the case and let it play its little tune before he would turn it over. I reckon he was afraid it would get shot to pieces when they finished me off.

I didn't know exactly what I was going to do when I got to the river. I figured the only real chance I had was to make a wild sashay and jump into the water before they could stop me. Naturally they would shoot at me every time I came up for air, but I would just have to try not to breathe much. I had already seen that they wasn't very good shots.

It bothered me about the gold. I couldn't swim across with that big sack; it would take me under. But maybe that little bag wouldn't hurt. I says to the captain, "Been thinking I'd sure like to carry the gold."

He looks at me like I'm crazy and says, "You have not signed yet. You get the money when you sign."

"The little bag at least," I says. "Just let me enjoy the feel of it."

He handed it to me. Maybe he felt like it would keep my greed fired up and I wouldn't give him no more trouble about the deed. I kept feeling the gold, which I knowed was what he wanted me to do. The seat of my britches was all itchy from wanting to get this over with, from wanting to get away from them. But I did enjoy the smell of the good clean air. It was the first time I'd been out in the open in three days.

The captain made it a point for us to ride by the government house and to call out the magistrate so he could see me with his own eyes. He told him we was all on our way down to the office of the lawyer to sign some papers. I spoke up to invite the magistrate to go along with us, but the sergeant stuck a pistol in my back where the magistrate couldn't see it, and I had to give up on hospitality.

There wasn't no bridges over the river in them days, nowhere on the whole Rio Grande. There wasn't even a ferry at this point. There was just a place about fifty yards wide that you could swim a horse across. Wagons and carts and such had to go down the river a long ways to where there was a little cable-operated ferry.

Texas looked pretty good to me, laying over yonder across that little stream of muddy water. Sure, the law was hunting for me over there, or at least I thought they was. But looking across, I couldn't see a sign of anybody on the other side. I didn't hardly expect that there would be somebody come over and help me out of the predicament I was in.

The captain was getting awful impatient. He turns to me and says, "Here we are, just the way we promised you. Now, the deed . . ."

I had kept edging to the front, getting as near to the river as I could for my big break. But that sergeant outguessed me. He rode in close and taken the reins of that sorry plug I was on. If I ran for the river now I was going to have to do it afoot. I sort of measured the sergeant with my eye, figuring how to climb right over him.

I says to the captain, "Do I have your word that when I sign, I can cross the river and you won't shoot me in the back?"

You ever see a rattlesnake curl his lips back? That's the kind of smile the captain gave me. "You have my word. The word of an officer and a gentleman."

He was lying like a candidate. The soldiers began to back their horses away and form up a line. I knowed what was coming to me the minute I signed that paper. I had got to the river all right, but I was never going to cross it.

One word you never want to say is *never*. All of a sudden the whole thing was taken out of his hands.

There come, in the wink of an eye, a volley of guns like the Fourth of July. For a sorry old plug like he was, that horse of mine must of jumped four feet straight up. The sergeant fell off with his face all bloody and hit the sand and just laid there. His horse taken out in a panic and swam across the river. I finally got my spooked plug under control and looked around and seen half of them soldiers down just like the sergeant was. The rest of them was running off, all but the captain. He just sat there looking sort of foolish and drained out.

Down to the riverbank came a dozen or so ragged-looking Mexicans with guns smoking in their hands. I didn't know the faces, but I sure knowed the type. They was a bunch of them cattle-stealing rebels. Directly I seen a friendly face coming. At least, I thought it was friendly. Felipe Rios rode down to where me and the captain was. With him was that rebel leader that I'd had such a cuss fight with over them running my cattle off.

I was never more glad to see a Mexican in my life, hardly. I says, "Felipe, you sure have a way of turning up when a man needs you."

The captain just looked at them and swallowed. He still held the deed in his hand. I noticed that the hand was trembling a right smart. He says, "I was about to release this man." Which was true; he was about to release me from all worldly cares. Felipe reached up and jerked the deed away from him, looked at it and handed it to the leader. I remembered then that Felipe couldn't read. But that rebel could.

Now that I seen the two of them together, the resemblance was considerable. I would of bet they was first cousins, at least.

That rebel studied the paper and knowed in a minute what this whole thing was about. Says he, "*Gringo*, we thought they were simply going to take you out and kill you. But it appears there was more."

I ought to've knowed not to talk so much, but I was so glad to see them that I had no caution. I told them what Santos had figured on doing, and what I was planning to try to do.

He didn't look a bit pleased. He says, "You would have turned your property over to this butcher to save your own neck?"

I told him it was the only neck I had, and the property wouldn't of helped me much if I was dead.

He looked at the canvas sack on the captain's saddle. "You were going to sell it to him for money. That is like a *gringo.*"

Where I came from it was always customary to sell things for money. It was the best medium of exchange anybody had ever come up with. But I got a strong feeling that I wasn't in no position to argue details. I wasn't in no position to argue *anything.* The look in his eyes told me I'd better do a lot of listening.

He filled my ear with a lot of stuff about how they was fighting to stop oppression and bury the butchers like Santos and so forth, and about how hard it was for them to understand a *gringo* whose only interest was in money when there was people bleeding and dying all around.

The only ones I could see bleeding and dying right then was Santos's soldiers. They was in a bad way, the ones that hadn't gotten clear. I wouldn't of given a well-used chaw of tobacco for Santos's chances of leaving that riverbank alive, either. I think the only question they had about him was whether to slit his throat from the left or from the right. And he knowed it, too, because his face was drained from a nice brown down to about a *gringo* color.

The rebel shoved the deed back at me and says, "You were going to sign it for him. Sign it for me!"

I looked at Felipe. He wasn't going to be no help this time, I could tell. All his sympathy was with them others. We had come to the parting of the ways. I reached up and taken a lead pencil out of Santos's pocket, one he had brought for that purpose, only things hadn't turned in quite the direction he had intended. I signed the deed and handed it to the rebel. I asks, "Who gets the ranch?"

Felipe says, "María."

I couldn't argue much with that. It seemed proper, since she had been a partner in it anyway.

I says, "And who gets María?"

Felipe says, "I do."

I figured he already had, maybe even while Jackson was still there. Well, that meant he would get the ranch too, which was better than having it go to Santos. Or to that rebel leader, who didn't look much like a cowboy to me noway. He had that wild eye you see in people who are always going around over creation looking for something to raise hell about.

I reached to get the canvas bag of gold off of Santos's saddle. "That belongs to me," I says.

The rebel clamped his hand over mine. He says, "No! You have just given it to our cause. We have use for it."

He started telling me again about their great crusade, and about all the hungry and shirtless and barefoot ones, and I knowed damn well there wouldn't none of them ever see any of this money. It's always been my observation that the feller who hollers loudest about helping the downtrodden poor is usually counting himself at the head of the list. Soon as he gets his hands on some money of his own, the poor don't look near as hungry to him anymore.

I told him it didn't hardly seem right to leave me without a thing to show for all my trouble. I was giving up my ranch; I ought to have *something*.

They didn't know about that little bag of gold in my shirt.

"You have your life, *gringo*," he says. "It is not worth much, but it is more than Santos was going to give you. Now go, before we take that too!"

Everybody's eyes was on me right at that minute. Santos taken what little chance he had. He jabbed his spurs into that horse and jumped him off into the water as hard as he could run, taking gold and all. He caught them rebels by surprise. When they finally started shooting at him, he slid out of the saddle to make less of a target. Somewhere out there he got separated from the horse and had to try to swim by himself. I don't know if a bullet caught him, or if his clothes pulled him down, or if he just plain couldn't swim. In a minute or two there wasn't no sign of him anyplace. He was gone, under that muddy water. Next time he ever came up, he was going to be a long ways down the river, and deader than yesterday's fish.

His horse must of been boogered by the shooting. It went right on swimming across toward the Texas side.

I had shaken hands with Felipe and said good-bye to my ranch, so I started swimming that plug of mine across too. I kind of halfway expected them rebels to decide to send me along after Santos, but they didn't. I got to the Texas bank without any holes in me that wasn't natural.

I had it in my head that luck was with me, and that I'd wind up with that canvas bag of gold and silver after all. I caught up to Santos's horse where it had stopped to rest itself on the Texas side. The sergeant's horse was standing there with it.

The bag was gone. It had slipped loose somewhere out there in the river.

Santos might float to the top, eventually, but that bag never would.

At least I still had the little sack of gold I had hidden in my shirt. And I had three horses, if the plug I was riding was to be counted as a horse. The captain's was a well-built black with an American brand. He had a pretty good Mexican-style saddle on him, and a carbine in a scabbard, so that I wasn't plumb unarmed. There was a saber on the saddle. I started to throw it away, till I decided maybe I could trade it later for supplies. Waste not, want not.

The shooting was liable to draw somebody curious. I didn't want to be there to explain things to them when they showed up, so I got on the captain's black horse and led the other two and taken out for the thickest brush I could see.

I was glad to be in Texas again. Hell, I was glad to be *alive*.

CHAPTER 3

Of course I was still Joe Peeler then, and you the world know me now as Joe Pepper. You want to know how come me to get to be Joe Pepper? Well, I'll tell you if you'll be patient.

For a while there I was in an awful uncomfortable situation. There wasn't but two sides to the river, and I was in some demand on both of them. The best bet I had was to go west as far and as fast as I could without doing me or the horses any real hurt.

The Texas and Mexico border had a lot of variety in them days, same as it does now. Down on the very lowest part, toward Brownsville, there was getting to be a certain amount of farming on both sides of the river, and the country was settling up. It was a good fertile land where cold weather didn't bite very hard or very long, and just about anything you wanted to plant would grow. Go up the river a hundred or so miles, though, and you start to get into a desert type of country where a man trying to farm had better have himself some awful big buckets to carry water out to his crops. You'd find that the farmers, especially over on the Mexico side, would dig irrigation ditches to carry water to fields about three times the size of a postage stamp. Back away from the river it was mostly just ranchland. Good ranchland, everything considered, only you had to give your cattle lots of room and not let them see too much of each other or they would soon be overstocked.

It was a big old wide-open country where you could go for a long time and never run across a lawman, or where you might—if your luck ran sour—turn a corner in a wagon road and run into a whole covey of Texas Rangers.

There was a good many people in that section them days that wasn't very popular where they had come from and couldn't go back home without some risk of winding up as guests of the state. But down in the border country they might go for years—maybe forever—and not have to answer any embarrassing questions. As long as they didn't raise any undue hell, people didn't worry overly much about where they had come from or what the homefolks might of thought about them.

If I had been in trouble in some other state, or even up in East Texas, I might of stayed in that lower border country and never had to worry about old times. But I had shot Jesse Ordway in South Texas, not far from the Rio Grande. I felt like the risk was too much for me to put up with. Sooner or later, the way people had of drifting west, I'd come face to face with somebody who knowed who I was and knowed about Jesse Ordway. It stood to reason that Mrs. Ordway had posted a reward on me. She was rich enough to've made it a big one.

A lot of people are good about minding their own business as long as it don't cost them nothing, but you put money into the situation and they come down with a bad case of public responsibility.

I had three horses on my hands, and a saddle for each of them. A man leading two saddled horses just naturally attracts attention. People get to wondering who used to fill the saddles, and they think maybe he knows something he ain't telling. A few miles from where I had crossed the river I came upon a young Mexican boy herding a bunch of spotted goats on a paint pony, bareback. I gave him the sergeant's saddle. He was a little dubious about it till I told him it had come to me in a vision that I was supposed to give it to the first boy I came across herding goats on a paint pony. He was a religious boy, evidently, because he taken it.

I was kind of tempted to keep the captain's saddle because it was made of good leather and had some fancy silver on it. But a man that ain't used to them big-horned Mexico saddles generally has trouble with them at first. They'll pinch right where it grabs you the worst. I came onto a Mexican packtrain loaded down with contraband Mexican liquor heading north to San Antonio. I traded that saddle to them smugglers for a sackful of *tamales* that they had packed in lard to eat along the way, and a goatskin full of raw *pulque*. I tell you, a man that drinks a little old-time *pulque* every day ought not to ever have to worry about a tapeworm. There ain't nothing could live bottled up amidst that stuff. It taken a right smart of it to burn the stench of that cell out of my nose. There I was with a little leather pouch full of gold coins, and all them *tamales* and that *pulque*, plus two good horses and one plug. I was rich, when you figure the times.

But a man can get tired of *tamales* pretty quick when they're all he has to eat. It was mostly Mexicans living along the border then, whichever side of it you happened to be on. One evening I reined in to a place and found a young Mexican woman there all by herself without so much as a pony to ride if she had to go anyplace. She said she was married, and her husband was off someplace on business. By the conversation I got a pretty good notion what kind of business it was; there was people on the Texas side that used to raid the ranches there and sell stolen cattle and horses and mules down in Mexico, and people on the Mexican side would drive up stolen stock from Mexico to sell in Texas. Sometimes the same horse might change ownership three-four times and wind up back where he started from. It made for a lot of business, anyway. Like I was saying, the woman had been by herself a good spell, and I found her mighty lonesome, same as I was. She never said it in so many words, but I figured she had already made up her mind that her husband was dead. Oftentimes when them outlaws got shot, whichever side of the river it was on, the people who killed them just left them laying where they was, and nobody ever heard from them again. It wasn't no easy life.

I stayed there with that woman three, maybe four days, resting up the horses, filling up on her cooking, comforting her in her loneliness. When I left there I just taken two of the horses with me. I left her that plug.

Past Laredo, and especially beyond Eagle Pass, things got pretty thin on the border. It started to getting into Indian country, and things tended sometimes to be a little wild for a man of genteel tastes.

The government had a military post on upriver that they called Fort Clark, and the troops there was kept busy most of the time running after Indians and renegades that had learned how to use the border to their advantage. There was Lipan Apaches and Kickapoos and the like down there, all of them kind of having it in for the *gringo*. Folks told me the Kickapoos had been friendly Indians one time, never gave nobody any trouble till a bunch of Confederate soldiers—this was during the war, you know—mistaken them for a bunch of hostiles and plowed into them on one of the creeks that run into the Concho. It came as a surprise to the Indians, first, then a big surprise to the soldiers because them Indians turned around and whipped the britches off of them. After that, they was enemy Indians like all the others.

I'd never fought no Indians up to that time, and hadn't lost any, but I figured it would be about as unhealthy for me to run into a bunch of soldiers as a bunch of Indians, so I tried to skirt around all the posts and towns and such. I was on one of them wide sashays when I got the name of Joe Pepper.

I hadn't seen any Indian sign that I could recognize. Up to this time I'd never even seen or been around Indians anyhow, except them few on the cattle trail to Kansas, and they wasn't really wild. Maybe I didn't know what to look for. But to play it safe I would stop early of an evening and build me a little campfire while it was still light, cook me some supper, kill the fire and move on a ways till it got dark, then make a cold camp. I didn't want Indians finding me at night by seeing my campfire or by smelling the smoke from it.

So one evening a while before sundown I was cooking up some *tortillas* out of ground corn I'd got from the woman, and boiling coffee in a can, when I seen a feller come riding in from the east. I could tell right off that he wasn't no Indian, and I had a feeling by the looks of him that he wasn't a lawman. You get a sixth sense about lawmen if you spend long enough avoiding them. So I hailed him to come on in and invited him to share what vittles I had. He was a tallish sort of a gent, with stubbly whiskers—rusty-colored—that hadn't felt a razor in quite a spell. I could tell by the way he wolfed down them *tamales*—cold lard and all—that he hadn't eaten a good square meal in a while.

You never seen a man more needful than he was, or so grateful for what he was given. It kind of gave me a glow inside to know how much good I was doing for a needy and grateful stranger.

Now, if you've ever heard anybody cock a hammer back on a pistol, and that pistol is pointed at you, it's a sound you'll never forget the rest of your life. It's like a rattlesnake's rattle—you can hear it a hundred yards away. I whirled around and tried to grab my rifle. But I was too late.

That grateful stranger shot me.

I can't swear that I heard it. I seen a flash, but I can't even swear it was from the gun. It might of been from the pain when that thing hit me in the ribs. I remember feeling like I'd been kicked by a Missouri mule—a big one at that—and I went down like I had been sledged. I remember fighting for breath and not getting any. I remember that grateful stranger feeling around over me, finding that little bag of gold in my shirt and stripping me to the waist to see if I had any more money. And I remember the warm feel of the blood running down my hide.

It's bad enough having somebody shoot you. It's that much worse when he makes you feel like six kinds of a fool for letting him. I remember laying there trying to get a breath so I could cuss him, and cuss myself for letting him into my camp.

Better it had been the Indians. They wasn't in the habit of repaying a kindness by killing you. Of course, there wasn't many people them days bent over backwards to be kind to Indians.

For a long time I figured I was dead, and I wondered how it was that I could be laying there thinking about it. I couldn't move . . . couldn't even breathe, hardly. I couldn't see enough to tell, but I was satisfied he had run off with everything I had.

It was getting on dark when somebody came along and found me. Things was so hazy by then that I couldn't tell much. I knowed they lifted me up onto a big wagon or something, and I could tell it hurt like thunder. They probed around my gizzard with a knife. By this time, of course, I knowed I wasn't dead—yet. I figured they would kill me off, though, the way they was doing. The pain got so bad that I passed out.

Next thing I remembered, I was riding on my back in something that felt like a wagon, and every time it hit a bump it was like somebody had jabbed me in the ribs with a crowbar. It was an awful bumpy road.

I got clear enough in my head to know they was talking Mexican, not *gringo*. It didn't make much difference at the time. Way after dark they stopped and lifted me down. They laid me on a blanket and gave me a big drink of some kind of liquor and covered me up.

Come daylight I could see that I was amongst some Mexican freighters. They had a bunch of oxen and them old big high-wheeled carts that you still see now and again down in the border country. They asked me if I felt like having any breakfast. I didn't, but I wanted another drink. Turned out it was *tequila*. You probably wouldn't know about this, preacher, but *tequila* ain't half bad when you're in need of it.

I gradually sat up and began to take stock. My ribs was sore as the devil, but I wasn't near as bad off as I had a right to be, getting shot in the side that way. I asked them what they had done to me. They said they had dug out a bullet that was laying in beneath the skin, up against the ribs. One of the Mexicans—a boy of fifteen or sixteen, I'd judge—brought it to show to me. It was flattened out, like if you'd laid it on a rail and let a train run over it the way kids will do sometimes with a coin, when they don't know the value of money. I knowed old Joe Peeler was tough, but I didn't see how I could of taken a slug and flattened it out that much and lived to look at it.

Then I realized that grateful stranger had shot me in the gold pouch. I had that leather bag under my shirt, and as I wheeled around his bullet had caught it. The gold coins taken up most of the force so that it was nearly spent by the time it got through to me. I had bled like a stuck hog, though. He must of figured I was near dead or he'd of seen to it.

Every move I made brought a little jab that made me use the Lord's name in vain. I always figured that was one of the lesser Commandments, and since I had already broke so many of the bigger ones, I didn't see what harm could come of it. It helps a man feel better sometimes to cuss a little, like you'd stick a knife into a bloated steer to let the gas out and relieve the pressure on him.

Them Mexicans was good to me. I felt bad that I didn't have a thing I could pay them with. The stranger had taken the gold, my horses, my rifle, my *tamales*, my *pulque* . . . everything but my boots. My feet must not of been his size.

I've always had a kindly feeling toward Mexicans since that time. Them freighters was God's people because they could just as well of left me laying where they found me. They sure didn't owe me nothing, a *gringo* stranger like I was, and trouble to boot. They wasn't of your church, preacher; maybe they didn't go to no church. But they was God's people.

I laid on top of the load on one of them big carts and rode all day. Along toward night we come to a settlement named Catclaw. It had some older Mexican name, but the *gringos* had come along and changed it. It was still Mexican, mostly. But I could tell by the names on the stores that it had a share of *gringos* in it. It was a county seat, too, because it had a frame courthouse up on the town square. It takes a *gringo* to want to build something frame when the lumber's got to be hauled three hundred miles, and when they've got all the material within a mile that they need to build out of adobe or rock. Next to the courthouse, almost as big and a lot stronger built, was a rock jail with walls that must of been a foot and a half thick. Looking at it even from a distance, I could almost smell that Mexican cell again. It always made me a little sick to my stomach if I thought about it much. You never know what freedom is really worth till you've done without.

I hadn't made any plans. I was broke, afoot, and for all I knowed had a price on my head. I had it in my mind that I would wait till way up in the night, then steal me a horse and cross back over the river into Mexico again. I was far enough west that I doubted my troubles from downriver would find me.

It never occurred to me that them freighters would take matters out of my hands. I was sitting around the fire with them at supper, eating a bite and trying to figure out exactly what I was going to do, when somebody came up from behind me. I thought it was one of the freighters till he spoke out in *gringo*. He says, "I understand you've had some trouble."

I turned around right quick, and there stood a man with a badge on his shirt. That badge looked as big as the lid on a five-gallon bucket. I let my hand drop down to my belt where my six-shooter would of been, if I'd had one. I figured he had me.

I says, "No, I ain't had no trouble to speak of."

The sheriff says, "They tell me somebody shot you and robbed you and left you to die. If that ain't trouble, I'd hate to see what trouble is." He acted kind of out of patience.

I told him I had no earthly idea who the grateful stranger was, or where he had gone to, so there wasn't much either me or the law could do. I thanked him kindly and told him I was sorry he had bothered himself.

By then he was getting suspicious, because most people in my shape would of been hollering for the law to drop everything else and help them. He says, "What's your name, friend?"

Him being a sheriff and all, I sure didn't figure he had much cause to be calling me friend. And I sure wasn't going to tell him my name was Joe Peeler. I looked across the fire and saw one of the Mexicans pop a hot *chiltipiquin* pepper into his mouth. Right quick I said my name was Pepper . . . Joe Pepper.

If I'd said my name was Smith, like so many of them do, he'd of knowed I was lying. But I suppose Pepper sounded natural enough, because he taken it for the gospel truth. He says, "Well, Joe Pepper, how would you like to come down to the office with me?"

I can tell you, I didn't like the idea atall. I figured he had a nice little cell waiting for me, and there wasn't a blessed thing I could do to protect myself. I says, "Any particular reason?" Seemed like a foolish question at the time.

He says, "I've got a stack of flyers over there with descriptions of various and sundry fugitives. Maybe you'll find your man on one of them. It would help, at least, if we know who we're hunting for."

I could think of twenty-seven places I had rather of gone than to a sheriff's office, but he had a gun in his belt, and that gave him a right smart advantage.

I figured at the time that he knowed who I really was and intended to slam the door shut on me soon as he got me inside. But he didn't. His office was a little box of a room in the front end of the jail. He motioned for me to sit down. He went to rifling through a drawer of a big roll-top desk and brought out a stack of papers. He says, "I'm taking it for granted you can read."

Lots of people couldn't, you know. But I told him sure, I'd been reading since I was ten-eleven years old. Slow about it, sometimes, but I could read. He handed me the papers and told me to go through them. While I was reading he would go rustle us some coffee.

By then I decided he didn't suspicion who I was. And all of a sudden I figured it would be an advantage for me to go through the flyers. I could find the one on me, stick it in my pocket when he wasn't looking, and he would never miss it. Soon as he left the room I went through the papers right fast, looking for one on me. When I got to the last one in the stack, I hadn't found anything. I went back through them again, a little slower. But it wasn't there.

At that time I still had no idea that Mrs. Ordway never had pressed any charges against me. I figured maybe the mail was slow; it wasn't fast and efficient like it is now. They even lost stuff, sometimes. Well, I thought, if I could stay out ahead of the reward notices, maybe I would be all right till I got out of Texas. New Mexico and Arizona was big places, and California was even bigger. A man could lose himself.

I went back through the notices a third time, taking it slow and reading each one. When I got through, I had pulled out three that sort of fit the grateful stranger. The sheriff came in with a pot of coffee he had made or had had made for him someplace else. He looked at the three and wadded up one of them. "I ought to've pulled this one," he says. "I got word he was killed in Laredo. Killed by a wagon. A hundred law officers after him and he got run over by a beer wagon." He studied the other two. Especially one of them.

"Owen Rainwater," he says. "He could sure be the one; he's ornery enough. He's got a brother that lives up north of here. Owen's bad. Harvey's a lot worse."

I figured that wherever I could find Harvey Rainwater, I could probably find Owen Rainwater too. And my horses. And maybe my gold, if he hadn't already spent it. I says, "How do I get to Harvey Rainwater's?"

"You ain't going," he says. "Whatever he stole, it ain't worth the trip."

I told him I had already made a fair trip; a little extra wouldn't hurt me. But he says, "It'd be the longest short trip you ever made. If you need money, Pepper, I can probably find you enough work around here to get you a little road stake. You don't want to be messing around with them Rainwaters."

I told him I didn't intend to mess around with them; I just intended to get back what belonged to me. He told me to forget about it; I was probably still running a fever from that wound and I would get over it in a few days.

The Mexican freighters moved on next morning, soon as it was daylight. I thanked them all very kindly for what they had done for me, and they wished me all the best of luck and went with them big carts. You could hear the wooden wheels squeaking for a mile.

The sheriff had it fixed up for me to sleep in a wagonyard and help fork hay to the horses and such in return for three meals a day till I was feeling better and could either move on or get me a better job. It wasn't much, but I decided to stick with it a few days till my side quit hurting and I felt like I could handle a long ride. I was still figuring on borrowing me a good horse some dark night.

I didn't have to go. The second day, I was raking spilled hay up off of the ground and putting it back into a wooden rack when my eye was caught by a man riding one horse and leading another down the street. At the distance I couldn't tell much about him except that he was tall. But I knowed the horses; they was the Santos black and the bay I had inherited from the late sergeant.

I dropped the rake and went into the barn. I had already noticed that the feller who owned the wagonyard kept a big rifle in there on a rack. It was some kind of handmade rifle, manufactured for the Confederacy by a homegrown armory over in East Texas. He just stared at me when I taken that rifle down and asked him for the loan of two-three cartridges. Naturally he wanted to know what I was going to do with the gun, and I told him I thought I had seen a coyote.

He went on to tell me the rifle wasn't none too accurate at long range . . . it was one of them hurry-up war jobs. I told him I figured I'd stalk this coyote and get up close. He gave me half a dozen cartridges. I figured I wouldn't use more than one, if I used any atall; I never was wasteful with high-priced ammunition.

The two horses was tied in front of an adobe saloon, which was to be expected, I would've found it funny if that grateful stranger had tied them at the church. The stable man followed me out and watched me start down the street. I don't suppose he had ever seen a coyote shot in town.

I stopped and looked at the horses. They wasn't any the worse for wear as far as I could tell. They looked the same as when I had lost them. The black had my saddle on him. I didn't see no sense in waiting; that stranger was in the saloon spending my money. I cocked the hammer back and stepped through the door.

I don't suppose you ever watched a man look at a ghost. That was my rusty-bearded friend, all right; I knowed it the second I laid eyes on him. He sat there staring at me like he couldn't believe what he seen. He dropped a glass that was half full of whiskey and let it spill all over the little square table he was sitting at. There was another man sitting with him. He couldn't figure out what the trouble was.

I says to the stranger, "You borrowed some things that belong to me. I come to get them back."

Along about then he decided I wasn't no ghost, and I wasn't dead. He didn't have anything to say for himself. He just reached down for the pistol at his hip.

That "wanted" notice in the sheriff's office had said something about Owen Rainwater being dangerous with a gun, and I suppose he was when he stood behind a man, like he had done with me. But face to face he just wasn't much. He never did get his pistol clean out of the holster.

One thing about it, when you shot a man with one of them big old rifles close up, they didn't have to hold an autopsy over him to find out if he was dead. He just laid there on his back on the dirt floor with one leg all tangled up in his chair.

I always figured the reason people like Owen Rainwater shot men in the back was because they knowed their limitations.

That friend of his at the table with him was considerable agitated. I reloaded the rifle real fast in case I might have to reason with him. But he wasn't much on this face-to-face business. He ran mostly to talk.

He hollers, "You know what you done? You killed Owen Rainwater!"

I says, "That was sure my intention."

He goes on hollering about what a big man Owen Rainwater was, and what a big man his brother Harvey was, and how bad Harvey was going to feel about this. I told him I was sorry if I had caused anybody any undue inconvenience; I had just come to get back what was mine.

I felt of Rainwater's pockets, and sure enough he had my sack of gold. I had to take it out kind of careful to keep from spilling coins. The sack had a big hole in it. It also had a dark stain that I knowed was from my blood. It didn't make me feel atall sorry for what I had done. I held the sack up for the bartender and a couple of the customers to see.

Says I, "I'm just taking back what's mine. He stole this from me."

They didn't seem disposed to argue about it. They was as agreeable a bunch as you could ask for. That friend of Rainwater's, he seemed to decide he wasn't thirsty anymore, because when I looked around he was gone. I taken Rainwater's pistols . . . figured they was fitting interest for the use of my horses and gold.

You've probably noticed how a gunshot or two tends to draw a crowd. In two or three minutes that little saloon was jammed so full of people that it was hard to draw a breath. There wasn't anything left in there that I was interested in. I went out front to see after my horses. Pretty soon the sheriff came trotting up, puffing pretty good. He was carrying some extra weight for what frame he had. He says, "What's going on in there?"

I told him nothing was going on in there now; it was all over with. I told him I had just got my property back. Seemed like he pretty well pictured the rest of it, because he said for me to stay right where I was at, and he went inside. In a minute he was back outside with me, awful flustered.

He says, "Do you know you just killed Owen Rainwater?"

I told him I'd already had that pointed out to me. I told him I was reclaiming my horses and hoped I wasn't going to have to argue with anybody over it, because I was getting awful tired. He said if they was my horses I was welcome to take them.

Then he said something that I ought to have remembered for myself but had somehow forgot. It was a thing that kind of set the pattern of Joe Pepper's life for a long time afterwards.

He says, "You know, there's a reward for Owen Rainwater."

He had gotten me interested. I says, "How much?"

He scratched his head and wrinkled up his face like it hurt him to think so hard. He says, "About five hundred dollars, best I recall. Maybe it was a little more. I'd have to go look at the flyer." Then he twisted up his face even worse. "But it'd take several days to get it cleared and paid to you. You'll need to be moving on. That's too bad, because I'll bet you could of used that money."

You know how it feels to have somebody wave money at you and then take it away? Sort of grates at you, it does. I says, "I ain't in no hurry."

"You ought to be," he tells me. "When Harvey Rainwater finds out about this he'll come looking for you. He ain't no man you'll want to fool with."

"I wasn't fooling with his brother Owen," says I. "Is there a reward on Harvey too?"

The sheriff's jaw dropped down to about the second button. "You don't think you're going to take him *too*?"

"Well, sir," says I, "as long as I got to wait around anyway, I'd just as well turn my hand to a little paying labor."

He stared at me like he couldn't figure out what breed of horse I was. Finally he says, "You know what I ought to do? I ought to deputize you so whatever you do'll be legal."

I would of had to study on that some; the idea of me carrying a badge didn't set real good with me right then. But in a minute he taken it all back anyhow. He says, "I can't afford to do that. Harvey'd kill you, and then he'd be mad at me because I had pinned a badge on you. I don't think I favor getting him mad at me."

I says, "If he's such a wanted man, why ain't you been out there hunting for him yourself?"

"Three reasons," says Sheriff Smathers. "First place, he's in another county. Second place, he's never caused us no trouble here, up to now. Third place, he'd shoot hell out of me."

I questioned the sheriff pretty sharp on whether he really thought Rainwater would be coming into town looking for me. He said he would bet his life on it. Seemed more like he was betting *my* life. I could think of lots of things I'd rather do than sit around there waiting for somebody to come in and kill me on his own terms.

One reason I had gotten Owen so easy was that I had taken him by surprise. That gave me a little advantage. I figured maybe the smart thing to do was surprise Harvey Rainwater, too.

I asked the sheriff where to find him. For a lawman talking about an outlaw he was supposed to go out and get for himself, he sure seemed to know a lot of details. He told me about every wagon track, every cowtrail and rat's nest between town and the adobe *rancho* where Rainwater was holed up.

I asked him how I would know Harvey when I seen him. He says, "Just remember what his brother looked like. Add ten or fifteen pounds of flesh and thirty pounds of meanness. That'll be Harvey."

I bought me a few traveling supplies and some fresh cartridges. I told the sheriff to get things moving on the rewards for both of the Rainwater boys, because I would be back to collect.

He seemed to doubt me.

The way I figured it—and the sheriff had agreed with me—the friend who had been in the saloon sipping whiskey with Owen had probably lit a shuck to tell Harvey. Brotherly love being what it was—it always seemed to me that the worst of kinfolks stuck together better than respectable kinfolks—Harvey Rainwater would probably not waste no time heading for town to hunt for me. He would figure it was a cinch I'd leave, so he would move at a good clip. From the sheriff's description it was going to take that friend till way up in the night to get to Harvey. More than likely Harvey would start for town as soon as it was daylight.

I rode till a while before dark, then stopped and fixed me a bite of supper over a small fire that wouldn't put out much smoke. Folks said there wasn't much to worry about from Indians in that part of the country, but there was worse things than Indians. I put the fire out and rode a ways more into the dark, like had become my habit. I knowed where I was going. The sheriff said the wagon trail led up to within a few miles of where Harvey was staying. All I had to do was keep on the trail.

I had me a good night's sleep with that gold sack in my shirt. Odd, how much comfort a man gets out of a handful of coin, especially when it's got that yellow color. I've had pretty women sing good night to me, and their songs wasn't half as sweet as the clinking of them gold coins, one against another.

Next morning I had me some coffee and bacon and started up the trail. Outside of cattle, I didn't see much till upwards of dinnertime. Then I seen half a dozen horseback riders way off in the distance. I watched them till I decided they was sure-enough coming my way. I knowed within reason who they'd be—one of them, anyhow. I slipped Santos's carbine out of the scabbard and pulled off into some brush and settled myself down to wait.

You'll find lots of people who like pistols, and I always carried one, but if you want something to really display your authority, show them the front end of a rifle or a carbine. That'll get their attention every time. I just sat there amidst the greenery of the mesquite and catclaw and let them ride on past me. They didn't see me, of course, because people don't generally see me when I don't want them to. I didn't have no trouble recognizing Harvey Rainwater. He was Owen Rainwater all over again, and about two collar sizes bigger around the neck. He had a look on his face like some of them old vigilantes must of had a long time ago when they was getting ready to break in a new rope.

I pulled my horse out into the trail, stepped down behind him so I didn't show too much of myself, and I hollers, "Harvey Rainwater!"

My voice always carried good. He turned his horse around real quick. I don't know which he seen first, me or my carbine. He didn't know me, of course, but a shooting iron has a way of introducing itself.

He couldn't see me very well, which is the way I wanted it. I never was one to take undue advantage, just enough so I'd be sure to win. He says, "Who are you?"

Says I, "My name is Joe Pepper. I believe you're hunting for me. I come out to save you a long trip."

The tall feller was riding alongside him, the one who had been with Owen Rainwater in the saloon. He recognized me right off. I heard him say, "That's him, Harvey. That's the gink that done it."

I says, "Owen taken what was mine, and I taken it back. He shot me once when I wasn't looking. He was looking straight at me when I shot *him*. Now, I ain't asking for trouble with you, Harvey, but if you want me I'm at your convenience."

He just looked at me like he couldn't believe none of it. A lot of them old boys earned a reputation for being quick oh the trigger and dangerous, but most often that was only when they had everything going for them the way they planned it. Catch them on their left foot and they're uncertain which way to turn.

I says, "You other boys, if you ain't relatives of his, I'd advise you to stay out. I don't like hurting a man when it ain't necessary."

He said something to the men that was with him, and they all pulled off to one side except the tall one. Harvey reached for his pistol. I let him get a grip on it and start bringing it up before I squeezed the trigger. I didn't want it said afterwards that I killed a man whose gun was still in the holster. That bullet taken him about six inches under his chin. His pistol went off and grazed his horse's right forefoot. That horse broke to pitching and sent him sailing out there like a big old floppy bird.

I doubt as Harvey Rainwater ever knowed it.

My own horse was cutting up, too. He didn't like the way I had used the seat of my saddle for a gunrest. I levered another cartridge into the chamber and brought it back up to my shoulder because I didn't know what the rest of Rainwater's crew was apt to do. All of them just sat there looking dumb except the tall one. He drawed a gun and was bringing it down on me when I let him have what was in the carbine. It sure seemed to come as a surprise to him. His horse made a couple of jumps, and the tall man wound up laying on top of Harvey Rainwater.

I watched the other four real close, afraid one of them might take a notion to do something rash. But they was all well-behaved.

I says to them, "I've had about enough of this. Any more kinfolks amongst you?"

They was quick to let me know they wasn't kin, just friends. And friendship has its limits. One of them pointed to the tall man. "Slim yonder, he was the only one that was kin. He was a cousin to Harvey and Owen. They wasn't too bright on his side of the family."

I didn't say so, but it seemed to me like the whole Rainwater tribe had been shorted some on brains. I says, "Well, if you boys are sure you ain't got no further quarrel with me, I'd be much obliged if you'd all drop your guns right where you're at." They seemed agreeable to that. It didn't take but a minute. I says, "Nobody's going to disturb them guns. You-all can come back here in an hour or two and get them. But right now I'd like to see how far you can get in the shortest possible time, right back the direction you came from."

They done pretty good, I thought.

When they was a fair distance and still going, I commenced catching up the Rainwater horses and petting them and talking to them gentle to calm them down. You can talk to a horse a right smart easier than you can talk to some people. They was a little skittish about me putting the Rainwaters back up onto them. They was used to a man riding head up instead of head down. My side was still hurting me a little, too, from where Owen Rainwater's bullet had hit me in the ribs. But directly I got the two tied into place. I looked back once to be sure where the other four was at and found they had understood me real well. They was still riding off.

I've always had a suspicion that Sheriff Smathers turned in for the reward on Owen Rainwater and figured to keep it himself. The last thing he expected was to see me come riding back down that street with two more Rainwaters tied across their saddles. I pulled up in front of his office at the jail and hollered for him to come out. He just stood there leaning against the doorjamb like he thought he might fall, otherwise. He finally came down the steps and walked around and pulled up the two Rainwaters' heads to take a good look at the faces.

He kept saying over and over again, "I'll be damned! I'll be damned!"

Says I, "I got one more here than I figured on. They called him Slim. You know him?"

He just nodded. "Slim Rainwater. A cousin."

Says I, "He got a reward on him too?"

The sheriff shook his head. "Not that I know of. Just Owen and Harvey. Slim never done anything much but tag along and drink bad whiskey."

I told the sheriff I was sorry to hear that. I hated to kill a man when there was no reason for it.

That seemed to strike him odd. He says, "If there'd been a reward, would you of felt better about killing him?"

I told him I would. A reward made a pretty good reason.

In such a case as that, when nobody knowed of any more family, it was customary to sell the horses and guns and saddles and such, and whatever was left over from the expenses of the burial was divided up by the sheriff amongst them he felt was entitled to it. In this case it was a fifty-fifty split between him and me. I never did see that he really had it coming to him, but it wasn't no big lot of money, and I had to depend on him to get me the reward for the Rainwater boys. I didn't feel like quibbling. Most of the sheriffs and marshals them days didn't draw much salary for the kind of job they did. A little extra money was always appreciated.

It taken me about ten or twelve days to get the reward because there wasn't no telegraph there, and the mail service wasn't none too peart. Meantime I just hung around town and played me some poker and taken a drink or two when I wanted it. I didn't sleep in the wagon-yard no more, or fork hay. People came from a long ways to see Joe Pepper, the man who killed the Rainwater boys, and funny as it seems,

I found this was good for business. They all seemed like they felt honored to get to play a hand of poker with Joe Pepper. I can't say as I favored their reasons much, but the main thing was the money. Taking them as a whole, they was a pretty miserable bunch of poker players. By the time the reward came in, I had cleaned up around there pretty good.

The sheriff came one day and says, "I got the authorization in today's mail. If you'll walk down to the bank with me, I'll see that you get paid."

It was a nice, refreshing walk. I enjoyed it a lot. I had already met the head man of the bank, a friendly old German by the name of Dietert. I had met his number-two man, too, a sour-faced, sour-tongued gink by the name of Clopton. Lord knows what *his* pedigree was.

I preferred old man Dietert myself. He had come out west from San Antonio a few years earlier and had established this bank and a mercantile and lumber and wool-buying and hide-buying business, and no telling what else that might turn him a dollar. He had sat in with me on a couple of games of poker at one of the saloons. He was good at handling money, all right, but he didn't have much knack for cards. I had thinned him a little. Them old Germans, they wouldn't play long enough to let you trim them to the quick. Some folks thought because they talked a little funny that they wasn't very smart, and that's how they generally bested you in business. They was thinking in two languages and out ahead of you in both of them.

Of course old man Dietert knowed what the letter was about; he had knowed it would be coming. But he read it over and looked at the draft real careful to be sure everything was in proper order. Them Dutchmen was always particular about proper order. He might make mistakes at the poker table, but he didn't make none at the bank. He says, "Vell, Mister Pepper, by the looks of this you're fifteen hundred dollars richer."

I told him that was the way I figured it, too.

He went on to tell me about the bank and how stable and safe it was and how fast the country was growing and how much bigger the bank was going to be in another five years. He suggested maybe I'd like to put my money there on interest and watch it grow with the bank. I told him I hadn't made plans to stay that long myself, and that I'd rather just get the cash money and go.

He said he was right sorry to hear that. He thought a man of my talents might find it profitable to stay around awhile and help out the sheriff. There was still some desperate sorts in the country who needed to meet up with Joe Pepper, and whose apprehension or demise was likely to be worth money to somebody, someplace.

The way he put it, I couldn't help but get to thinking. I wasn't going noplace special. Since the sheriff didn't already have my real name and description on a flyer, maybe he never would have; maybe they wasn't being mailed this far west. And even if one *did* come, there was a good chance I'd be the first to see it. It would be real easy to fold it up and shove it into the stove.

The banker's remark kind of taken the sheriff by surprise. I says, "What do you think about it, Sheriff?" I could already tell by the look on his face that he wasn't real keen on the notion. But the banker was a man of influence, because he taken on like he thought it was the best idea to come along since bourbon whiskey.

And that's how come Joe Pepper to wear a deputy sheriff's badge.

CHAPTER 4

It didn't take me long to learn some things about the sheriffing business, things that ain't wrote down in the statutes. Sheriff Smathers taken pains not to antagonize me about it, but he just the same let me know sort of kindly that the idea of me being a deputy was the banker's, not his. He had as soon I hadn't stayed because a feller like me tended to draw lightning, and he was getting to be an old man. He wasn't sure he could dodge fast enough when it struck. Another thing, since I was working out of his office and had his official stamp on me, so to speak, he said it was clear to him that any rewards I came up with ought to be divided with him, share and share alike. I didn't see his case quite as clear as he did, but I told him we would talk about it when the time came. His part of any split, I told him, ought to be calculated according to how much effort he put into the job, the chances that was taken, and such like. I've always been one that believed a man works best when he's got a proper incentive. Give him the same whether he works or sits down, and he'll wear out the seat of his britches before he wears out the knees.

There was some other things about sheriffing that came as a little of a surprise to me. There was some places around town that didn't operate strictly according to the statutes. There was laws that said it was illegal to gamble. There was laws about a saloon being open till way late at night or on a Sunday. And there was laws about them fancy houses down on Red Lantern Row. Most of them laws, I found out, was honored mainly in the breach. About once a week the sheriff made him a little round of all them places, and when he came back his pockets was fuller than when he left. You know as well as I do, that ain't the normal order of things with most folks that patronize them kinds of businesses.

If I'd of wanted to put the boot on the other foot I could of asked him to share that with me, same as he wanted me to share rewards. But at the time the thought of taking a percentage off of them poor unfortunate girls went against my grain. Being partial to the cards myself, I thought I could see the gamblers' side of it, too. Later on I learned better; I learned that the smart one takes what he can while the rest ponder Scripture. But wisdom ain't born in you; you got to cultivate it.

Catclaw was an agreeable kind of a town, once I got used to it. There was a little farming along close to the creek, but not enough of it to be any real setback to the community. People had a way of tending to their own affairs and not crowding in too much on other folks'. Big part of the town was Mexican, of course, and the sheriff being white, he didn't mess around much in the south part of town as long as the trouble there didn't spill over. The way he seen it them people had been keeping their own laws since long before the rest of us came. If a man was wronged, he taken it on himself to set things right. If a man was killed, his kin taken it on themselves to balance the books and take an eye for an eye. It wasn't anybody else's business, sure not the government's.

I used to wonder if that wouldn't be a good policy for us *gringos*, too. It would sure starve a lot of lawyers to death.

There wasn't much money to be made over in the Mexican section, which is another reason why Smathers didn't care to go over there. What little real money there was, it accumulated in the Anglo section. Texas was still dirt-poor. Main thing it had was land and cattle, and neither one of them worth real specie. They was hard times for us honest men, and none too easy for all them other folks. About the only actual money that had come into the state had been brought back by cattlemen taking their herds north, and by the carpetbaggers who had come in to steal everything that wasn't bolted down tight. No matter how hard they tried, they couldn't keep some of their money from getting into circulation.

The town had a fair to middling trade territory, selling goods to the ranchers and farmers and what-not on down to the Rio Grande on the south, way out into the edge of Apache country on the west, and north up to where there was nothing but Comanches. A couple of big general stores did business to the outlying country, and seven or eight saloons did business without having to go anywhere. Them days, no matter how hard the times, the last man to starve out was the saloon-keeper. When *he* left, you could take down the town sign.

There wasn't too many ways for people to move west without going through this town or some other one like it. Most of the people from San Antonio or points south had to come through unless they made it a point to leave the main road and go around. It was them roundance people I mostly kept a lookout for. I memorized all the "wanted" fly-ers, pretty near, and kept notes in a tally book in my shirt pocket, the way I've seen Texas Rangers do. One of them Rangers ever come upon a suspicious-looking bunch of strangers, he would take out his note-book and flip through it and check descriptions. If any looked like they might fit, he invited them to go with him. They hauled in a lot of the innocent along with the guilty, but one of them Ranger invitations was hard to refuse.

I made me a regular patrol north and south of town, cutting sign on people that taken the long way around. As scattered and few as the towns was, any man that taken pains to go around instead of coming through was naturally suspect. Biggest part of the time it was for noth-ing. Either I never would find them, or they would turn out to be Mexican cowboys looking for stock, or like once happened, some black troopers out of Fort Clark hunting for a couple of deserters. The army was always asking us to help find these runaway boys, but I didn't feel like it was my place; them damnyankees could hunt for their own. I felt like any soldier that had gumption enough to run was beginning to display some good sense.

Besides that, the army didn't usually offer any reward.

Once in a while I would strike paydirt and catch me somebody that was on the dodge. Generally they would come peacefully enough, once I showed them the seriousness of my intentions. Getting them to town was only the first part of the trouble, like as not. Them upstanding citizens that put up reward money was always looking for some excuse not to pay it, once you done your part of the job. They would claim that the time had run out or that the reward wasn't meant for no regularly paid officer, or some such dodge, trying to rob an honest lawman of his due.

I remember one time I caught an old gotch-eared boy that had robbed a carpetbag bank in one of them settlements over east of San Antonio. They had put up a thousand dollars on him. It wasn't just that he had robbed the bank which bothered them so much. He didn't really get off with much money. But afterwards he had taken the head banker for a hostage. He taken him along with him for maybe twenty miles, then made him strip off naked so he wouldn't be in no hurry to run to somebody's house for help. It's bad enough to lose your money, and even worse to lose your dignity on top of it.

Of course I didn't know the whole story when I went after him. All I knowed was what he looked like, and that part about the thousand dollars. The rest was just unnecessary details. I found him hiding out in the same general part of the country where Harvey Rainwater had been. I knowed him on sight; a man with a gotch ear just don't hardly melt into a crowd. I figured right off that he was a likable sort because he hadn't been there more than a couple of days, and he already had made friends that was willing to risk getting punctuated with my gun to protect him. But friendly don't count for much against a thousand dollars. I persuaded him, you might say, that he ought to come and go with me and not cause them new friends of his any undue grief. He came around to my point of view after I put a bullet through the fleshy part of his leg. I was kind of sorry about that later, seeing the way them people there made a fuss over him and patched him up so neat and fixed him a lunch to eat on the way to the jail. They didn't fix *me* nothing.

After he had time to get over the pain in that leg, and after the fever had run out, I could tell what the people seen in him. He had a grin wider than a pasture gate, and he could tell the biggest and funniest lies. If lies get a man sent to hell, I reckon he wouldn't have a chance.

But they was healthy lies, the kind that make you laugh and don't hurt nobody. He asked for a guitar, and we brought him one. Worst guitar player you ever heard in your life.

Naturally I sent word back where he had come from that we had him in jail, awaiting their pleasure. Well sir, they didn't lose much time getting their selves over there . . . the county sheriff, a deputy, and the banker himself, a fat, whining kind of a Yankee. I knowed from what Gotch had told me that he was one of them carpetbaggers who had come down on us like a plague of locusts after the war, working in cahoots with their reconstruction laws to freeze people off of their land and then buy it up cheap for the delinquent taxes. He had cleaned out Gotch's family that way, which was why Gotch picked on him so. Gotch had told me all about walking that banker home, barefoot plumb to his chin, and I don't know which of us had laughed the hardest at the story.

The sheriff wasn't a bad sort, as them scalawag officeholders went, but that banker was one of them dollar-nursing kind that wouldn't spend two bits to watch a bumblebee whip a bald eagle. Soon as he seen we had his bank robber safely behind the bars, he craw-fished on the reward. Said it had been for Gotch's capture within a month, and this had been two-going-on-three. I looked real close at that flyer. It didn't say a word about no time limit. He said it was supposed to have, and it was the printer's mistake, not his. If I wanted my thousand dollars, I would just have to take it up with the printer. I've seen enough printers in my time to know they're always broke.

On top of that, he had the nerve to ask us for the borrow of a horse that they could take Gotch home on.

I've been shot at in my life, and I've been cheated, and I believe I was always maddest at being cheated. I used the Lord's name in a shameful manner. It didn't change nothing. They still had the legal papers to take my prisoner, and they wasn't going to pay me a dime.

On top of that, I had come to like old Gotch. The truth wasn't in him, but neither was there any real harm.

They was going to leave at daylight the next morning. The banker had a hotel room. The sheriff and the deputy slept in the hay at the wagonyard because their county wasn't allowing them much in the way of expenses, and the banker sure wasn't paying. I sat in the front office, stewing over the situation and listening to Gotch abusing that Mexican guitar. All of a sudden it come to me. Gotch hadn't tried to shoot me when I taken him; he had just refused to go with me. I went in there and says, "Gotch, you ever shot a man in your life? You ever tried to?"

He said he hadn't. I says, "If somebody was to slip you a loaded pistol through that window, would you shoot that fat banker to get yourself free?"

He says, "No, I'd maybe try to scare him to death, but not shoot him."

There was maybe twenty pistols in a drawer that had been taken off of one man or another and never given back. I didn't get Gotch's because that would be a dead giveaway, and his wasn't much account anyway. If you're going out of your way to give a man something, you ought to give him something good. I picked me one and taken several cartridges and loaded it, then got to thinking. Now and again I'd been fooled about people. Maybe I oughtn't to take any undue chances. I taken the cartridges back out and pulled the lead from them, poured the powder into a spittoon and fitted the lead back in place. Then I reloaded the pistol with them, walked around back of the jail and rapped on the bars with the barrel. I seen a hand reach out, and I put the gun in it.

In a little while I heard Gotch playing on that guitar again.

I didn't go next morning to unlock the cell for that visiting sheriff and his deputy and the banker. I just gave them the key and told them I was going down the street to have me some breakfast. I seen that they had their horses, plus one they had had to buy at the wagonyard for Gotch to ride. The liveryman owed me a split on that.

I walked down the street a ways, then ducked behind a corner where I could look back. Sure enough, I seen them three come out in single file with their hands up, and old Gotch bringing it up behind them with that pistol in his hand, grinning like a dog licking clabber. They rode out of town, heading west instead of east.

I went on and did what I had said I would ... had me a thousand-dollar breakfast. It was one of the best meals I ever ate. Old Sheriff Smathers came around later in the morning, and I never let on to him.

Way after dark that night, the three of them came a-limping back into town sorefooted, all of them as naked as the day they first come into the world. And a whole lot smarter. They hadn't only lost their prisoner, but they had lost four head of horses and their guns and whatever cash and truck they had brought with them.

I think that banker suspicioned what had happened, because he tried awful hard to get me fired. But old Smathers wasn't keen on it, seeing as he would of shared the reward with me if there had been one. The banker finally offered to put up the reward again, a thousand dollars alive, two thousand dollars dead. But by then his welcome had plumb worn out. I told him it was a little like trapping coyotes. If you ever catch one in a trap and he gets loose, he's trap-wise from then on and ten times harder to catch. I wanted to hunt easier game.

That banker had to float a loan from old man Dietert at the Catclaw bank to buy them some clothes and horses.

I always had a hunch Smathers smelled a rat about Gotch, but he never said nothing. The only thing he ever wondered about was what happened to his spittoon. He pitched a smoked-down cigar butt in it and damn near caught his britches afire.

By and by I had added five or six rewards to my bank account, probably two or three thousand dollars in all. I still had it in my head that I wanted to be a rancher, even though all my attempts at it had come to considerable grief. That wasn't the part of the country I especially wanted to do it in, though. For one thing it was a heap dryer than the land I was used to, back home. It was really a lot better than it looked, I know now, but it always appeared to be in the midst of a drouth if you was from a greener part of the country. Another thing, I still figured they was looking for me back yonder, and sooner or later somebody might come straying through who knew me. I'd already had to leave a ranch in South Texas and another in Mexico. I didn't aim to leave one here.

Time came when one office seemed a little close for me and Sheriff Smathers. We come to something of a disagreement over a five-hundred-dollar reward on a feller that had shot a woman back in East Texas. Now, you're probably wondering how me, on the dodge myself, could go out and bring in other people on the dodge and keep my conscience clear. Truth is, I didn't. Like with old Gotch there; if I'd of turned him over to that fat banker and his laws, I'd of lost some sleep over it. I always hurt a little over most of them, and I couldn't of done it if money hadn't been such a cool balm for a troubled conscience.

One like that woman-killer, of course, didn't trouble me a bit except that he hadn't given me any excuse for shooting him. I always figured the best cure for a man like that is a deep burying. The reward was the same dead or alive.

Anyway, I had to catch him all by myself. I didn't get three cents' worth of help from old Smathers or anybody else. So when the reward came through, naturally I was inclined to figure I ought to keep it myself. Old Smathers seen it different. He wasn't overly strong at sharing danger, but he was real apt with pencil and paper when it come to sharing money.

Things didn't improve a bit when some old boy breezed into town one day and robbed our old Dutch banker in broad daylight. I was off at the time, looking for suspicious tracks on the trails south of town. First I heard of it was along late in the day when I was heading back toward town, tired and in bad need of a drink. I ran smack into a wild-eyed citizen posse, carrying more guns than Lee had at Gettysburg. You take the majority of them posses, they're more danger to each other than to the people they're hunting.

Feller in charge was that sour-faced loudmouth, Clopton, from the bank. I always figured he had a grand notion that one day he was going to be the high muck-a-muck in charge of all the money, when the old man died. He wasn't ever very civil, and that day none atall. He asked me if I didn't know the bank had been robbed, and of course that was a silly question because he knowed I'd been out of town.

He gave me a lecture about how a peace officer was supposed to be on hand when he was needed instead of out pleasure-riding around over the country, and I told him I was hot and thirsty and tired, and it had sure been no pleasure. Besides, bank robbers wasn't in the habit of making an appointment before they favored us with a visit.

I had been told that this Clopton was an officer in the Confederate Army, which didn't overly surprise me. It helped explain his extra airs, and some of the reason why we lost. He had been in the bank when the robber came in. Of course he didn't tell me all of it, but I found it out later when I finally got back into town. The robber was a youngish sort, no different from a hundred or two others you'd of met on the ranches and in the army and on the freight wagons. What Clopton didn't tell me was that the old banker Dietert stayed cool and just about had the robber bluffed into thinking the bank had sent nearly all of its cash out in a payroll. But Clopton was scared for his life, and he opened up the safe. The robber got off with maybe a thousand dollars in paper money; the silver was heavy, and he must not've wanted to get his horse loaded down. Clopton was afraid the boy would kill all of them when he got through, so as to leave no witnesses. When he left without doing anybody any harm, Clopton went and shut the safe—a little late to be doing that—and then went into a crying jag.

By the time I met him on the trail he was over it, and he was talking and acting tough. He was probably trying to make up for the show he had put on earlier.

The robber had come south; they generally did them days, because it wasn't far to Mexico. Clopton said if I'd had my eyes open I was bound to've seen him. But I hadn't seen anybody all day except a couple of Mexican oxcart men and a little detail of them black soldiers out of Fort Clark with a consumptive-looking white lieutenant who probably *needed* to rob a bank.

There wasn't nothing I could do but turn around with that posse and help them hunt. It was a big rolling country of mesquite and catclaw and *guajillo* and all that other half-desert kind of growth that could swallow a man up with you looking straight at him. We cut for signs but didn't find any. Sheriff Smathers had gone out with another posse, in a little different direction. I found out that the boy had man-aged to cover his trail just a little ways out of town, and nobody could tell where he went to.

We hunted till full dark. By then I was glad it was a town posse, be-cause they was all ready to turn around and go home. One of them *se-rious* posses, now, they'd of stayed out two or three days without a bite to eat. I wasn't ready to do that, not for an amateur robber who hadn't gotten off with but a thousand dollars and hadn't shot anybody.

I changed my tune when I found out what else got taken. I went down to the bank early next morning to see if old man Dietert could give me a better description than that idiot Clopton. I found the old Dutchman busy trying to convince several people that their money was still safe, that he would stand good for any loss out of his own per-sonal pocket. But for me he had to make an exception.

"I'm sorry to tell you this," he says, "but you vill remember that leather pouch you vanted me to keep in the safe? It is gone."

Well sir, I couldn't help cussing a little. I had almost got myself killed getting hold of that gold in the first place. And I had had to take it away from a thief and kill him. I swear, it began to look like the good Lord didn't intend for me to have it.

The cash money I had on deposit was all right, but it sure made me sick to lose that gold pouch again after all the trouble I had been to.

I didn't wait around for anybody to form up a fresh posse. I set out by myself. But it was too late to pick up that old boy's trail. There had been so many people riding around over that country looking for him that it was hopeless. I rode on south, all the way to the river, hoping to pick up some kind of a clue. I found lots of tracks, but there was no way of knowing which one of them might be his, or if any of them was. I brewed it over in my mind for a long time before I finally got up nerve to cross that river into Mexico. I had thought once that I'd seen enough of Mexico to do me for a lifetime. But I decided to take the risk. This was so far upriver that they had probably never heard of Santos, much less of Joe Peeler.

I hunted around down there for several days, looking over all the suspicious characters. Just about every *gringo* I seen that was past seventeen looked suspicious, the frame of mind I was in. About all I had to go on was the description of the horse, a smallish mustang-type bay with a little streak on his nose. I must of found a hundred like that, but no *gringo* riding any of them. I finally gave it up and went back across the river where I belonged, tired out and feeling low. I wasn't ready for the griping of old Sheriff Smathers. He was saying I must be turning lazy, that I ought to've stayed down there till I found the robber because by this time the bank had put up a five-hundred-dollar reward on him.

He sure hated it, not getting a cut of that reward. But he didn't hate it half as bad as I did, because he hadn't lost a sack of gold coin that he had become attached to.

He kept grousing, and it was a pleasure to get out of town again. I kept on for a while working that country between town and the river, not getting nothing for it but a saddlesore.

That old boy was gone, and there was nothing to do but accept it. The hell of it was, I was the biggest loser of anybody in town.

CHAPTER 5

One thing about me, I could always tell when the gravy was running thin. I knew my time in Catclaw was about up. It was getting so every time old Smathers opened his mouth, I had to open mine too. The strain between us got considerable. He would of loved to've sat in the office and watched me bring in the feller who taken the bank, so he could share in the reward. But some games are meant to be won and some are meant to be lost. That time we had a busted flush.

It was a good thing for me, I guess, that Samantha Ridgway came along when she did.

Actually she came the second time before I chanced to see her. I was off on one of them wild goose chases when she first came through with one of them little emigrant wagon trains that seemed to pass there about as regular as a man washed his socks. It wasn't a big one like you read about, the kind with a hundred wagons. There wasn't ever as many of that kind as folks seem to think, at least not down in our part of the country. Most of the time they was more like five or six, maybe eight or ten wagons. Those was the easiest managed. The folks in the front wagon could always look back and see the hindmost, and vice versa. The last ones didn't eat near as much dust as on a big train. An outrider could see the fore and aft wagons all at the same time and knowed right away when anything went wrong.

Oft as not when you came onto one of them little wagon trains, you found a lot of people was kinfolks. I always had a fondness for families myself, growing up in a big one the way I did.

Like I say, I missed Samantha the first time. If it hadn't been for some Apaches off out to the west, she would of never left any foot-prints on my life. The wagons camped at the edge of town one night while the folks picked up some supplies, then headed west toward old Fort Davis, way off out across the Pecos River country.

This, you got to understand, was before Mackenzie made his big cavalry raid out of Fort Clark and tore up the worst nest of them border-jumping Indians in northern Mexico. These Indians would stay in Mexico most of the time because the Mexicans was too busy with problems of their own to bother them much. Now and again they would cross the river, hit somebody with some devilment, then not let their breechclouts touch them till they was safe south of the Rio Grande. Mexico didn't care much, seeing a bunch of *Tejanos* get blood-ied up.

Well sir, this emigrant train never made it to the Pecos. Them Indi-ans came skinning out from behind one of the flat-topped mountains you find in that desert country, and before the folks could get the wag-ons circled the red devils was amongst them. Things got fiercesome for a few minutes till the Apaches took what they mainly wanted, the loose horses and mules. They would always kill a few people if it came handy, but the stock was the main thing.

When the dust cleared, the emigrants had three men to bury out on that greasewood flat. Before they could get back to town they had to stop and bury another one.

I was west of Catclaw a few miles, scouting around for suspicious sign, when I met a feller pushing his horse pretty hard, heading east. He asked me how much farther it was to Catclaw, and I told him. "Thank God," he says, and points back over his shoulder. "There's a wagon train behind me needing help. There any doctors in the town?"

I told him there was two, one *gringo* and one Mexican. Told him to get the Mexican because he didn't drink much. He allowed as they would need them both.

He went on toward town, and I followed the mail road west till I came finally to the wagons. A more desperate, hard-whipped bunch I never seen. Not only did they lose their loose stock, but the Indians killed some more in the traces. That was the way with the Indian when he went to war: kill what he couldn't steal, and leave the white man afoot if he couldn't leave him dead. So these people had to double up with what stock they had left. They even doubled some of their wagons in tandem, one behind the other like freight wagons. The wagon canvas was shot full of holes, and a couple was partly burned. They was a confused and staggered lot of people, I'll tell you. Some people went west them days that shouldn't of ever left hearth and home.

It was Samantha that caught my eye, sitting up on a wagon seat, driving the wagon all by herself. She wasn't a lot to look at just at the time, I'll grant you, but somehow she sort of grabbed me. Her face was smudged with dirt and ashes. There was streaks down her cheeks where the tears had run. Her hair was all blowed out and wild-looking. But with all of that, she taken my breath.

I says to her, "You're kind of small to be driving that team all by yourself. You need some help?"

She says, "My mother's the one that needs help. You a doctor?"

I told her I wasn't. I stood up in the stirrups and looked into the wagon. A woman was lying in there on a pile of blankets, white and pale as if death was knocking on her door. And it was. A big middle-aged woman was sitting in there with her, holding on to her hand.

As things unfolded, I found out that her husband had been more or less the captain of the wagon train, a family leader and all that. He had been out front trying to get the wagons circled when the Indians hit, and he was the first one to get killed. The old lady—Samantha's mama—went running out to try and help him. She grabbed up his rifle and tried to fire it, but it was empty. She swung it like a club till one of them put a bullet in her.

They was a strong, loyal bunch of women them days, preacher, not like them little bicycle-riding, croquet-playing dolls you see around nowadays. Why, just a little while back I even seen a woman smoking a cigarette . . . a *cigarette*, mind you . . . and she was supposed to be a lady, not a saloon girl. Some people these days don't know the first thing about morals.

But that's got nothing to do with what I'm telling you. I rode back to the lead wagon. A big, stocky farmer was sitting there on it, looking grim as death. And he had plenty to be grim about. I found out his name was Zebulon Wentworth. They was great on Bible names in them days. Of course the ones that knowed him called him Zeb, which kind of took the Bible back out of it. Zebulon was for Sunday, like the Bible generally is.

Old Zeb's wife was a sister to Samantha's mother, and now people looked to him to head up the wagon train. He was one of them tough East Texas farmers that had spent so long behind a plow that his hands was shaped to fit the handles. Big hands, like a ham hanging up in a smokehouse. He could knock a man rolling if he was of a mind to, though generally him and his kind had no such inclinations.

He asked me if I had met his man on the road. Then he told me they had had some trouble, which I could plainly see for myself. But I reckon he needed somebody new to talk to, because he commenced telling me all about the Indian raid. I found out that the big woman sitting with the wounded lady back in that other wagon was his wife Addie. Zeb was sore afraid he was fixing to lose his sister-in-law. He was telling me how hard that was going to be on his niece Samantha, both of her folks getting killed and leaving her to shift for herself, a young and innocent girl of nineteen, facing the cruel world. My heart kind of weakened as I listened to him.

By and by I could see a bunch of horses coming. Old Zeb tensed up like he thought it might be Indians again, but I told him it was likely a bunch from town, coming to meet them. And that's what it turned out to be. That Mexican doctor was in the lead with a black bag tied on behind his saddle. The *gringo* doctor couldn't come, somebody said, but he would be waiting when the wagons got to town. I'd seen a good bit of him since I had been in Catclaw, and I figured somebody was getting him sobered up.

They stopped the wagons so the *medico* could look at the wounded. He started with Samantha's mother. She was fevered and talking out of her head. I had seen enough wounded men in the war to know that she didn't stand much chance. The doctor must of knowed it too, but he didn't tell the folks so. He looked at her pretty good, then went to the other wagons. There was two men wounded, and one little boy

that got a broken arm by falling out of a wagon while the fight was going on. They wasn't in any big danger of dying unless it was from
embarrassment because of so many of them people from town, crowding around looking at them.

The doctor went back to Samantha's wagon. He told Samantha and
her aunt Addie and Zeb that old lady Ridgway was in a bad fix, and
that the bullet needed to come out of her right away. He hated to do it
there, but he was afraid to wait till they could get to town. So we
spread some blankets on the ground in the shade under the wagon,
and unhitched the team so they couldn't spook and accidentally run
the wheels over her. I helped a couple of men lift her down from the
wagon and put her on the blankets. Then the doctor shooed all the
extra folks away so there wouldn't be a bunch of people watching
when he opened up her dress. He kept me and Zeb there to help him,
and of course three or four of the women. He didn't have anything to
put her to sleep, so he gave her all the laudanum he thought was safe.
Then he commenced.

I watched that girl while the operation was going on. She stood back
out of the way. The tears ran down through the dust on her face, but
she didn't let out a whimper or break down and get to be a problem like
lots of women would've done. She had her head down some, praying. I
thought to myself how lucky that woman was to have such a daughter.

I see people nowadays who get more loyalty out of a yellow dog than
out of their kids, but there I go talking about things that have nothing
to do with the story.

We had to hold Mrs. Ridgway tight because it hurt her. That bullet
was in there solid. The worst part was that it had already been in too
long. By and by the doctor finally brought it out. Old Zeb gave a sigh
of relief, and his big wife Addie said, "Thank God," but I knowed from
the look in that Mexican doctor's face that it had all been for nothing.

The poor woman had fainted from the pain, and I personally had
some doubt that she would ever come to. The doctor got the blood
stopped and the wound taken care of the best he could. We put the
lady back into the wagon, and the train started moving again toward
Catclaw.

A big lot of people had gathered to watch the wagons come in. I pointed Zeb toward a big open piece of camping ground next to the wagonyard.

There was one thing about people in them days: They might quarrel and raise hell amongst theirselves, but when trouble came most of them was there to help each other. Being summer, the schoolhouse was empty. A bunch of people had already rushed over and fixed the place up to make a kind of hospital out of it. The woman teacher normally stayed in a little room in the back, where there was a stove and a bed and dresser and such. The women in town had already fixed this up for Mrs. Ridgway to give her some privacy. Cots had been brought in and set up for the wounded men and the boy in the main schoolroom. The benches and tables was shoved back against the wall.

They had the *gringo* doctor sobered up pretty good, but his hands was still shaking. I was glad the Mexican had already done the operation on Mrs. Ridgway because folks would of naturally chosen the *gringo* doctor over him. That would of been a bad mistake.

Like I said, people was good to pitch in and help where they could. The liveryman over at the wagonyard had all the people's stock brought into one of his corrals, and he put out hay for them. Said he wouldn't let the people pay him for it. Later on I figured out that he already sensed he was going to get to sell these folks a bunch of horses and mules to make up for the ones that the Indians had killed or got off with. That would make a little hay look cheap. But maybe what he done was all out of the kindness of his heart; it ain't for me to say it wasn't.

The wagon people made camp but didn't have to cook supper. People from the town kept coming out, bringing them stuff. I circulated amongst the wagon folks, talking to the ones that felt like talking. I found out that most of them was kin. They had come out of the old colonies of deep East Texas. The carpetbaggers had taxed them out of most of what they owned, and they was going west for a new start. They had heard farming land could be had cheap along the Rio Grande west of El Paso. They had elected Samantha's pa to head up the bunch. He had never done no Indian-fighting, but he had stood up against his share of Yankees in the war. He knowed a man's duty.

After he was killed, folks naturally looked to old Zeb Wentworth to lead them. He hadn't been off to war, but he had been in the home guards. He was there when the Yankees tried to invade Texas by way of Sabine Pass and got the pants shot off of them. I watched him there at the wagon, going around to the folks to be sure they all got camped all right, seeing that the stock was all cared for. I knowed he would of rather been down at the schoolhouse with his wife, seeing after his sister-in-law and his niece.

There might of been a lot he didn't know about westering, but he had the nerve to give it a good try. He had the look of a mild and gentle man, and mainly that's what he was. But one of the wagon people told me something that made me study him closer. Seems like the carpetbaggers and scalawags wasn't content to just take the land away from these people, but they tried to stop the wagon train and take away what little else they still had, claiming it was due on back taxes. One carpetbagger made a bad mistake, though. He laid his hands on a woman, trying to make her open a big wooden trunk so he could see if there was any money in it. In just the time it taken him to fall, he was laying on his back with a big hole between his eyes, and old Zeb was standing there with a rifle smoking. The rest of them thieves ran as fast as they could, back to the county seat.

That's the kind of people them farmers was. They minded their own business and was no worry to anybody except those that tried to mess with them.

It stood to reason there was probaby a reward out for Zeb back where he came from. But I wasn't tempted to do anything about it, not a particle.

I went up to Zeb finally and asked him if there wasn't something more I could do to help. He said if I wasn't a minister and wasn't a doctor, he guessed not. I had helped patch up a few wounded in my time, but I sure wasn't no minister.

I says to him, "What'll you-all do now? You're too crippled to go on."

He looked at me like he didn't understand what I said. He says, "We're crippled, but we ain't all dead. Sure we'll go on. We ain't finished what we set out to do."

That was their way; if there had just been one of them left alive, he would of gone on for the rest of them, or died making the try.

I rode down to the schoolhouse with him, partly because I knowed I'd see that girl and partly because something about this old man and his tribe had sort of got to me. I noticed that the first thing Zeb done when he walked in the door was to take his hat off, like it was a church or somebody's house, instead of just an empty school. His eye was on the door to the room where his own closest family was, but first he went to the wounded men and the boy and inquired after their health.

Samantha heard his voice and came out the door. She shut it behind her, kind of a sign that it was closed to the public in there. Real gentle, old Zeb asked her how her mother was. She didn't say anything; she just kind of answered him with her eyes.

All that time I had been trying to figure what it was about her that had hit me so hard. All of a sudden I knew. She reminded me of my Millie, my lost Millie. She was just about Millie's size and build, and with her face all smudged up like it was with dirt and grime and soot, the differences didn't show. Even her eyes was like Millie's.

She was, right at first, like Millie come back to me alive.

By the time I finally seen her with her face clean, and could tell she was a whole different woman, it didn't matter anymore. I was hooked tighter than a catfish on a trotline.

The old man hugged her, which I would of loved to of done, but of course that was unthinkable. I'd of wound up like that carpetbagger, trying to see out through a third eye. And I'd of had it coming to me.

Sometime during the night Samantha's old mother just drifted away in her sleep. Looking for her husband, I reckon. She never came back. Next afternoon they buried her in the town cemetery, over on the side with the "good" folks, away from all the hardnoses who had died wearing their boots. I'd have to say for the credit of the town that just about everybody turned out. Even the saloons closed. Not a soul there had knowed her, but they all done her honor. They went up on the hill after the hearse and sang about amazing grace and the blood of the lamb, and a few of the womenfolks cried like she was an old friend. They done right by her.

Samantha wished her mother could of been buried with her pa, but
that wasn't practical. Old lady Addie told her they would find each
other in heaven; it didn't make much difference where they laid the
clay.

Well sir, I kind of appointed myself an unofficial guardian and as-
sistant to Zeb Wentworth. I made out like I figured it was my duty as a
law officer. Mainly what it done was to give me a chance to see a right
smart of that girl.

One thing was clear to me: These folks couldn't start out again
the way they was, weakened so much. They had lost four men and a
woman. It was going to be a few days before the two wounded men
ought to have to suffer the hardship of the trip. Besides, they needed to
heal up some so they could help if things came to another bad pinch. I
told Zeb if he would wait a few days maybe there'd be some more emigrant wagons come along to reinforce them. A man might make
twenty trips across that desert and not see an Indian. Then, on the
twenty-first trip, one would raise up from behind a little greasewood
bush and take his hair. It was all a matter of chance. The Indians came
and went like the weather, and didn't leave many tracks.

All this time Sheriff Smathers was plaguing me about that bank
robber. Even if I caught him and got the reward, after I split with old
Smathers I wouldn't have but two-fifty for my trouble. By then I was
interested in something worth a lot more than any two-fifty. I wanted
that girl. So I spent most of my time with the wagon people.

I didn't intrude myself on her or nothing, you understand; I just
made it a point to always be around, so that if she needed anything
she didn't have to call on nobody else.

The waiting was bad for me in one way, though, because it gave the
town women time to get acquainted with the train women and swap
gossip. You know how women will talk. Some of their opinions of me
wasn't near as good as the opinion I had of myself. Well, that's natural. People sometimes need a hard man to do their fighting for them,
and take the worst of the risks for them, but he don't fit in with parlor
society, or even front-porch society. He stands outside someplace,
needed too much to turn loose of but not enough to bring him into

the family. It's like they're never quite sure of him, afraid maybe he'll
go bad on them one day. It's happened, plenty of times.

You'll often find that the man doing the hunting is more like the
man he's after than like the people that pay him to do the job.

The wagon people wasn't loaded down with specie, but they had
enough cash for the absolute necessaries. Main thing they needed was
some extra draft animals to take the place of the ones they had lost.
The people in town was friendly enough and sympathetic, but they was
like most folks . . . when it comes to business, friendship don't cross
over.

During the time I had been at Catclaw, traveling around looking
out for the snorty breed, I'd got to know a lot of the ranchers. I
thought I knowed some who might have horses and mules they would
sell cheaper than the wagonyard operator and the folks in town was
asking. A couple of the wagon folks needed oxen, and I had gotten
acquainted with enough Mexicans to know where some such could be
had. So I went with Zeb Wentworth and a couple of others, trying to
help them spend where the dollar was biggest.

Naturally that left some of the townfolks thinking sour thoughts
about me, and speaking sour words. The keeper of the wagonyard had
seemed like a pretty good friend of mine, but he cooled off after I done
him out of the sale of twelve horses and mules. I figured he wasn't
hurt none. There would be plenty of wagon folks coming through after these was gone, needing stock to replace some that went lame or
died along the way. I wouldn't care if he stuck *them*, but these was *my*
wagon people.

Doing this little chore gave me a chance to get these wagon folks on
my good side—the men, anyway—and maybe offset what some of the
town people might be telling them. Of course the people in Catclaw
didn't know nothing about me except what I had done while I was
there. They didn't even know Joe Pepper wasn't my real name. But
some of the women told Addie Wentworth that I was now and again
seen down on Red Lantern Row in broad daylight, where a respectable
man wouldn't go except in the dark of the night. They told her I was a
man who went out and hunted people down for money, like a wolfer

killing varmints for the bounty, as if that was a bad thing. The men I went after was always somebody they wanted to get rid of anyway.

Each family on the wagon train done its own cooking. Since Samantha was alone now, Zeb and Addie taken her under their wing. They was her closest kin, so it was the Christian thing to do. The old lady always seemed like she went out of her way to keep Samantha busy when I came around. She said it helped keep the girl's mind off of her grief. I figured it was to keep her mind off of *me*, if she had been thataway inclined.

I didn't try to press her. I just always tried to be somewhere close in case she needed somebody to talk to. I never tried putting my arm around her or kissing her when she wasn't expecting it, or stuff like that. I had a notion that would scare her off. I had intentions toward that girl, and they was all honorable.

I started dropping suggestions to Zeb that it looked like they was going to need some extra men to go with them. I didn't volunteer, exactly; I thought it would look better if he asked me instead of it being the other way around. And I figured that if I played the cards careful and easy, he would do it. Old Zeb and Samantha was alike in some ways. I could tell they both liked me.

But not Addie Wentworth. A more suspicious old woman you'd never find. She could see through me like a pane of window glass. Every time me and Samantha was about to strike up a conversation, the old woman thought of some chore that wouldn't wait, and she'd put Samantha on it. Then she would give me a look that would turn sweet milk into clabber. I tried to take it kindly and tell myself she was just interested in Samantha's welfare, same as I was, but I couldn't help wishing sometimes it had been *her* that got in the way of the Indians.

She was a hefty sort of a woman. Two or three times when I watched her climbing into her wagon, I almost let the devil talk me into pushing her just to see how hard she would fall. Of course I never actually done it, but thinking about it was pleasuresome.

She kind of taken me by surprise one day. Another time I might of told her off, but Samantha was there and I couldn't afford to say anything she might take bad. The old lady bored a pair of holes through me with her eyes. She says, "People tell me you're a gunfighter who kills for money."

She caught me on my left foot, so to speak. All I could do for a minute was stammer. Finally I says, "I never shot no man that wasn't looking at me, and never one that didn't need it."

She didn't let up. She says, "I suppose you always considered that you did the world a favor."

I hadn't thought of it in quite that way. Any time I ever done a thing like that, the notion of doing the world a favor was a long ways from my thinking. I says, "I never been one to brag. But yes, I expect the world is better off without the ones I've put away."

I taken a long look at Samantha. I couldn't tell that I'd hurt myself in her sight. But I sure hadn't helped myself with old Addie.

It was pretty soon decided that the wounded was in shape to travel. And along about that time there come two more sets of wagons. One was some emigrant wagons with white folks. The other was a bunch of them old big wheeled Mexican carts, traders headed out for El Paso with goods come all the way from ships that unloaded at the mouth of the Rio Grande. Naturally when the settlers on that mover train heard what the first wagon train had run into, they wasn't hard to talk into all joining together for the trip across the Pecos River country and out into the Davis Mountains, and then on to El Paso. There was a little discussion about maybe they could get along without the Mexicans. Some of the emigrants didn't know nothing about Mexicans except that they remembered the Alamo. But old Zeb asked me and I told him they wasn't *marrying* the Mexicans, they was just traveling with them. That kind of tickled the old man; he always loved a joke.

I suppose I had planted enough seed so that the idea seemed to sprout in Zeb's head all by itself. He comes up to me after having a powwow with men from the other wagons, and he says, "Anything keeping you here, Joe?"

I acted like I didn't know what he was getting at. He told me flat out that he'd be pleasured if I was to come and go along with them. He had a notion I could be of help to them in that wild country. I told him I never had been out that way very far, and I didn't know the trail.

I had played enough good poker that I figured my eyes wouldn't show how much I really wanted to go. I wanted them folks to figure it was all their own doing, so they would feel grateful to me instead of it having to be the other way around.

Zeb told me they had some maps that was supposed to be reliable, and he figured the trail had been beaten out so well that we wasn't apt to get lost. Main thing he wanted me for was as a guard, to help be sure they didn't get slipped up on again.

I told him I sure did feel bad about having to leave Sheriff Smathers, him depending on me so much. That was all a poker bluff, of course. Far as I was concerned old Smathers could go soak his head in a trough till he quit bubbling. He had about wore out his welcome with me.

I told Zeb I didn't have a wagon. He said it was better that way. They wanted me to be an outrider, a scout. A wagon would be in my way. "We can't afford to pay you," he says, "but you can take your meals at my wagon with me and Addie and Samantha. Addie'll be right tickled."

I figured Addie would only be tickled to feed me some ground-up glass. But the idea of sharing a campfire with Samantha made the whole thing sound fine.

Zeb still thought he was the fisherman. I didn't intend to let him suspicion that he was the fish. He says, "When we get out yonder to the valley, I expect there'll be farmland enough that you can get a share for yourself. We'll be pleased to have you for a neighbor."

I could still remember my boyhood pretty good. One thing I didn't share with these emigrants was their feeling for the plow. But I had begun to picture me having a ranch out there, with cattle running all over the hills, and a little ranchhouse with Samantha in it, fixing my supper every night. So I told Zeb if they really felt like they needed me, I'd make the sacrifice and settle up my affairs in town.

Old Smathers had already sensed that I wasn't long for that place. He didn't act very pleased when I laid the badge on his desk, but he didn't seem surprised none either. He says, "Throwing in with them farmers, are you? Anybody can tell by looking at you that you ain't no farmer. Maybe you figure you can get ahold of their money somehow."

That was about what I had expected of him. He always thought of everything in terms of money. I didn't tell him about Samantha because she wasn't none of his business, and he wouldn't of understood anyhow. He was long past the point where a good-looking woman stirred him up much.

I went over to the bank to draw my money. Old man Dietert seemed like he was sorry to see me go, especially since I was pulling a right smart of cash out of his safe. He told me how risky it was to carry all that cash around and offered to write me a draft on a bank out in El Paso. I told him no thanks. I knowed what to do about a man that tried to rob me with a gun, but it wasn't so easy to keep a man from robbing you with pen and ink. I was looking at Clopton when I said it, just being sure he got the message clear. The old man was all right, but one of these days he was going to die of his infirmities, and this town would be at the mercy of Clopton.

I got me a money belt and put all that money in it where it belonged, just under my heart.

The next morning at daylight we pointed them wagons west. There I was, way out yonder with a whole train of farmers, standing in some danger of contamination. You know what a wagon scout is, don't you? He's a fool who rides way out in front of everybody and says to the Indians, "Here I am, come get me." Of course he hopes there ain't none of them around to take up the invitation.

Well, there wasn't, not for a while. The wagon people was pretty tense for the first two or three days, till we got to where the battle had taken place. They sure didn't let the wagons stretch out much; they had the lead horses or mules of every team sticking their noses over the tailgate of the next wagon. Zeb hadn't figured to stop at the battle site, but it was late in the day, and everybody just naturally quit. There was fresh graves out there, and they wanted to pray over them one more time, since it wasn't likely any of these people would ever pass this way again. I think Zeb was more worried over the state of mind this would put them in than over the time they might be losing.

It was an awful quiet supper. Afterwards Samantha got up and started walking real slow out to where her father was buried. I went to follow her, but old Addie stepped in front of me. "She'll want to be alone," she warns me, meaning that *Addie* wanted her to be alone.

"I won't bother her," I says. "I'll just go out there and make sure no Indian slips up and joins her."

I just stood back and watched her. I could see her shoulders shake a little and knowed she was crying, and I wanted to go up and take her and hold her so bad I couldn't hardly stand it. But I knowed old Addie was watching from over by the wagons, and she would be out there like a hornet. Finally Samantha says, "You'd of liked him, Joe."

I told her I knowed I would've, which was likely true. I liked Zeb, and from what I could hear, Samantha's father had been cut out of the same timber.

She says, "It scares me, going on out yonder alone."

If she had any doubt before how I felt about her, I didn't leave her any. I says, "You ain't alone. If I have anything to do about it, you ain't ever going to be."

I don't know what I expected her to say to that. Maybe I thought she would come and fall into my arms. She didn't. She just turned and looked at me, and I couldn't read what was in her eyes. She smiled, just a touch, and she says, "I know that, Joe." And then she walked back toward the wagon.

As far as I was concerned, I had asked her to marry me. She hadn't said *no*, but she sure hadn't said *yes*, either.

We went on and never seen so much as a moccasin print. We had a little scare one day when a bunch of horsemen showed up in the distance, and we got all the wagons and carts circled in a hurry. The riders, though, turned out to be a patrol of black troopers with a white lieutenant working out of Fort Clark. They was on their way in after a hundred-mile scout, and they hadn't seen a thing.

People began to get so relaxed and confident that a few even quit being nice to the Mexican freighters. Decided, I reckon, that they wasn't going to need them after all.

Nighttimes, when I could talk to Samantha after supper where her old aunt couldn't hear us, I'd point out to her that a young woman all by herself that way couldn't take up a farm. It was by way of trying to get her to say she would step into double harness with me. But she would always say the Lord would show her the way when the time came; she figured He had plans for her.

I sure had plans for her.

I never did get to talk to her very long at a time. That old Addie seemed like she had twelve eyes, and half of them in the back of her head. She wouldn't give the two of us much chance for any real serious conversation.

Once when the old lady was busy digging through a trunk in her wagon and wasn't watching us, I got Samantha out and we started for a walk around the wagon circle in the moonlight. We hadn't got fifty yards before I heard somebody come trotting up behind us. I had my pistol out before I had time even to think about it. When I spun around I seen the old lady catching up to us. She didn't pay any more attention to that pistol than if it had been a matchstick. She says to Samantha, "You better get back to the wagon, sugar. It's dangerous out here."

Samantha says, "There ain't any Indians."

The old lady tried her best to kill me with a look from them two hard eyes. She says, "All the danger ain't from Indians."

Samantha done as she was told and started for her own wagon. The old lady hung back. When Samantha was out of hearing she turned on me like a mad cow hooking a wolf away from her calf. She says, "The rest of them don't see through you, Joe Pepper, but *I* do. You're trying to turn the head of a poor little orphan girl."

I pointed out to her that Samantha wasn't a little girl.

"She ain't old enough yet to know her own mind," Addie says. "Till she is, I'll help do her thinking for her. And *you* have no place in my thinking."

I didn't have anything but the best of motives in mind for that girl. I wasn't going to do a thing till the words had been properly read to us out of the Book. But I knowed there wasn't no use trying to convince Addie of that fact. I figured I would just keep working on Samantha, kind of slow and easy, and maybe by the time we got to El Paso I'd have her in a frame of mind to run off and look for a preacher with me. *That* would fix the old woman.

It was the next day, or the day after that, when Pete Ogden showed up.

I was way out in front of the wagons, kind of edging over toward some flat-topped mountains. We kept the wagons as far back from the mountains as we could because it was a favorite stunt of the Indians to hide till the wagons got to the closest point, then come charging and catch the wagons strung out. I worked over fairly close, but not so close that they wouldn't have theirselves one dandy horserace trying to catch me.

That's when I seen the Indians, coming at me through the greasewood, running hard. One looked like he was a good ways out in front.

First thing I done was fire my pistol into the air three times to let them wagon folks know they was fixing to have a visitation. Then I put spurs to that Santos black and figured to see just how fast he could really run. He was even better than I figured. He had seen them other horses coming at us, and I reckon he sensed that I was some excited. Horses have got a way of knowing. If it had been a matched race on some country track, we could of taken the whole pot.

The farmers didn't waste no time. When I got to the wagons they had already circled up and put all the loose stock inside. They had left a little gap for me to ride through, was all. The second I loped in, they pushed the wagons up tight.

I had left them Indians like they was caught in the quicksand. But the odd thing was that one man was still way out in front of the others. It finally struck me that he wasn't with them; they was chasing him. And he was coming for the wagons as fast as he could travel.

Old Zeb hollers, "That's a white man!"

Sure enough, I could tell now that he was wearing a hat, something the Indians hadn't commenced doing at the time. And under that hat was a wad of hair he was fixing to lose. His horse was giving out under him.

Samantha all of a sudden got to remembering seeing her father shot down in front of her eyes. She started hollering, "Somebody save him!"

I tried to tell her that anybody who went out there might not come back. I didn't feel like going out and risking my life to save a fool. It was damned obvious that the man was a fool or he wouldn't of been out there by himself in the first place. But she wasn't listening to that kind of argument. She was hollering for somebody to do something, and then she grabbed a rifle and started out there herself.

Way I seen it, that man could take care of himself or take what was coming to him, but I wasn't just about to let that girl get herself killed for some stranger. I ran out and grabbed her. I turned her around and pushed her back toward the wagon. Then I dropped to one knee and started shooting past the man, into that bunch of Indians. At the distance I couldn't do them any great damage, but maybe I was looking good to Samantha. In a minute several other men came out afoot and joined me, and we all started walking to meet the rider, shooting our rifles as we went.

The Indians kind of wavered at all that fire. I don't think we was hitting any of them, but we had sure got their attention. The rider was in a pretty fair way to make it, then, but his horse went down. He was still out there a hundred yards or so past us, afoot. That gave the Indians a last chance, and it looked for a minute like they was going to get him. Old Zeb got up and started running out to meet him. I couldn't do no less with that girl watching, so I jumped up and followed after him. A couple of the Mexicans was right up beside me, and one or two of the farmers. I suppose I'd of looked better to Samantha if I'd been out in the lead. But I'd always believed that the Lord helps them that help theirselves, and I couldn't see where I was helping myself much out there so far from the wagons. Not with a dozen or fifteen Indians out there looking mad.

That feller was coming in to meet us even faster than we was going out to meet him. The Indians had stopped out there a ways and was taking potshots. Only three or four had rifles, and it was way too far to send an arrow. One of them got lucky and put a bullet in that feller's leg. He went down like he had been hit with an ax. He got up again, cussing like a politician who has just lost the election. You'd of thought, after the narrow escape he had, that he would of been more considerate of the Lord's feelings. He kind of hopped on his good leg and went down again.

Zeb hollered for him to lay still, that we was coming. But he kept right on crawling and scrambling toward us on his hands and knees, still looking back over his shoulder. A man don't rightly respect fear, I suppose, till he's had a bunch of Indians breathing on the back of his neck.

He was in a right smart of a panic when we got to him. I thought he was going to fight us right at first, like he couldn't tell for sure if we was Indians. I told him if he didn't behave himself I was going to stomp him a little. I grabbed him under one arm and a Mexican grabbed him under another. We lit out with him toward the wagons. Zeb and the others followed along behind us, walking and running backwards, keeping their eyes on the Indians. I was too busy to look, but I was satisfied they kept edging on in toward us till we got them up to good rifle range of the wagons. Then they stopped.

As we got to the wagons I turned for a quick look. I seen one of them Indians a hundred yards away. I didn't know much about sign language, but I got the gist of what he was telling us. The wagon people started shooting at him, and he decided to leave.

We laid the feller down in the shade of a wagon. He was groaning and cussing a little and wasn't feeling too good. That leg was bleeding. It wasn't flopping, though, so I felt like the bone hadn't been busted. All in all it wasn't much of a wound. I've been gouged near as deep by a cactus thorn.

There was more than enough people around to do the doctoring, so I didn't make no effort to help out. I had already done a right smart more than I figured was my duty to a damn fool. I stood in front of the wagon and kept my eyes peeled on the Indians. I didn't figure they was likely to make a charge at the wagons, knowing how they was out-manned, but I also knowed that Indians would sometimes do the opposite of what you expected. It never hurt to be ready.

Well sir, first thing I knowed Samantha was there with a pan of water and a towel, and she was washing that feller's face and talking soft to him while Zeb and a couple of the men was pouring whiskey into the wound and holding him down. He used language that ought to never fall on a good woman's ears, but I suppose he wasn't thinking along them lines at the time. Pretty soon Zeb had the bleeding stopped and the wound tied up and was telling everybody the damage was nothing very serious. I could of told them that from the start. The feller had calmed down considerable. Samantha was still putting that wet cloth to his face and trying to make him feel better.

It didn't make *me* feel any better, I'll tell you.

Now that I had time and the inclination for a closer look, I could see that he was young, a good deal younger than me. He had several days' growth of whiskers, but there wasn't no tracks around the corners of his eyes yet. When he finally managed to tear his eyes away from Samantha he looked at me. He says, "You're the one that dragged me in here, ain't you?"

I already felt like that could of been a mistake, and I didn't want to claim all the credit. I says, "One of them. Soledad Martinez was the other one."

He thanks us both and says, "That was sure a tight spot you-all got me out of."

I was about half mad, thinking how easy it would of been for some of us to have gotten ourselves killed. If it hadn't been for Zeb and Samantha, I'd of let him take his chances out there with them Indians.

I was about to walk off and leave him, but I decided to ask him, "What the hell was you doin' off out yonder by yourself, anyway? Didn't anybody ever tell you that Indians are dangerous?"

He says, "There's other things just as dangerous."

I seen the way Samantha was looking at him, with enough pity in her eyes to drown a gray mule, and I thought, *There sure is.* I walked out between the wagons and looked toward the mountains. The Indians was still out there, riding away but taking their time about it, kind of tempting the foolhardy to go chasing after them. There wasn't no fools with our wagons, though, unless you count that stranger.

When the Indians was clean gone I caught up my black and rode out to the stranger's horse. It was a little bay, still alive but too badly wounded to live. I pulled the saddle off of him, then put a bullet in his brain. I carried the saddle back to the wagon circle. A saddle ain't ever a cheap and easy thing to come by. I figured this stranger would need his to ride out of here as soon as he was able, which I hoped would be *real* soon.

Well sir, if you think you already begin to see the turn of things, you're plumb right. Just about the time I was beginning to have some dreams about buying me a ranch out west and settling down in a nest with Samantha, she gets a patient to worry about and mother-hen over. I've never understood it, but I've seldom seen it fail. Watch a nurse, and nine times out of ten she'll marry one of her patients. You can be as big as a mountain, stout as a bull, brave as a bear, rich as old Croesus, and chances are you won't get no more than a passing glance from a woman. But get yourself sick or hurt to where she can wait on you and play nurse to you, and you've got her in the palm of your hand.

I got to wishing it had been *me* with a wound in my leg. Then maybe I'd of got some attention. Way it was, I hardly even got a thank-you-sir.

There wasn't nothing to do but camp right where we was till we could tell about them Indians. We figured there was some risk they might go for some of their friends. If the subject was to be pursued any further, this was as good a place as any to do it. They had to come at us over a big open greasewood flat where they made a lot better target than we did.

Time I got all the necessaries took care of and went back to the Wentworth wagon, Samantha already knowed a great deal more about the stranger than I was interested in finding out. His name was Pete Ogden, she told me, and he had come from over around San Antonio someplace. He was on his way west to seek his fortune when he had run into the Indians, who had a little different plan worked out for him.

"You know something else?" she says. "He's a farmer."

Well, so had I been once, but I sure didn't brag about it.

She says, "If we try we might talk him into staying with us and locating in the same part of the country that we do."

I could tell by the way he kept looking at her that it wouldn't take any talking to convince him. It might take talking to keep him from it.

That old lady Addie was tickled to death over the way things turned out. She grinned at me like the jasper that's about to kick the stool out from under a man with the noose around his neck. I could've choked the old woman if there hadn't been so many witnesses.

Well sir, me and Soledad taken us a long ride early the next morning, swinging over to them hills to look for sign the Indians might be getting ready to come at us again. The country was as clean as a hound's tooth. We decided there wasn't anything to keep us from proceeding ahead except timidity.

Soledad was kind of the *caporal* over the Mexican part of the wagon train. Seemed like a decent sort, a man we could depend on. After that little set-to which gained us a new passenger, he got to acting as an outrider. I'd scout out front. He'd trail along behind the wagons, and far out toward the hills, making sure the train didn't get sneaked up on from behind. About all we ever seen out there was jackrabbits and *javelina* hogs.

You'd be surprised how fast Pete Ogden's leg started healing up. Of course he had him a good nurse that seen after his welfare every spare minute she had; he *ought* to've done good. Pretty soon he was getting around on a cane, then limping about without it. Looked to me like he was fit enough to start making some real use of himself around the wagons. But Samantha said he oughtn't to rush nature.

Nature was rushing along pretty good, it seemed to me. Nights, him and her would take out and walk around the edge of the wagon circle, the way I'd tried to do with her. Old Addie never would let us out of her sight when it was *me*, but she didn't seem to worry about Pete Ogden. Matter of fact, she would kind of stick the knife in me and give it a twist every time she seen the chance. She'd say, "Ain't they a handsome couple?" or such as that.

I'd remember the old Bible story about how the Lord handled all them sinners at the Tower of Babel by making them speak different languages so they couldn't understand each other, and I'd wonder how come He hadn't fixed it so men and women couldn't talk to one another. It would of saved a lot of grief in this old world, preacher. I'm surprised the Lord hasn't thought of it.

My eyes have always been pretty good. I could see by the look that came into Samantha's every time Pete Ogden passed in front of her that I could forget all them pretty little dreams I had been building up about her and me.

After a while Pete got tired of riding in a wagon all day and volunteered to help out however he could. I mentioned the loose stock, thinking how it wouldn't hurt to let him eat dust at the tail end of the wagon train, bringing up the extra cattle and horses. He got the borrow of a horse and fell in back there and went to work. I watched him a right smart, and I'll have to admit he made a hand.

I was some disappointed about that. I had hoped he would show up as one of them slough-off types, and old Zeb would run him off from the train first time we came to a settlement. But he showed himself to be a willing worker and acted like he understood stock. There's nothing leaves a man as frustrated as wanting to dislike somebody and not finding anything solid to dislike him about.

It's even worse when you wind up owing him a debt. And one day pretty soon I found myself owing Pete Ogden.

We was way off out in that old dry country west of the Pecos River, where the Davis Mountains come down and cut across the desert, and you either have to climb over them or go way around or hunt a pass through. All the old wagon and stagecoach trails led through the passes, which is fine except when the Indians come looking for horses and hair. A nice narrow pass is just made to order for an Indian, like buffalo hump and eagle feathers. We came up to one, and there wasn't nothing else to do except me ride in there and see if there was anything waiting for us that we might not want to meet.

There was.

Did you ever accidentally strike a hornet's nest and watch them hornets pour out after you? I doubt that you did much watching because you was too busy running. That's the way it was with me. These stories you read about the Indian always knowing everything that goes on within a hundred miles of him are just so much imagination on the part of some Eastern writer that never heard an arrow sing by his left ear. I think I surprised them Apaches about as much as they surprised me, or I wouldn't of had a chance for any kind of head start.

I've known a few old men in my time that had a reputation as Indian fighters. They always told me that one secret of getting to be an *old* Indian fighter was to know when to run, and always ride a fast horse just in case you come to one of them times unexpected. I was riding that Santos black and doing real good. I could see the wagons going into a circle ahead of me. Way out behind, Soledad was spurring like hell to catch up to the train.

I was making a dandy gain on them Indians. I was maybe three hundred yards from the train and at least a couple of hundred ahead of them Apaches when I seen somebody come spurring out to meet me from the wagons, firing a pistol as he came. Now, talk about useless . . . somebody shooting a pistol at Indians five hundred yards away is just plain wasteful.

Another old story you hear sometimes is that Indians couldn't shoot a gun straight. That's about as truthful as a lot of the other Indian yarns. I was looking back over my shoulder and seen one of those Indians stop his horse, jump off, drop to one knee and fire. I seen the smoke, and a second or two later that horse of mine turned a flip.

I hit the ground like some giant had picked me up and throwed me as hard as he could. All the breath was knocked out of me, and that horse's rump came down and pounded on both of my legs. I reckon it was imagination, but I thought I could already hear them Indians singing over my hair. I tried to get up and run, but I didn't have the breath in me, and my legs was both too numb. I sort of halfway pushed myself to my feet. My eyes was so blurry I couldn't see which was the way to the wagon train, and which to the Indians.

I heard a horse come running at me, and tried to shoot my pistol at it, but it was all jammed with dirt and wouldn't fire. I throwed my hands up to try and protect my head, because I figured I was about to get a stone ax right over my ear.

Somebody hollered. "Grab on! Let's get out of here!"

It was Pete Ogden. He leaned over and reached out his arm, and all of a sudden my legs didn't hurt me a bit. I grabbed onto him. He socked the spurs to that horse and held me as tight as he could up against the saddle. My legs was both hanging off on one side, dragging through the low brush. I could hear them Indians hollering behind us. I could hear that horse straining with the double load, and I could hear Pete Ogden promising him all kinds of good things if he wouldn't let the Indians catch us.

You never tried to hang on to a running horse when all the breath's been knocked out of you, I suppose. Under any ordinary circumstances it would be hard to do. But knowing what was back there to catch me if I fell off, I didn't have much trouble at it.

I heard the wagon people shooting, trying to drive the Indians back, but I couldn't see anything. The saddlehorn kept punching me in the ribs and knocking the breath back out of me every time I could get a little air in. We made it to the wagons. Pete Ogden jumped his horse over a wagon tongue and dropped me on the ground like I was a sack of oats. I was still in a daze when people picked me up and started hunting over me for wounds. By the time I could get enough breath back to tell them I was all right, there wasn't a secret birthmark about my body that half the wagon train didn't know. My clothes was pretty well torn off of me, first by the fall when my horse went down, and then by the brush Pete drug me through.

Directly I was laying under the shade of a wagon and looking up at Pete Ogden the same way he had looked at me the time before. Except that I didn't have any wounds for Samantha to fuss over, and get her all moon-eyed.

Saying "thank you" never was hard for me like it is for some people, but this time it was like pulling my own teeth out to get it said. I almost gagged over it. I finally told Pete I was right obliged to him for his little favor, and what the hell was he shooting up all that ammunition for? He said he was hoping he might scare the Indians away, which showed how little he knowed about Indians. I hoped he knowed more about farming.

You might think what Pete done just squared up a debt he owed me, but I knowed deep inside that it was more. The only reason I had gone out to rescue him was because Samantha shamed me into it, and I knowed the others was going out anyway. But Pete Ogden came after me all by himself, and without anybody shaming him. This young farmer was a *man*, and I resented him for it!

Talk about things turning out backwards . . . this time it was *me* that was laid up and needing help, and all Samantha could do was hug Pete Ogden's neck and tell him how brave he was, how scared she was that something might of happened to him. Nary a word about what might of happened to me.

A man who tells it around that he understands women is just letting everybody know how big a fool he really is.

I got my breath back awhile later. Zeb asked me what I thought we ought to do about getting through that pass. I told him it seemed to me that if them Indians wanted it so much, the neighborly thing was to let them have it and work on north. Maybe we could find us another one that wasn't being used. Soledad rode out and got my saddle back for me when the Indians was gone, the way I had done for Pete Ogden. The Indians had carried off my carbine. I sure hated to leave that black horse. He was as fast a one as ever I rode, excepting maybe my Tennessee gray. But they don't make horses that can outrun a bullet.

That was the last of the Indian trouble for us, though Pete Ogden didn't take Samantha outside the wagon circle for any more night walking. They just stayed at the wagon and spooned in front of everybody. Odd thing happened, too. Pete Ogden had always seemed grateful to me for helping drag him away from the Indians, and after he done the same thing for me he got downright friendly, like we was old partners or something. I didn't encourage him. Even if he didn't know it, I owed him a right smart more than he owed me, and owing a man a debt don't endear him to you.

It got to be common knowledge amongst the wagon folks that when they got to El Paso him and Samantha was going to hunt up a preacher. There wasn't nobody prouder over it than Addie Wentworth. She had finally got to where she would even treat me like a white man, knowing I wasn't no danger to her niece any longer.

But I could tell something was bothering Pete. I'd catch him sometimes watching her when she wasn't looking, and there was a worry in his eyes that got to worrying *me* a little. I got to suspicioning that maybe he already had him a wife back wherever he came from, and things had gone so far that he was afraid to tell anybody. I got to thinking maybe there was hope for me yet.

One night Pete tapped me on the arm and gave me a nod of his head. He motioned for me to walk out with him a ways, past the wagons. By this time we had got amongst some Mexican settlements along the Rio Grande, and we wasn't much concerned about Indians anymore. It wasn't far to El Paso.

Pete says to me, "Joe, I got something to tell you. If I don't do it now, I'm going to bust."

I figured he was going to confess to me about the wife he had went off and left behind him. I was going to hear him out and then do the manly thing: knock him halfway to El Paso.

He says, "You figured me for a stranger when I joined this train, but I wasn't, not quite. You never seen *me* before, but I seen *you*, Joe. I knowed who you was from the start."

That throwed me a little. I just looked at him and tried to think back to when I could of ever crossed his trail before. I was afraid he knowed I was Joe Peeler instead of Joe Pepper.

He says, "I rode into Catclaw one night, and I spotted you with your badge on. I made it a point to stay out of your sight. I needed me a stake to go on west; I was flat busted. I waited till you was out of town, and I taken it."

He didn't have to tell me any more. I guessed the rest of it. I says, "You're the bank robber I hunted all over hell and half of Texas for."

He just nodded at me. He says, "I was hungry, and it seemed like a smart thing to do. Now that I've throwed in with these good folks, and you and Samantha, I'm ashamed of myself. I can see that I really ain't good enough for her. I ain't worth much, Joe."

That wasn't exactly the truth. He was worth five hundred dollars to me, right there the way he stood. That is, when I delivered him in at El Paso and notified the bank at Catclaw.

I was a little put out at him. I says, "Have you got an idea how many miles I rode hunting for you? I wore saddle-blisters on my butt and went hungry so much that I had to punch a new hole in my belt."

He tells me, "I'm sorry, Joe. I didn't know you at the time, and I thought it would be funny to have people hunting for me and not finding me. It was the first time in my life anybody paid any real attention to me."

"If they'd of caught you they'd of paid you more attention than you really wanted."

Pete says, "I still got nearly all the money, Joe. I just spent a little dab in Mexico, is all. I'd like to get you to send it back to them for me." He reached inside his shirt and brought out a little canvas pouch. I ran my hands into it. I could tell it wasn't no big lot of money.

He says, "There's a shade over nine hundred dollars. I never spent more than twenty-thirty of it."

I thought about my little leather bag of gold. It wasn't in the pouch. I says, "There's something else, Pete. You got something that belongs to me personal."

He didn't act like he understood, so I told him. He just blinked at me. He says, "I didn't see nothing like that. All I taken was the currency."

Something about the way he looked at me, I knowed he was telling me the truth. Which meant that somebody else had lied to me.

Clopton! Old man Dietert's number-one helper had been the one who opened the safe for Pete, and the one who shut it afterwards. *That* crooked coyote had got off with my gold and blamed it on Pete Ogden.

I cussed a blue streak. Pete thought it was against him. He says kind of sorrowful, "I don't blame you for being mad at me. I got it coming. You want to turn me in to the law at El Paso, I'll stand ready to take my medicine."

There it was, the opportunity to get Pete Ogden out of the way, to maybe have a new chance at Samantha. To rub old lady Addie's nose in the truth. The chance I'd been waiting for, and I spoiled it.

I got to feeling noble and generous, which is a feeling I never had but a few times, and generally always lived to regret. I says to Pete, "You really love that girl? You really mean to try and make her happy the rest of her life?"

"I would if I could. But she won't want me when she finds out what I am. I ain't worthy of her."

"She don't have to know about it. I'll turn in the money for you. I'll send a letter back to Catclaw and tell them I found you and had to kill you. As far as they'll be concerned you're dead and buried, and the case is closed. Nobody ever has to know except me and you."

I don't reckon Pete had expected that. I do believe he was about to break down and cry. He says, "I'll owe you for the rest of my life, Joe."

Better *him* owing *me* than the other way around. What he didn't know wouldn't hurt him. I wasn't really all that noble. I knowed if I was to turn Pete in to the law, Samantha would blame me more than she blamed him. Chances was she wouldn't of spoken to me again, ever. All I would've got out of it would've been the reward. I figured to get the reward anyway.

Well sir, we got in to El Paso, and they had theirselves a wedding, and Pete Ogden moved right into Samantha's wagon. Old lady Addie grinned at me, so much as to say she was glad Samantha had got herself an honest, hardworking young farmer boy instead of a crooked, whiskey-drinking, gambling gunfighter. And I grinned back at her because I knowed a lot more about it than she did.

The wagon train pulled out for the valley where the farmers figured to sink their plows into new ground. I stayed in El Paso because it would of hurt too much to see Samantha and Pete Ogden together.

I really did intend to turn that money in at first. Then I got to thinking. They owed me a five-hundred-dollar reward for finding the bank robber in the first place. On top of that, they owed me for that bag of gold Clopton had got away with. I figured the money Pete had given me didn't quite cover all I had coming to me. But I was still in a generous mood and willing to accept my loss. I just kept what I had.

I did write old man Dietert a letter, though. Best I remember, I told him something like this:

Deer Mr Dietert,

Just a line to let you know I come across that bank robber and we had a fight and I am sorry to relate that I was obliged to kill him. Before he died he told me he had went and spent all the money so there aint none to send to you. I saved his ear to mail you as proof but it spoiled on me and I dont think you want it. He also told me he didnt get as much as was supposed to have been lost and that he suspected somebody in the bank must have helped himself and blamed him for it. I was thinkin maybe it might be smart if you and Sheriff Smathers was to surprise Clopton with a serch of his house, you might be surprised at what you come up with. He always looked kind of shifty eyed to me.

Best regards and yours truely.

Joe Pepper

I would of liked to have been there if they found my gold sack on him. I never did hear one way or the other, but years later I run across somebody from Catclaw and asked if they knowed old man Dietert or his helper Clopton. They said the old man had finally died of a heart seizure, and Clopton had long ago run off to Mexico. Seemed there was trouble of some kind, and he got away with nothing much more than his britches.

CHAPTER 6

I'm ashamed to tell you, preacher, but for a little while I tried to drown my sorrows in bad whiskey and sinful surroundings. Old El Paso was a good place for a man who wanted to do that kind of a thing. They had people there who was experts at helping you. I consorted with women of bad character and men who was worse. Pretty soon that fat money belt had shrunk to a little of nothing. One morning I come face to face with myself at the mirror and done some pretty stern talking. I had to get myself into some productive kind of labor.

So I went back to gambling. I know you don't approve of it, but the way I done it, there wasn't a lot of gamble in it. I cheated. Not all the time, mind you; just when I had to. Nine out of ten of them people didn't have to be cheated; they would just naturally beat themselves. Pretty soon I had built me up a first-rate stake again. Not as much as I had come to town with, but enough to set me up in a game where I stood a chance to come away with some real important money.

I had given up on my dream of a home with Samantha, of course, but the idea of another ranch hadn't altogether left me yet. I had a notion that if I could clean up good in El Paso I'd drift on out to Arizona and maybe buy me a ranch and live the rest of my life in peace.

At one place in town they had a high-stakes game in a back room almost every night. Big cowmen and big mine people would come there and try their hand against the best gamblers in town. Their luck wasn't usually any too good, but they would keep coming back, most of them, hoping the next time Lady Luck would turn her face on them instead of her back. That's what kept them high-stakes games going, was the hope that when a man lost big, he might go back and win big. Now and again one would, just enough to keep the others hoping. Meanwhile them gamblers skimmed the cream off of a lot of the cow business and the mining without ever getting cow manure on their boots or picking up a shovel.

The place was a saloon known as the Rio Bravo, which was the name a lot of the Mexicans had for the Rio Grande. Owner was a man named Frank Feller. He was a fair-to-middling poker player and sometimes sat in on the games, but mostly he was a shill for the real gambler of the outfit, a tall, spidery kind of a gent named Arthur Phelps. Folks around town called him "Slick" Phelps, but not to his face. He was said to be a good shot. He had long hands that had never known a callus, and tapering fingers that could make a deck of cards do almost anything except sing a hymn. Feller provided the place and bankrolled Phelps's games and got a percentage of the take, though they always pretended the game was Phelps's own, and Feller appeared to lose a right smart to him. That was just to bring the suckers in.

I had got a little rusty at the game, since them people in Catclaw hadn't been much of a challenge, but I polished it up in El Paso and bided my time till I thought I was ready to match up with Slick Phelps. Finally, after I had been there two months, I sat in on the game one night, figuring I was ready. Now, I considered myself a right smooth hand, but I could tell right off that I wasn't a match for Phelps. I lost a thousand dollars in one night and knowed he was cheating me more than I was cheating him, but I never once caught him at it.

So I went back to lower-stakes games in other places to practice up some more. I practiced cheating other people, then I would turn around and cheat myself on purpose so they wouldn't catch on to what I was doing. I wasn't after these small fry anyway, except for the practice they gave me. I had my sights set on cleaning out Slick Phelps. Finally I went back and sat in with him again. I thought I had improved to where I could give him a contest. It didn't take me but two hours and another thousand dollars to figure out I wasn't good enough to wipe the dust off of his boots.

I noticed a couple of things about Slick Phelps. One thing, he never drank. The only thing he ever taken was a cup of coffee, which seemed to sharpen him up. Whiskey was for idiots when it came to high stakes gambling. It just slowed the hands and dulled the eyes. Then Slick Phelps would come down his web and grab you like a fly. Another thing he always done was to excuse himself every couple of hours. He would walk outside and take a little air, and he would ease his kidneys. Little as you might think about it, the strain on a man's kidneys in a long game can be just the edge that a smoother player needs on him. Slick Phelps didn't give nobody any edge.

When Phelps was out, Feller would take over the game. He was no cowboy playing for matches on a saddle blanket, of course, but he wasn't a pimple on Phelps's backside when it come to the pinch. Often as not he would lose more than he taken in, and when Phelps came back it was up to him to recover the house losses. Some of them high-stakes players always kind of waited for Phelps to take his constitutional, then they would bet big against Feller, trying to get back what they could.

I knowed if I stayed in El Paso till I had a beard to my belly, I would never beat Slick Phelps. Not in any ordinary way, that is. But Joe Pepper didn't get his reputation doing everything the ordinary way.

They had an outhouse behind the saloon, up against the alley. I set myself out there one night in the shadows across the other side and watched Phelps. He done everything by habit. He would come out the back door and stand on the stoop two or three minutes, looking up at the stars. I figured he was probably looking for sign of rain, which was a waste of time at El Paso. Next thing he would do was to roll himself a cigarette and stand there and smoke it about half up. He never smoked inside, at the game. Cigarettes was a distraction, and he didn't allow himself no distractions.

Finally he would throw the cigarette away, walk to the outhouse, take care of nature's call, then stop at the washstand, wash and dry his hands, and go back in to the game. I watched him all that night, and never once did he vary from the routine.

I had sort of worked up an idea in my head. The sheriff was an agreeable sort of feller, considering the things he had to put up with, and he generally rode around town in a buggy. One night there was a disturbance in one of the fancy houses down toward the river, and he went trotting his horses down there to see about it. I trailed along behind him in the dark. While he was inside I fished in the back of that buggy and found a set of handcuffs. I didn't steal them, exactly, I just took the borrow of them awhile. I didn't have a key to them, but I kept pestering them a couple of days, off and on, till I learned how to open them up with a piece of wire.

The night I brought off my plan, I taken all the money I had been able to work up and shoved it into my shirt. I taken the handcuffs and a fair piece of rawhide rope, and I set myself up in the dark behind the Rio Bravo. I let Slick Phelps go the first time he came out. The second time I watched him smoke his cigarette, and watched him go to the house out back. When he went to the washstand and poured a pan of water out of the bucket, I stepped up behind him and gave him what people used to call a cowpuncher shampoo. That is, I fetched him a lick up beside the head with the barrel of my six-shooter. You never seen a tall man fold up so limber.

I had found where there was an old empty corral a piece off down the street. I drug him down there in the dark while he was still enjoying the benefit of the shampoo. I laid him on the ground, handcuffed him to the bottom of the fencepost and tied his feet with the rawhide rope. I stuffed a handkerchief into his mouth and tied another one around it to where he couldn't holler. Time he come to he was trussed up like a hog on a spit.

I dusted myself off, walked in the front door of the Rio Bravo and marched back to that high-stakes game in the rear room. I bought me a stack of chips and set in to see how much I could win from Frank Feller.

He didn't seem bothered right at first when I started beating him. He would glance over toward the door once in a while, figuring Phelps would walk in any minute and polish me off in short order. My stack of chips started growing right peart. Before long Feller was spending a lot of time looking at that door. Every time he did I taken the occasion to improve my hand a little. Sweat started running down into his eyes, and he would rub a sleeve over them, and I would see him pull a new card out of that sleeve. That didn't bother me much; as long as I could see what he was doing, I could do him one better.

He got to talking about how something must of happened to Phelps, and maybe we ought to wait up the game for him. I told him it didn't matter to me whether Phelps was in the game or not, that if Feller was able to play for the house there wasn't no reason why the game shouldn't go on. One by one the other players dropped out. By and by Feller had dropped so much money to me that he couldn't afford to quit. He kept thinking, I guess, that Phelps would finally show up and bail him out of trouble.

But Phelps didn't show up. I had picked me a good place to put him, where nobody was apt to come across him till daylight. By daylight I figured to have myself that ranch in Arizona.

What I *did* get was something different. By the time the sun came up and hit Feller in the eyes through the glass panes of the east window, he didn't own that window anymore. *I* did. The Rio Bravo was mine.

The story told around town was that somebody figured Phelps would have money in his pockets when he stepped outside that night. They waylaid him to rob him, then handcuffed him to give theirselves plenty of time to get away. Most people agreed it was probably Mexicans from over in Paso del Norte, across the river. It was the custom if you couldn't find out who had done something to just blame it on the Mexicans.

Most people accepted that theory, but Frank Feller never did. I think he had it figured out from the time they found Phelps where I had left him. He came to me at the Rio Bravo, where I was figuring what color I wanted to paint the front. He was loud and threatening; most people hadn't heard much about Joe Pepper at the time. He left there in a lot worse shape than he came, one eye shut and the other hard to see out of. He went then to Slick Phelps and convinced him it was me who had done him to a turn.

I wished he hadn't done that, because I figured on making Phelps a proposition to stay on and play for me the same way he had played for Feller. That loudmouth ruined it.

Phelps sent word he was coming to have satisfaction. I sent him back a note telling him I was already satisfied and didn't want no trouble. People around the saloon told me he was a man to watch out for; he had helped several undertakers across the country to get on their feet and pay their bills. I decided if that was the way it had to be, I didn't want anybody saying I wasn't ready.

I taken me a rifle and walked across the street to a little barbershop. I sat down where I could watch the front of the place through the window while the barber cut my hair. By and by Slick Phelps came walking down the street on them long, spindly legs. Just before he got there he shucked his swallowtail coat and laid it across a hitching rack where it wouldn't get dirty and wouldn't be in his way. He had a six-shooter on his hip.

Up to then I had entertained some notion I might still be able to talk to him. After seeing him I decided that talk was the last thing he had come for. He stopped in front of the Rio Bravo. He hollers in, "Pepper, you coming out here?" He drawed his pistol and held it.

Them fellers that drawed before they faced you was hard to beat.

I didn't say anything. I taken the barber's cloth from around my neck and got up from the chair.

Phelps waited a minute and hollered again. Then he walked inside. I reckon he didn't find me in there, because in a minute or two he was back. Meantime I had stepped down into the street, into the sunshine. It just so happened that this was late in the afternoon, and my saloon faced west toward the sun. Afterwards, some people accused me of working it all out this way. I never did admit to that.

He had been inside long enough that his eyes was accustomed to the dark instead of the light. I says, "Slick, how about me and you working out a deal? We'd make good partners."

He hadn't come there to talk business. He raised up his pistol, but the afternoon sun hit him in the eyes. I leveled my rifle and taken a good clean sight while he started to shoot wild. You can imagine, preacher, it wasn't no contest.

I sure did wish I hadn't had to shoot Phelps. Him and me could of made us a right smart of money together if he hadn't listened to Frank

Feller so much. If I had had my choices I would rather of laid out Frank Feller.

Well sir, that's how come Joe Pepper to start making a reputation in and around El Paso. Folks figured I must be something special to have beaten Slick Phelps, but I didn't take no credit and still don't. I'd still rather bring a man around to my persuasion than to kill him.

Them days they had a custom in El Paso. Somebody had nailed a big board to a tree in the middle of town, and it was kind of a bulletin board for everybody to see and use. Somebody had something he wanted to sell, he tacked a note on the board. Somebody wanted to call a man a thief or a liar in public, he wrote it out and tacked it up on the board. A friend told me there was a note on the board that I ought to go see. Frank Feller had wrote it. He called me twelve kinds of a cheat and a black-hearted killer. I looked all over town for him. I had it in mind to take him over to the board and persuade him to eat that note, with witnesses. But folks told me he had remembered some business in Mexico.

That Rio Bravo turned out to be quite a place. I'd never had me a saloon and gambling house before. Pretty soon I gave up any notions I'd had about a ranch. The cow business never was half what people sometimes made it out to be. A man can starve himself into a little bitty shadow trying to nurse along a bunch of money-losing cows. A man who has a good saloon is always popular, especially in a thirsty place like El Paso was. Any direction you came from, when you got to El Paso you was dry to the bone.

I taken over the run of the games. I handpicked me a couple of good house gamblers, bankrolled them and taken a split of the proceeds. Once in a while one of them would get to putting aside too much money for himself and start to feeling independent, and then I'd have to get into a game with him myself and teach him a little humility, and also take enough money from him that he appreciated working for me again.

There's an art to handling employees. Some people never learn it.

Things was running my way for a change. I won't try to tell you we run a hundred-percent honest house because you wouldn't believe me, and I don't see no point in telling a lie if there's no profit in it. But I will say we tried to give everybody as even a shake as they could get anywhere in town, and better than most. We had the odds with the house anyway because I didn't keep men around working for me that wasn't almost as good a hand with the pasteboards as I was. And we tried never to clean a man out of his last dime; we always quit in time to leave him a taw. That way maybe he would come back for another game. Take a man's taw away from him and you've lost a customer for good.

About the only worry I had was politics. I never seen a town so mean on politics as El Paso was. The Democrats and the Republicans was at each other's throats. And there was factions within both of them groups that was fighting each other almost as hard as they fought the opposite party. Me being an old Confederate veteran naturally leaned me a little toward the Democrats, but I tried never to worry about a man's politics when I played him. I taken money gladly from Democrat and Republican alike.

It was during that time that I first run onto Burney Northcutt. Folks told me he was a big rancher from west of the Pecos. He wasn't an old man then, the way *you've* knowed him in late years. He was just sloping over the hill into middle age. He had a pinch of gray in his hair and a dab in his mustache, but his eyes was pure fire. He had built a big spread by having the guts to take what he wanted and the iron will to hang on to it. He had fought Yankees and Apaches and bandits and drouth. He had a natural taste for combat; it was like fresh air and sunshine to him. When things ran quiet for too long he would take an itchy notion to come into El Paso, ream out his innards with strong whiskey, and see if his luck at the tables was as good as his luck on the range.

It never was. Folks told me he had always lost to Slick Phelps. Nothing changed when I taken over the Rio Bravo. He lost to me every time we ever played.

He would cuss like a muleskinner and threaten to shoot me, but as long as he kept his hand away from his pistol I didn't pay him much mind. I wasn't one of them people who rankled at every insult and called on a man to apologize or draw his gun, not if I knowed he still had some gambling money left in his pockets. Anger is bad for the digestion, and none too good for business, either.

Half a dozen times I could of shot Burney Northcutt, and not six people in El Paso would of criticized me for it. Maybe if I'd done it then, I wouldn't be in the fix you find me in here tonight.

But of course that's spilt milk, and there's no use rolling in it.

I found me a nice-looking girl down on the row. She had corn-silk hair and big blue eyes that seemed to touch a chord in me someway. I taken her out of circulation and kept her in my own private stock, so to speak. I got to where I didn't waste much time fretting over Samantha. She was just another game I had played and lost. If a man's going to be any kind of a gambler, he's got to get so he don't cry over his losses.

I had me some good times there in El Paso. Things rocked along pretty smooth for a long spell. That's not to say there wasn't little difficulties once in a while over a game, and once I had to kill a holdup man who tried to bulldoze the place and take all the money. But I went for a whole year once without ever having to draw a gun on anybody. Joe Pepper's reputation went a long ways toward holding down trouble.

One day that girl of mine told me she heard a rumor that Frank Feller had been seen in town. He was talking about getting even, some of the girls had said. I had got kind of careless in my good fortune, but I taken to sitting with my back to the wall and watching the doors and windows. I didn't figure him for a face-out shooter, not after what happened to Slick Phelps.

After a while I decided the reports must of been false, because I never did see or hear anything of him. Then all of a sudden I had something a lot more than Frank Feller to worry about. A new face showed up in the high-stakes games.

This feller didn't look a bit like Slick Phelps or I'd of taken him for his brother. He had Phelps's same techniques with the cards. He had the same kind of long, tapering fingers, the same quick and easy shuffle that left you convinced you had missed seeing something but never could tell exactly what. And every time he sat down at the table, the stack of chips in front of him growed while everybody else's got smaller and smaller. The gamblers that worked with me played him first, till he cleaned them out. I gave them a good talking-to about paying attention to business, but that didn't do no good. They was simply outclassed. So finally I sat in on the game with him myself.

It would of been better if the doctor and sheriff had come along and quarantined the place for smallpox. He taken me the way Grant taken Richmond. He got me in the same shape that I had got Frank Feller, in so deep that I couldn't afford to keep on but couldn't afford to quit, either. When it was all over, he had the Rio Bravo, and I had had me *some* experience. He left me with a hundred dollars—said he never liked to leave a man without a taw.

That's when I first seen the fine hand of Frank Feller at work. He showed up looking like a cat that's stole the cream and left the family nothing but the skim milk. He announced to all and sundry that he had gone all the way to California hunting a gambler good enough to take me to the poorhouse.

For a little while I studied on killing him, and I expect I would of done it if I could of decided on a way. No way I could think of seemed like it was quite bloody enough. Then after a while I began to see that he hadn't done nothing more to me than I had done to him. The more I thought about it, the more it got to looking funny, except I couldn't get myself to laugh much.

Sooner or later, I figured, somebody else would take him. He wouldn't die rich. I would live to see him flat on his butt again.

But while I was waiting for that, I couldn't just sit around. I had got in the habit of eating regular. That hundred dollars wouldn't take me far. In fact, I sat in on a low-ante poker game and lost most of it in about the same time as I would of spent eating a good meal.

Lady Luck had turned her back on me. I don't know what I done to sour the old girl on me, but whatever it was, it must of been something big. Got to where I couldn't hardly beat a bunch of cowboys playing on a saddle blanket.

My girl with the corn-silk hair was spending her nights with other people. I was eating *chili* and sleeping on a bedroll down by the river when somebody came to me with a story that Don Luis Terrazas was hiring guards on the big ranch he was building down in Chihuahua.

He was paying good money to *gringo pistoleros.* I borrowed a few dollars from some friends and bought me a few days' supplies and struck off across that sandy desert south of El Paso.

I didn't have no trouble getting the job. My only trouble was getting to like it. I never did. Terrazas had been a soldier under Juarez, people told me, and he grabbed up a big chunk of Chihuahua state after they run the Frenchmen out. I reckon that was his reward. Naturally there were already some natives there who didn't want to give up what they figured was theirs. He needed people who could use a gun and convince them they was wrong.

It was some of the easiest money I ever made, away from a gaming table, but the job always had a sour taste to it. Every time I brought back a runaway *peon* on a rope, or somebody they had classed as a *bandido*, I'd get a whiff of the cells they throwed them in, and I'd remember the one Captain Santos had used for me. They all had the same smell to them. It's a stench that, once it gets in your nostrils, it never quite leaves you the rest of your life. It marks you someway, like the smallpox.

I got sick of it. So one night I drawed my pay and slipped down to the cells. I gave the two guards there a cowpuncher shampoo. Then I taken the keys and opened all the doors I could get to and let the prisoners out. Some of them taken to running the way I expected them to. Others just sat there, afraid to try to get away. They had been *peons* all their lives to one *patrón* or another, and the idea of freedom was beyond their thinking. I didn't have time to stay around and give them any Fourth of July lecture. I figured Don Luis would probably have some of his gunfighters on my tail by daylight, and it was a long ways from the mountains of Chihuahua back up to the Rio Grande. I taken my horse, and a couple of Don Luis's that seemed like they wanted to follow me. When I looked behind me after sunup, I didn't see nothing back there but desert.

I tried the cards again in El Paso, but Lady Luck still had me on the list. I had to sell the Terrazas horses to be able to eat. I thought about going back to the kind of work I done at Catclaw, but the sheriff wasn't hiring. He didn't care much for retired gambling-house owners, or for men that had carried a pistol for Terrazas. Kind of a narrow-minded sort, he was.

I thought maybe I'd go bring in fugitives for the reward, but that turned out not to be worth all the wear and tear, either. I guess it taken an awful crime out in that part of the country to make them offer much of a reward, they was used to so much devilment anyway. Most people who had the law after them would run off down into Mexico, and I couldn't afford to cross the river. Don Luis and his *pistoleros* had a long memory for faces.

Like I've said before, one thing I always had was the sense to know when the gravy was going thin, and it was time to change. It was bully for me that I'd built up a right smart reputation. The word had passed around the country that Joe Pepper was a good hand with a gun. An outfit over in New Mexico was mining silver, and they had been having trouble getting their stuff out. A bunch of bold and brassy *hombres* kept riding in and taking it away from them. The law wasn't doing them much good, seemed like. Everybody knowed to their own satisfaction who was taking the silver, but they didn't have proof. Without proof the law couldn't do much—or wouldn't—so the mine owners came and asked if I could help them. I told them if they paid enough, there wasn't no practical limit to what I could do.

They was, I thought, kind of generous.

One thing people always use around a mining camp is dynamite. I taken me a bundle of it, rode back up into the mountains where the robbers stayed, and located their cabin. There wasn't much to it; they didn't expect no trouble with the law, and they didn't hardly even have a guard out. All I had to do was to tap the one lone sentry over the head kind of businesslike. The rest of them was inside, playing poker with the take from the last robbery. I planted that dynamite up beside the house, lit the fuse and moved out a little ways to watch.

You never seen a poker game break up quite as sudden. That cabin was poorly built anyhow. When the smoke cleared I only seen two of them come out of it, and I picked them off with my rifle.

After that the boys over in that district sort of lost interest in stealing other people's silver shipments. The local law was a little put out about it and said I had denied them boys the protection of a trial by jury. But the mine owners was happy, and they was the ones that paid me, so I just made a couple of suggestions to the local law, none of which they took.

I stayed on the payroll a good while, till the mine owners was sure their trouble was over. They knowed some people having similar difficulties up in the northern part of the state and sent me up there with a letter of recommendation. I was hired on the spot and told that anything I wanted to do, they would back me up. "Due process of law" in that country just meant that every man taken care of himself. After I had laid out three of them boys on a board, the rest decided the high altitude wasn't good for their health, and they moved out to a warmer climate.

There again I came in for a certain amount of slander. There was some folks who said I didn't give them boys a sporting chance, but I did. I sent them word before I came that they'd be a right smart healthier if they left the country before I got there. They didn't take my advice.

One thing, preacher, there never has been one of my bullets ever found in a man's back, except a couple of times when they was trying to run away to escape arrest. I always got a man from the front side, even if that exposed me to a little danger myself.

Naturally I had work in that part of the country as long as any of the wild bunch was still around. I done pretty good for some years, drifting from one mining section to another across New Mexico and Arizona, and for a time clear over into California. There was times when I didn't have to do anything except show up. The sticky-fingered crowd would hear Joe Pepper was in the vicinity, and they would just naturally go hunting for a different place to ply their trade. Couple of times the mining people decided I hadn't done anything to earn the money they promised me, and I had to use some persuasion to bring them around to my way of thinking. Last I knowed, there was still a "wanted" flyer out for me in California, charging me with robbery. But it wasn't me that done the robbery, it was *them*. They backed off from what they duly owed me, and I had to collect the bill the best way I could. I tell you, preacher, I found out a long time ago that all the people who go to rob you don't do it with a gun. There's some big-business men that needed planting about as much as the people they sent me after.

I read in one of them penny-dreadfuls where I was supposed to have been in the Lincoln County war, and ridden with Billy the Kid and such as that. A lie, every word of it. I had no part in that war atall.

Truth of the matter is, I figured there was money to be made out of that Lincoln County mess and went over there to see if I could hire on. Either side, it didn't matter. Way I figured it, both sides was a little shady, but their money would spend good.

It was a wasted trip. Each side figured I was a spy for the other, and I was damn lucky to escape from there with my life.

I never stayed in one place long enough to ever get elected as a sheriff. Once in a while a sheriff would hire me for a deputy, but seemed like there was always somebody against me. They would hear or read some wild story like them lies in the newspapers and the penny-dreadfuls, and some righteous citizen would raise up in indignation and want me run out of the country. Times, it got awful hard to make an honest dollar.

Such as that would occasionally lead me to have to take jobs that I would as soon of left alone. Like that Johnson County war in Wyoming. Now, *there* was a fiasco. You've probably heard of it.

There was a bunch of big cattlemen up yonder that claimed a considerable part of Wyoming as their range. And there was a bunch of homesteaders and nesters and little cattle raisers and so forth that sort of figured they also had a right to some of the land. A thing like that naturally leads to a certain amount of unpleasantness. It also leads to jobs for people like me.

I was sure needing work at the time. I'd been back in El Paso, finding out to my own dissatisfaction that Lady Luck still hadn't eased up on me for whatever it was I done that offended her. Every once in a while I would hope to catch her looking the other way, and I'd sit in on a high-stakes poker game. But she always looked around and seen me before my stack of chips got too high.

I had a visit from an old friend who had put me onto a job or two before. If I would take the train to Paris, over in East Texas, he said, and meet a man there by the name of Tom Smith, I was a cinch for work. The pay was to be good. I just barely had me enough money left for a train ticket and a few days' eating, so I went. This Smith had rounded up a bunch of other people, same as me, all of them supposed to be men of nerve and good with a gun. He didn't tell us what we was to do except that we was supposed to serve warrants on some bad characters and to draw five dollars a day and expenses. On top of that we would get a bonus of fifty dollars for any man we had to kill. Them days, five dollars wasn't bad, especially when your axle was dragging on the ground.

He told us to be quiet and say nothing to anybody. We went up to Denver and then on to Cheyenne with a cattleman named Wolcott. He was one of them that had decided to hire us for the job. I taken a disliking to him right off, because I could tell he didn't like *us*. He let us know that we wasn't nothing but hired gunfighters, and not in the class with the "gentlemen" who was paying us to take care of the work they was too clean-handed to do by themselves. He was an old man by then, which I reckon lots of people would of said *I* was, too. He had been an officer for the Union during the Civil War. That might of been another reason I couldn't take to him much. There had been a whole new generation growed up since that war; they had never smelled powder. I think maybe they put too much faith in him because he *had*. The truth is, he was probably too old to lead an expedition like ours.

They fixed us up with horses and ammunition in Cheyenne, and we pulled out for Casper on a special train with all the blinds down so people wouldn't notice us. We got to Casper in the cold dark of the morning, caught our horses from the stock car and headed out so we wouldn't be seen by the townspeople after the sun came up. The whole thing was a bad go, right from the start. A bunch of the horses got away. It had been raining, so the wagons kept sticking in the mud, and it was cold enough to bite a Texas man to the bone, especially if he was running to gray hair the way I was.

It wasn't till about this time that they ever really told us just what we was expected to do. Seemed like the cattlemen had been having lots of trouble with thieves. What we was supposed to do was make a roundup of these thieves and arrest them. If they resisted arrest we was supposed to shoot them. Seemed like the cattlemen hoped they would *all* resist arrest. It would of been a lot simpler that way.

You've probably read since that a lot of the men they was after wasn't really thieves at all, but just people who was resisting them and laying claim to lands that the cattlemen had been using. We didn't know nothing about that at the time. Way I looked at it, I was working for the man who paid me. If he said a man was a thief, that man was a thief. If I thought different, I asked for the wages I had already earned, and I rode off.

I'd never been to Wyoming in my life. I had no reason to think these cattlemen might be lying to us. For five dollars a day, which I needed pretty bad, I didn't question their word.

There was a regular little army of us—fifty or so, best I remember—moving out from Casper toward the town of Buffalo. It was supposed to be a secret, and everybody we come upon was made prisoners to be sure they didn't leak to anybody.

First night's camp, I would of pulled my freight if I hadn't been so broke, and so far from home. The leaders of the army was all drinking and arguing with one another over what to do next. Some of them wanted to go to Buffalo like the plan called for. Some others wanted to go off on a tangent and hit a bunch of rustlers at the cabin of a man by the name of Nate Champion. They figured him for one of the biggest rustlers. They taken a vote, finally, amongst theirselves. We didn't get a vote; we was just the hired hands. A man's reputation back home didn't count for nothing up there. The vote was that we go to Champion's cabin. We had to pack up and leave in the middle of the night.

I was getting to the point in my life where I needed my rest. I sure hadn't had much of it on this trip, and it looked like I wasn't going to get any for a while. I got to thinking to myself that five dollars a day wasn't much. Many's the night I've bet fifty times that much on one hand of cards. If I hadn't been so far from Texas I'd of told them what they could do with all of Wyoming, and I'd of gone south to a warmer climate.

It was a miserable ride, a regular blizzard blowing against us all the way. We stopped to build some fires and thaw out a little, then went on to Champion's cabin. We surrounded the layout.

Somebody had made a mistake, not the only one made on that deal by a long shot. There was supposed to be a dozen or more rustlers staying at the place. There wasn't but two, the way it turned out, plus a couple of trappers that had dropped in to get out of the storm. When the trappers came out at daylight, they was made prisoners. They told us there was just two men left inside, Nate Champion and a friend of his called Nick Ray. We had orders to get them dead or alive, best way dead.

Ray came out and looked around, hunting for the trappers, I suppose. Somebody gave an order to fire on him, and a bunch of them did. My hands was so numb from the cold that I couldn't handle my rifle. Ray crawled to the door, and Champion reached out and pulled him in. No telling how many bullets was chipping at the wood all around him, but he didn't let his friend die out there alone.

There wasn't nothing to do but wait. We figured it would be worth a man's life to try to rush that cabin because you would have to cross too much open ground. For five dollars a day they could have it. That feller Champion, somebody said, was an old Texas cowboy. You don't monkey around with that kind until you find out whether they can shoot or not.

By and by somebody came along, one on a horse and one in a wagon. One of the ranchers hollered that the man on the horse was one of those we was supposed to arrest. A lot of shooting broke out, but none of it was any good because both of them got clean away. Everybody's hands was too cold, I reckon; I know mine was.

The wagon had been left behind. We piled it high with wood, set it afire, and some of the boys run it up against the cabin. Pretty soon the place was burning. We didn't know it then, but Ray was dead. Champion was the only one left alive in there. All of a sudden he busted out running with a rifle in his hands and tried for a ravine. He nearly made it. A couple of the boys was posted back there and brought him down.

I felt kind of low about the whole thing, especially after hearing he was a Texas man. Seemed to me like anybody that game deserved a little more of a show.

But like I say, I was working for wages, and when a man pays me I don't ask a lot of fool questions. I do what he asks me to, or I draw my time.

Seemed to me like we never did stop riding, and the leaders of the crew never stopped bickering and arguing amongst theirselves. That one thing alone was enough to tell me we was in for a hard time. Them two that got away from us was our downfall. They had rode on ahead and given the alarm. We got word that a big gang of rustlers was coming to meet us and would wipe us out like them Indians had done Custer, not too far north of where we was. There was another big argument over whether we ought to go on or back up.

The backer-uppers won. We retreated back to the JA Ranch.

You talk about mad! The cattlemen wasn't half as mad as them rustlers or settlers or whatever they was. They come in on us like a swarm of bees. Before they was through they must of numbered three or four hundred men, which meant there was six or eight of them to every one of us. We forted up at the ranchhouse, and they set up a siege.

We had a good place to make a stand. The house had been built solid, back when people still wasn't sure of the Indians, I reckon, and the logs was thick and square. We found a lot of big timbers and built us up an extra fort outside. We thought we could stand just about anything. But we couldn't. They waited us out, shooting every time they seen something to shoot at and lots of times when they didn't. We done the same.

Finally we was about out of ammunition and plumb out of anything to eat. A man can stand up to almost any kind of a fight when his belly's full, but let him get hungry and he falls down on you. Seemed to me about then that the damnfools had taken over, because it was ordered that we would all make a break at the same time and try to shoot our way out of the trap.

I never was one to consider suicide. I've never shot a man I didn't think needed shooting, and I never was that mad at myself. Running out in front of that mob would've been about the same thing as killing yourself, because we'd of lasted about as long as a snowball in a fire-box.

Just about the time we was fixing to send ourselves to hell, the army showed up. The cattlemen had friends in high places, but they hadn't come more than five minutes too soon. Any later and they'd of slapped dirt in our faces with a shovel.

Two of the Texas men died of gunshot wounds. I got this bad scar on my cheek from a big splinter, when one of their bullets grazed a log I was behind. We was a pretty hard-used bunch, all in all. They hauled us off to jail. Us Texas boys was moved around from one jail to another and finally even to the state pen while they waited to put us on trial. We hadn't even knowed what the whole thing was about.

The cattlemen that hired us was all out on bail, walking around free and talking big.

The shooting had been in April. We was turned loose on bail finally in August and put on a train for Fort Worth, Texas. We was supposed to go back later for the trial, but I don't suppose any of the boys ever did.

I sure as hell didn't.

CHAPTER 7

How did I finally come to get into *this* fix? Well, preacher, I'll tell you.

I've had some mighty lean years since that Johnson County episode. I got awful tired of them gun-carrying jobs, but what else could I do? I never did seem to have any more luck with the cards, especially after the years taken to putting arthritis in my joints. Look at them swelled knuckles! Sometimes it's all I can do to even hold a deck, much less to deal with any kind of grace. Old age has its dignity, I reckon, but it's damned inconvenient.

I tried cowboying, but who's going to hire an old man whose joints creak on him when he gets on and off of a horse? And you take most of these cow outfits, they think it's a sin for a hired man to ride anything except a raw bronc. Truth is, they're so tight, most of them, they don't want to buy a horse that costs them over twenty-thirty dollars. Soon as one gets to where he knows something and won't pitch anymore, they sell him to a farmer. Claim they don't want their cowboys getting lazy. I'm way past the bronc-riding stage as you can plainly see.

I tried a little more freelance manhunting, but the day is over. I even hunted for Butch Cassidy and his Wild Bunch once, till they crossed over into Wyoming. I knowed my name was still on the list there, so I tipped my hat and turned back, hungry.

I done some wolfing for a spell, too. Now *there's* a dirty job for you, wolfing. But when you look at it, killing wolves for a bounty ain't much different from doing it to men, except wolves don't shoot back at you. Cattlemen had trouble with them big lobo wolves pulling down their calves. And *sheepmen* . . . there just wasn't no way a sheepman could operate in the same part of the country with them wolves. They would get all the lambs first and then take in after the mamas.

A lot of people looked down on the wolfer as a sort of scavenger, like the men that gathered buffalo bones. But it was a living. Hard times, a man can't be choicy.

I done a little bartending, one time and another. It's no life for a man who's known better things. You have to deal with such a low class of people. Nothing I hate worse than wrestling with a drunk. The only time I could ever tolerate a bunch of drunks was when I was drunk myself. In late years I ain't been that way much. My stomach's gone to the bad, and it gets real put out with me when I eat anything or drink anything that it don't approve of.

So, when you come down to it, there ain't been much else for me except *pistolero* jobs of one kind or another. Sometimes I'd get on as a guard for a mine or a bank or an express company, or for some big-shot who thought somebody might want to shoot him. Jobs like that don't have much dignity to them, and you have to swallow a right smart of dirt.

An old man gets used to a certain amount of dirt, but not *that* much. I've walked off of jobs and told them where they could go with it, when I didn't even know where supper was going to come from.

But that gets expensive. Now and again I got so hungry I just had to take a job that I wouldn't otherwise of touched. Like once I was guard to a fat politician from back East who was taking him a long vacation in a big *hacienda* down the river from El Paso. The voters back home was paying his expenses and was being told he was on a long trip out West examining the prison systems. What he was really doing was bathing himself in whiskey and having the women brought to him two at a time, white and Mexican both. It was my job to keep any outsiders from finding him. But one sneaked in anyhow, one of them nosy newspaper reporters. He taken a picture of old Big-Gut with one of the pretty *señoritas* on his lap, and neither one of them wearing anything much except a surprised expression. It run in one of the El Paso papers, and then got back to that politician's home state.

I lost my job, of course. That's another reason I never was partial to them newspaper reporters, always poking around where they ain't got no business.

Them kind of jobs would gag a gut-wagon dog. But when you're in my shape you got to take them or go hungry.

That's why when I got word awhile back that Burney Northcutt wanted to see me at his ranch, I came down here as quick as my little Mexican pony could travel. I remembered how I used to play poker with him in El Paso, back when Lady Luck still approved of me. I remembered how he would cuss and stomp and swear to have me killed, but next time he came to town he'd try to best me again. We wasn't ever what you'd call friendly. In fact, I never did particularly like him. I reckon he felt the same about me. But we had a respect of sorts, one for the other. We was both pretty good at what we done.

I remembered he was a big operator. He came out into this West Texas country right behind the Indians. He fought old Mother Nature when she was at her meanest, and taken from her when she was at her best. He had carved himself an almighty big country. It wasn't the finest grazing land in Texas; fact is, it's probably some of the sorriest. But it'll do the job if you have enough of it to give your cows plenty of room.

I had heard stories about how he had throwed people off of country he wanted, how he had bought up the law in some counties to where nobody jumped till they heard him holler "frog." But I never gave it much thought because it didn't pertain to me.

But you know, preacher, about Texas and its four-section law? A big part of this land out here belonged to the state, and they passed a law that said a man could homestead four sections of it, and if he could stay there three years without starving to death he could buy it dirt cheap. Well sir, the biggest part of the land that old man Northcutt had, he got on a cheap lease off of the state. When the new law came in, he found people, claiming four sections here and four sections there, generally out of the best parts of his ranch. They was four-sectioning him to death. Now, he'd of been right pleased to have bought the whole thing from the state if they'd of let him, but they said he couldn't buy no more than anybody else, which was four sections. Hell, the old man probably had *that* much in corrals.

I got down to the ranch and went to see him. It had been a good many years since we'd laid eyes on each other, and I expect we was both a little surprised. He looked at me real sour-like and says, "By God, Joe Pepper, you've turned into an old man. If I'd of knowed how old you was, I wouldn't of sent for you."

I told him he wasn't apt to turn no schoolgirl's head either.

For a little while I thought I had wasted a long trip. He scowled at me like he was thinking about throwing me off of the ranch. I bristled up a little, just thinking about it. I doubted he had anybody young enough or tough enough to do that to me; I could tell by looking at him that *he* couldn't.

We glared at each other till it seemed like both of our faces would break and fall off. Finally he says, "Well, you ain't likely to scare them with your looks anymore, but maybe you can scare them with your name."

"Who am I supposed to scare?" I asks him.

I didn't know how much raw hate that old man really had in him until he told me about the four-sectioners. I'm glad you wasn't there to hear him, preacher; that language would of shamed you. And the look in his eyes . . . well, I'm not one to scare, but that look made a cold chill run down between these hunched old shoulders. I do believe if he'd of had one of them there in front of us, he would of choked him to death with his hands, or tried to.

I says, "You're hiring me to scare the four-sectioners?"

He cut his eyes at me, and they stabbed like the point of a Bowie knife. "I want you to *kill* one. That'll scare the others."

It had been a good many years since I had killed anybody, though I'd scared a few within an inch of killing themselves. I wasn't sure I needed his money quite that bad. I decided to test him out and see just how serious he was. I says, "You know I'll protect myself if one of them comes at me."

He says, "I want you to make sure one of them *does* come at you. I want you to crowd him till he loses his head, and then you kill him."

I can't say the idea was a new one. But I'd always used it against somebody I figured the world wasn't going to miss, somebody who had it coming to him. I'd never used it against somebody who had done nothing but steal land away from an old thief. Of course I had seldom ever been quite as hungry before as I was right then.

I says, "We ain't talked price yet."

He says, "I ain't got time to horsetrade or quibble with you. It's worth a lot to me to get rid of them nesters, and get rid of them fast." He walked over to his safe. I noticed he didn't move any too quick, and he was dragging his right leg just a touch. The years hadn't been kind to him. If this trouble had come on him twenty years earlier he wouldn't of hired anybody like me to take care of it; he'd of done it for himself.

I could hear his knee joint crack as he eased himself down to work the dial. He gave me a hard look back over his shoulder like he was afraid I'd watch and see the combination. The idea *had* occurred to me, just in case he was a little reluctant afterwards to pay me what he agreed to. I looked off out the window till I heard the door squeal on its hinges. He got out a little tin box and thumped it down on the table. He opened it and taken out a bundle of the prettiest green bills you ever seen. He pitched them across the table at me. "Five hundred dollars now," he says, "and five hundred more when the job is done."

I hadn't seen that much money in one pile in years. My poor old hands began to tremble, just wanting to get in there and feel of the bills, the way when I was younger my hands used to tremble every time they got close to silk. But pardon me, preacher, you wouldn't know about them things.

I wanted to be sure we understood each other. I says, "How will we know when the job is done?"

"When they've buried the nester you shot," he tells me, "and when the rest of them have loaded their wagons and left the country."

I told him I hadn't seen his four-sectioners, but it might be that killing one man wouldn't put them all to flight. I might have to kill more than one. I figured that ought to call for more money.

He cussed a little and told me I was a black-hearted holdup man. I told him that was my natural upbringing, and if I hadn't been that way he wouldn't of wanted to hire me. So he upped the ante. That thousand was to cover the job if it went as easy as he expected it to. He'd put up another five hundred apiece for any extra four-sectioners I had to kill.

Five hundred dollars was probably more than some of them ever got in one bundle in all their lives. Here they was, bringing that much dead.

"All right, done," I tells him. "You got any special man picked out, or do you just want me to shoot one at random?"

That hate came back to him the way I've seldom seen it in a man. He let the breath out between his teeth real slow, and then he says, "There's one. His name is Clayton Massey. You kill *him* and I'll give you a two-fifty bonus."

I drawed old man Northcutt out about this Massey that he seemed to have such a special hate for. Seemed like this was a young fellow from back over in the Concho country. Not only did he have the nerve to come out and file a claim on some of the old man's best water, but he had the extra nerve to bring *sheep* with him. Now, you got to understand that Burney Northcutt was one of them old-time cattlemen who thought all a sheep had to do to ruin a country for fifty years was to walk across it. Sheep outfits trailing west had learned to go forty miles around his place if they wanted to get where they was going without leaving a hundred dead sheep for every mile. The old man had taken a bunch of his cowboys over to throw Massey off of his place, and Massey met them with a gun and a set of state papers out of Austin that said the four sections was his, and he could run anything he wanted to on them . . . even giraffes, if he had any. The old man tried to ride over Massey, and Massey shot the horse out from under him.

The old man owned the sheriff of the county. He had Massey arrested for killing the horse and for trespassing. But the case got transferred out of the county, and the court held that Massey acted in self-defense, and that the old man was lucky it hadn't been him that got shot instead of the horse.

I knowed then why he hated the four-sectioners so bad, especially Massey. What made it even worse was that some of Massey's friends and kinfolks came too, out of the Concho country, and some of them brought sheep as well as cattle. First thing the old man knowed he had him half a dozen little sheepmen sitting on land he thought was going, to be his for five hundred years. And it wasn't the nature of them people to homestead the worst land; they always picked the good places, where the water was.

He gives me a description of this young Massey, and how to get to his place, and he tells me, "The quicker you go on over there and kill him, the quicker you can get your extra money and be gone."

I asked him if it would be all right with him if I waited till in the morning. It had been a long ride, and my horse was tired. I was a little weary myself. One thing I didn't want to do was to come up against somebody when I was tired, especially if he had the advantage of being young:

Caution is what makes *old* gunfighters.

I had me a good supper at Burney's expense, a good night's sleep in his bunkhouse, and a good breakfast the next morning. When you get to my age you'll realize how important such small compensations can be. Next morning I set out to Massey's place.

Now, you know this ain't the best ranching country in the world, but I couldn't help thinking as I rode that if my life had taken a different turn in the beginning, I might have had a big spread like Burney Northcutt to pleasure me in my declining years. I wouldn't be riding around all over the country selling my gun to people I didn't particularly like. I'd look at Northcutt's cattle—all colors of the rainbow, half leg and half horn—and think how all this could of been mine. I could understand how he would hate to see it cut up and given to people he didn't think was good enough to shine his boots.

I got to thinking back through all them bygone years. I got to thinking of the time just after the war, and me and Arlee Thompson and our first start, mavericking cattle, making them our own. I thought of me and Millie and our place, of things that hadn't crossed my mind in years and years. A feeling came over me that I'd forgot I ever had, a feeling of being young and having somebody and someplace that belonged to me, something I was a part of, something where I wasn't just an outsider looking in. For a while there it was like I was back in South Texas, and all this was mine, and I wasn't just a lone and lonely old man.

It was a big country, so big that it taken me all morning at a pretty good trot to get to Massey's place. I came to a creek that was the way Northcutt had described it and knowed I was either on the place or close to it. I followed it upstream to the spring where Massey had built him a house. I kept watching all the way for sign of the four-sectioner and his sheep, but I didn't see them. First thing I came to, outside of a scattering of improved Durham cattle, was the house and pens.

You couldn't call it much of a house; there wasn't two wagonloads of lumber in the whole thing. It was one of them little box-and-strip outfits that says "hard times" the minute you look at it. It wasn't more than maybe fifteen feet square, sitting up on sawed-off cedar posts to keep it off of the ground. An old dog came out from under the porch and barked at me. I seen a woman come to the door and stand there, shading her eyes with her hand.

I almost fell out of the saddle.

I tell you, preacher, you couldn't of hit me harder with a tow-sack full of red bricks.

That woman was my Millie, that I had buried nigh forty years ago.

Now, I know you're going to laugh at that, and say it was just an old man's bad eyesight failing on him, and maybe a little of the heat, too. You're going to remind me that I thought the same thing the first time ever I seen Samantha Ridgway. But say what you want to, it happened. There she was, the spitting image.

I rode on up to the house. She spoke to me, but I couldn't hear what she said, and I couldn't say anything back. My tongue was all stuck to the roof of my mouth. She spoke to me two or three times, and finally it got through my thick head that she was telling me to get down and have myself a drink of cool water, because it looked like I was suffering from the heat.

I finally managed to say, "You're Millie!"

She looked kind of surprised. She says, "No, I'm Jill. Jill Massey. I'm afraid you've found the wrong house."

I was still confused. I says, "But you're Millie. Don't you know me?" The whole thing had hit me so sudden that I had a hard time remembering Millie would've been near sixty years old by now, if she had lived. This woman wasn't much over twenty.

I think I must of scared her a little, and that kind of brought me up. I finally got it through my head what she was saying, and that this couldn't be Millie.

I *did* notice then that my head was swimming a little, and that the sweat was running down my face like I'd been caught in a rain. Maybe the heat *had* got me. I eased down from the saddle and leaned against my horse for a minute. I asked her where I could water him, but she told me to go sit in the shade on the step and rest a little. *She* would water him for me.

But first she brought me a dipper of good cool water out of a barrel. I sat down there like she said, and I watched her lead the pony down to the creek and loosen the girth and let him drink. She made him take it slow, which showed she knowed something about horses. Sometimes when they're dry and hot they'll drink enough water to give themselves a bellyache. Same way a man does. I watched her all the time, and I'd swear—if my mind hadn't cleared some—that she was my Millie, born again.

Directly she led the pony up to a corral and pulled the saddle off of him. She turned him loose where he could roll in the dust. She hung the bridle on a post and came back to the house. She says, "You're staying for dinner."

That hadn't been my intention, but I was still too numb to argue. She says, "Clayton'll be in after a while to eat. He's ranging the sheep over to the east. They won't stray much during the heat of the day."

I'd never made any big study of herding sheep. I didn't care to learn any more about them than I already knowed, which wasn't much. I says. "Where'd you come from, Jill Massey?"

"Over in Concho County," she tells me. "Close to Paint Rock."

I knowed Paint Rock was on the Concho River east of San Angelo, but that didn't answer my question. I says, "I mean, where did you come from originally? Where was you a girl at?"

"Right there," she says. "Where I grew up, you could see the cupola on the Concho County courthouse."

I got to questioning her about her forebears, whether any of them had ever come out of South Texas. I kept thinking maybe she was blood kin of Millie, but as far as I could ever tell, she wasn't. Seems like her folks had come over out of Tennessee before she was born, but after the time of Millie Thompson.

While she was cooking up some red beans and mutton for dinner, I taken my watch out to see what time it was, figuring probably her husband would come riding along pretty soon. All of a sudden I remembered that I carried Millie's picture in the back of the watch. Lord knows how long it had been since I had last looked at it—twenty years, probably. Time does get away from a man. I opened the back. It had been shut so long that I had to prize it with a knifeblade.

There she was, my Millie, just the way I remembered her. Now that I looked at her picture, and compared it to Jill Massey, I could see where this girl didn't look all that much like her after all. Time was playing tricks on me again. When you get old, your mind's eye starts failing on you, same as the ones on the outside.

I got to wondering about myself. I decided I had got to letting my mind wander when I was on the way over from Northcutt's. I had got to thinking about the old days, and I guess without me realizing it, Millie had taken to haunting me again, trying to come to the surface in a way I hadn't let her do in many and many a year. The minute I seen this young woman, I also seen Millie. They wasn't the same atall; they just seemed to be to an old man whose eyes and mind was getting confused.

But I sat and listened to her talk, and it was like it had been the time I found Samantha; the years just rolled away. It was like I was sitting in my own house with Millie again, most of forty years ago. It was like I was a young man, just starting out on the road of life instead of coming up on the end of the trail. For a little while there I think my arthritis quit bothering me, and my shoulders squared up. It was a good feeling.

Her husband came along directly. He seen the strange pony in the corral, and he came rushing to the house to make sure his wife was all right. He seen me sitting there at the table, drinking coffee, and he was sure relieved. I might of been feeling like a young man right then, but all he could see was a harmless coot too old to be a danger to anybody. He shook hands with me and told me he was Clayton Massey, and he hoped I was staying for dinner.

Naturally I was, or my horse wouldn't of been unsaddled. I didn't tell him my name; I wanted to size things up first. He would find out soon enough who I was.

I watched him kiss his wife, kind of gentle and self-conscious. I had the notion he would of done it some different if I hadn't been there. That taken me back a long ways, remembering when it had been the same with me. I figured him for a man of maybe thirty, young enough to have all the energy in the world and old enough to know how to use it.

Jill Massey got dinner finished and put it on the table. She had baked bread in the oven, Mexican-style, flat in the bottom of the pan. Clayton Massey says to me, "It ain't much, but you're welcome to what there is. The whole place ain't much yet, but it'll be a lot more someday when I've had time enough to work on it."

I got to thinking how he sounded a lot like I had when I was his age, when I had a pretty woman to work for, the way he did. By and by I asked him why he had come way out here instead of staying in Concho County where he started. He said there wasn't room anymore. His daddy had settled in that country when it was still young. Now the son had to move out to a country that was still young and do like his daddy did. I pointed out to him that when his daddy went to Concho County there probably wasn't nobody else claiming the land he settled up, except maybe the Indians. But out here, there wasn't an acre that somebody hadn't already claimed before him.

He said that was the truth, but the law had decided it wasn't enough anymore to have all this big open country in the hands of just a few men. It wanted to have people settle and towns grow; the frontier was gone and wasn't coming back. He said the country had already more than paid the first people here for their pains, and it was in its legal rights to ask them to move over and make room. I suppose that made sense to an ambitious young man, but I could also see how it would seem hard to an old mossback like Burney Northcutt who had dripped sweat and sometimes blood all over this land.

I mentioned Northcutt and how I had heard he wasn't too partial to the things that was going on around here, that he felt like they was taking away what belonged to him.

Massey told me a little history that Northcutt had neglected to mention to me. He told me that in the early days there was Mexican settlers—squatters, of course—all up and down these creeks, and North-cutt had come along and run them off. He had even killed a couple or three in the process to show his intentions was serious. He told them their day was over, and it was time for a new deal all around.

Massey says to me, "Now it's *his* day that's over, and it's *us* that have the new deal. You watch, we'll make this country support fifty people for every one that it used to have. This country is meant to grow, not to stand still."

Somehow time kept running backwards for me. I kept thinking about the old times in South Texas, and of the trouble I had with Jesse Ordway over the piece of land that I had and he wanted. I got to trying to see Jesse Ordway in my mind, but it had been so long that I couldn't hardly remember anymore what he looked like. I kept putting Burney Northcutt into the picture in his place.

Massey says, "He's tried a lot of things to get us out of here. He's tried to buy me out, and run me out. He's tried to stampede my sheep, but sheep don't stampede very good. He's tried shooting into them, but he's found I shoot back. He's even had his cowboys ride in here at night and shoot into the house."

I taken a sudden chill. It all came back to me in a rush. I remembered the night they had killed my Millie. It was forty years ago, but it seemed like it had been yesterday. I closed my eyes and I could hear them riding around the house, shooting into it. In my mind I heard Millie scream. I got to shaking and couldn't quit.

Clayton Massey grabbed hold of me. He says, real worried, "What's the matter, old-timer? Jill, get that bottle of whiskey, quick!"

He handed me the bottle, and I tipped it up and taken a couple of long, hard slugs of it. Gradually I got to feeling warm again, and I quit shaking. He says, "Better take another, old-timer." I told him I had had enough. I tried to get to my feet, but my old knees just couldn't do it. I sat back down and tried to take a grip on myself. I tried to get the old times and the new times separated from one another, so I could think. It was hard, because they was all so mixed up.

Directly I had a grip on myself. The two of them was sitting across the table, looking like I had scared them half to death. With an old man, you never know when he's going to kick over and leave you.

I says, "I'm all right now."

"It's the heat," he tells me. "Man your age has got to watch himself and not overdo it. You better stay with us a day or two and rest. Then you can go on about your business."

I figured it was time to tell him. "I came *here* on business. I came here to kill you."

His mouth dropped open, and his eyes got like a saucer. He shook his head like he didn't believe none of it. "You better go lay down, old-timer. You're sick."

I says, "You ever hear of Joe Pepper, son?"

He nodded his head. "Sure, everybody has. He used to be a gun-fighter, long years ago."

"He's *still* a gunfighter," I says. "I'm Joe Pepper."

You know how it is, I reckon, when you have a raving old man on your hands; you try to humor him. The Masseys didn't believe a word of it. I could tell they figured the heat had got me.

Massey says, "Joe Pepper died years ago. He *must* have."

"Not unless I'm a ghost," I tell him.

Gradually he began to come around. I guess there is still a little of the old-time Joe Pepper in my face, if you look hard enough. Finally he gets kind of nervous and says, "Jill, I believe him."

I could tell she did too. All of a sudden I seen fear laying way back deep behind her eyes. Massey taken a quick look toward the corner, where his rifle was propped. He wasn't wearing any pistol; I had taken note of that when he first came into the house. I says, "I wouldn't do what you're thinking, boy. I'd just sit real still."

He didn't look like one who would try to run away. Grab for the
rifle, maybe, but not run away. Either choice wouldn't of done him
any good if I'd decided to shoot him. He says, "You figuring on killing
me right here?"

I says, "That's what I was sent here to do."

"What about Jill?" he says. "Whatever you do to me, don't hurt her,
please."

The thought had never entered my mind, but it laid heavy on his.
He says, "She's carrying, mister. For God's sake, don't hurt her."

Millie had been carrying, too. I remembered now. Lord, I hadn't
even thought of it in years.

The tears commenced to well up in Jill Massey's eyes. She started to
plead with me to let her husband be. She said they would move; they
would turn this country back to Burney Northcutt if he wanted it so
bad.

But Clayton Massey stood up and pushed his chair back. He says to
her, "Hush, Jill. Don't you tell him that. The only way Northcutt gets
this place is to kill me. I'll never give it to him." He taken a couple of
steps backwards, and I knowed he was about to make a try for that rifle.

I had real quietly pulled my pistol out of my belt. I brought it up
where he could see it real good, and I pushed to my feet. I was afraid
my old knees would betray me, but they stood me in good stead. When
the pressure comes, I ain't as old as I look. I told Clayton Massey to
stand where he was and not do anything that him and me would both
be sorry about. I stepped around him, went over to the corner and
picked up his rifle. I taken it and pitched it out the door as far as I
could.

"Just removing temptation," I tells him. "Thing like that can get a
man killed."

By this time I reckon he was convinced that he was as good as
dead. He looked at his wife, and back at me, and he says, "If you've got
to do it, at least don't do it here in front of *her*. Let's go outside where
she doesn't have to see it."

I wasn't going to do it, not there or anywheres else.

I says as harsh as I can, "Now you sit back down at the table and listen to me, boy." He was a little slow about it, so I nudged him with the muzzle of my pistol. "Sit *down!*"

He did. I could see the girl's knuckles as white as flour, gripping her chair. Her face didn't have much more color than that, either.

I says, "Now listen to me, both of you. I said I came here to kill you. But I'm an old man, and an old man's mind is always changing."

"You said Burney Northcutt hired you."

I patted my pocket. "I got the money right here, five hundred dollars."

He says, "You mean you're going to take his money and *not* kill me?"

I shook my head. "No, I'm a professional man. I don't take money on false pretenses. That would ruin my reputation. I'm going to take his money back to him and tell him I've thought it over and changed my mind."

"He won't like it," says Massey. "He's set in his ways."

"He don't *have* to like it. I'll tell him that times have changed for *me*, and they'll just have to change for *him*. I don't like what's happened to me, but I've learned to live with it. He can too."

Jill Massey says, "If he wants my husband dead so bad that he hired you, he'll just go and hire somebody else."

I says, "Not if they know Joe Pepper is here. My name still stands for something in the trade."

Massey says, "What do you mean, if Joe Pepper is here?"

I told him I kind of liked their place, and I was about to be out of a job, and if he could use an old man's help I would hire on real cheap.

He argued that he couldn't pay me much, and I told him an old man didn't need much. A little to eat, a little to drink . . . a lot of time to sit in the sun.

They never did understand what had made me change my mind, and I couldn't tell them because I didn't altogether understand it myself. All I knowed was that them two young people was me and Millie, given another chance to start over. I wasn't going to let Jesse Ordway . . . I mean Burney Northcutt . . . do them out of that chance.

It was a little before dark when I rode up to Northcutt's big frame house. He was sitting on the gallery, taking his evening rest and his pipe. He was some surprised to see me back so quick. He taken his pipe out of his mouth and stared at me. He says, "You always had the reputation of being a fast worker, Joe Pepper. But damn if that ain't the fastest five hundred dollars I ever spent. I reckon you've come for the rest?"

I reached in my pocket and taken out the roll of greenbacks that had felt so good in my hands. I pitched it over into his lap. I says, "No, I come to give your money back to you. I don't take pay if I don't do a job."

I reckon it was typical of him that he thought the worst. "Taken a look at it and got cold feet, did you? I ought to've knowed better than to hire a man that's got so old the nerve has gone out of him. Time the word gets around about this, there won't nobody hire you to slop hogs."

I shrugs my shoulders and tells him, "Don't matter, I already got work."

"Doing what?" he says real nasty. "Washing out spittoons in a bar?"

"Herding sheep," I tells him.

He stood up, and when he did I seen the pistol in his boottop. An old badger like Burney Northcutt wasn't going to get caught without a six-shooter, not even on his own front gallery. He says, "You sold out. I've heard of you doing lots of things, Joe Pepper, but I never heard of you double-crossing anybody before."

I says, "I never needed to before, Jesse."

It occurred to me that I had called him by the wrong name, but somehow it didn't matter. Standing there like he was, he looked to me like Jesse Ordway of almost forty years ago. All of a sudden the front gallery of that old ranchhouse was the bank where I had met Jesse. I was a young man again, and full of grief and anger because I had just buried a young wife that I had loved, and Jesse Ordway was the man who had been the cause of it.

Burney Northcutt reached down for the pistol, but it wasn't Burney Northcutt I shot . . . it was Jesse Ordway. I shot him once and seen him fall back against the wall, and all the grief and the anger and the pain came rushing up from forty years' burying, and I shot him again, and again and again. I kept shooting till the pistol was empty.

I could hear men hollering around me. I was still in that South Texas town, running for my horse. I got on him and started down the street, only it wasn't really a street atall, it was just a ranch yard. I managed to get some cartridges back into the gun and shoot at Jesse Ordway's men who was shooting at *me*. I looked around for Felipe Rios, but he wasn't there. I couldn't understand why he wasn't; he was *supposed* to be.

They came after me, but I was still ahead of them when dark came.

I wasn't familiar with the country. I rode way into the night, trying to tell myself I wasn't lost but knowing I was. Finally these weary bones had all they could stand, and I had to get down and stretch out on the ground and rest.

I remember dreaming a lot through the night. There was a woman . . . she was Millie awhile, and then she was Samantha, and then she was Jill Massey, but always the same woman. And there was me and Clayton Massey, all mixed up with one another so that I never did know for sure which one of us was which.

Finally I felt something touch me. I opened my eyes to the sunlight, and there was a man leaning over me. He had just lifted the pistol out of my belt. He had a badge on his shirt. It looked as big as a washtub. So did the muzzle of the rifle he held down to my nose. I seen then that he had a bunch of men with him, all of them pointing guns at me.

Well sir, that's how come me to be where I am now. They hauled me here and throwed me in this jail. Ordinarily there wouldn't of been a term of court for two months, but because old man Northcutt was a power in this country, and because Joe Pepper had a name for himself too, they rushed things a mite. They brought in a district judge that Northcutt had helped get elected, and picked them a jury of Northcutt cowboys.

It didn't make no difference to them that the Northcutt power died when he did. Without him, the old ranch of his won't be long in breaking up. The people who talk so bitter about me killing him won't let him get cold in the grave till they start filing on his lands to grab what they can of the leavings.

Clayton Massey came in and testified about Northcutt hiring me to kill him, and me changing my mind. That didn't change the jury's mind, though. They'll all be out of work pretty soon on account of me. They'll have to be drifting off and hunting jobs somewhere else, unless they decide to file on four sections of Northcutt land themselves.

That's about all there is to the story, preacher. I don't know if I've told you what you wanted to find out.

They've finally quit hammering on that scaffold out on the square. I reckon they got it finished.

I feel kind of sorry for them boys, having to work on it most of the night. They'll be disappointed when they come down here in the morning and find out they won't get to use it after all.

That noise out yonder? Just some friends of mine, come to get me a change of venue. Friends of yours, too, I expect, so if you recognize any of them I'd be obliged if you keep quiet about it. I wouldn't want to get them four-section people in trouble.

Better stand back here against the door, preacher, away from the outside wall. They're fixing to pull the window bars out with that team of mules, and I'd hate to have a stone fall on your foot and cripple you.

There it goes. Mind giving me a lift up through that hole?

Well, been nice talking with you, preacher, but I got to be hurrying along. Tell the boys I'm real sorry about their jail. Next time they ought to build it stronger. This one won't even hold an *old* man!

LONG WAY TO TEXAS

CHAPTER 1

Death, when it finally came, would be savage and swift. But the waiting seemed eternal. For more than two hours Lieutenant David Buckalew had huddled with his nineteen tired and ragged men in this vulnerable hilltop redoubt and had wondered when the Indians would come shrieking up that barren slope to take them.

What in the hell were they waiting for?

A chilly wind swept across the low circle of hastily piled rocks. Buckalew fastened the three remaining buttons of his gray coat, the only remnant of a uniform that had been new and proud a few months ago in Texas. The wind searched its way through a long rent beneath his right arm. He held the arm against his body and shivered. He wondered if April was really that cold or if the chill came from within.

This, he thought bitterly, was an unfitting place for twenty men from Texas to die, and an unfitting way. They had come to an unfamiliar land to fight a just and honorable war against the Union Army, not to be cut to ribbons by a band of Indians with whom they had no quarrel, whose tribe they didn't even know.

The hard-used Texans had come upon the warriors while working their way along the fringe of scrub pine timber, moving southward through the mountains of eastern New Mexico. The confrontation had surprised the Indians as much as the Texans. The Indians had brought their horses to a sudden halt and gazed uncertainly at the white men across the space of perhaps a hundred yards. There had been at least thirty of them, and probably nearer forty. The number had been growing since. Buckalew had seen additional warriors trailing in.

Perhaps that indicated a respect of sorts. He hadn't seen much respect lately. Since he had been assigned to this unit against his will and theirs, he had encountered difficulty in getting the men to obey his orders, or even listen to him. But when they faced the Indians he had merely pointed toward the top of this hill. He had had to put spurs to his big brown horse to keep from being left behind. There had been stragglers earlier along the trail, but there were none on this hurried climb. The Indians had followed along, shouting challenges but firing no shots.

At the top of the hill the men had quickly, and without directions, set about building what fortification they could. They stacked rocks into a rough circular wall as a shield.

That the Indians could sweep up that hillside and wipe them out, David Buckalew had no doubt. But it wouldn't be done cheaply or easily.

The men had tried to dig down behind the crude wall but made no headway in the stony ground, for they had no real tools for the job. For the twentieth time he expanded his spyglass to full length with cold-sweaty hands and took a long sweeping look downhill. For some time he had watched Indians working in and out of a narrow pass. Now he saw little movement.

If they'd caught us in there, we'd be dead already, he thought, shivering. Weighing heavily upon him was the hard realization that he had almost led the men into that pass. He hadn't given Indians a thought at the time—he had seen no need to—and he had been reasonably sure no Yankee pursuit had passed them to set up an ambush. But solid old Sergeant Noley Mitchell had saved him from that fatal mistake. He had suggested they climb up over the rough side of the hill. David had seen no need for it, but the men started to follow Mitchell's suggestion anyway. There had been nothing left for the lieutenant to do but make it an order and salvage whatever dignity he might from a situation already out of his hands.

It had been clear from the start that although David Buckalew had the commission, Noley Mitchell had the men.

Mitchell had evidenced no malice that David could see as he

watched the men climbing the hill. He said simply, "Call it a notion, Davey."

That was the way it had been since he had been assigned to this unit in Albuquerque: *Davey*. Not *Lieutenant*, not *Sir*, but just *Davey* to Noley Mitchell, as if David were some kid, not a man already in his twenties. It was little wonder the rest of the men didn't respect his rank.

Mitchell had said as they started bringing up the rear, "I just don't like gettin' caught in tight, narrow places. Goes back to ridin' a rough horse through a narrow gate when I was a boy and crushin' my leg against the post. I never forgot it, though it was a long time ago." It had indeed been a long time, because Noley Mitchell was twice David's age, and perhaps a bit more. In deference to that age, David gave him the benefit of many nagging doubts.

Now that Mitchell had been proven right about their not going through the pass, David knew the men were thinking and perhaps even saying among themselves that it was the old sergeant—not the young lieutenant—who had saved them from dying in it. Of course it had been only a temporary reprieve, for it looked very likely that they would die on the hilltop instead.

He could clearly see both ends of the pass. When the Indians came against them it would probably be from the south end. He kept bringing the spyglass to his eye and searching in that direction. Eventually he caught a flutter of movement to the north. He blinked and looked again. Because of the distance, the image jumped and danced. He knelt to brace the telescope against a boulder and very slowly swung the end around until he could focus on what he had seen.

"Yankees!" he said aloud and in surprise. "A bunch of them, ridin' straight into the pass."

He knew suddenly why the Indians hadn't yet bothered the little Texas group huddled behind their miserable pile of rocks. They had easier prey to trap, and more of them.

Sergeant Mitchell, kneeling down carefully on stiff knees, could see little with his naked eyes. David judged that he probably needed spectacles. "Let me have the glass a minute, Davey."

David grunted. Rank meant no more to Mitchell—or to the rest of these men—than it meant to a packmule. Mentally they were civilians, and they would never be anything else. So, for that matter, was David. But at least he *tried* to be a soldier. Lately he felt he was the only one left who did.

Mitchell growled about his difficulty in bringing the glass to bear on the target. He rubbed a ham-sized fist over his eye and tried again. "Yep, it's bluebellies."

David said, "They've taken the pressure off of us for now. Might be a good time for us to clear out."

Mitchell ran stubby fingers through a gray-salted two-inch tangle of beard coarse as porcupine quills and shook his head. "They'd just come after us later, if they're of a mind to. Where they caught us might not be half as good as the place we've got right here, button."

Mitchell had a Texan's way of referring to any young person as *button*, no matter how much military rank he might carry. Texans stood in awe of few things, and certainly not the gold bars of a second lieutenant. David understood that Mitchell had served many years as sheriff in some county south of Austin. Nothing fazed him much.

The men had heard Mitchell's comment. If David ordered them to go, most would probably stay here anyway. He saved himself the humiliation.

The chilly wind kept finding its way through the split seams of the gray coat his mother had made for him. The piping, stitched with great hopes by loving hands, hung loose and useless. The left sleeve showed a dark stain, and a hole that had been carelessly darned by male hands unused to needle and thread. David let his mind run back to a time when it was new, to that grand marshaling day in San Antonio, a fine day of fiery speeches and patriotism. With the stirring words still echoing in their minds, an intrepid band of Texas Confederates had started westward on a march meant to carry them all the way to the Pacific.

This was the Territory of New Mexico in April of 1862. The Civil War had pitted white man against white man, and red men against them all. It had been less than a year since flamboyant Captain John R. Baylor, famed for his exploits as a Texas Ranger, had recruited his Second Texas Mounted Rifles in San Antonio and had led them across the desert to begin the conquest of the Western territories for the greater glory of the Confederacy. It had seemed a splendid idea at the time, and to David it still did. The Union forts in New Mexico and Arizona were poorly defended. A preponderance of their officers and a fair percentage of their enlisted men had been Southerners who had resigned at the outset of the war. They had returned to their homes to help raise an army for the Confederacy, leaving their former posts short on men and shorter on leadership. Moreover, because these forts were so far from the East and adjoined on one side by Confederate Texas, they were virtually isolated. They were considered beyond help if any concerted effort were made against them.

Behind Baylor's fast-moving cavalry had moved the huge but slower brigade of Henry Hopkins Sibley, late of the Union Army post in Santa Fe, now a general for Jefferson Davis. He knew the western military installations by virtue of his service there; he knew the weak points of every one. The Texans had first taken Fort Bliss at Paso del Norte without bloodshed. Poorly equipped from the standpoint of arms, and mostly dressed in civilian clothes because nobody had the time or the material to supply proper uniforms, the Texas force had overcome distance and heat and cold and hunger through eight hard months on alien ground. They had marched from one victory to another, plucking Union apples from the tree . . . Fort Fillmore, San Augustine Springs, Valverde. They had raised the Texas flag over Albuquerque and ancient Santa Fe.

Total victory had seemed in easy reach, for the Arizona side of the Territory presented no challenge. Tucson was in Confederate hands. Beyond Arizona lay California, ripe for the taking. Its goldfields would finance the Confederacy's armed might. Its great open seacoast would provide an outlet to the world, an outlet so huge no Union blockade could seal it.

With all that in Confederate hands, how long could the gangling Abe Lincoln and his upstart Yankee Congress continue to deny the Southern states their right to secede from the Union, their right to govern themselves in a new and sovereign nation?

It had been a daring plan, conceived in the first flush of Texan euphoria at the outbreak of the war and sustained by the ease of victory over one weakened Union post after another.

But the Texans had considered New Mexico isolated because it was so far from the Union East. They had not taken into account that help might come from the west and north. They had only dimly known about the column of Union volunteers who had marched out of California to challenge the great desert, and of another which had ventured across the Rocky Mountains of Colorado and down through the San Luis Valley.

Disaster had come suddenly. On the twenty-seventh day of March the Confederate volunteers and the Union volunteers had slammed together at Glorieta. Badly overextended, sustaining themselves in a hostile land by supply lines which stretched hundreds of miles back into Texas, the Confederates were vulnerable to any interruption in these supplies. "Preacher" Chivington's Colorado men caught a vital ammunition train in the middle of Apache Canyon and destroyed it without mercy.

That great column of black smoke had cast a fatal shadow across the Confederate dream of Western conquest. The taste of victory turned to ashes in Texans' mouths. Splintered into dozens of disorganized and almost leaderless groups scattered over half of New Mexico and all of hell, short on ammunition and shorter on food, they had little choice except to retreat south under the pressure of determined Union pursuit, to try to reach Texas and hope the Californians and the Coloradans wouldn't hound them all the way back to San Antonio.

On the map, if David had had one, Texas lay a relatively few miles directly to the east. But that part was as hostile as New Mexico, for it was still firmly in Indian hands. The maps left the Panhandle region of Texas almost a total blank, marked only as "unknown Indian land." Beyond the cap rock stretched the great staked plains, familiar only to Comanche and Kiowa and to a relative handful of Indian traders operating out of eastern New Mexico. No white men known to the Texans had ever traversed it, had ever seen its hidden watering places or traced out its rivers and streams, had ever traveled the dim trails stretching across that vast and markless tableland of grass.

To David Buckalew and his men, and to other scattered units like them, the real Texas lay to the south. If they could ever reach Fort Bliss, they could then strike eastward along the military, immigrant and stagecoach road which would lead them to the Pecos, to the Conchos, and eventually to the safe and settled lands just west of San Antonio.

But it was a long way to Bliss, and Union scouting parties had been doing their best to seek them out and cut them to pieces. To the Yankees this was insurance against the Texans' ever again trying to carry the war across the Western territories. David's group was a remnant of many which had been ordered to lag behind and fight a rearguard action, to delay Union pursuit long enough so that the larger bodies of men, particularly the walking infantry, could have a long head start.

David watched the mirror flashes as the Indians talked to each other across the near end of the pass. He could no longer see the Union troops; they had moved into the trap. The gunfire started, echoing off the ragged mountain walls. David shivered. He was too far away to hear the shouts and the screams with his ears, but he heard them in his mind. Through the glass he saw riderless horses galloping out of the pass, some on this side, some going back through the far end. He saw two men spurring desperately and watched the mounted pursuit that inevitably caught up. He saw the men fall, and the Indians jump down around them.

He had seen much of death in New Mexico, but he had never managed to harden himself against the coldness that settled in the bottom of his stomach. The gunfire became scattered. Finally it stopped altogether. He licked his dry and wind-chapped lips as he trained the spyglass on the near opening of the defile. At last he saw Indians begin to spill out of it. He could count at least fifty; there might have been more. Many led extra horses that he knew carried cavalry saddles.

The Indians moved toward the hill where the Texans crouched or lay waiting in dread, gripping their rifles. A young soldier who had never shaved out of necessity recited the Lord's Prayer over and over.

At length a dark-stubbled, hawk-featured man said irritably, "Richey, I wisht you'd shut up."

Pete Richey glanced at Luther Lusk with stricken eyes. "Luther, I'm just askin' the Lord to help us."

"If He didn't hear you the first time, He ain't listenin'. You're makin' me almighty nervous."

David said, "Let him alone. A little prayin' a long time ago mightn't of hurt *you* any."

"He'd do better to save his breath for the fight."

David looked at the boy, a seventeen-year-old farm lad who had lied about his age to get into the volunteers, and lately had had ample cause to regret it. "You go on with it, Richey, if you want to."

Pete Richey gave David a grateful look, then glanced uneasily at Luther Lusk. For a moment David thought he might finally have made a friend. But Richey was over-awed by the frontiersman Lusk, too much to challenge him. He turned back to his rifle. His lips moved again, but his prayer was silent.

David frowned at Lusk, a thick-set man wearing a fancy Mexican-style coat over a tattered homespun cotton shirt. Lusk had appropriated the coat out of a store after beating up the Mexican storekeeper, a man burly enough to present him a challenge. He had defended himself on the grounds that the man had a Union flag draped on the wall, and besides that, his father had probably fought in the battle of the Alamo. If he hadn't, he probably was friends with somebody who had. Nothing came of the incident except an admonishment from higher officers. From what David had seen, Lusk was something of a wild man. Admonishing a wild man was like using a willow switch against a bear.

"Sergeant," David said to Noley Mitchell, "you'd better give Lusk his rifle. He'll need it directly."

He had taken the trooper's rifle after a set-to three days ago. David's orders had been to retreat gradually, harassing the Union troops wherever it was practical without undue risk to his men, slowing down the Union advance. He had orders not to take suicidal risks, but to get his small command back to Texas intact and safe if he possibly could. He had been hitting small Union details from ambush, then running before they had time to react.

They had sighted a Union force much too large for them, Luther Lusk had wanted to charge it anyway and "get in one more good lick against them damnyankee bastards before we turn tail and run." David had seen it as a clear case of suicide and had forbidden it.

"I'll go by myself, by God!" Lusk had shouted angrily. "If there's any man here with sand, he'll go with me."

David had seen fit to club Lusk over the head with the barrel of a pistol and tie him to his saddle. He reasoned that he had saved not only Lusk's life but those of the other men.

The troop as a whole was not keen on following Lusk into a moment of glory and an eternity of sleep. Nevertheless, their sympathies were clearly with him. David had made no friends by his rough but effective method of stopping Luther Lusk. He kept telling himself he shouldn't worry about it. These were not the men with whom he had campaigned through most of his time in New Mexico; he had recently been assigned to them against their will and his own. His original outfit had been badly shot to pieces, David himself falling among the wounded. These volunteers had lost their lieutenant, elected by them back home and willingly followed by them until his death. Instead of allowing them to elect another of their own choice, the higher-ups had chosen to impose upon them this stranger, a green young officer from the old and peaceful Stephen F. Austin colony way back in what was now considered East Texas. What could a young upstart like that know of battle? There hadn't been anything bigger than a crossroads fistfight down in that section for at least twenty years.

Lusk grasped the rifle as Mitchell extended it to him. He jerked it roughly from the sergeant's hands and said caustically to David, "Thank you, Lieutenant, for all your generosity. I thought you was fixin' to make me throw rocks at them."

"When this is over," David said evenly, "that rifle goes back to Sergeant Mitchell."

"When this is over," Lusk replied in a cold voice, "this rifle will go to some redskin. You know it and I know it."

One Indian rode out in advance of the others. He stopped a hundred yards short of the hilltop. He was in easy range, but nobody shot at him. The warrior waved a rifle and began to yell. The wind was blowing the wrong direction for David and the others to hear him. They would not have understood the words anyway.

Lusk said bitterly, "Go out there and arrest him, Buckalew."

Several more Indians moved up even with the first one. They waved muskets and some newly captured Yankee rifles. Fresh scalps dangled from the firearms. David knew little of sign language, but he understood the more graphic gestures.

Suddenly the Indians wheeled their horses around and rode away, shouting victory to the mountains, carrying their trophies with them.

David watched in disbelief. After a minute he stood up, his mouth hanging open. He studied the mountains with the spyglass, hunting for a sign of other Indians lying in wait.

Young Richey prayed again, this time giving thanks.

David knew little about Indians. He had been a boy when the last raid occurred in Hopeful Valley. He had heard many stories and doubted half of them. He distrusted people who claimed to know all about Indians, because his father said such people were all talk. He glanced at Mitchell, who had never made such a claim. "What do you make of it, Sergeant?"

Mitchell replied in a gravel-voiced drawl. "I fought Indians down home in the wild old days. All I ever learned for sure was that you never do know. They hunt people for sport, the way me and you would hunt a deer when we wasn't really hungry. When they've satisfied their appetite they're ready to go off and celebrate. Maybe tomorrow they'll get the notion to come lookin' for us. But today it looks like they've had glory enough."

Luther Lusk pushed to his feet and headed for his horse. "Well, I come here to fight Yankees; I ain't lost no Indians."

"Lusk!" David shouted. "You halt right there. You give that rifle back to Sergeant Mitchell."

Lusk turned on his heel. For a long moment the big man's hawk eyes glared at the officer, challenging him. The muzzle was pointed vaguely in David's direction. The temptation showed strongly in his face.

"What if I choose to do otherwise?"

David said tensely, "Then I'll kill you!" It was an empty statement, for he knew he wouldn't. But he stood and bluffed because he had already lost too much ground with these men.

Lusk had all the advantage, if he chose to use it. Chances were small that he would ever be prosecuted back in Texas for something done here in the mountains of New Mexico. But in a moment he handed the rifle to Mitchell. "Hell, let some Indian kill him; then nobody'll stretch *my* neck."

David said, "Don't anybody rush: We'll leave here with order."

"Order?" Lusk was incredulous. "What does order mean to an Indian? If we want to live to fight more Yankees, we'd better forget about order and get the hell away from this place."

David's back was rigid. "You seem to've forgotten how it was the day we all rode out of San Antonio. Like as not you were drunk. But *I* remember. We rode out of there proud. Well, we've been beaten, but we're not whipped. We won't go back to Texas *lookin'* whipped." He knew most of the men just wanted to leave there. He would not have admitted it, but his own britches were burning him. "Mount up."

That was another order he had to give but once. The men began edging their horses south, but David motioned for them to follow him. He moved down the east side of the hill toward the pass.

Noley Mitchell spurred up beside him. "I don't mean to question your judgment, button, but Texas is yonder-way."

"Those Yankees might've brought somethin' we can use."

"Davey, you can bet them Indians picked up every gun, every knife, every cartridge."

"But maybe not all the rations. Indian tastes don't run to military issue. And maybe we'll find some canteens. For what's ahead of us, we can use every water container we can find."

Mitchell would have argued further, but David showed no disposition to listen. His eyes were set firmly on the pass, and the old lawman took that sign for what it was. He rode quietly, glancing over his broad shoulder to be sure everybody was coming.

David wanted to look back but feared that could be taken as a sign of doubt. He held the lead, sitting straight in the saddle the way his father had taught him. Joshua Buckalew had been one of the early "Texians," those who came before the revolution. He emigrated from Tennessee in 1830, taking up land in Austin's colony, fighting in the revolt against Santa Anna and Mexico. He had been a survivor of the massacre at Goliad and had found his way to Sam Houston's army in time for the final victory at San Jacinto.

Joshua Buckalew had been a soldier, a hard man for a son to follow in the eyes of the people in Hopeful Valley, and those elsewhere who had ever known Joshua.

David's father had never expressed pride in the battles he had fought; on the contrary, he hated even to talk about them. But other people talked, and exaggerated. Joshua Buckalew was a reluctant hero in the land where he had chosen to live out his life. People expected much from his son. That was why David had been elected lieutenant of the Hopeful Valley volunteers . . . not for himself but because of his father.

Up to now, David had to consider himself a failure. It was a hard thing to be a son of Joshua Buckalew and still be a failure.

Joshua hadn't said much as David had prepared to ride away to San Antonio with the valley's other recruits. "There's a lot you ain't seen yet, and you've got a lot to learn about life," he had cautioned, his eyes glazed. "You'll find a lot of it ain't the way you expect it to be, and sure not like people say. You'll find a lot that ain't just and fair. But set yourself straight and ride always in the service of the Lord. You'll owe no man an apology if you do the best that's in you."

The Lord had precious little to do with this *war*, David thought with some bitterness. There had been a certain amount of public praying at the muster in San Antonio, and calls upon the Deity for His guidance in the righteous campaign. But it had not taken David long to decide that the Lord had no great leaning to either side. He had let both suffer horribly, and the suffering was far from over.

The speeches and the music had been fine, and the flags had waved gallantly as they had set out upon the first long march. But shortly after coming into New Mexico he had watched a man die screaming, trying to hold his shattered guts in place.

There had been no music then.

Now David was increasingly certain that all this suffering had been for nothing. Wasted were all those hard miles they had fought, all those days they had ridden until their tailbones were numb and their dry tongues stuck to the roofs of their mouths. All those men who had died, all those men who had gone home maimed for the rest of their lives . . . they had done it for nothing. The campaign was lost.

It hadn't been what he had expected. It was hell being a soldier.

A dull ache worked through his shoulder, a reminder of the price he himself had paid. The wound had never completely healed; he was not sure it ever would. They had pulled him out of the makeshift military hospital in Albuquerque too soon, for they had badly needed officers. It had been his doubly bad luck that he was assigned to this outfit which didn't want him. Had the men been allowed an election, David did not doubt that they would have chosen Noley Mitchell, and he would be the one leading them back to Texas.

The irony was that he knew the old lawman would probably do a better job of it.

Leadership had been an easy thing in those early months of the war. All the Hopeful Valley men were his friends, and all knew what needed to be done. He didn't have to give orders. Being an officer was more an honor than a responsibility. It was no great challenge to lead when they were winning, and winning easily.

The crisis of leadership came now, when they were losing. This was the true test. Ever since he had been with this outfit, David Buckalew had fallen short.

God, for one more chance!

Before riding down into the pass he sent Noley Mitchell up on one side of it and a Mexican trooper named Fermin Hernandez up on the other to scout for Indians. David had never been comfortable about the Mexican; it was an old ingrained prejudice from his part of the country, where Anglos and Mexicans had fought two official wars and many unofficial ones. Yet he had found that Hernandez possessed the best eyesight of any man in the outfit. The Mexican could not read words written on a page, but he could read tracks on the ground and describe in considerable detail the circumstances of their making. He could see riders a mile away and tell if they were soldiers or Indians or what. He was useful as an interpreter, too, for David's knowledge of Spanish was rudimentary at best, geared to the limited vocabulary he had needed in his chosen trade, the buying, training and selling of horses and mules.

Harnandez gave the "clear" sign, and a moment later Mitchell did likewise. David left half the men posted in the mouth of the pass to stand guard. He took the others in to look over the battleground.

Battleground was not exactly the word for it. It had been more slaughter than battle. The blueclad troops had had little chance to fight back. The Indians had been well hidden in the rocks on either side and presented little target. The Union soldiers lay scattered along the pass, heaped like bloody rag dolls, scalped and mutilated. David's stomach started to turn, and he shut his eyes for a moment until the feeling passed.

At a glance he knew the Indians had taken all guns and ammunition; he had expected that. He came upon a dead packmule. The Indians had ripped the pack off, looking for anything they could use. David motioned to the youth Richey to go through what was left. He saw a dead horse with the saddle still on, and a canteen tied to it.

He glanced behind him at a farm lad named Ivy, who had always been eager but was considered by the others as a bit slow in his thinking. "Ivy, you been needin' a better saddle. Get somebody to help you take that one."

Ivy was dubious. "There's blood on it, Lieutenant."

"It'll wear off."

David turned away, then stopped abruptly. Staring up toward him with sightless eyes was a man wearing captain's bars on a bullet-torn, faded-blue uniform. David dismounted. Kneeling, he shuddered a little as his fingers lightly touched the man's face and closed the dulled eyes. He began going through the pockets. There might be papers.

Inside the coat he found an envelope, its corner stained a sticky red. As he opened it he heard a noise behind him. A frontier trapper named Jake Calvin was going through the pockets of the Union soldiers nearby.

"Calvin!"

Calvin looked up, startled. "You say somethin', Buckalew?" He had made his living with a skinning knife. Dead things brought him no dread.

"Don't you draw the line at robbin' bodies?"

"Who's robbin'? I'm just salvagin', same as you."

"I'm lookin' for dispatches, orders . . . nothin' else."

"And I'm just lookin' for tobacco and such. Them must of been tradin' post Indians, because they ain't left a two-bit piece in the whole damned bunch, far as I can find out."

"They were soldiers. They probably didn't have two bits. Get back on your horse."

Calvin showed some disposition to argue, then shrugged it off. "Wasn't findin' nothin' noway."

David read the letter through. His first reaction was surprise. He had taken it for granted that this was a Union detail out simply to harass straggling Confederates. It was more than that. The letter, addressed to Captain Tad Smith, was an order for Smith to take a detail to the Owen Townsend ranch west of the Pecos River. There he was to prepare for immediate shipment a store of rifles, ammunition and powder which had been cached by Union troops as they fled northward the year before. They had not wanted it falling into Confederate hands but had not wished to destroy it, either. Now, the letter said, they had use for it in the pursuit and chastisement of the Texan invaders.

A train of ten wagons will be dispatched from this point on the 10th instant, and should reach the Townsend rancho within two days after your arrival. Townsend and his household have already left here and should be returned to their place of residence before you reach it.

They are loyal to the Union; therefore you will render all possible service and show utmost courtesy. Townsend was a valued scout for General Kearney's incursion into the Territory fifteen years ago, and the family has been of material aid to us in the current difficulties. You may place fullest reliance in the word and advice of my friend Owen Townsend.

I need not remind you how badly this cache of munitions is needed for the continuation of our successful campaign to push the rebellious Texans from our borders and to pursue them into their own lair.

Benj. Stahl,
Colonel, Commanding

David looked around him at the dead men. They would never finish that mission now, or any other. When those wagon people got to the cache, they would probably wonder why the escort never showed up.

The young trooper Richey rode up to David. He was visibly shaking. His eyes apprehensively searched the rocky sides of the pass. "We done picked up everything we think would be of any use, Lieutenant. We've found some tinned rations, a few canteens and such. If you're waitin' on us, there ain't no use you wastin' any more of your time."

David nodded. "Nothin' is keepin' us here."

Richey glanced at one of the bodies and turned his face quickly away. "We goin' to leave them layin' here this-away?"

"You want us to take time to bury them?"

"Anywhere else it would seem like the Christian thing. But this ain't no Christian place."

"No, it sure isn't." David made a signal and led the men out of the pass, heading south. Hernandez came down from his post on the west rim and looked at David. David signaled for him to go ahead and take the point. Hernandez hunched a little and went on. Sergeant Mitchell rode off of the east rim and fell in beside David as they proceeded in a stiff trot, putting the pass as far behind them as they could without overtaxing the horses.

Mitchell said, "I spotted a packmule out yonder a ways. He must've stampeded out of the pass, and the Indians either didn't catch him or forgot about him."

"We'll pick him up." David was only half listening. His mind dwelt on those Yankees back there. He still held the letter in his hand, crumpled. He unfolded it and glanced over it again. Gradually he realized something that he had passed over lightly the first time: a detail of wagons was on its way to collect the cache. Unless good fortune should strike twice and the Indians should eliminate the wagon train too, the mission probably would still be accomplished, even without the captain and his men.

David reflected on the potential destructive power in ten wagons of munitions. If those Yankees recovered the cache they would use it to guarantee that some Texans never saw home again.

Sergeant Mitchell was talking, but David only nodded, agreeing to comments he didn't really hear. He noticed some lines on the back of the letter. They were a crude map, directions for finding the Townsend place. They were probably enough for someone who knew this part of the country, but to David they were a little vague.

His pulse began to beat with an excitement different from the kind he had felt facing those Indians. He looked up, his eyes widening. Sergeant Mitchell continued to talk, and David had not heard a word he said. He studied Mitchell now, still not hearing. He had never been comfortable in the sergeant's presence, but the feeling was of a personal nature, a realization that he was in a position that morally belonged to Mitchell, and some doubt whether he was worthy of it. It had nothing to do with Mitchell's ability as a soldier. If he had nineteen men like Noley Mitchell, he could turn around and give the damnyankees a whipping right here and now, and make them yearn for Colorado and California.

He frowned, wondering what Mitchell would think about the idea that was beginning to build in his mind.

He turned and looked back at the other men. He saw Gene Ivy, gazing worriedly toward the hills where the Indians had disappeared. The lad meant well and could perform if told exactly what to do, but he seemed unable to initiate anything on his own.

Pete Richey. Willing also, but young, green, perhaps of less potential even than Ivy. The two boys, he had been told, had come from neighboring farms, had ridden together to the appointed marshaling place for recruits, had listened to the same patriotic speeches, and had told the same lie about their ages to join.

T. E. Storey, who rode almost sideways now, looking back toward the pass they had left. From what Mitchell had said the day David had been assigned to this unit, Storey had been a town policeman. That, in David's view, should have been a good background for a soldier. But Mitchell had been disparaging. "When they can't make it anywhere else, they become city policemen," the ex-sheriff had said. David was vaguely aware of the traditional rivalry between county and city officials. He tended to regard Mitchell's judgment as colored by prejudice. Storey, David thought, should be a man he could rely on in a pinch.

Aaron Bender, from whom David had not heard a dozen words. Maybe quiet men were the best soldiers. Certainly the loud ones usually were not.

Jake Calvin, David had already decided, was not one to count on in time of trouble. In a couple of skirmishes with Union details Calvin had hung back, staying low and out of the line of fire as much as he could. He became fierce after the battle, but only in his talk.

He was still in doubt about Homer Gilman, a miller by trade, a tall, gaunt man who had little to say but always stuck close by Noley Mitchell. He was very plainly a Mitchell partisan.

There were Patrick O'Shea and Otto Hufstedler, an unlikely pair to be close friends. O'Shea was fairly freshly arrived from the old sod. Hufstedler had come to Texas with a tide of German immigrants in the 1850s, the young men like himself trying to avoid conscription into a German Army they hated. Now he found himself in an army anyway, a volunteer fighting for a cause he probably did not understand, struggling with a language still difficult for him. He and O'Shea seemed always to be together. The only common bond David could see was that both were immigrants. Perhaps that was it, that they felt shut out to some degree from other company. That was a feeling David understood very well.

Fermin Hernandez. Accounts indicated he had been an oxcart freighter on the road between San Antonio and the Rio Grande by way of rowdy Helena and points south, no place for a weak or timid man. It was said that Hernandez had done some smuggling when it came handy. That was against the law but was hardly considered a moral offense in that time and place; everybody beyond the age of seven did some of it. They saw no way a government could be harmed by a bit of trading between people of two neighboring countries and regarded the customs laws as principally designed to provide wages to lazy government employees who should have been lending their minds and muscle to honest endeavor. Hernandez never volunteered to talk about himself, and David hadn't asked. A Mexican's affairs were his own business so long as they did not encroach on those of the Anglo. That was the code of the times.

Luther Lusk. David's face pinched as he gazed at the man. From fragments he had heard, he gathered that Lusk had had some disagreements with the law back home, represented by Noley Mitchell, but that they had come together willingly against a common enemy. It was said they had been enemies once, but here they were friends, and David had sensed a bond of sorts between them, a respect that honest enemies sometimes develop for one another. Exactly what Lusk had done for a living was unclear. David had heard or seen indications that he had some experience at freighting, as had Hernandez, and at scouting on the Indian frontier for the Ranger service. If the latter were true, David doubted that it had lasted long. Lusk showed little inclination to follow orders from anybody, and the Rangers were a quasi-military organization. They could not have depended upon a man of such independent mind for very long, David reasoned. Certainly he knew that *he* could not depend upon him.

The other men were of varied stripe and hue. David had not come to know them much in his limited time with the outfit. They were still little more than names to him, names and faces but not personalities.

They showed little interest in becoming anything more, at least for him.

Sergeant Mitchell stood in his stirrups periodically and searched the hills with his eyes. He took off his threadbare remnant of a gray coat, for the sun was beginning to warm him. He rubbed a shirtsleeve across his sweaty forehead. "How long you figure now to Fort Bliss, Davey?"

David was paying so little attention that Mitchell had to ask him twice. David said, "I don't know." He was still crumpling the letter in his hand. He frowned, glancing back once more at the men behind him.

They could do it. Hell, yes, they could do it, if they put their minds to it and had the will.

"Sergeant, I wish you'd read this and tell me what you think."

Mitchell held the letter out at arm's length, squinting. When he had read it, he turned it over and examined the map. He traced with his finger and pointed to a spot. "I'd say we're somewhere along here, wouldn't you?"

David didn't care to let it be known, but he had more faith in Mitchell's sense of time and position. "I would imagine so."

"And . . ."—Mitchell traced the map on down toward the bottom— "there is the Townsend place. Some east of our present line of travel, wouldn't you say?"

"I'd say so," David agreed, leaning again on Mitchell's judgment.

"I believe I know what you're thinkin', Davey."

"That we could stop those munitions from fallin' back into Union hands. That we could keep them from bein' used against Texas."

Mitchell pondered. "Some of these old boys might not like it much, us goin' out of our way. They can already smell Texas in the wind."

"That's why I'd rather not tell them till I have to."

Mitchell's heavy eyebrows knitted. It was clear that he did not relish being a partner in any conspiracy. "They may not take it kindly."

"They haven't taken kindly to anything else I've done. It's a soldier's place to carry out orders, not to ask questions."

"That's when you're winnin'. But when you're losin', a man starts watchin' out for his own hide."

"So we tell them when we have to, and not before."

"You're the officer. I just ain't sure it's totin' fair."

"If we told them, how many would we lose?"

"A few might take and leave us. But they'll have to know sooner or later. You can't fool them all the way."

"Maybe I can fool them to a point that they have no choice."

"They've always got a choice, Davey. Anytime it gets dark, they have a choice."

David glanced back at the men trailing him and felt a moment of quiet envy. All they had to do was follow. They didn't have to take responsibility or make decisions. They didn't have to take the blame for an officer's mistakes, if they could live through them.

Times like this he wished he were back in Texas trading horses and mules, able to fall back on the comfort and security of his father's name.

But it was a long way to Texas.

CHAPTER 2

If there had been any talk in the men, the bitter day had worn it out of them. They rode in stolid silence through the dry and alien hills. Hernandez was out front as scout, the lieutenant and Mitchell next, riding together. Before sundown they stopped to cook a light supper at a spring they came across, using rations from the pack of the Yankee mule they had picked up along the way.

They brewed their first coffee in many days. Lacking any grinder for the Yankee coffee beans, they put them in a leather pouch and beat them to pieces with a rock.

No man here was acquainted with this region. They filled the canteens, for there might be water again across the next hill, or this might be the last for a hundred miles. The sun's warmth faded quickly in the late afternoon, and by sundown most of the men had their coats on, buttoned against the chill. After a brief supper they rode a few more miles to put the campfires behind them in case Indians or Yankees might smell the smoke. They made a dry, fireless camp in a cover of scrub timber.

No one argued about taking his turn standing guard, and David had little concern about someone falling asleep at it. The memory of those dead Yankees made it difficult to sleep even when off guard duty.

They brewed coffee in the cold light of a mountain dawn and chewed hardtack found on the packmule. By good daylight they were moving southward again, edging gradually eastward. In midafternoon they came across a tiny Mexican settlement, surrounded by a few small fields just starting to get their spring work. Across the valley David saw a scattered band of sheep trying to find the first green picking of spring but crowding the season a little. He had seen dozens of these villages spread across this territory. They were largely self-sufficient, producing almost everything the people needed for their own survival. In the days of Spanish colonialism and later Mexican rule, they had been too far removed to receive much help from the government; virtually the only officials they ever saw were the tax collectors, who always seemed to find them about once a year. The government agents brought nothing but took much away. These villages were only minimally affected by the trade that went on between New Mexico and the northern Mexican states such as Chihuahua. If they couldn't grow it or make it, they did without.

The people were usually wary of strangers. David had found in them little inclination to fraternize with the Confederates. He doubted that they had been warmer to the Yankees. They were sufficient unto themselves.

As a precaution he spread the troopers in skirmish-line fashion rather than let them ride into the village in a tight group, an easier target. He signaled Hernandez to wait for him, and the two rode toward the little plaza side by side, suspiciously eyeing the houses and the corrals, looking for any sign that there might be people here beyond the native villagers.

The women and the children who had been outside seemed to melt quietly away, disappearing into the houses. By the time David and Hernandez reached the plaza, only two persons remained in sight, one an old man with a gray, stringy beard, perhaps the village patriarch, and a *padre* standing in the door of the little mud church.

David raised one hand in a sign that he came in peace and reined toward the old man. The *viejo* eyed him with suspicion and a trace of fear. Through long generations, strangers had seldom brought good tidings to these settlements. The old man could clearly tell that these bedraggled *Tejanos* brought nothing with them that would enrich his village. The people would be most fortunate if these foreigners did not bring misfortune of some description; most did.

"Tell him we're friendly," David said to Hernandez. He had been around Texas Mexicans enough to sense that Hernandez was translating faithfully. But the old man's half-whispered reply meant nothing to him, and he could tell even Hernandez had trouble with it. Hernandez had complained before that these New Mexico people spoke a brand of Spanish different from his own. They had been isolated for generations, and their little contact was with a different part of Mexico than that known to the Texas Mexicans. It stood to reason that the dialects were worlds apart.

"He says he is grateful," Hernandez translated. "He asks what we want of him."

"We'll take nothin' from his village and hurt no one. All we want is information."

As Hernandez relayed the message, David saw the old man ease a little, though still wary. Texans had been portrayed to these people as first cousins of the devil, and some had gone to considerable lengths to prove it.

"Ask him if he has seen any Union troops."

The old man assured him that none of the *Americanos* had been seen here in many months, not since the *Tejanos* had driven them north.

David was inclined to believe him, though he could never be certain about these people. They were Mexicans, and as a Texan he would always remember the Alamo. "Ask him how far it is to the ranch of Owen Townsend, and what direction it lays in."

Hernandez glanced at David with surprise. This was the first he had heard of a Townsend ranch. He asked David to repeat the name, then translated the question. For a moment David thought he saw recognition in the watery brown eyes. But when the answer came back through Hernandez, it was to the effect that the *viejo* knew no Owen Townsend.

David frowned. "Ask again. Be sure he understood the name."

The answer was the same. Clearly, Townsend was a *gringo* name. The people in this village rarely saw a *gringo*.

David's instincts told him the man was lying. He was certain he had seen recognition, just for a moment. To know nothing was a form of defense these people had long used to avoid involvement in events which were none of their affair. What they did not know, they could not tell. What they did not tell would bring no reprisal.

Hernandez shrugged. "He lies, I think. But if he don't want to tell, he don't. Who is this Townsend? What for do you ask of him?"

"*I'll* ask the questions."

Hernandez ignored David's reply. "Is it for this Townsend that we go always a bit to the east, instead of only to the south? To get to Paso del Norte we should be closer to the Rio Grande, but we move toward the Pecos. Since yesterday I have wanted to ask you about this."

"I have my reasons. You will not talk of this to the other men."

Hernandez made no attempt to hide his suspicion. He gave David no response, neither promise nor denial. David knew that in all likelihood every man would know as soon as they stopped for supper.

He looked again at the old Mexican and resisted a moment of violent temptation. If the patriarch did not choose to speak, he would not, and that was the end of it.

As always, they rode until an hour before dark, then stopped to fix a hot supper over tiny fires they hoped would make little smoke and be unseen. During this time he noticed several of the men in conversation with Hernandez and glancing in the lieutenant's direction. Eight or ten of them converged on David. Luther Lusk was in the lead, bristling.

"Buckalew, who's this Towser you was askin' about?"

David gave Hernandez a hard look. "Townsend," he corrected.

"Why are you askin' about him? What business have we got anywhere besides Fort Bliss and Paso del Norte?"

David saw that the rest of the men were watching curiously from afar. He was reluctant to give it all away because he didn't trust their reaction. He stared at the fire a little and then asked, "Are you proud of the way we're goin' home, Lusk, chastised by the Yankees?"

"You know I ain't. None of us are."

"What if we were given one last chance to hit them a lick—not a flea bite but a hard lick that would really hurt them?"

Lusk frowned at Sergeant Mitchell, then looked back at David. "Have you talked it over with Noley?"

"It's not his decision to make; it's mine."

Lusk's frown deepened, along with his suspicions. "If Noley don't like it, I don't."

Heat began rising in David's blood. He repeated what he had said, about it being his decision, not Mitchell's. Lusk ignored him and looked to the sergeant.

Mitchell had listened quietly, sipping his coffee. Reluctantly he said, "You'd better tell them, Davey."

David didn't think so, but he felt himself hemmed in.

Lusk continued to push. "If it's a decent idea you'll tell us about it. Let us decide what *we* think."

Resentment fired David's face. This was not the way a military unit was supposed to operate. The more time the men had to think about it, the more arguments they might raise against it. But he bowed to the inevitable. "All right, since everybody wants so damned bad to know, I'll tell you." He waved for all the men to gather around, including those still fixing their suppers.

One lesson old officers had drilled into him was that to keep control of the men you always start out on the offensive and never take a defensive tack with them. "By rights," he declared sternly, "I ought not to tell you a thing, and you ought not to ask. It's a soldier's job to follow orders and ask no questions." He saw that the lecture was lost on these men. They were soldiers only by their own consent, and that consent had been but tentatively given. They had responded patriotically and on impulse to a call that their country needed them. That need, in their view, had involved whipping hell out of the Yankees, not relinquishing their individuality and manhood.

David took the letter from his pocket and read it aloud, allowing time for its import to soak in on the men. He remembered that it had taken a while before he had seen its potential. "So there it is, ten wagons of arms and powder. All that, lyin' there waitin' for them to use against us. We're the only Texans who know about it. It's up to us to blow it to Kingdom Come."

Trooper T. E. Storey looked at Luther Lusk, as if assessing his possible support. "What if there's already Yankees there, guardin' it?"

David said, "That bunch of Yankees the Indians killed . . . they were bein' sent to do that and to wait for the wagons. There's no reason to expect anybody to be there except the ranch people."

"And how many of *them* is there likely to be? I've known of ranch people in Texas that stood off a hundred Comanches, just maybe three or four of them, forted up good. How many would it take to stand off the twenty of us?"

David challenged, "How many of us stand likely to be killed if the Yankees get ahold of all that ammunition?"

"None, if we move fast enough and beat them back to Texas."

Stiffly David said, "We came out here to do a job for our country. As it stands right now, we got our butts kicked. When we signed up in San Antonio we took a pledge to do the best that was in us. Well, I think there's still better in us than we've shown. Till we've done this job or busted a gut tryin', how can we say we've done our best? We won't be able to look people in the face and say we've tried."

Storey was not converted. "Who we goin' to look in the face if we're dead? What if we decide not to go?"

David's eyes narrowed. "You'll go. I'll lead you if I can. If I can't, I'll drive you."

Storey stared at him in sullen silence.

Luther Lusk turned to Noley Mitchell. "It's up to you, Noley. What do you say?"

At that moment David resented Noley Mitchell, but he tried not to show it.

Mitchell didn't hesitate. "I think we ought to go and do it."

Lusk nodded. "That's good enough for me. If you say so, Noley, we'll follow you."

Follow the sergeant, not the lieutenant. David gritted his teeth. "We can make some more distance before dark." Most of them hadn't finished supper yet, but he motioned for Hernandez to lead out and pointed the direction, southeast. They rode into the darkness.

Mitchell kept his horse beside David a long time before he

volunteered, "Davey, I know you and the men have got off on the wrong foot with each other. But they're a good bunch, mostly. You got to have patience and trust them more."

David didn't reply.

They made a quiet, dry camp, the night chill biting to the bone as David wrapped his one woolen blanket around him and stretched on the ground. He slept fitfully, the arm bothering him a lot. Dreams came to him in patches and fragments. The pain took him back to the army hospital in Albuquerque. For a time he dimly saw a woman bent over him, wrapping the wound with gentle hands, trying not to hurt him. He tried to see her face, but it never came clear. It never had.

He awoke to the realization that someone was shaking his arm, bringing on a stabbing pain. Noley Mitchell was kneeling beside him, the first pink light of dawn reflected in his grim face. "Davey, we've got two men gone."

Casting off the blanket, David moved quickly to his feet, looking around him in the semidarkness He hoped one of them was Luther Lusk.

Mitchell said, "That's the way with them city policemen. It was T. E. Storey and Aaron Bender. They must of left durin' Storey's watch."

Two men! David clenched his fists in frustration. The odds had been long enough when they were twenty. Now they were eighteen.

Mitchell scowled. "I ain't told you the worst of it yet. They taken some of our rations with them. We've got little enough as it is. You want me to detail a patrol and trail them?"

David wanted to trail them. He wanted to catch them and perhaps shoot them as an example. He gave way to a string of profanity such as a horse trader is likely to pick up in the course of that uncertain career. It served as a release for the anger and allowed him to regain his balance. Time they spent in pursuit of Storey and Bender would be time lost from the more important job at hand, and perhaps time given to whatever Union troops might be coming along behind them.

"The hell with them. Let's get the men up and move out."

Through the day the men kept quartering eastward, watchfully crossing canyon after canyon, ravine after dry ravine that snaked out in search of the alkaline waters of the Pecos River. Late in the day they came to the turbulent brown stream that etched its way between the mountains and the dreaded plains, the uncharted Llano Estacado. Noley Mitchell went to the edge, filled a canteen and tipped it up to taste of it. He spat most of it out and rubbed a sleeve across his mouth. "Anybody doubts that's the Pecos, just let him drink a little of it. I remember how it tasted when we crossed it before, on the way west."

"That was a long way south of here," David reminded him.

"Distance don't improve it."

Soon afterward, following the river, they came in sight of a Mexican herder tending a large band of Merino sheep. David spurred his horse to catch up to Hernandez, and together they rode to the sheep. He took the herder to be in his mid-twenties. With the country at war, it struck him odd that a man of that prime age should not be serving in the Army—either Union or Confederate—instead of herding sheep out here in a desolate land that to David was little more than desert. These people, so remote from the heavily settled sections, knew little or nothing of the bloody wars fought by civilized men. They were backward in many ways.

The young herder studied the troopers intently, and it occurred to David that among other things he was counting them.

"Ask him about the Townsend ranch," David said to Hernandez.

To his surprise an answer was freely given, without the hesitation he had seen in the old man in the last village. Hernandez turned. "He says he has heard of it but he was never there himself, so he cannot tell just where it is. But he says there is a trading post south of here where we can ask, and he thinks those people will tell us. He says there is food to buy in the post, and much whiskey."

"Last thing we need right now is whiskey," David said darkly, looking toward the men behind him. He had never been with them in a place where they had been tested by whiskey; he had no idea who or how many might give him a problem. "Ask him if he has seen any Yankees."

Hernandez relayed the question, then turned with a quizzical expression. "He asks, what is a Yankee?"

Backward! David thought again. How could these people exist way out here, cut off from all that was important in the world?

Later the Texans stopped for supper, then made their customary ride into the first hour of darkness. David quietly studied each man, looking for signs that would tell him who might be contemplating desertion tonight, following the example of Storey and Bender. David slept a little early in the night, but the worry over desertions brought him fully awake with every changing of the guard, and during the last two shifts he slept none at all. He sat up with the blanket pulled around his shoulders. He shivered from the chill and counted the sleeping men time and time again, looking sharply every time one turned or groaned in his sleep. At daylight he still had seventeen men.

The one cup of hot coffee failed to take the chill out of his bones. Riding along, he kept glancing at the rising sun, wishing it carried more warmth. By now, down in his part of Texas, the nights would be passable, and the days would even be getting a little hot. There would be a good green tinge in the grass, and the brush would be putting on leaves. Here, farther north and at a higher altitude, it was still more winter than spring.

He could not help wondering, at such a time, what he was doing so far from Texas.

At midmorning Hernandez topped over a rise and reined up suddenly. He turned and looked back, his eyes searching out David. He did not have to signal; his manner was enough. David spurred up to him.

Hernandez pointed. "The trading post, Lieutenant."

It lay a quarter mile down the slope, just far enough from the river to be out of the flood plain. David took out the spyglass. He looked first for any sign of Yankee troops. He saw a scattering of horses and a fair number of mules, mostly of the Spanish type he had seen all over New Mexico. He saw few he thought were of army caliber.

It wasn't much of a settlement, even by the standards of this sparsely settled country. He saw one long L-shaped adobe building and a squat storehouse behind it. Beyond that was a brush corral where some of the Spanish-looking ponies stood listlessly as if waiting for somebody to fetch them a handful of hay, and doubting that anybody would. Scattered all about was the litter of filth accumulated during years of careless living.

A sleepy-looking place, an unlikely place for trouble. Yet it gave him a feeling of uneasiness that earlier villages had not.

It came to him that he saw no women or children out stirring, as would usually be the case. It struck him that this place looked different from the family villages he had seen so much; it lacked the scattering of adobe and brush houses.

Hernandez seemed to share David's misgivings. "You know what I think, Lieutenant?"

"I'd like to hear it."

"You have heard of the Comancheros?"

The word was dimly familiar. That it had to do with Comanches was obvious, but he could not remember the connection. He had never moved in real Indian country, and he knew only what he had retained from things he had been told.

"I have heard talk of them up here," Hernandez said. "They are people—Mexicans mostly—who go out on the *llano* and do trade with the Indians. The Comanches and Kiowas and whatever others there are, they steal far south in Texas, and down in Mexico. They bring here what they have taken, or near here, out on the plains. The Comancheros trade them what they want—blankets and guns and whiskey. They get horses and cattle from the Indians . . . sometimes even women and children slaves the Indians have stolen. That is what the people in the villages have told me. This is a very old thing, a very old trade. Maybe so these are Comancheros. It could be a very bad place."

Noley Mitchell had ridden up and heard most of it. David looked at him, asking a question with his eyes that rank made it awkward to ask in words. Mitchell said, "I've heard of them too, Davey. He could be right. Smart thing would be to go around."

David considered that. "But we might go around the Townsend place too and never know it. We'll ride in there and ask, just Hernandez and me. You'll stay here with the rest of the men."

"You may wish you had us."

"Give us ten minutes, then spread out wide and come in closer to the village. But don't come all the way in unless you see or hear signs of trouble. If that happens, come runnin'."

Mitchell clearly had reservations, but he nodded. "However you want it, Davey."

David thought of the spyglass. He handed it to Mitchell and moved forward. He and Hernandez rode side by side, two tired, dusty men who had little in common except the country they came from. David Buckalew was dressed in the leavings of a smart gray uniform, designed by no pattern other than his mother's imagination, because the Confederacy was new and had not settled upon a common style; every officer outfitted himself according to his own fancies, and what was available. Fermin Hernandez, a private soldier, had not even that much outward appearance to tie him to the military, for he had ridden to war in what had been his Sunday mass suit, of black homespun wool. It had been hell through the summer campaign, and by winter, when he really needed it, the fabric had been patched and re-patched and worn so thin that it hardly turned back the sharp, cold wind. But Hernandez rode like a soldier, his back straight, his chin out, his eyes alert.

The people at the post would quickly recognize them for what they were, soldiers of the Confederate States of America . . . more specifically, Texas. People in this part of the country had gotten so in the last few months that they knew a Texan as far as they could see him.

David's suspicion about the adobe post did not diminish as he approached it; if anything, his uneasiness grew. His eyes shifted from the building to outlying corrals, to every clump of brush and every pile of trash that might hide a man. Ahead of him he saw two men come out of the long adobe's front door and stand beside it together, waiting. Other men, six in all, scattered on either side, watching the two riders come in. David took most of them to be Mexicans, but as he neared he could see that two, at least, were Indians.

He assumed the two in the middle to be in charge. He gave his major attention to these, though none of the others made a move that he did not see. He doubted that anything was getting past Hernandez either, for the Mexican was as tense as a trigger spring.

David tugged gently on the reins and halted the brown horse about three paces in front of the men. He raised his hand with the palm outward, signaling peace, though he had reservations about it. The hard way these men looked at him said little of peace but much of war. His first thought was that they were probably all Yankee sympathizers. On reflection he doubted that. Indians had shown no inclination toward politics; they killed either side with equal fervor.

He stared at the two men immediately in front of him. Because of the portly middle and the liberal sprinkling of gray strands in the man's otherwise black hair, David assumed him to be the *major-domo*. "Tell him we have come here in peace to ask only for information."

Hernandez translated and got back a standard salutation. "He says we are all friends here, that his house is our house."

"I wouldn't have it if he gave it to me," David said. "The whole lot of them would as soon cut our throats as look at us. Tell him I'm pleased at his gracious reception, and that we want to ask directions."

Hernandez started the translation. The man who stood next to the older one took a step forward and said in plain English, "Friend, there is no need for you to work through an interpreter."

David was at first startled, then a little chagrined because this man had understood everything he had said. He still looked like a cutthroat, even if he did speak English.

"You're Texans," the man said. "You're a long way from home."

"But tryin' to get there as quick as we can," David said.

"Seems to me you've lost your way, moving this far east. This can be a poor country for a man who loses his way."

A poor country all around, David thought. He refrained from saying it aloud; he figured he had already said enough of a provocative nature. These people looked as if they might want something to be provoked about. The longer he studied the faces, the less he wanted to prolong the stay.

The man who spoke English was burned dark by the sun, and David had assumed him to be Mexican. Now that he looked closer he saw that the eyes were gray rather than brown, and the features were different from those of most people he had seen here. "You're not Mexican. What are you?"

"I am not anything except simply myself," came the easy answer. "I am Floyd Bearfield."

"Where do you come from?"

"That doesn't matter. What matters is where I am, and I am here. I have been here—or hereabout—for a long time."

An exile, David sensed. Usually a man becomes an exile for something he has done. "These aren't your people."

"They are my people now. I have chosen them and they have accepted me. Probably you are a Texan by accident of birth; you just happened to be born there. I am here because I have *chosen* to be."

Damned poor choice, David thought. But each man to his own taste. "Have you seen any Yankee soldiers?"

"None," said Bearfield. "There is little here to interest soldiers of any kind . . . Union or Southern. We have our own community, our own commerce. We do not need a great deal from the outside, and certainly the outside has little business with us. We do not see many people."

David stared at one of the Indians. He knew little of them, but he assumed this one to be Comanche. He found something incongruous in the coat the man was wearing. It was a white man's. He even imagined he saw something familiar in the coat but knew that could not be so.

David said, "We are lookin' for a certain place. We hoped you could tell us how to find it."

"Perhaps. But you do not want to travel any more today. Get down and we will see what we can find for you to eat, and to drink."

"We haven't the time."

"We might even find other pleasures for you."

"We have to go."

Bearfield was letting his displeasure start to show. "Look to your horses, man. Two good horses, by the look of them, and almost ridden down. They need rest and feed. Get down, and we'll see to it."

The man reached out suddenly and took David's bridle reins. As if by signal, an Indian quickly grabbed the reins of Hernandez' horse.

Hernandez looked at David in alarm but made no move, waiting for a sign.

The other men moved in closer. David read the intention in their faces. They were about to pick up two Texas horses, cheap.

Hernandez' hand dipped and came up with a knife from his belt. An Indian dropped a blanket from his shoulders, revealing a hidden rifle. He pointed it at Hernandez.

David stiffened. "Easy, Hernandez. They'll kill you."

"We might." Bearfield nodded, pleased. It had been an easy catch. "Step down easily. Give no one cause to do you violence."

David swallowed. He was not totally surprised at the treachery, but he didn't know what to do about it other than to stall for time. Ten minutes, he had told Mitchell.

"I am an officer of the Confederate Army," he said imperiously. "You will turn my horse loose."

Bearfield shook his head incredulously. "I've found you *Tejanos* to be a thick-headed lot. There *is* no Confederate Army, not out here. You've been slashed and shot and beaten to pieces. Do you think the long arm of Jefferson Davis will reach all the way to the Pecos River because of *you*?" He spat on the dry, powdered ground. "Don't try our patience, Texas. We'll let you walk home if you'll not provoke us. Otherwise we'll drag your bodies down to the river and let *it* carry you back."

David felt cold as he looked into the hard faces. The men had formed a semicircle, trapping him and Hernandez. He looked at the rifles that had materialized, and the knives. It struck him as improbable that these men would let them walk away from here. He made no move to dismount.

Tightly he said, "You're mistaken about the Confederate Army. There *is* one, and part of it is very near. Draw our blood and they'll level this place, and you with it."

Bearfield smiled coldly. "We'll accept that risk. Do you get down, or do we *cut* you down?"

Time for stalling had about run out.

David heard running horses. He saw surprise strike the men on the ground. Some stepped back, confused, fearful.

Mitchell had rushed his ten minutes.

Bearfield turned loose of the reins. Only then did David risk glancing around. Mitchell had deployed the troops in a broad line. They came in with rifles up and ready, trapping Bearfield and his men in the open.

David took his first good breath. Hernandez sighed in relief, still holding the knife. He jabbed the point of it at the hand of the Indian who held his bridle rein. The Indian turned loose, quickly raising the hand to his mouth to suck at the bleeding wound.

David looked at Bearfield again. Grimly he asked, "Was there anything else you wanted to say?"

Bearfield didn't look at him. Sullenly he watched the soldiers come in close. Some of the men around him raised their hands in response to the rifles pointed at them, but Bearfield stood with arms at his sides. The portly *majordomo* said something angry to him. Bearfield did not reply.

Noley Mitchell rode up beside David. David said, "Thank you, Sergeant. Your watch must be runnin' fast."

"I watched you through the glass, Davey. Looked like you might be glad to see us."

Luther Lusk reined up by Fermin Hernandez. "You all right, *chili*?" Hernandez assured him he was. Lusk looked accusingly at David. "Noley told you it was risky to come in here, Buckalew. We could've lost ourselves a good interpreter."

David smarted under the reproach but did not intend to lose dignity by arguing reasons. He said to Hernandez, "Call for everybody in the buildin' to come out, or we'll shoot these men."

Three more Indian men and two Mexicans came from inside. Two slatternly women followed, and finally a young Mexican girl. All the women were frightened, the girl most frightened of them all. Her face was bruised and swollen. Her clothing was ragged, barely enough left of it to cover her.

"Ask if that's all of them," David said sternly. "Tell them we'll search the place. If we find anybody hidin', we'll shoot him. And we'll shoot anybody who runs."

Hernandez relayed the message. The response from the people in the yard was that all were here.

"All right, men," David said stiffly, "pair up and make a search. If you find any people, do what I said. Shoot them." The last part of the order was made in anger. It was quickly regretted but not withdrawn. Mitchell left four men outside to stand guard. In a few minutes the soldiers came out. They found no people hiding in the long building, though out in back they discovered an old man working in a crude blacksmith shop and fetched him around.

Young Pete Richey said, "You don't really want us to shoot him, do you, Lieutenant? He's awful old."

David shook his head, glad the men hadn't taken him literally. "He's probably deaf . . . didn't hear the order."

The old man asked worried questions in mumbled Spanish; he didn't understand what was going on. He plainly expected to be killed. He turned to Pete Richey and began to plead.

Richey grabbed the old man's arm. He grasped the lapel of the coat the old man was wearing; the coat was much too big.

"Lieutenant," Richey declared, "I know this coat. It's the one T. E. Storey was wearin'."

A couple of the other Texans agreed, now that it had been pointed out to them. David saw what appeared to be a blotch of dried blood on the coat. Some attempt had been made to wash it out.

The old man couldn't understand what was being said, but he understood very well the angry tone of the voices. He turned and tried to break away, but his legs faltered. Richey quickly caught him, grabbing a handful of the loose coat.

In panic the old man reached down and picked up a rifle one of the others had dropped on the ground. He whirled. Luther Lusk fired, sending the old man sprawling backward, dead.

It had been so sudden that no one else moved; everybody seemed frozen for a moment. Then Jake Calvin said, "It's plain they killed Storey and Bender. I say we ought to shoot and kill every one of them right where he stands."

David thought Calvin was probably right. His own inclination was to shoot them all, other than the women, on general principles and for the good of the country. But he knew he wouldn't. He glanced at Sergeant Mitchell. "Gather up all the horses and mules into one corral."

Mitchell gave an order and took half a dozen men with him. In a few minutes they were back. The tall Homer Gilman was troubled. "Lieutenant, we found Storey's horse out yonder, and Aaron Bender's."

David and Mitchell gravely exchanged glances. David turned to Bearfield. "Would you like to explain how that came to be?"

Bearfield shrugged defensively. "How would I know? Indians come into this place all the time to trade. You don't ask an Indian where he's been or what he's done. It's nobody's business."

"Which ones came in on those horses?"

Bearfield shrugged again. "I don't know. I wasn't paying attention."

David was fairly sure he could pick out one of them, the one who had worn the coat that had caught his eye as he first rode in here. He knew now: it was Bender's.

He said for all the men to hear, "You see now why we have to stay together. You see what happens to men who go out by themselves."

Jake Calvin's eyes were narrow and angry. "I say we kill them all!"

The Texans' faces showed a majority in the same mood. David remembered his father's account of the difficulty Sam Houston had in preventing his victorious Texan soldiers from killing the captured Mexican general Santa Anna. "I'm tempted like all of you, but we can't be sure they were all in on it." His gaze shifted to Bearfield. "We came here to ask for directions."

"Ask. I'll tell you whatever I know."

"I feel sure you will, because we're takin' you with us."

Bearfield's mouth dropped open. "You'll kill me."

"If we have to. It's up to you to be sure we don't have to."

Bearfield looked quickly at his friends, anxiously seeking help. Evidently none understood what was said. "Where is it you want to go? I'll tell you right here."

"And maybe beat us there, and take a lot of friends with you? You'll come with us, and you'll tell us when I get ready to ask you. You'll stay with us till we get there, so that if you lie to us we can cut your throat."

David turned to Mitchell. "Sergeant, take a couple of men and catch out a few of the best horses. We'll need one for Bearfield, and we ought to take four or five more to spare."

Mitchell nodded. "We'll run off the rest, then."

"No. These people could soon catch them. If they try to follow after us they'll have to do it afoot. Shoot everything we don't take."

Bearfield protested, "You wouldn't do that!"

"I'd do worse, if I could. I'd burn this place like some kind of a pest-house." He knew the adobe building wouldn't catch fire, except perhaps its roof. Even if it did, the smoke might draw unwanted attention.

Mitchell took four men to the corrals. They carried some of the guns the trading-post people had dropped. In a few minutes the firing started. The trading-post men hadn't understood the order, but they understood the shooting, the screaming of horses and mules. They shouted their protests in vain. Bearfield watched in bitter silence.

Presently Mitchell and the men came back leading five horses, one saddled for Bearfield. David noted with satisfaction that the stirrups were taken up close, evidently for a short man. Bearfield was going to ride very uncomfortably.

Mitchell said, "We smashed the rifles. We figured that's what you'd want us to do."

David hadn't thought of it, but he said, "That's fine, Sergeant." He had the men take what they wanted of the weapons lying on the ground, then smash the rest. He told Bearfield to get onto the horse. Bearfield stood sullenly until Mitchell prodded him with a rifle. Mitchell took a short piece of rawhide he had picked up somewhere and tied Bearfield's hands to the big horn of the Mexican saddle.

When the troopers had mounted, David gave Fermin Hernandez a signal to lead off. They began stringing out, most looking back. They would have preferred to leave this post razed, the men all dead.

The Mexican girl shouted and came running after them. David saw one of the trading-post men grab at her, but she eluded him. She came on, running like a frightened rabbit, crying out in excited Spanish. David intended to keep riding, but Hernandez heard her and turned back. David halted reluctantly.

The girl grabbed David's leg and pleaded. Hernandez listened, his face darkening. He said, "The Indians, Lieutenant, they stole her out of Mexico. They sold her to the Comancheros, who have kept her here, prisoner." Eyes narrowed in hatred, he looked back at the post. "They do much bad to her. If she stays, they do bad to her some more."

David was about to explain that they couldn't take care of a woman.

One or more of the trading-post men had gone inside and fetched out hidden rifles. A shot was fired, possibly at David. The girl gasped as the bullet smashed into her back. She rolled forward against David's horse, then collapsed. The brown horse danced excitedly, trying to step away from her. David started to swing down but caught himself. One glance told him she had died instantly.

A cry of rage tore from Hernandez' throat. He brought up his own rifle and fired a quick shot at the crowd at the post. A man pitched forward. With a shout, Hernandez spurred back toward the building. In an instant, half the Texans were beside him, shouting in blood anger, firing as they rode.

David shouted vainly for them to stop. Of those who had hesitated, almost all rode back as a second wave, sweeping across the open ground, cutting off the trading-post men before they had time to reach the safety of the adobe building.

Floyd Bearfield thought it was his chance. He started tugging against the rawhide that bound his hands to the horn. David shoved the muzzle of his pistol against Bearfield's ear. "Try and I'll kill you!"

Only Noley Mitchell and Jake Calvin had held back with David. The rest had charged in, shouting, shooting.

Calvin held his ground, his face twisted. "I hope they don't kill them all. I hope they save one for me."

The shooting was over in a minute. The men came drifting back in threes and fours. They gathered around David and the sergeant in a rough circle, their faces still flushed with the outrage which had driven them. Fermin Hernandez dismounted and knelt silently by the girl. He looked up furiously at Bearfield.

Bearfield saw murder in the Mexican's face. He drew closer to David. "I'm your prisoner. You're not going to let him . . ."

David held his hand toward Hernandez, palm outward. "We need him."

Hernandez seemed strongly moved to do it anyway. But he stopped.

Luther Lusk was one of the last to ride up. He was holding someone in the saddle. "Noley," he called, "we got trouble."

The men pulled quickly aside. Pete Richey was slumped over, blood spreading down across his saddle and over his horse's shoulder. Gene Ivy and Homer Gilman, on the ground, got hold of him and eased him down. Lusk dismounted quickly and knelt by the boy. "Step back a little. Let me see to him." He ripped the coat and shirt away. The wound was in the left shoulder. The bullet had gone all the way through.

Gene Ivy cried out at the sight. He and Richey had grown up together.

Patrick O'Shea said, "I saw whiskey in the building. I'll go and fetch it."

David called after him to come back, that he didn't want another man shot there. Luther Lusk said, "Don't worry about him, Buckalew. Ain't nobody alive down there except the women."

In minutes O'Shea was back with a jug. Lusk tipped it up for a long swallow and shook his head violently. "Vile," he gritted. "But it'll clean out a wound."

Richey was still conscious, though the color had drained from his face, leaving it a bluish white. David felt cold, looking at him. The thing had been unnecessary; they shouldn't have charged back on that place. But it was done now. Recriminations wouldn't help anything.

Lusk finished the bandaging. "He oughtn't to ride."

David cursed under his breath. "We can't stay, and we can't leave him here. He's got to ride."

Lusk declared, "We didn't have to come into this post in the first place, Buckalew. Noley tried to tell you we oughtn't to."

David shouldn't have answered, but he couldn't help it. "I didn't order that charge. I tried to stop it." The words were hollow; the thing was done. "Get him onto his horse."

He saw Bearfield staring grimly back toward the post. Everything down there was quiet and still.

David said, "Bearfield, you're as safe as any of us so long as you try no tricks. Behave yourself and we'll turn you loose when we're through. Cross us and we'll leave you layin' like your friends back yonder."

He gave Hernandez a nod. The Mexican took a last look at the girl, her small, fragile body lying smashed on the ground. Then he set out again to point the way south.

CHAPTER 3

They rode a long time in moody silence. David did not want to set new directions too quickly lest their destination be anticipated by anyone following behind them. Late in the afternoon they made their usual stop to fix supper. Over a steaming cup of coffee, David stared coldly at Bearfield. The trader kept his gaze on the ground, but a gnawing anxiety showed in his face.

"Hernandez says you're a Comanchero. It strikes me that you're probably a man with a lot of blood on your hands."

"I never liked that word *Comanchero*. But Comancheros are simply traders. That's all *I* am. I buy and sell. I never kill anybody, Buckalew."

"But you make a market for those that do. You buy bloodstained goods. That makes you part of the killin'."

"I don't kill people."

"You were about to kill me and Hernandez." He decided the exchange was a waste of time. He asked, "Do you know Owen Townsend?"

He saw instant recognition in Bearfield's eyes, and perhaps even more than that. But Bearfield chose not to acknowledge it. "Townsend? What does he do?"

"He has a place somewhere. Either you know him or you don't. If you don't, you're of no use to us. The guarantee is off."

"I know him," Bearfield admitted grudgingly. His dislike was evident.

David's father had taught him that a man should be judged by his enemies as well as by his friends. Bearfield's enmity spoke favorably for Owen Townsend, Yankee or not. David said, "You're takin' us to his place."

Bearfield looked sharply at him. "Me, to Townsend's place? You don't know what you're asking. Anyway, I can't imagine what he has that you would want. If I know Townsend he's no friend of yours. He probably raises the Union flag in his bedroom."

"All you have to do is take us there."

Bearfield plainly disliked the prospect. "I would go around his place if I were you. He has nothing you need."

"Eat your supper. We'll move on in a few minutes."

The look of anxiety clung to Bearfield. "Even if he doesn't try to kill you, he'll probably try to kill *me*."

"What have you done to him?"

Bearfield's jaw tightened. He didn't answer.

David didn't care whether Bearfield ate supper or not. He was considerably more concerned about Pete Richey. The boy had been stretched out to rest on a blanket. Luther Lusk squatted beside him, chewing hardtack and sipping coffee, his eyes on the boy. David studied Lusk in silence. In the time he had been with the outfit he had not seen one thing in Lusk that he liked, one thing to give him any idea that Lusk was capable of concern over anyone except himself. But now he hovered over Pete Richey like some mother hen.

Richey lay still, his eyes closed. David couldn't tell whether he was conscious or not. "Has he eaten anything?"

Lusk grunted. "Did you think he would?"

"I hoped he might. He'll need his strength."

"How's he goin' to have any strength? He's been losin' blood, and he'll keep losin' it if he has to ride again."

"We can't stay here. We might *all* lose blood."

Lusk's eyes showed he was spoiling for a fight. "If there's anybody comin', this is as good a place as any. We can whip them here."

David said dubiously, "I never noticed you take an interest in this boy before."

"He never was hurt before." Lusk clenched his fist and cast a threatening look at Floyd Bearfield. "I've known his old daddy down home for a long time. He done me a favor once. A lifesavin' favor, you could call it."

David said, without conviction, "We'll get his boy back to him."

Lusk scowled. "I wisht I thought so."

Noley Mitchell eased over close, asking with his eyes if David needed help. David shook his head and walked away. "Finish up," he said loudly to everybody. "We'll travel a ways before dark." He could feel Lusk's hard eyes on his back; he didn't have to look. He motioned for trooper Homer Gilman to tie Bearfield's hands to the saddlehorn again. Gene Ivy was closer, but David wasn't certain of the youth's competence; he didn't want Bearfield taking advantage and getting away.

Bearfield said resentfully, "I won't run off."

"You bet you won't. Now, which way do we go from here?"

Bearfield cursed under his breath but did not otherwise resist. "Down the river. He built close to the water. There isn't enough water in this country that a man can locate just anywhere he wants to."

As he rode, David watched Bearfield. He began to notice that Bearfield sat straight in the saddle, with the style of a military man. He regarded the thought as an unlikely one. Why would a military man be living in the middle of nowhere with a set of cutthroats and thieves? But the notion kept nagging at him. Finally he asked.

Bearfield replied with bitterness. "Do I look like a soldier?"

"As a matter of fact, you do."

The wind was out of the south, and presently it brought David the faint smell of smoke. He saw that Mitchell had caught it too. "Not a grass fire, Davey," Mitchell said. "We'd see the sign of it, I think. This smells more like wood."

David turned in the saddle. "Bearfield, how far to Townsend's?"

Bearfield looked him in the eye without wavering. "Not far."

"Close enough to smell the smoke of their fires?"

"Perhaps."

David tried to read something in Bearfield's face, but the man had the air of a card player, his eyes a mask. Hernandez was about fifty yards out in front, moving up a steep rise in the fading red light of the afternoon sun. David was on the point of sending someone up to tell him to stop. Suddenly Hernandez halted at the top of the hill, turning his horse quickly and coming down. He was frantically signaling for the troops behind him to halt as he spurred back toward them. He pulled up in front of David, his horse's hind feet sliding, raising a little cloud of dust.

"Indians, Lieutenant! A camp of them is there, just over that hill." His face was flushed. He looked back over his shoulder as if he expected pursuit.

David asked urgently, "You think they saw you?"

"I don't know. I see *them*, and that is enough."

For a moment Bearfield was forgotten. He seized the opportunity to drum his heels against his horse's ribs. The horse started south in a run. David dropped his hand toward his rifle, then realized the danger in firing. "Don't anybody shoot!"

Several men spurred after Bearfield. Luther Lusk was in the lead. He caught up and grabbed at Bearfield's reins, at the same time ramming Bearfield's horse. The jolt bounced Bearfield up onto the cantle of his saddle. While he was out of balance Lusk gave him another hard bump, almost knocking the horse off of its feet. Bearfield slipped from the saddle and then began dragging, his hands tied to the horn, the brush tearing at his legs. He cried out from the pain.

Lusk got hold of the reins and took the horse into a wide circle, then brought him back toward David in a smart trot. He let Bearfield drag. He stopped beside David and held out Bearfield's reins as an offering. His voice was cold. "Here, Buckalew. You lost this."

Bearfield tried to pull himself up, tugging against the big horn of the Mexico saddle. The lower legs of his trousers were shredded. Blood showed on the frayed cloth around the knees.

"You lied to us," David accused. "Our deal was no tricks."

"I didn't lie to you," Bearfield said in a subdued voice, pinched with pain. "The Townsend place is down the river."

Maybe it was and maybe it wasn't. "But you didn't tell us about that Indian camp."

"Indians move around. You never know where they'll be."

"I'm bettin' you knew these were here. You figured to lead us into the midst of them and get us all killed, and yourself set free."

Bearfield's chest heaved; the jolting had pounded much of the breath from him. "Are you going to leave me dragging like this?"

David's foot was in the right position to kick Bearfield in the face. The temptation was strong. He turned. "Smith, you have a rope. Put a loop over Bearfield's neck."

Bearfield stared with wide eyes. "You wouldn't hang me."

"I would if I saw a tree big enough. The next time you run, we'll see how far your neck stretches."

David kept glancing at the hill beyond which Hernandez had seen the Indian camp. He could still smell the wood-smoke, drifting on the south wind. He was beginning to feel that the Indians hadn't seen Hernandez. A scouting party would have been here by now.

He considered his options. To cross over the Pecos at this point would be relatively easy, for it was not wide or turbulent here. But it was some distance east to any hills that might hide them from view of the Indian camp. Moreover, he considered it probable they might run into more Indians in that direction, toward the open plains. That possibility would probably be lessened if they moved back toward the New Mexico settlements. He looked at Hernandez and pointed west. "We won't let you get so far out in front from now on. We'll be close behind you if you run into anything."

Hernandez said nothing to indicate any gratitude.

They rode long into the darkness, putting miles between themselves and the Indian camp. For a time David kept Homer Gilman as a rear guard trailing some distance behind them out of concern that Indians might even yet ride in upon them. This concern did not leave him until night. The moon was late in rising, so they rode in almost pitch-blackness. As the moon came up, David spotted a dark motte of brush in the silver light. He gave quiet orders for pitching a dry, cold camp. He had Bearfield's hands tied to a tree. Bearfield complained that he could not sleep that way. Jake Calvin suggested that he knew how to put him to sleep. The complaints stopped.

Some of the men were without blankets. Several had volunteered their own in an effort to make Pete Richey as comfortable as they could. The boy was in considerable pain.

At daybreak Bearfield still lay where David had put him, his hands securely tied. If he had tried anything, half a dozen men would have fought over the privilege of killing him, and he knew it. His body was cramped from the uncomfortable positions to which his bonds had limited him. His eyes were streaked red; he hadn't slept.

Pete Richey lay awake, face pale and twisted with pain. David said, "You just keep ahold. We'll get there."

He judged that they could cut back toward the river now. A southeasterly course should bring them in well below the Indian camp. He hoped it would not bring them in below the Townsend place as well. Bearfield assured him it would not, and David had little choice but to gamble along. Perhaps by this time Bearfield was fearful enough of these Texans not to try springing any more traps.

They came back onto the river at midmorning. Bearfield was looking around with considerable agitation. David had an uneasy feeling he might know something he wasn't sharing. But presently Bearfield said, "You'll find the ranch just a short distance now, straight down the river."

"How far?"

"You'll see it soon. When are you going to set me loose?"

"When I get ready."

"I don't want to go all the way in to that ranch."

"We haven't seen it yet, much less gotten there."

Bearfield had told the truth. Hernandez stopped when his horse topped the next rise. He took a long look and rode back. "Settlement, Lieutenant."

David motioned to Noley Mitchell. The two of them accompanied Hernandez back up the hill. Below them perhaps a quarter mile lay an adobe ranch headquarters up the slope from the banks of the river, just safely beyond danger of flood. The buildings were clustered as in a fort, an open space around them, surrounded by a cedar picket fence four to five feet tall. The main building was large and in a hollow square with a typical Mexican patio in the center. David studied it a long time through the glass. He saw only one outside door facing in his direction. The outside windows were few and small, just large enough to let in a minimum of sun and fresh air and to give shooting room for riflemen inside in case of an attack.

The outer picket fence was far enough from the buildings that anyone who scaled it would have to face into open fire while running something like thirty to forty yards. Townsend—or whoever had built it—had intended to be well prepared for hostilities. There had been many enemies to worry about fifteen years ago. There probably still were.

He shuddered, thinking about the fearful price his men would pay if forced to attack that fortification by simple frontal assault, against even half their number of determined riflemen. That smacked of suicide and had no place in his plan.

Outside the picket fence but adjacent to it were two small adobe outbuildings and a pair of adobe-wall corrals, built thick to withstand Indian efforts at cutting them or breaking them down. David saw no gates into them except from within the picket-enclosed compound. To his considerable relief he saw only four horses in the pens. Several more grazed at some distance along the river, sharing the short old grass with some long-legged, long-horned cattle of the Mexican type.

He took that as a hopeful indication they would find few people here. At the distance he couldn't tell if the corraled horses might be military. Probably not, or there would be more. He handed the glass to Mitchell.

Mitchell made a long and careful study. "Looks all right."

David signaled for the rest of the troop to move up. "We'll ride down there in double file like we didn't expect trouble, and chances are there won't be any. If there is, spread out and attack while they're still off balance."

Lusk said sarcastically, "You want Pete Richey to attack too?"

David ignored Lusk and said to the whole command, "We're on a military mission. Let's look like soldiers."

He signaled for Hernandez to stay with the others this time, not to ride out in advance. David himself led the two columns down the hill.

He carried his rifle across the pommel of the saddle, his right hand around the trigger guard, ready in event of fire. He consciously straightened his back, trying to give the illusion of military bearing if not the reality.

For a moment his mind went home to his father, and back in time to another war in another place. If Joshua Buckalew were here, he wondered, would he handle this differently? Could he?

The Texans' approach was seen. Three men stepped out of the arched doorway that led into the patio. They moved into the sunlight but stayed near enough that they could quickly dart back into the relative safety of the patio. At least one carried a rifle, but he made no belligerent move with it. This gave David stronger hope that there would be no violence here.

One of the men took an extra couple of steps forward as David came within hailing distance. He carried no rifle. One of his arms hung stiffly at his side. He was an Anglo. The other two men, both younger, were Mexican.

David reined up and saluted. The one-armed man stood stiffly, in a manner suggestive of the military. He responded only with a nod. He raised his left hand in the Indian sign of peaceful intentions.

David said, "You'd be Owen Townsend, I suppose?"

The man seemed mildly surprised at the use of his name. "I am. I did not realize I was known in Texas." His sharp eyes searched David's face for something they didn't find.

"I am David Buckalew, Lieutenant, Confederate Army. My compliments to you, sir." For what, he could not have said.

"And mine to you, sir, and to your men."

Again, David would have been hard put to have found much for either side to compliment the other about. The Texans were a hard-used bunch, and this cedar-picket and adobe civilian fort was hardly a thing of classic beauty.

Townsend's voice was civil but not friendly. "Get down. I imagine you're all hungry. There isn't much here, but we always willingly share whatever there is."

"Much obliged, Mister Townsend. Our first need is some medical supplies. We have a wounded man."

Townsend's gaze immediately picked up Pete Richey. "Of course." He turned to one of the Mexicans and spoke in Spanish. The only word David understood was *Martha*. That, he assumed, would be Townsend's wife.

Townsend walked out to Richey's horse. The boy was hunched in the saddle, taking the punishment of the long ride with a stoicism David would not have suspected he possessed.

Townsend asked, "A brush with Union troops?"

Luther Lusk took it upon himself to answer. "No, sir, it was Comanchero traders. We put in at a tradin' post north of here." His eyes met David's. "That was a mistake."

"I know the people," Townsend said with bitterness. His gaze landed upon Floyd Bearfield. He took a startled step backward, then hatred filled his face. "Is that where you got *him*?"

Lusk nodded, mildly surprised at Townsend's reaction. "Yes, sir. Picked us up a prize, didn't we?"

Townsend noted with evident approval the rope around Bearfield's neck. "If you are looking for a place to tie the other end of it, there are some good strong trees down on the river. I'd be glad to escort you down there personally. In fact, I'd take it as a personal favor."

Lusk looked coolly at David. "I'd be pleasured, myself. But the lieutenant is given to makin' promises."

Townsend turned back to David. "Lieutenant, my invitation extends to you and all your Texans. It does not extend to that man. If he makes any attempt to set foot inside my home, I'll be obliged to kill him!"

Bearfield was anxious. "You promised me, Buckalew. I brought you here. Now turn me loose."

"When I'm ready." David shifted his attention to Townsend. "Bearfield is our prisoner, sir. You'll have to indulge us a little. We'll not impose on your hospitality any further than we have to."

Townsend said firmly, "I don't know what promises you've made, but I hope you're a practical man. I hope you recognize realities. Your word to a man like this is nothing, because *he* is nothing."

David thought, *If it's my word, it remains my word no matter who I give it to.* But he kept the thought to himself. He had more important business on his mind than to argue morality with a Yankee.

The corner of his eye caught a movement, and he quickly turned his head. A young woman stepped through the arch, shading her eyes with her hand. The wind caught her long skirt and boogered a couple of the nearest horses. She picked out Pete Richey and walked toward him.

Something about her jolted David. For a moment it was as if he knew her, as if the sight of her tried to summon up a memory hidden deeply in some dark recess of his mind. He stared, puzzled. There was no way he could ever have known this woman.

Her eyes were cold as she studied the boy slumped in the saddle. "How many of our men did he kill before they got him?"

David couldn't find voice to answer her.

Owen Townsend said, "It wasn't our men. He was wounded in a brush with Floyd Bearfield's people."

The name Bearfield seemed to hit her like a fist. She turned quickly, her eyes wide as she looked at Townsend. "They fought with Bearfield?"

Owen Townsend pointed. "He's their prisoner, Martha."

Her face seemed to drain of color as she saw Bearfield for the first time. Her hands lifted involuntarily to cover her mouth, as if to keep her from crying out. They turned to fists, and she suddenly ran forward, holding the fists together and using them to beat at Bearfield. She screamed at him.

Bearfield tried to pull back but was hemmed in. "Will somebody get this crazy woman away from me?"

The men were too startled to do anything except watch her. Owen Townsend stepped forward and grasped his daughter's shoulder. He pulled her around. "It'll be all right, girl. He's their prisoner."

She laid her head against his chest, her shoulders trembling. He held her with his good arm and said, "I apologize for my daughter. But she has good reason. We both do."

When she gained control, she turned again. Her eyes purposely avoided Bearfield. "Where's that wounded boy? Let's get him into the house where we can tend to him."

Luther Lusk and Gene Ivy lifted Richey down from the saddle. Carefully they carried him through the arch and toward the adobe building, following the fast-walking girl.

David stared after them, taken totally by surprise. It took him a minute to recover and get back to the pressing business. He found Townsend staring at Bearfield again, the hatred strong.

"Mister Townsend, how many people do you have here?"

"No Union troops, Lieutenant."

"How many of your own people?"

Warily Townsend hedged. "If I told you that, then you would know as much as I do."

"I *need* to know as much as you do, at least on this subject."

"I needn't remind you, Lieutenant, that we are on opposite sides. I'll give you whatever aid I can in a humanitarian way, and see you started on south. But that's as far as I can go."

David's voice firmed. "How many people, Mister Townsend?"

Townsend considered a moment, then relented, evidently seeing no way the information could be of great value to the enemy. "Just a few of us . . . my daughter . . . half a dozen Mexican ranchhands. Three of the men are married and have wives and children here. There's an old Mexican woman, too, mother to one of the men. She helps my daughter in the house."

"And *Missus* Townsend?"

Townsend seemed to flinch. "She's up the hill yonder. Buried."

"Oh. I'm sorry." David frowned, not fully trusting. "Doesn't seem like many people for a place of this size."

"We went north last year when you Texans came. Most of our help scattered. The thieves—red *and* white—took off a big part of our cattle. We haven't been back long enough to get our help together again." He added pensively, "As you've surely noted by now, Lieutenant, war is a very expensive enterprise. I wish we could get by without it."

"We didn't ask for it either."

"Then who did? I keep asking myself."

Townsend started toward the patio entrance. "I'll get some women commenced cooking. We don't have much except beef. I imagine you'll be anxious to get on your way. You never know when Union troops may show up." The last, David thought, was said hopefully.

David followed him into the shade of the patio. "You're a long way from any real settlement here."

Townsend considered, suspicious of the comment. "Tolerably."

"Come right down to cases, you're pretty far out onto Indian territory. How do you manage to keep your scalp on?"

"With care, Lieutenant." Townsend gazed back out the archway toward the spread of far blue mountains and across the valley that was beginning to show the first tinge of green for an observer who used imagination. "Out here you don't look to other people to help you much; you take care of yourself. Government means little to you . . . Mexican, American, Confederate . . . You fight your own battles or avoid them. You make your own treaties, your own compromises. I've lived around Indians for most of thirty years. I came out here in the early times and trapped beaver when this was still part of Mexico. A man had to be watchful then. If he got careless his scalp wound up on an Indian lance or he wound up in a Mexican prison. I learned to be watchful and to get along. I've made my own treaties and kept them, even when armies couldn't do it. The only real trouble I've had has been from men like Bearfield, who know no truth and no law."

David did not try to hold back his curiosity. "What did Bearfield do to you, sir?"

Townsend's face pinched. An old anger was in his eyes. But he said only, "Enough." He knotted his good hand into a fist. "You wouldn't think so now, but he was a soldier once. I knew him then. He was an army supply officer, and a good one until he became addicted to some of the major vices. You can't afford those on military pay. He began converting government supplies to his own use. Some army rifles fell into Indian hands and were traced back to him. He deserted just ahead of a court-martial. I suppose his skill as a supply officer has been good use to him in his present trade." Townsend looked around.

"When you're through with him, I don't suppose you would turn him over to me?"

"For the U.S. Army?"

"No. Just for me."

David shook his head. "No sir, I reckon not." He followed Townsend through a doorway and into what he found was a parlor. The adobe wall, he noted, was fully two feet thick. He stopped and measured the door facing with his hand.

Townsend said, "We built the place to last through my grandchildren's time."

"How many do you have?"

A momentary sadness passed over Townsend's face. "None." He turned away. David sensed that he had touched him where he hurt.

Women's voices were speaking Spanish in the next room. David walked to the doorway to look. Pete Richey lay on a cot. His shirt had been removed. Luther Lusk stood holding it, evidently waiting for orders from the Townsend girl. Martha Townsend, wearing a white apron tied snugly around a slender waist, was washing Richey's chest and shoulders with a large wet cloth. By the smell of it, David judged she was using alcohol. Her hands were gentle but sure.

The setting and the smell took him back. For a moment he was in the makeshift military hospital in Albuquerque, trying to fight his way through a painful fog to the light, trying to see the faces of the people who hovered over him, the people to whom belonged the hands which worked on him as Martha Townsend's worked on Pete Richey now. David thought of a girl he had seen so dimly, a girl whose hands had been gentle but whose face had been a blur to him, a girl he had wished ever afterward that he might see again, to know if she was really as beautiful as she had seemed.

He studied Martha Townsend, wondering if Pete Richey saw her now as David had seen that girl in Albuquerque. David saw her clearly enough to know she was not beautiful. He was not sure he would even call her pretty. Perhaps he might, if he had not seen the snap of hostility in those blue eyes as she had first stepped out of the house and looked upon the Texans.

Joshua Buckalew had admonished him never to judge by beautiful features or beautiful skin. Real beauty, real character was to be found in the eyes, he had said. *The eyes tell the truth when the face lies.*

She noticed him standing in the door and gave him an impatient flash of those blue eyes, seeming to suggest that he find gainful employment elsewhere.

David said to Owen Townsend, "This is not a job I enjoy pushin' off onto a woman."

"She knows what she's doing. She was a volunteer in the military hospital while we were in Albuquerque."

David frowned. *Could it have been her after all?* Somehow he hoped not. The dream had been a thing of beauty to him, one of the few good things he had found in all these months in New Mexico. That girl across the room fell far short of the dream.

He watched her skillful hands wrap a fresh bandage securely around Richey's wound. A Mexican woman helped, handing her what she asked for. Luther Lusk turned Richey partway over when Martha Townsend told him to.

David held silent until the job was done. "What about Pete? How's he goin' to be?"

She only glanced at David, then looked back at the boy. "He should live, I think, if you don't kill him making him ride. But I suppose you will. Taken as a whole, Texans are a thoughtless lot, from what I've seen of them. The Union should have been glad to let you secede, and good riddance."

David forced down the quick anger that stirred in him. Anger was of no use to him here. *Attitudes like hers were the reason for this war in the first place*, he thought.

She said, "It's time we all got out of here and let this young man have some rest. We can't go with you standing in the middle of the door."

David quickly stepped aside. Thinking about it then, he wished he had taken more time. It would have been more seemly. What galled him most, he thought, was that Luther Lusk had seen him move at the girl's command.

But Lusk showed no sign that he had noticed. He seemed pleased. "Looks like old Pete's goin' to make it."

The girl nodded. "But he'll need a lot of rest."

David shook his head. "I'm afraid he can't rest long. We have to be movin' south pretty soon."

"You could leave him here. He would be well cared for."

"And be a prisoner the first time Union troops came by."

"Hardly anyone ever comes by, Lieutenant."

"We did. And chances are good that we're bein' trailed by Union cavalry. I wouldn't like the thought of that boy spendin' the rest of the war in a Union prison."

A dark humor came briefly into the girl's eyes. "When we were in Albuquerque I heard some of you Texans brag that the war wouldn't last three months."

David felt anger stirring again. He tried not to give her the satisfaction of seeing him rise to the bait. "I'm surprised you'd even offer to keep Richey here and take care of him, as little as you think of Texans."

"Your Mister Lusk told me about the skirmish with the Bearfield people. That helps outweigh the fact that you're Texans. Incidentally, he mentioned that you didn't take part in it."

David flinched.

She went on, "Anyway, this boy is wounded. That makes him different."

"*I* was wounded, once." He said it with a motive, thinking perhaps she would look closer, perhaps recognize him.

She showed no sign that she did. "Evidently you got over it."

Owen Townsend seemed to decide his daughter had said enough. "Martha, I wish you would get a few of the women together and start cooking up something for these men, so they can be on their way."

She protested, "You know that boy in there needs rest."

"They may *all* have a long rest if Union cavalry should find them here. We don't want this place turned into a battleground."

David said, "Neither do we. That's why we'll stay no longer than absolutely necessary. The cooking can wait, Mister Townsend. Right now I'll have to ask you to get all of your people outside."

Townsend's eyes showed alarm. "What are you going to do?"

"We won't harm anybody unless we're forced to it. But we need to have all your people outside where we can watch them."

Townsend demanded stiffly, "Watch them do *what*? Nobody here is going to make any move against you or your men."

"I hope not, because we've got to search your place."

Townsend darkened. "This is a gross abuse of our hospitality."

Martha Townsend's face was flushed crimson, her arms folded tightly across her breasts.

In a few minutes the ranch people were gathered in the open patio. Most were fearful, a couple of the Mexican men belligerent, looking to Owen Townsend for leadership. David sensed that if Townsend gave the word, they would put up a fight. David counted and tried to remember just how many people Towsend had told him there were. "Is this all of them?"

Townsend's civility was gone. Tautly he said, "All but two men out on horseback, looking for cattle. They'll be in before dark."

David took him at his word; he could do little else. He turned toward his own men, who were watching the Townsend people distrustfully. "Now I want you all to spread out and go through the house. You know what you're lookin' for. That's *all* you're lookin' for, except guns. Whatever guns you find, bring them out."

His gaze swept their faces. Whatever he might think of them in other respects, he had no reason to believe any of his men were thieves. As the soldiers disappeared into the house, David turned back to Townsend. "My apologies, sir. This is my first war. I've already found out we have to do things we'd rather not do."

Martha Townsend demanded, "What do you think you'll find in there? Do you think we've hidden a troop of Union soldiers?"

David looked her straight in the eye. "I think you know what we're lookin' for, Miss Townsend. Your father does."

He saw the quick look that passed between father and daughter. Up to that moment he was not certain that she did know. Now there was no question in his mind. He said, "I wouldn't insult you by askin' you to tell us where to look, Mister Townsend. We'll find it ourselves without compromise to your patriotism."

Martha Townsend said harshly, "That is very considerate."

"Your father can take comfort in knowin' we didn't find out through him."

He could see the question burning in Townsend's eyes: how *had* they found out? But to ask would be to admit of knowledge. Townsend held silent.

Floyd Bearfield leaned against the wall in a corner of the patio. Fermin Hernandez had remained to keep him under guard. Hernandez kept his rifle aimed loosely in Bearfield's direction, not directly at him but close enough that Bearfield could not forget about it for a minute. Bearfield studied David and Townsend with much curiosity. He never had been told why the Texans were looking for the Townsend ranch; he still didn't know. David saw no point in telling him.

In a little while the soldiers began coming back empty-handed. David counted them off, one by one. His confidence, at a high point when the search had started, began to ebb sharply. The last one out was Noley Mitchell. The old peace officer shook his head. "Sorry, Davey, but it looks like we've come up dry."

Uneasily David protested, "It's got to be here. Maybe there's a cellar under the house."

"We found the cellar all right. There wasn't nothin' in it but some supplies of one kind and another. No munitions."

Bearfield pushed away from the wall and stood straight, suddenly highly interested. His lips formed the word *munitions*, though he did not speak aloud.

Luther Lusk spat. "I could of told you we wouldn't find no such thing in the house, or under it either. If somethin' had ever touched it off, there wouldn't of been enough left of this place to build a chicken coop. If there ever *was* any munitions—which I doubt—they've hidden them someplace out away from here."

"It's here," David argued. "If it wasn't here they wouldn't have sent a Union detail out to recover it."

Townsend's jaw dropped. "Detail? What's this about a Union detail?"

David considered before answering. "I don't guess there's any reason we oughtn't to tell you. Indians wiped out a Union detail. I found a letter on the officer." He fished the letter from his pocket and read the first part to Townsend. The ranchman clenched his fist.

David said, "I didn't intend to ask you, Mister Townsend, but now I've got to. Where is that cache at?"

Townsend looked at him with a strong measure of doubt. "You sure it was Indians? You sure *you* didn't do it?"

"It was Indians."

Townsend was frowning. "We're in a war, Lieutenant, and you're my enemy. If I told you anything, that would be treason . . . giving aid and comfort."

David's fists knotted in frustration. He wished he knew the man well enough to be aware of a weakness. "Mister Townsend, if I had more time I might be able to play with you, but I don't. I'm askin' you again."

Townsend gave no ground. David looked at the Mexicans, wondering which of them might be easiest to break.

Townsend was ahead of him. "No use wasting your time on my people. They know nothing. They had no part in it. Even if you tortured them, there's nothing they can tell you."

David took him at his word. "Then, that just leaves you."

Martha Townsend said bitterly, "There's also *me*. Why don't you torture *me*, Lieutenant?"

Owen Townsend turned on his daughter. "This one time you'd better hold your tongue, girl. It could get you into more trouble than you can handle."

She started to say more, but David cut her short. "I was taught a long time ago—honor thy father."

Sarcastically she said, "So you know a little Scripture . . . Somehow I'm surprised."

"This might be a good time for a little Scripture. We're on serious business here. We mean to find that cache."

But the determined look in the Townsends' eyes told him he wasn't going to find it by asking them. And he and his men didn't have time to dig holes all over this ranch.

Floyd Bearfield took a step forward. "You never have asked *me*, Buckalew." He had an air of confidence he hadn't shown since losing the advantage at the trading post.

"What do you know about it?" David asked, suspicious.

"I know things about this ranch that you wouldn't find out if you prowled around here for a month. And you don't have a month."

"You know where the stuff is hidden?"

"I know a logical place where it *might* be hidden."

David saw a flicker of concern in Townsend's eyes. That was enough. "Go on, then. Tell me what you know."

Bearfield shook his head. "Not that easy, Texan. I don't just give it to you. I trade."

"Trade for what?"

"Freedom."

"I've already promised you freedom."

"I want a good fast horse to be sure I can keep that freedom after you've delivered it." He glanced at Townsend; murder was in the rancher's eyes. Bearfield said, "You see why I need the horse."

"You'll have time to get away."

"But I want something else, too. I want a percentage of the goods."

David shook his head. "A horse, but no percentage."

Bearfield asked, "How much munitions do you expect to find?"

David didn't answer.

Bearfield said, "It must be a fair amount if you're willing to go to so much trouble for it. You could spare me some. We need it, the business we're in, the people we deal with. It's a dangerous life."

"A lot *more* dangerous for the people you come across. No guns or ammunition for you, Bearfield. Just the horse."

"I don't see that you're in a position to argue. You can't afford to go hunting for it; you're fighting against time. Any hour now, Union soldiers may come riding over that hill."

David couldn't help himself; he glanced at the hill over which he and his men had come.

Luther Lusk scowled at Bearfield. "Lieutenant, if you'd just turn him over to me and the boys, I believe we could persuade him to take a more liberal view."

It was the first time, offhand, that David could remember agreeing with Lusk. He gave the matter some consideration.

Bearfield discerned the drift of David's thinking. "You promised. You promised you'd set me free."

David looked him in the eye. "I'm a horse trader by profession. Horse traders have been known to lie. Sure, I promised to set you free. But I didn't promise I'd keep some of my men from trailin' right after you. I'll give you freedom, but it'll be up to you to try and keep it."

Luther Lusk rubbed his powerful right fist into the palm of his left hand. "Give him his freedom now, Buckalew. Give him a hundred yards head start."

Bearfield seemed to wilt a little. He could see that David was considering the proposition seriously. "All right, no share. Just the horse. And nobody follows after me, is that agreed? Nobody follows after me."

"I can't speak for anybody but my men and me. *We* won't come after you. What Townsend and his people do is somethin' I can't control after we leave here. You'll have a good head start."

"An hour. Give me an hour on Townsend and I'll make it from there."

Townsend warned, "You'd better think hard before you make promises to him, Buckalew. He might be lucky and find some of his Indian friends out yonder. He would turn around and come after you."

"Do *you* want to tell me where the goods are hidden, Mister Townsend? Then I wouldn't have to trade with him at all."

Townsend paced in a tight circle, brooding. "You know I can't do that." David gave him a little time, hoping the rancher might weaken. Townsend halted and looked back at him. "Lieutenant, I'm not admitting to anything. But if there *were* a store of goods such as you're talking about, what could you do with it? You couldn't haul it away from here on horseback. There's no way you could get any good from it."

"I'm not worried about gettin' any good from it, sir. All I intend to do is to take the harm out of it. I'm goin' to blow it up."

Bearfield protested, "Blow it up? Good God, man, do you have any idea what that stuff is worth today?"

David brought his hand up to his half-healed arm and replied with bitterness, "I know what it's worth, turned against my people."

"I'll buy it from you, Buckalew. Depending on how much of it there is, I'll pay you in gold, and I'll swear to you that no Union troops will ever use a pound of it."

"And what would you do with it, Bearfield? How many stolen cattle and horses would the Comanches trade you for it? How many stolen Mexican girls? And you know what the Indians would do with those goods. They would raid down into lower Texas, and plumb into Mexico, to bring you *more* stolen goods. And how many of my people would they kill in the process?" He knotted his fists and took a step forward. "You said you'd take us to it. Do it now or I turn you loose with a hundred-yard start . . . afoot!"

Bearfield sullenly gave in. He pointed his chin. "Yonder, down the river. There's a cave down there, a big one."

"A cave?"

"Indian traders used to store goods in it before Townsend came here and took over this part of the country for himself."

Anger boiled in Townsend's eyes. David sensed that Bearfield had struck upon the truth.

Townsend's voice was barbed with fury. "I already owe you for blood, Bearfield. Now I owe you for treason." He turned away, his face dark. With his back to David he said, "You've found out what you wanted to know, Lieutenant. Now I'd be obliged if you'd get that man away from here. I can't stand to look at him or to smell him."

David should have felt exhilaration, but he didn't. He felt like a participant in some dark and unsavory conspiracy. "Mister Townsend, under better circumstances . . ." He let it trail off, hoping Townsend would know what he meant to say.

Townsend still didn't look at him. "Am I a prisoner, or am I free to go back into my house?"

"It's your house. But I'll ask you not to leave it."

David saw a grin on Luther Lusk's face. For the first time, this contrary frontiersman was beginning to believe. And he saw a gleam of approval in the eyes of Noley Mitchell. "Davey," the sergeant said, "you just may make an officer yet."

David didn't have time to bask in the glow of this unaccustomed approval. He turned to Lusk. "I want you to stay here with most of the men and watch over things."

Lusk shook his head. "No siree, Buckalew. I'm goin' to take a look in that cave."

"I'm givin' you an order, Lusk."

"And I'm tellin' you to take your order and go to hell with it."

The two men glared, each waiting for the other to back down. David said, "When we get back to Texas, you'll have a lot to answer for."

"We ain't there yet by a good ways."

The farm boy, Gene Ivy, volunteered, "Lieutenant, I'll stay here and watch after things."

David realized he could not let the thing pass; Lusk had challenged him, and he must meet that challenge if he expected to keep any discipline in this command until he could get the men safely home. He kept his eyes grimly on Lusk, finding no evidence that the frontiersman was going to back away. He slowly drew his pistol from its holster and brought it up to bear on Lusk. "I gave you an order."

Lusk tried to hold his gaze on David's eyes, but finally he was forced to look down at the pistol. David knew then that he had him. He held his hand rock-steady. Lusk looked back into David's eyes and swore under his breath. "You'd do it. I believe, by God, you'd do it."

"I'd do it."

Noley Mitchell decided it was time to take a hand. "Luther, we've got more to do than watch you try to match determination with the lieutenant. If he says stay, I reckon you'll stay and try to act like it was your idea in the first place."

Lusk hunched. "I was just tryin' him out."

The sergeant impatiently shook his head. "Looks to me like you'd get tired of that. You've already found out he'll do what he says he will."

"*You* wouldn't shoot a man like that, would you, Noley?"

"I don't know. I ain't a lieutenant."

David wished at that moment that Mitchell *were* the lieutenant. But he could see that Lusk's resistance was over. How many more tests would he have to surmount before he could get these men home and rid himself of this unwanted responsibility?

Gene Ivy said again, "Lieutenant, I'll stay here."

The lad's eagerness to please somehow lifted a little of the burden and made David's spirits rise a little. "Thanks, Ivy." He looked around. "Where's Homer Gilman?" The tall miller stepped out from behind some of the other men. "Here, Lieutenant."

"Gilman, I'm leavin' you in charge. I want you to post guards around the place and see that no civilians leave here till we've finished the job. I don't want them findin' help and bringin' it down on top of us. Other than that, you don't hurt anybody and you don't bother anything. Is that clear?"

Gilman looked at Mitchell, then said, "Sure is, Lieutenant."

David, Mitchell and Hernandez saw to their horses. Two other men, the immigrants O'Shea and Hufstedler, were picked to go along. Mitchell said to the Irishman, "Patrick, there is a rope on Smith's saddle. I wish you would put a loop around Bearfield's neck."

The Irishman hummed some kind of a chanty as he moved gladly to comply. Bearfield's eyes narrowed resentfully as the rope was placed around his neck. O'Shea drew it up tighter than was necessary, enough perhaps to give Bearfield's skin a burn. The man flinched and started to voice a protest but thought better of it and said nothing. He slouched in the saddle, smoldering.

They rode down to the river, the Texans and Floyd Bearfield. Then they turned south, following the flow of the water. Half a mile down, Bearfield pointed. "That's it, just under that little bluff."

David squinted. At first he didn't see it and suspected that Bearfield lied. When he finally spotted it he realized how easily he could have ridden past without discovering it. A scattering of low brush obscured the opening.

Bearfield said, "An old Mexican told me he hid in there once for two days from some Indians who had bought bad whiskey from him. They were from out on the plains and didn't know this piece of country. Afterwards he used this place to hide his trade goods."

Riding up to the cave, David decided it would have been feasible for the Yankees to bring their wagons within twenty or thirty feet of the small opening. They wouldn't have to carry the goods by hand very far. He dismounted. The opening was large enough that he could walk into it by bending at the waist; he wouldn't have to get on his knees and crawl.

Noley Mitchell stared speculatively at the cave. David was mildly surprised to see a stirring of excitement in the sergeant's eyes. "By God, there *is* a cave," Mitchell said.

"You doubted it?"

"To be honest with you, Davey, I've doubted this whole thing all along. It's been such a long time since I've seen anything work out right in this crazy country . . ."

"You saw the Yankee letter."

"Saw it, but somehow I couldn't ever quite believe in it. I guess I figured when we got here we'd find that the Yankees had already taken everything away, if they had ever left it here in the first place. You've been away from home long enough to see how armies operate. One hand never knows what the other hand is up to. Mostly they just stumble along like a man in the dark and hope the other side stumbles worse."

David said, "We found the cave, but we still don't know if there's really anything in it."

Mitchell nodded. "You want me to go in first?"

"No, I'll go."

"I'd move a little slow, was I you. For all you know a bear might've taken a likin' to it, or a mountain lion. They may not take a likin' to *you*."

"Then you'd be rid of me."

"You think the boys would breathe easier for that?"

"I know they would."

He handed his reins to O'Shea and told him to keep an eye on

Bearfield. "Hufstedler, you go up on top and keep a lookout. Hernandez, you go upriver a ways and watch. We don't want anybody slippin' up on us."

Bearfield said sullenly, "I've done everything you brought me for. I've shown you the ranch, and I've shown you the cave. It's time you turned me loose."

"When I'm ready."

Bearfield glared at him in hatred. "You don't intend to turn me loose. You're goin' to kill me, or let Owen Townsend do it."

It wasn't in Bearfield's nature to trust anyone, or to accept a promise for what it was, David decided.

"Bad as I hate to," he said, "I promised to turn you loose, and I will. But in *my* time, not in yours."

He stooped and moved slowly into the gloom of the cave, sniffing for animal scent that might indicate he was not alone. He found only the dry smell of ancient dust, bitter to his nostrils. It seemed to rise up each time he moved his feet. He heard a noise and turned quickly, half expecting something to jump at him. Noley Mitchell had followed him into the cave.

David paused, letting his eyes adjust slowly to the poor light. He could get no clear idea of the cave's size. Farther back the ceiling appeared high enough that he could stand erect. Wind never reached far into this cave, and moisture never touched it. He saw old boot tracks in the dust, disturbed only by a crisscrossing of newer animal tracks. Beyond them was a dark and shapeless bulk, covered in grayed tarpaulins. David wished for a torch that he might see better, but he knew that was a foolish notion. If this *was* the cache, one spark in the wrong place would blow him and the others to the far side of the Pecos River.

He found the corner of a tarp and raised it. Behind it was a stack of kegs. He rolled one out and saw the word painted on it: *powder*.

He forgot about dignity and decorum. He forgot all the rules that had been drilled into him about proper conduct for an officer and a gentleman. He whooped loudly and danced half a dozen jig steps across the dusty floor.

A voice from the cave opening said, "Noley, I do believe the boy's human after all."

Luther Lusk was standing there. David started to ask how, but he already knew. He said, "You just don't follow orders, do you?"

Lusk shook his head. "Not worth a damn." He took several strides across the dusty floor and threw the tarp back farther. He glanced at the sergeant, his eyes wide with surprise. "You see that, Noley? By God, the kid was right all the time. It's here. It's here!" He turned to David. "How much of it is there?"

"They're supposed to be sendin' ten wagons for it."

"Ten wagons." Lusk stared at the cache with those dark hawk eyes and rubbed his mouth and chin fiercely.

David said, "Lusk, as long as you're here you'd just as well set in to makin' a hand. Let's roll a few of those powder barrels out. We'll make a trail of powder across the floor and down toward the river. That'll give us time to get clear before the whole thing goes up."

Lusk blinked. "Ten wagonloads. That's enough to move this hillside down and dam up the whole Pecos River."

David nodded. "Then Mister Townsend will have himself a real fine lake."

"Maybe right up into his bedroom."

David repeated, "Lusk, let's get movin' with those barrels."

Noley Mitchell had been staring silently at the cache. He held up the palm of his hand. "Let's wait a minute, Davey. I think maybe we ought to stop and talk this thing over."

David looked at him, puzzling. "I don't see how we can go wrong. It'll be the easiest thing in the world to touch it off."

"I wasn't thinkin' about touchin' it off, Davey. I was thinkin' about *not* touchin' it off."

"We've got to. You know how much damage the Yankees can do us with all this stuff."

"If they get it. But it occurs to me that they don't have to get it, and we don't have to blow it up, either. Instead of the Yankees usin' this against us, we could use it against them. All we've got to do is haul it out of here to where it'll do us the most good."

David blinked in surprise. "How? On horseback? We couldn't carry enough with us to spike a cannon. Townsend doesn't have but one decent wagon that I saw. I'd figured to take that with us to haul Pete Richey."

"Accordin' to your letter the Yankees are sendin' ten wagons. We could just wait and use those."

"The wagons aren't comin' by themselves. There'll be soldiers with them, maybe a lot of soldiers."

"Strategy, Davey. When the other side's got the biggest strength you use strategy. I'll bet if we put our heads together we can figure out a way to persuade them Yanks around to our way of thinkin'."

David turned and looked at the large store of munitions. For just a wild moment . . .

Mitchell kept pressing him. "Ten wagonloads of shot and shell. Think on it, Davey. A whole damned war could be fought with that, if we could get it to the right place and at the right time."

The notion was contagious. David let his imagination run unbridled. For a moment he pictured a narrow pass, perhaps somewhere to the south, an entrapment like the Yankees had made against the Texans in Apache Canyon, except that this time it would be the other way around, the Yankee Army being euchered into a trap from which they couldn't escape.

Mitchell said, "We been goin' towards home with our tails between our legs. You think you're the only man in this outfit who's felt that way, Davey? We've all felt it. Now here we stand, lookin' at a chance to stay in the fight after all. We've got one last chance to come out of this thing with some dignity and pride. Hell, who knows? If everything broke for us just right we might even turn this war around and start a whole new push to the north again. We might drive them people clear back into Colorado, and back out to California. We almost done it once. Who's to say we couldn't do it again with a little luck? A little luck and ten wagonloads of ammunition?"

The vision was staggering. The temptation was almost overwhelming.

Almost. But David saw the flaw. "There's too many *ifs* in it, Sergeant.

It works *if* we can take the wagons away from the Yankees. It works *if* some other Yankee force doesn't catch up to us before we can get clear of the country. But supposin' one of those *ifs* goes against us? The Yankees recover the whole thing, and we've made this trip for nothin'. Some of us—probably most of us—will die, wasted. No, it's safer to do what we came here for. Blow it up." He turned to roll out a barrel of powder.

He heard a shot. For a second he froze, thinking this whole cache was about to explode, with him and the others on top of it.

Lusk declared, "Outside! Somethin's gone wrong outside!" He stooped and rushed back out through the opening. David sprinted across the cave. As he went, he heard another shot, and still another.

The sunlight blinded him for a moment. He saw Lusk standing with his arm outstretched, trying to take aim at something moving. Lusk's pistol roared.

Floyd Bearfield was getting away.

From on top of the hill, Hufstedler fired his rifle as Bearfield came into his view. It was a forlorn hope; David had been told Hufstedler was the poorest shot in the command. David called for him to cease fire. He turned, knowing what he would find and dreading it.

Patrick O'Shea lay in a spreading pool of his own blood. He coughed painfully, struggling for breath. David could tell at a glance that he had few left to him.

"I'm sorry," O'Shea rasped, "I tried . . . to look in the cave . . . He . . . surprised me . . ."

Luther Lusk and Fermin Hernandez had spurred after Bearfield, but David knew the chase was hopeless. Bearfield had too long a start. He cursed softly. "He didn't have to do this. I was goin' to turn him loose."

Mitchell said, "*He* didn't believe that."

"But I was . . ."

Hufstedler half slid, half ran down the hill, shouting, "Patrick! Patrick!" From where he had been he probably could not have seen what was happening down here. David had sent him up there for a better view of different terrain. The German stopped, staring with wide eyes, then dropped to his knees beside the dying Irishman. "Damn you, Patrick," he said thickly, tears streaking his cheeks, "I ought to kick for you your butt! What for you let him shoot you?"

O'Shea was past answering him, or even hearing. He lived a few more minutes, gradually falling back further and further beyond reach. The breathing stopped, and the only sound was from Hufstedler, alternately crying out in grief and in rage.

Hernandez and Lusk came back in a little while, their horses lathered from the fruitless run. Lusk's face was dark with frustration. "He lost us over in them hills. He knows them, and we don't."

David turned to Noley Mitchell. "It was a great notion, Sergeant, for a few minutes. But now we've *got* to blow up that cache."

"I don't see why."

"Bearfield will listen for the explosion. If he doesn't hear it he'll pretty soon figure out what we're up to. He wants that stuff as much as we do. He'll come after it sooner or later. We're just seventeen men now, sixteen when you count out Pete Richey. We can't fight off Yankees and Bearfield both."

Mitchell looked at Lusk, who knew what he was talking about, and at Hernandez, who hadn't heard any of the earlier conversation. "There might be a bunch of us willin' to try."

"Not at the risk of lettin' these goods fall into the wrong hands. We're goin' to set fire to it and run like hell." He turned and started back for the mouth of the cave. He heard a few half-whispered words pass between Mitchell and Lusk. Someone stepped up quickly behind him. David felt something poke him in the back.

Lusk's voice spoke firmly, "You'd best raise your hands, Buckalew. I'm takin' the borry of your pistol."

David stiffened. He might have expected many things, but not this. He lifted his hands and felt the pistol being drawn from his holster. He turned, easing his hands down, knowing they wouldn't likely shoot him. Lusk still had a pistol aimed his way and held David's pistol loosely in his left hand.

David turned accusing eyes at Noley Mitchell. The sergeant stood straight, his jaw grim and determined.

"Sergeant," David said, "I wouldn't be surprised at anything from Lusk. But *you* . . ."

"Sorry, Davey. But this time I reckon we're goin' to have to do things my way."

David looked to Hernandez and Hufstedler. Neither comprehended the run of events, but neither showed any disposition to help David. He knew their first loyalty was to Mitchell. Both seemed to be waiting for the sergeant to explain.

David looked into the muzzle of Lusk's pistol and shivered involuntarily. He was not afraid; he was confident that nobody intended to kill him unless he crowded them into it. More than anything he felt frustration. Everything had gone sour in this damned war, for the Texas forces in general and for him individually. He hadn't wanted to be put in charge of this detail in the first place, and he had never been able to win anything better from most of the men than a grudging tolerance. Now even that little seemed lost.

He said tautly, "This is rebellion."

Lusk replied, "I thought that's what the whole war is."

Noley Mitchell motioned for Lusk to lower the pistol. "No need to point that thing at him, Luther. It might go off."

David turned to Mitchell. "This'll go hard with you, Sergeant, when we get back to Texas."

Mitchell smiled, a little. "Davey, you're young, and I make allowances for the young. Time a man's my age he's seen most of what the world has to offer, and seen *through* a lot of it. You're too young to've seen through much. They make all them fancy speeches and tell you how it's supposed to be, and it's too much to expect of a young feller to know what's real and what's talk. They tell you you're an officer and a gentleman, and that everybody else has to obey you because they've put a gold bar on your coat. That's all right, when everything is goin' the way it ought to. But there comes a time, when nothin' goes right, that somebody has to step in and show you what the real world is."

"And you've taken it on yourself to do that?"

Mitchell nodded regretfully. "I've stood by you and done what I could to keep you from makin' any real bad mistakes. And I'll have to say that, considerin' your limited experience, you ain't done bad at all. But this time I believe you're wrong. I believe we've got a good chance here to strike a blow for Texas. Since you *don't* believe it, I've got to bring you around to my way of thinkin', or I've got to take the command away from you."

"Looks to me like you've already done that."

"Maybe. Maybe not. It depends on you."

"You mean you'd give the command back to me, provided I do what you tell me to?"

"Somethin' like that."

"It wouldn't really be command then, would it?"

"Nobody ever has total command, except for God. I have no wish to shame or belittle you, Davey. But I want us to take this chance for the good of Texas. For the good of the men in this detail. For me and you."

"It's a long risk. If it doesn't work, how is it for the good of any of us?"

Mitchell's eyes took on an intensity David had not seen in them before. "You've never really thought much of these men, have you?"

David hesitated about answering, then decided the truth probably showed anyway. "No, I can't say I've been much impressed."

"This was a good outfit, a better one than you can imagine. Every man in this bunch thought the world of old Lieutenant Satterwhite. All he had to do was snap his fingers and everybody was lined up and ready for whatever come. We always said we'd ride into hell if he led us." A remembered sadness touched Mitchell. "And that's what happened, finally. We rode into hell, and a lot of the men didn't come out again. Satterwhite, God bless him, was the first to fall because he was out in front, where he always was. It's taken a lot out of this crew, gettin' whipped like we did. Maybe it was the same in the outfit *you* was with."

David didn't answer, but he remembered.

Mitchell looked upriver, the painful memories pinching his eyes. "The spirit was gone. I kept hopin' we'd get it back. When I found out they didn't intend to let the men elect a new officer for themselves, I at least hoped they'd give us one who could lead us the way *he* did. Well, they gave us you." Mitchell turned his gaze back half apologetically to David. "I ain't sayin' you haven't tried; you have. I ain't sayin' that under better circumstances you wouldn't be a good officer, even for this bunch. But you joined us when the men was already feelin' whipped, and we ain't done a thing since but retreat or get chased halfway across New Mexico. All we've had is dirt and sweat and fleas. It ain't your fault, it's just how things go.

"Now we've got one chance to win back that spirit we had, to stir up the pride we lost. I intend to see us get that chance. *With* you, if you'll agree. *Without* you, if you don't."

"What'll you do if I don't? Shoot me?"

Mitchell frowned. "No, we'd let you go on south without us. Anybody who feels like he don't want to be part of what we're fixin' to do, he can ride along with you. If you won't help us, we don't want you in our way." He stared at David a moment. "Davey, I ain't told you, but I met your old daddy once. I think I know how you've tried to live up to him. I'm wonderin' how you'd feel—how *he'd* feel—if you rode back to Texas by yourself, and we come along later with that whole wagon train of war goods?"

David looked away from the sergeant, afraid his thoughts would show. Mitchell had stepped on him where his foot was sorest. Joshua Buckalew had won *his* war. Worst of all to David these past weeks had been the realization that he was going home a loser.

He said, "There are just so many things that could go wrong . . ."

"You ain't a coward, Davey. I think I know you well enough to be sure of that."

"I've already told you what I'm scaredest of. If this doesn't work, everything falls back into the hands of the Yankees. Or worse, it might even fall to Floyd Bearfield."

Mitchell shook his head. "I've got that thought out. We'll cover all our bets. For precaution we'll string out powder just like you said. We'll keep a man posted out here all the time. If he sees we're losin' our gamble, or the wrong people come after the goods, he can touch off the powder and ride away. If *we* don't get the cache, then nobody does."

David couldn't fault the plan much, as far as it went. "Have you thought out just how we're goin' to get those Yankee wagons?"

"Not yet. But you're a bright lad. I figured maybe me and you could work on it together."

David grimaced. Hell of a note this was . . . rebelling against him, taking his command away, then turning him into a co-conspirator. "You goin' to let me have my gun back?"

Mitchell glanced at Luther Lusk. Lusk said nothing, but his expression made his recommendation for him. Mitchell replied, "Later, Davey, later. With a lot of spilt powder around, there's no use askin' for an accident, is there?"

CHAPTER 4

Owen Townsend stood in the open, dusty yard, his good arm folded across his chest, fingers tightly gripping the sleeve that covered the stiff arm. His daughter stood beside him. They watched in grim silence as the Texans who had been left on guard moved out toward the returning men. Homer Gilman and Gene Ivy trotted out to meet them, for they had seen the body tied face-down across the saddle on a led horse. Ivy said in a chilled voice, "It's Pat O'Shea."

There was no need for questions. The absence of Floyd Bearfield was testament enough.

The rest of the Texans gathered as the returning men reached the gate. Some spoke darkly of trailing after Bearfield, but David said nothing. He knew they would realize the futility of it when the first anger had run its course.

Townsend asked the question, though he didn't need to. "Bearfield?"

David nodded.

Townsend said, "I told you you should have killed him when you had the chance. I suppose he got away?"

David nodded again. He swung down from the saddle and looked back at the horse on which they had returned O'Shea. The other Texans listened in silent anger to Otto Hufstedler telling in his broken English what had happened.

"Mister Townsend, we'll bury him here, if it's all right with you. If it's not, we'll take him somewhere else. We wouldn't want to bury him in hostile ground."

Townsend said, "It'll be all right." His daughter started to object, then changed her mind. Townsend continued, "We have a small ranch cemetery up the hill yonder." He pointed to a grove of trees at some distance. "Floyd Bearfield is responsible for some of those graves too."

David studied it a moment, wishing it were Texas. He had seen too many Texans buried, too far from home. "We'd be obliged. I hope you have some spare lumber."

"It's scarce, but there's an extra wagon box in a shed."

David turned, looking for somebody to detail to the job. Noley Mitchell said, "I'll see to it, Davey."

The men carried O'Shea into the house. In a minute, only David remained outside, with Townsend and his daughter. Townsend studied him with questioning eyes. "I expected to see you blow up that whole hill."

"It was my intention. But the men see it differently."

"The men? What have they to say about it? You're the officer in charge."

"I'm the officer, but it would be a shameful abuse of the truth to say I'm in charge."

Townsend grunted in surprise. "What kind of an army do you Texans have, anyway?"

David shrugged. "I don't know. It's the only army I was ever in."

"How you people ever got this far, I'll never understand. An officer commands and men obey. That's the only way an army can be run."

"A regular army, maybe. But there's nothin' regular about an army like ours."

They put O'Shea's crudely built coffin onto Townsend's wagon and carried it up the hill. David looked back every so often toward the north. Sooner or later . . . maybe today, maybe tomorrow, maybe next day . . . a Union detail would come down that long grade with a string of wagons.

The grave had been dug by a couple of Townsend's ranchhands, who waited now, sweaty and begrimed, removing their hats as the wagon pulled up to the site.

David had only the vaguest idea about the differences between Catholic and Protestant. Somebody had told him O'Shea was Catholic and should have a priest for his final services. There was no priest here, and not even a country Baptist preacher. Many a Texan had been buried in this New Mexico soil without benefit of clergy. Sooner or later, some of the ranch Mexicans had told Hernandez, a priest would come through and they would bring him here to give the appropriate rites. Even a *Tejano* deserved a chance at heaven, they said, because he had been so far from it while here on earth.

Next to Pete Richey, who still lay on a bed down at the ranchhouse, Gene Ivy had seemed the most inclined toward strong religion. David had him read a few appropriate passages from the Townsend family Bible. That was all of the service. David shoveled a little dirt into the grave, then passed the shovel to Noley Mitchell, who in turn passed it on.

Owen and Martha Townsend had come along to honor an enemy who was beyond hurting them. David counted eight boards and crosses in the little cemetery. In the center he saw two which stopped him. One bore the simple inscription: *Amelia Townsend 1819–1861.* The other said: *Patience Townsend Chancellor 1840–1861.*

He glanced at the Townsends. Martha Townsend saw the question and answered before he asked it. "My mother . . . my sister."

The boards had not yet weathered to the point of being gray. David saw tears well into the girl's eyes, and he had no more questions. He thought now that he understood several things.

The group strung out down the hill, following the empty wagon back toward the adobe buildings. David dropped to the rear. The two Townsends waited and walked along beside him. Townsend asked, "Since you didn't blow up that stuff, what do you intend to do with it?"

"I can't tell you that, Mister Townsend."

"You must be planning to try to take it with you, at least some of it. But how? You couldn't carry much on horseback, and yonder is the only good wagon you'll find on this place."

David hadn't read him the entire letter. Possibly Townsend was unaware of the Yankee wagons. If so, it would be wise to leave him in his ignorance.

Martha Townsend declared, "We just finished burying one of your people. How many more will be killed before you go back where you belong?"

David made no attempt to answer. Frustrated, she declared, "All you people have brought to New Mexico has been death and destruction."

David looked back once at the tree-shaded cemetery on the hill. He could not argue against her statement. "We didn't ask for this war. It was forced on us by people who thought they could walk over us and dictate to us from two thousand miles away. The South has pride, Miss Townsend."

"Is pride worth dying for?"

"A lot of people have thought so."

Owen Townsend said, "I won't argue politics with you, Buckalew. I'm just arguing military realities. You've already lost. All you have left is a lot of political talk. You're a country boy, I take it. What's the largest city you've ever seen?"

"San Antonio, I guess."

"They made a lot of speeches to you there, didn't they?"

"Yes sir, they did."

"I've heard a lot of speeches in *my* time, too. When I was your age I believed most of them. But I'm older now. I find that politics is mostly lies and delusion. They talk to you about glory and duty and honor, all those political people. But at the worst you'll find them to be liars and hypocrites, and at best you'll find them to be damnfool zealots who talk of things they know nothing about. I used to listen to them, but I learned better."

"You don't believe in honor and duty?"

"Real honor, yes, and real duty. But not this empty brassband variety. You remember what I tell you, Buckalew, and if you can stay alive you'll finally come to see I'm right. I've watched too many soldiers over too many years. I've seen them fight their hearts out for what some politician said was duty and honor. And when they had given all there was to give, the politicians would betray them. They would steal the fruits of it. Or they would just throw it away because the public had lost interest, and the average politician won't waste three minutes on something that doesn't help him with the voting public. The soldier does the fighting, but in the end he's at the mercy of the politician. The politician *has* no mercy. He's false, an empty shell. You think the politics of your Confederacy will be any different? The politicians of your government were politicians before there *was* a Confederacy. They'll still be politicians when the Confederacy is gone. To hell with them. Save yourself, son. In your place that's what they would do. It's what they *always* do."

David didn't comprehend half of what Townsend was saying. Probably Townsend was talking about Yankee politics, and maybe he was right. But David was certain government didn't operate that way in Texas; it never had. Sam Houston, in his time, wouldn't have allowed it.

"Mister Townsend, all I know is that we came to New Mexico to do a job. Win or lose, it's our duty to do the best we can. We won't bother you or your people if you'll pledge not to try to interfere with us."

"You know I can't give you such a pledge. You're still the enemy."

David perceived a minor victory. "You *do* believe in duty, after all."

Townsend's mouth pulled down at the corners. "Sometimes we're trapped by our loyalties. We tolerate things we had rather not, because the alternative is disloyalty. Any duty I have is to my country, not to its politicians. The politicians are all back where it's safe and comfortable. I have a duty to our soldiers, because they will suffer if you get away with that ammunition."

That much David could understand. "Then we'll have to watch you and your people. Nobody leaves. Anybody who comes in has to stay in."

"Spoken like a soldier."

That was what David had tried hard to be. "I'll take that as a compliment, Mister Townsend."

"It wasn't meant to be, not altogether. I've been a soldier myself. I find that in many respects soldiers are like sheep. Never ask questions, even when you should. Just believe, and follow orders."

"My people don't always follow *me* too good."

"That's your weakness as a military unit. But it may be your strength as *men*."

Several times during the remainder of the afternoon David walked out to visit with the guard posted on a rise a couple of hundred yards south of the buildings, and east of the small cemetery. David had left his spyglass to be passed from one guard to the next. Each time, he took the glass and looked past the ranch headquarters to the trail which led in from the north. A little before sundown he found the miller, Homer Gilman, on duty. Gilman did not stand at attention as David approached. He gave a civil enough nod, but that was all.

"No sign of anything?" David asked, as he had asked each other sentry.

"Buckalew, there ain't nothin' moved out yonder except jackrabbits, and not many of *them*."

David took the spyglass and trained it on the road. He was divided between a hope the wagons would show up today and a hope that they wouldn't. Every hour the Texans spent here was another hour that some Union command was moving closer to them, or that Floyd Bearfield might use to his advantage. Yet, David had not yet thought out a good plan for taking the wagons away from the Yankees without getting some people killed. Perhaps it would be better if the wagons showed up before such a plan *was* worked out. Then maybe the men would agree to do what he had intended in the first place: blow up the ammunition and go south.

He handed the glass back to the miller, whose face was troubled. Gilman said, "Buckalew, I ain't real sure we can take them wagons."

David grunted. "Neither am I."

He walked back down to the house and entered the room where Pete Richey lay atop a cornshuck mattress on a frame cot. Richey seemed to sense a new presence in the room. He opened his eyes, sighted David and tried to rise up onto one elbow.

David said, "Lie back, Pete. Take all the rest you can."

The boy eased. David seated himself in a chair by the cot. He studied Pete closely but was unable to determine much from his face. It was dark in this thick-walled room. The only large window opened into the patio, and that side was already in the deep shadow of evening. The window to the outside was tiny, just large enough for a defending rifleman to take aim but difficult for someone outside to shoot through.

"Feel any better, Pete?"

"It hurts like hell."

"It'll be better," David said, knowing the words were empty against Richey's pain. But he felt obliged to say *something*.

Pete said, "They tell me we're goin' to capture them Yankee wagons."

His use of the word we *was much too optimistic*, David thought. "Seems like most of the boys want to try."

He caught a tone of fear in the boy's voice. "Sir, if we don't win . . . they'll throw us into a Yankee prison someplace."

"We'll win," David said, thinking himself possibly a liar.

"They'll lock us in some dungeon and let us rot. I don't think I could live if they done that to me."

David became aware that Martha Townsend stood in the doorway. He had no idea how much of it she had heard. He stood up. "Don't you fret about prison, Pete. We'll get you home."

He walked past Martha Townsend. She followed him until they were beyond the boy's hearing. "You don't really intend to try taking him out of here?"

"You heard him. If he stayed it would mean a Yankee prison for him. He'd rather die than face that."

"They wouldn't have to know he's a Texan. We could tell them he's one of our ranch people. They wouldn't doubt us."

David couldn't quite believe. "You'd do that for one of us?"

"Knowing how he was wounded, and where, yes . . . we would. Besides, he's nothing more than a boy. What's he doing here anyway?"

What are any of us doing here? he thought with a clenching of his jaw. He kept looking at the girl, considering what she said. It had a lot of appeal, but he knew he couldn't accept. "I promised we'd get him home."

"Then go now," she said urgently. "Put him in our ranch wagon and go, tonight. Get him out of here before the troops come, and the wagons."

He blinked. She must have heard. "The wagons?"

"Of course, wagons. You crazy Texans are going to try to take over the wagons that come to carry the ammunition and powder away. You'll get yourselves killed, and maybe some of our people too. Please, Buckalew, give it up and go on tonight. Go blow up that cave, if you must, and then get out."

He could not tell her how much he would like to do exactly that. He said, "I'm grateful for what you've done for Pete. You're good folks. I'm sorry that circumstances have set us crossways."

She didn't soften. She said curtly, "I wish circumstances could have set you up a little brighter."

After supper he sought out Owen Townsend. "Mister Townsend, I apologize for the discomfort I'm about to cause you, but I've got to ask that you gather up all your people. You'll all go into the cellar for the night."

Townsend frowned. "It's musty down there. The air's not healthy, especially for the children."

"My men need some sleep. They can't stay up all night and guard you."

It occurred to him that Townsend accepted the situation with a minimum of protest. He expected more argument from Martha Townsend, however, and got it. She pointed out among other things that the cellar was a single room, and there was no way to observe the proprieties if both men and women had to sleep in it. David sympathized but saw no ready answer. He suggested that all the men could face north and all the women face south. Her opinion of that idea was expressed in a word that he could not remember having ever heard a woman use before. She was still talking when the top of her head disappeared down through the opening in the floor.

Noley Mitchell had silently counted off the Townsend ranch people as they went down the ladder.

"You sure that's all of them, Sergeant?" David asked. "We can't afford to miss even one who could slip away and go for help."

"That's all of them, Davey. You need not fret yourself."

David looked down the opening and apologized again to the people there for their discomfort. After letting the heavy door down into place and noting that there was no way to lock it, he pushed a large wooden trunk across the floor and left it sitting squarely atop the door. The strain set his weak arm to aching.

He doubted that anyone standing on the ladder could budge the trunk, pushing upward against its weight. But to be safe he found a couple of clay water pitchers, balanced one atop the other and set them over the corner of the door. If the door lifted as much as a couple of inches, they would tip over. The top one, at least, would be smashed.

"We'll have a couple of the men sleep in here," he said. "The noise will wake them up if anybody messes with that door."

Mitchell appeared at least mildly impressed. "Davey, you're gettin' better. You're liable to make a good officer yet." The smile lasted only a minute. "Now, before we waste any time, I'd best show you what Hufstedler found a while ago."

David followed the sergeant out beyond the adobe wall which surrounded the buildings. The Dutchman leaned on a rifle beside a clump of low brush some distance behind the big house. He straightened as the two men approached him. He pointed silently to the ground.

Hidden by the thorny tangle of low growth was a small wooden door, set almost flush to the ground. David's eyes widened.

"Some of the old houses back home still have these," he said. "Left over from the Indian-raid days."

Mitchell agreed solemnly. "Back where you lived, I don't reckon you ever had the occasion to need one of them getaway tunnels."

"No, but my father says they were handy in his day."

Mitchell's eyes narrowed as he looked toward the house. "In a manner of speakin', them Townsend people are under siege. Come dark they'll try to slip somebody out to go for help."

David looked around for something heavy to put over the door. Not far away was the wagon they had used to haul O'Shea up the hill. He and Mitchell and Hufstedler pulled and pushed it across to the brush by hand and set one of the rear wheels to rest on top of the door. Hufstedler began picking up large rocks and putting them in the wagon bed to add weight. David tried helping him but gave up because of the ache in his arm.

Night was upon them. The air was cool, even crisp, but David found it pleasant. He pulled himself up onto the wagon bed, favoring the arm. He let his legs hang over the empty endgate.

Mitchell left awhile to see that the first shift of sentries were on duty. Presently he came back. "You still here, Davey?"

"Yes. It'll get chilly after a while, but right now the air feels good."

Mitchell squatted on his heels on the ground. The two men sat in silence. David listened for sounds of trace chains and wagons and horses but knew they were unlikely to arrive here in darkness. Even if they were close by, they would probably have camped for the night rather than risk accident to the wagons on a poor trail. No lamps or candles burned anywhere in the house; the place was totally dark.

Mitchell said finally, "I hope you're not still sore, Davey."

"Why should I be sore? All you did was take my command away from me. I'd just as well tear the lieutenant's bars off of my coat."

"Don't do that. You'll need them again, once we get that stuff somewhere that it's useful."

"You know I can file charges on you when we get back to Texas."

"You won't, though, if we're successful. You won't need to if we're not."

"I'll admit that I've been as green as a gourd vine. I've made mistakes since I've been with this outfit. I'd have made more if you hadn't been along. I'll even admit that you're the one who should've been the officer over these men instead of me."

Mitchell nodded. "I'm glad to hear you say that, Davey."

"But the choice wasn't left up to me or you or the men. It was made by higher authority against the wishes of all of us. I don't see that you've got a right to go against that."

"Where is that authority now? Do you see it out here anyplace? Out here we have to make our own authority if we think it's necessary. And today we decided it was, Davey, to keep you from throwin' away our chance to win back some glory for Texas."

David pondered awhile before he asked the question that had been nagging him. "What about glory for Noley Mitchell?"

"Well, sure, Davey, there'll be glory in it for all of us if we can make it work. A little glory wouldn't hurt none of us when we get home. It wouldn't do no harm to the Buckalew family, would it? Like father, like son."

"What do *you* need it for, Sergeant? From what they tell me, you've already had it. They tell me you've been a sheriff for years in your home county. I would imagine you've already had all the glory a man would ever need."

Mitchell was silent a moment. "You're right about one thing; I *was* sheriff down there for a long time. But did any of them tell you why I'm not sheriff anymore?"

"I figured you resigned to join the invasion."

"I was already out before that. They voted me out of office, them people back home. They said I'd been in long enough, that I was gettin' too old for the job, too set in my ways. They voted in a new man, a young feller not much older than you are. Green, he was, greener than grass, takin' over a job I'd worked and sweated and spilled my own blood for over the years."

"So you joined the volunteers to prove to them they was wrong?"

"I figured by the time my enlistment was up, and we'd taken everything clean to the Pacific Ocean, they'd be sick and tired of that upstart. They'd be tickled to see me come home. It seemed like for a long time it was workin' out that way, till Glorieta. Since then there ain't nothin' been right. We've taken one lickin' after another, and we was sneakin' back home with our tails between our legs. Till today. When I seen all that powder and ammunition . . . when I reached out there and touched it and finally realized it was real and not just another wild daydream . . . I could see that I had been given one last chance . . . *we* was given one last chance."

David stared at the outline of him in the darkness. "You were always civil to me, Sergeant, more than most of the others. But I always felt like even you resented me a little, deep down inside. Now I think I know how much. To you, I was that young man back home, all over again, beatin' you out of a place you felt was rightfully yours."

"I tried not to let it show. I'm sorry if it did, because you're not that same feller. With a little more time and experience you've got a chance to be a damned good officer. I hope you can live that long."

"I sure do intend to try."

He became aware of vague rustling noises. Noley Mitchell heard them too, and pushed to his feet. David eased down from the wagon and waited. The noises continued, intermittently, from beneath the wooden door.

The dry wood creaked a little as someone pushed against the door from beneath. It stopped a moment, then a stronger effort was made. The door raised slightly, perhaps an inch, then dropped again. Whoever was down there lacked the strength to lift that wagon and its load of rocks.

David called, "Is that you, Mister Townsend?"

No one answered, but the door no longer moved. David heard a muttering in Spanish, and at least a couple of voices. He said, "Mister Townsend, this is David Buckalew. There's a wagonload of rocks sittin' on top of the door, and I don't believe you folks are goin' to be able to lift it. If I was you, I'd go back and try to get some sleep."

After a long silence Townsend's voice came up, muffled by the small earthen tunnel and the wooden door. "Why didn't you tell us you knew about the opening? You'd have saved us a lot of work."

"I decided you'd take us more seriously if you found out for yourself that we're awake. Maybe you won't take chances that could get somebody hurt. Good night, Mister Townsend."

The voice carried a tone of resignation. "Good night."

———◆———

At daybreak David scanned the northern horizon for a sign of wagons. Seeing none, he let the Townsend people out of the cellar so they could go about their preparations for breakfast, and whatever else they needed to do. He warned that none were to go beyond the yard.

Soon Luther Lusk, sleepy-eyed from a long tour of guard duty, brought a young Mexican ranchhand into the house at the point of a rifle. "Buckalew," he said gruffly, "you'll want Hernandez to give this *hombre* a lecture on the dangers of not payin' attention. He slipped past the outhouse and was headed over the back fence."

David eyed the Mexican carefully. "You didn't hurt him?"

Lusk lowered the rifle. "Surprised him, is all. He fell off of the fence and landed on his belly instead of his feet. He didn't lose nothin' but his dignity, and most of his breath."

"I don't want to hurt any of these people. They don't know anything about our war."

"They know enough about it to try to help the Yanks."

David had Hernandez ask the Mexican why he tried to get away.

To get word to the Yankee wagon men, he said.

"Why?" David asked. "You don't owe anything to the Yankee soldiers."

The Mexican replied that he owed much to *el patrón*, Owen Townsend.

"He asked you to get word to the wagon people?"

He had asked all of them, the Mexican said, to get away if they could and carry a message north.

David ate his breakfast—what there was of it—nervously and in a hurry, not knowing when a guard posted uptrail would come loping down to the house with news that he had sighted the wagons. But breakfast went by and then the noon meal. In the daylight, David and Mitchell kept only a minimum number on guard, letting as many men as possible rest and catch up on sleep lost to long hours on duty last night, as well as perhaps putting a little on account for the hours they would likely lose in the nights to come.

He made it a point not to interfere more than necessary with the Townsends and their people, though keeping them confined to the house and yard was undeniably a major interference. David looked in occasionally upon Pete Richey. Pete seemed to spend most of his time asleep, or at least half asleep. David supposed this was good; he wasn't sure.

Martha Townsend sat in a straight chair not far from Pete's cot. Her shoulders were slumped. David saw her eyelids gradually close, then come suddenly open as she caught herself. She looked accusingly at David. "Did you ever try to sleep in a closed-up cellar?"

David had no comfort to offer her.

Two hours into the afternoon, the rider he had expected loped into the yard. David stepped out the door in time to see Hufstedler rein up and twist his body half around in the saddle, excitedly pointing back behind him. "They come, *Herr Leutnant*. Those Yankees, they come."

Noley Mitchell trotted up. "How many, Dutch? How far away?"

"Ten wagons that I count for sure. So much dust, could be more. They are over the hill perhaps two miles coming." In his agitation he was getting the words all mixed up. "There are men riding horses, Noley. A . . . what do you call it . . . an escort. They come out in front. They come much sooner than the wagons."

David's mouth had gone dry. He found his voice a little shaky. "Good work, Hufstedler. You go pass the word to the others. They'll all know what's to be done."

Noley Mitchell stared at David Buckalew. "You sure *you* know what's to be done?"

"I know what we've talked about. If it doesn't work . . ."

David went back inside the house. A grim Owen Townsend met him in the front room. Townsend said, "I heard enough to know they're coming. How do you intend to do it without getting my people hurt?"

"We'll try to take those wagons without any fightin'. If we *do* have to fight, you and your people will be out of it. You're all goin' back down in that cellar again, I wish you'd call them together, Mister Townsend."

Townsend's frown deepened. "You really believe you're going to do it, don't you?"

Martha Townsend had lost that tough shell. Her eyes were a little frightened. This was no longer something abstract, a distant possibility they could discuss with detachment. The time was here. Her bluster was gone. She seemed somehow vulnerable for the first time since he had met her, unsure of herself. He told her, "However it goes, it'll be over in a little while. And you'll be all right."

Her eyes met his for a moment, and they held no hostility. Then she was gone down through the trap door. Townsend waited until the last of his ranch people had descended before he went into the cellar. He paused as his shoulders were level with the trap door. "You know I can't wish you victory, Buckalew. But I do hope you come out of this with your life. I'll say this for you Texans: what you lack in intelligence, you make up in nerve."

He went on down, stopping once as another thought struck him. "I suppose you still have the other end of this tunnel blocked?"

"Yes sir."

Townsend sighed and disappeared. David closed the door behind him and slid the trunk over it.

He remembered that he still wore his ruined coat, the only thing left of his original uniform, the only thing that marked him as a Confederate soldier. He draped it across a high-backed chair. It was warm enough outside that he needed no coat. His hat was of a nondescript kind that anybody might wear. It bore nothing of the military except the dust and grime of a long and hard campaign.

David walked into the yard. Luther Lusk followed him. He glanced up toward the hill, where five riders were still a quarter of a mile away. He turned, looking for Noley Mitchell. The sergeant materialized from nowhere. It seemed he was always there when David needed him, and sometimes when David didn't.

"Everything ready, Sergeant?"

"As ready as it'll get." Mitchell's eyes were on the distant riders.

David nodded. His hands were suddenly cold, the palms wet. He ran his right hand over the Colt Dragoon he carried in his belt. Mitchell had given it back to him last night. "Then I'll go out and invite the company in." He glanced at Lusk. "I won't ask you to come with me."

Lusk's eyes seemed to laugh. "But you'd be tickled if I did."

David hated to admit it. "I don't fancy bein' out there all by myself." He started for the gate. Lusk trotted to catch up. The black-bearded frontiersman matched him stride for stride. David walked past the gate six or eight paces so he could clearly be seen. He tried to look relaxed, offering no evident threat to the soldiers who approached. A hundred yards from the gate the five halted. They parleyed a moment, then two came riding on while the other three stood their ground.

"They're suspicious, Davey," Lusk said. It was the first time anyone in the command except Mitchell had called him that. Rather than an affront, he took it now as a sign of progress.

This was the closest David had seen a Union uniform on a live man in some time. One was an officer. The other was a corporal, two big stripes on each of his dusty blue sleeves. The officer's saber bumped against his leg as the horse trotted roughly toward David and Lusk. David had never seen much logic in the saber. In the fights he had seen, a man was likely to be shot before he ever got close enough to use one. The officer, thirty or older, tall and very lean, had several days' stubble on his face. It had been a hard trip, from the weary look of him and the corporal. The Yankees had suffered as much here as the Texans, David thought. Somehow the realization surprised him a little.

He lifted his hand Indian-style as the officer drew rein. The man studied David with a measure of doubt, then let his gaze rove quickly over what he could see of the house and yard.

"Where is Owen Townsend?" the lieutenant demanded.

David had considered posing as Townsend, but he decided some of these men might know him, or at least have been given a description. "He's in the house. He's been taken with a fever."

The lieutenant's eyes narrowed. "And who are *you*?"

"Name is Buckalew." David saw no need to lie about that. There was no reason for a Yankee to recognize the name; he hadn't done anything glorious enough to attract attention. "I'm with Mister Townsend."

"Where are the other troops?"

"Other troops?"

"Another detail was supposed to be ahead of us, under Captain Smith."

"No other troops have come. You sure they're ahead of you?"

"My orders said they would be."

David's heart was hammering. Any minute now, he thought, this officer was going to see through him, and there would be hell to pay. "Some clerk's mistake, more than likely. Would you like to come in and see Mister Townsend?"

The officer frowned at the noncom and took a look back at the three men he had left posted farther out. "Before we move any further, I think that's exactly what I'd better do." He stepped down, handed the reins up to the corporal and waited for David to lead the way.

David said, "I didn't get your name."

"Chancellor. Lieutenant Tom Chancellor. I'm ... I *was* ... Mister Townsend's son-in-law."

David shivered, glad he hadn't tried to pass himself or Luther Lusk off as Owen Townsend. That would have been a disaster. "He'll be mighty glad to see you, then." He walked into the house, the lieutenant close behind him. He moved into a second room, well beyond sight or sound of the corporal. David slipped his pistol from its holster and turned, thrusting it toward the officer.

"I'll be obliged if you'll raise your hands."

Chancellor stiffened, his eyes wide. Surprise gave way to anger, and to concern. "Who are you? Where's Mister Townsend?"

"I'm Lieutenant David Buckalew, Second Texas Mounted Rifles. You're my prisoner."

Chancellor had not yet raised his hands. He demanded again, "Where's Mister Townsend? What've you done with him?"

"He's all right." David pointed his chin toward the trunk. "Move that trunk over. You'll find him under there."

Chancellor appeared to know about the door because he shoved the trunk aside and pulled the door up without hesitation. "Mister Townsend," he called anxiously. "Are you down there? Are you all right?"

Martha Townsend's voice cried out, "Is that you, Tom? Tom, this place is surrounded by Texans. They've set a trap for you."

Chancellor glanced back resentfully at David. "I know. I caught both feet in it."

David said, "I'll thank you for your weapons first. Then you can go down and have a reunion." Chancellor grudgingly gave up his pistol and saber, then started down the ladder. As David closed the door and pushed the trunk over it he could hear the anxious exchange between Owen Townsend and Chancellor. He heard Martha say in a breaking voice, "Thank God you're safe."

About that time, Luther Lusk came through the front door with his pistol in the corporal's back. He said, "Here's the next one for you, Davey."

David said sharply, "If you flushed those other three . . ."

"They're still way out yonder. I done this so gentle that they didn't see a thing."

The corporal's face was flushed with chagrin. "I don't understand this. I don't understand this at all."

David studied him a minute. He was not so tall as Chancellor. "I don't believe his uniform will fit you, Lusk."

"It ought to fit *you*, though, Davey."

The next step was somehow to bring in the three riders who waited far beyond the gate. David said to the corporal, "I don't suppose you'd step out there and wave them in?"

The corporal's voice firmed. "No, I would not."

"Then," said David, "I'll need the borry of your uniform."

Lusk watched with interest as David finished putting on the corporal's blue. "Ain't a bad fit," he volunteered. "You'd of made a fair-to-middlin' Yankee if your politics had been different."

David found something a little awry in the fact that even a Yankee corporal had a regular uniform when a Texas lieutenant did not. He said to the corporal, "You can wear my clothes awhile, so you don't have to go down in that cellar in your underwear. Don't worry, I'll be glad to swap back with you in due time."

He stepped out into the yard and into the open gate. The three horsemen still waited a hundred yards farther on. At the distance, he figured, they could not see that he was not the corporal. He waved his hand over his head in a signal for them to come in. He watched until they had ridden part of the distance. He glanced once at the hill. The wagons had not yet appeared. That, he thought, was just as well. He turned back into the yard before the three riders were close enough for a good look at him. He waited just inside the gate, pistol in hand. Lusk crouched on the other side, holding a rifle. They listened to the hoofbeats as the horsemen approached. When the horses stopped, David could tell by the sounds that the men were dismounting.

He nodded at Lusk. The two jumped through the open gate, guns pointed.

"Just raise those hands to your shoulders," David told the astonished men, "and walk on through the gate."

From out of nowhere came three Texans to take charge of the cavalrymen's horses. The Union soldiers were quickly disarmed and conducted into the house. David studied them and looked at Noley Mitchell. "We need three men who come nearest to fittin' those uniforms."

Luther Lusk was one. Homer Gilman was another. Fermin Hernandez would have been a third, but David reasoned the wagon soldiers might be suspicious of a Mexican in Union uniform; there weren't many. So Otto Hufstedler was chosen as the third.

The three soldiers, dressed in Texas tatters, resentfully went down into the cellar with their predecessors. David walked out front and looked toward the hill. The first wagons were appearing. "All right," he said to Lusk and the others wearing the Yankee uniforms, "we'll ride up there and direct them toward the cave. But we'd better change horses. Those wagon people will recognize these."

The cavalry saddle felt odd to him, though he was riding his own brown horse. He had been using a saddle of his own because Texas had not had funds to equip its soldiers, even if the military goods had been available.

Approaching the strung-out wagons, David counted eleven. One was probably carrying provisions for men and animals. He turned to Luther Lusk. "You've never seen fit to call me by my rank before, but you'd better call me *Corporal* this time. They've got discipline in the Yankee Army."

A dark humor showed in Lusk's eyes. "Been kind of demoted, ain't you, Davey, from lieutenant down to corporal?"

Two escort riders were out in advance of the lead wagon. A burly, dusty-faced one wore sergeant's chevrons. He gave a weary half-salute as the Texans approached. "You must be from that advance detail," he said.

Lying had never been countenanced in the Buckalew family, and

David had never had much training at it. This had been somewhat of a hindrance to him in his chosen profession, trading horses and mules. But now that he had started, it seemed to come easy. "Yes, we are. Your lieutenant sent us up here with orders to turn the wagons down toward the river. We're goin' to load them right away."

The sergeant frowned. "Why didn't he come himself?"

"They're feedin' him and the others, down at the house."

Resentment quickly flared in the sergeant's round, bewhiskered face. "I could stand some feedin' myself. These men are all tired. They could stand a good night's rest before they commence loading the wagons."

David noticed that the man spoke rapidly and pronounced his words without slurring them or cutting off a "g." The Townsends did the same way. It sounded odd to him, but it set him to worrying that his own manner of speech might give him away. "My captain says he wants the wagons loaded now so we can start in the mornin' and be gone at first light."

The sergeant cursed, every word given the clarity and polish that comes from a long and fond familiarity. "I think I'll go talk to the lieutenant about this."

"My captain outranks your lieutenant," David said.

The sergeant cursed again. "Never saw it to fail. Damned headquarters outfit always takes the best of everything. Any dirty work and sweat job comes along, they always give it to *us*. One of these days I'm going to transfer out of this department and go where the *fighting* is."

David turned away, trying to hide the nervousness and doubt on his face. If he made a wrong move, he thought, the sergeant might find all the fighting he wanted, right here.

He pointed toward the hill where the cave fronted on the river, and he started riding, not looking back or carrying on with the sergeant's argument. Behind, the sergeant groused some more and then sent a private back to carry the word to each of the wagon drivers. "Tell them that damned headquarters bunch has done it to us again," he shouted, making sure David heard.

Luther Lusk winked at David. Quietly he said, "If we keep him mad enough, he won't think about gettin' suspicious."

It was considerably more than a mile down the slope and around the hill to the entrance of the cave. The wagon men seemed in no hurry to finish the trip. David turned a couple of times to look at the afternoon sun. He tried to judge how much daylight time remained, and whether they could get all the goods loaded before dark. All that powder would make it too risky to use torches or lanterns for light.

David and Lusk stayed out well ahead of the wagons, where they would not be drawn into needless conversation that might create suspicion. The sergeant seemed in no mood for anything more than a one-sided harangue anyway. The other two Texans split up along the trail, outriders for the procession.

The entrance to the cave was not visible until David and Lusk went around the hill, the river lying to their left. As they did so, they saw a rider spurring downriver as fast as his horse would run. David and Lusk glanced at each other, not comprehending for a second.

"That was Gene Ivy," Lusk said.

Realization hit David like a mule kick to the stomach. Ivy had been on guard at the cave. Nobody had thought to go tell him what to expect. He had his orders in case the wrong people showed up. And David and Lusk looked like Yankees.

"He's touched off the powder!" Lusk shouted. He dug the spurs into his horse's sides.

David yelled, "No, Lusk! You'll be blown to pieces!"

But Lusk kept riding, spurring at every stride. David held back a moment, trying to think, wondering how far out from the cave Ivy had sparked the powder, wondering how long it would take that racing flame to reach the cave and the explosive cache inside.

David doubted he could help Lusk now, and he owed the man nothing. No, that was wrong. He owed him for being a soldier in the same cause. He owed him for being willing to gamble all he had on a venture he believed in. David spurred after him.

Lusk had a long lead. Ahead, David could see the black smoke racing along the ground, following the trail of powder they had strung out as a precaution. *Hell of a precaution that turned out to be!* he thought, holding his breath as the brown horse raced ahead.

For a few moments he was certain Lusk was going to lose the race. If he did, there wouldn't be enough left of him to bury, and probably not of David, either. But Lusk slid his horse to a stop and was instantly on the ground, down on hands and knees, then scrambling desperately to his feet, shouting God knew what. A few feet ahead of the oncoming flame he began raking sand desperately with his hands, throwing it atop the string of powder, the flame. David could hear him shouting, alternating between curses and prayer. David jumped to the ground and rushed to help him, moving a few feet nearer the cave entrance, his heart in his mouth and choking him; he couldn't have shouted if he had wanted to.

The sparkling, hissing flame sputtered, jumped over and found a spot of powder to burn. Lusk attacked the flame with his bare hands while David leaped down to his aid, kicking sand with his boots. Some if it went into Lusk's eyes, but neither man slowed because of that.

The flame sputtered, flared, sputtered again and went out. Lusk remained where he had quit struggling, on his hands and knees, blinking at the sand, staring at the spot where the fire had burned to a stop. It struck David that the frontiersman's face had gone three shades whiter than normal. Lusk's mouth hung open. Finally one of the man's hands went to his chest, and his face twisted as he struggled for breath.

David realized that his own lungs were afire. He had held his breath too long. And when he took in a long breath the burned powder seemed to sear him. He began coughing, fighting to stop the burning, the constriction of throat and lungs. He dropped to his knees.

For a minute or two he and Lusk knelt there, facing each other, both trying to get a fresh handhold on life.

When finally he had regained his breath Lusk said, "Davey, that was a hell of a lot closer than them Indians."

David only nodded, his chest still heaving.

Lusk said, "If I ever pull a stunt like that again, I hope you'll shoot me."

David nodded again. "That is a promise." Slowly a grin spread across his face, mirrored on Lusk's.

Lusk began pushing to his feet, swaying a little. "Somehow, I wouldn't of thought you'd do it, Davey."

"I wouldn't have thought so either."

Lusk reached out his hand. David took it, and Lusk pulled him to his feet. They began looking for their horses. Both had ended up down near the river. They had stopped and turned back toward the cave, both watching with ears pointed forward, still frightened by the sudden run, the flame and the smoke. They would be hard to catch for a man afoot.

The Yankee sergeant came around the hill and rode up to David and Lusk. The black smoke still clung, fiery to the nostrils. He waved his hand in front of his face as if he thought he could fan the smoke away. "What the hell is going on here? You headquarters idiots been playing with fire?"

Lusk eyed him disgustedly. "There was damn little play in it."

David said, "Confederate. A Confederate tried to touch it off. They're all around us here."

The sergeant looked about quickly, suddenly alert. "Where is he now?"

Lusk grunted. "He left."

David looked downriver, wondering how far Gene Ivy would run before he stopped, and before he began working his way back toward the Townsend headquarters to find out what had become of his comrades. "That is why we need to get those wagons loaded as soon as we can."

The sergeant's face had turned grim. "All right, but don't you think we ought to have some help? How about sending some of your headquarters outfit up here?"

"Most of them are out on patrol," David replied. "They're scoutin' for Confederates, and for Indians."

"Indians too? Goddamn!" the sergeant gritted. He turned and rode back to hurry the wagons.

Lusk grinned again. Those hawkish eyes seemed almost friendly.

Gradually David was becoming used to seeing that uncommon expression on the frontiersman's face. "I think we'll get them wagons loaded all right."

David nodded. "Soon's somebody catches our horses for us, how about you ridin' back to the house and seein' how many men can be spared to come out here and help?" It struck him that he hadn't given it as an order; he had said *how about?* "Tell them to remember that they're workin' hands from the Townsend ranch. Anybody says anything about Texas, we've got a battle on our hands."

They lined the wagons up as near the cave entrance as they could. David warned for everybody to hear: "Don't anybody even think about smokin'. One spark in the wrong place and they'll be huntin' for us on the other side of the river. And not findin' us."

The sergeant came up to him and said stiffly, "I'll remind you that you're only a corporal. As the sergeant, I'll give the orders here." He turned toward the men. "No smoking now. That's an order. Do you hear me?"

David had given a good deal of thought to the proper way to load the wagons. He had decided that the powder, being the most explosive, should be concentrated on as few wagons as possible and these kept separated from each other. If one were for some reason set off, distance would help prevent the explosion from starting a chain reaction in the others. He made that suggestion to the Yankee sergeant and added, "That's the way the captain ordered us to do it."

The sergeant growled, "That's the way with those headquarters officers. Full of orders but not of fight. Comes time for the fighting to be done, and the work, who do you suppose they send? *Me*, and my outfit."

David soon found that although he complained with every step he took, the Yankee sergeant had evidently earned his rank with good effort and ability, for he marshaled the wagon men into a very effective work force. Lusk was soon back with several of the Texans, whose status as ranchhands went unquestioned. The sun was just going down as the last keg and the last wooden box were loaded onto the final wagons. The hoops were put in place and the tarpaulin covers spread and tightly secured against the rain that David doubted would ever fall in this drouthy-looking country. He quietly circulated among the Texans as the job was finished, passing orders in a whisper.

As the wagons were strung out around the hill and moved toward the ranch headquarters, the Texans spread themselves strategically on both sides of them. David had feared that sometime during the loading process one of his men would let a careless word fall and betray the whole masquerade, but none did. As the wagons started up the long slope, he began to feel strongly that they were going to get away with it.

Just outside the adobe wall that enclosed the yard, he rode up beside the sergeant and pointed. "We'll circle the wagons here."

The sergeant gave him a look of disdain. "Who the hell says so?" He looked around for signs of other soldiers. "Where is your captain?"

David shrugged. "Out on a scout, maybe. Or eatin' supper."

"I'll be damned glad when *we* get to eat some supper." The sergeant pulled away momentarily and made a motion for the driver of the lead wagon. "We'll circle here."

David waited for him to come back. When he did, David asked, "You have a cook with you?"

"Such as he is," the sergeant said without enthusiasm. "Jones, down on the end, driving the provision wagon. He's a real belly-robber. I hope you've got a decent cook with *your* outfit."

"We've got no cook at all."

"The hell you say! You mean we've got to put up with Jones again? What's the matter with those idiots at headquarters, anyway? Don't they know that men in the field have got to have something decent to eat or they can't keep going?"

The wagons were circled and drawn in tightly, so that the mules which pulled them would be corraled within the circle made by the wagons themselves. No fences or hobbles would be needed. David watched while the mules were unhitched and unharnessed and a ration of corn put out for them.

The sergeant looked toward the house. "I thought sure they would come on out, now that the work is all done. I'll bet they're sitting in there laughing at us. Always the dirty details, that's what *we* get."

David took a long, careful look. As he had ordered earlier, his Texans had made it a point to scatter out so that each stood beside a Union soldier. All were watching David for a sign. Lusk was eyeing him closely, his expression saying, *This is the time.* David reached up with his left hand and removed his hat, bringing it down to waist level. As he did so, he drew his pistol with the right hand and trained it on the sergeant.

The other Texans drew their pistols and covered the Union men. Anger surged into the sergeant's round, bestubbled face. "Now, just what in the hell do you call this?"

David said, "I call it *capture*. You're our prisoners, Sergeant."

The sergeant didn't comprehend. "I always knew you damned headquarters people were crazy . . ."

"We're not from your headquarters. We're from Texas. You're prisoners of the Second Texas Mounted Rifles."

The truth filtered through the sergeant's anger. He sobered. "What about my men? I don't want you hurting my men."

"Just tell them to do what we say and nobody has to be hurt." David motioned toward the house. "You'll go in there single file, hands up. Lusk will show you where. You'll find all your friends down in the cellar, in good shape."

A touch of hope flickered in the sergeant's eyes. "I suppose you've got that headquarters outfit down there too."

"They never got here. They were ambushed by Indians."

The sergeant regretfully shook his head. "That's too bad. Probably had an officer that didn't know anything except shuffling papers. They ought not to be allowed out by themselves."

David held back the cook Jones and a soldier the cook said customarily helped him. The others went down into the cellar. The four whose uniforms had been borrowed were brought back up to change again. David was glad to shed the blue uniform. The color had not suited him, and the fit was none too good.

He walked back outside to view the wagons in the twilight. He looked a moment to the west, where a faint red glow still clung to the clouds above the distant ragged mountaintops. Now that he had time to pause and reflect, he found his knees weak and shaking. He sat on a wagon tongue and stretched his legs out, rubbing them with his hands.

He heard Noley Mitchell's voice behind him. "It'll pass, Davey. The excitement has caught up with you, is all."

David could not quite believe what had happened.

"We did it, Noley. It was impossible, but we did it."

Mitchell stared thoughtfully across the circle of wagons. "The hardest part is still ahead of us."

David hardly heard him. "The hell of it is, it was so easy. I was wrong, Noley. You were right."

A faint smile tugged at Mitchell's mouth. "We'll know about that later. It's a long ways to Texas."

CHAPTER 5

The Yankee cook prepared supper in the open yard, his fire built well away from the wagons so that no stray spark could set off a disaster. David considered how best to feed the prisoners; that sergeant's complaint about hunger had been genuine. He decided not to risk letting them come outside to eat. He had a couple of his Texans help Jones move the food indoors and pass it down into the cellar that served as a convenient prison. They took enough for the ranch people as well as the Union soldiers. Then the Texans ate.

David was hungry, but he postponed his meal. He climbed down the ladder and found himself the object of many hostile eyes. In the lanternlight Owen Townsend, his daughter Martha and Lieutenant Tom Chancellor sat together on an old wooden crate, plates in their hands.

David said, "I apologize if the food isn't good. It's the best we could do under the circumstances."

Nobody said anything; they simply stared at him. David cleared his throat. "I apologize to you, too, for havin' to sleep another night in this stuffy cellar. But this'll be the last one. We'll be gettin' started at first light."

Still nobody said anything. He gazed regretfully at the girl a moment. "Miss Townsend, you can sleep upstairs if you like. So can the other women. You'll breathe better up there."

Her voice was cold. "I prefer the society down here."

Chancellor touched her hand. "Martha, I don't believe those Texans would bother you. It *would* be better for you up there."

She looked at David. "Do you think you could trust us women?"

"Yes, I'd trust you."

"Then you'd be wrong. We would take any chance we saw, and somebody would be hurt. So we'll stay down here and ask for no favored treatment."

Tom Chancellor started to say something. Owen Townsend told him, "Best leave her alone, Tom. She's got the same strong will as . . ." He stopped there, the thought bringing him pain. Chancellor nodded and looked down at the floor.

The air *was* stale and dead in here. David gazed at the girl until her sharp eyes cut him. He climbed up the ladder, suppressing a wish to ask her again. An ungiving lot, these Yankees.

On top, he sought out Noley Mitchell. "It might draw some fresh air through if we leave this door open awhile and open up that escape door outside."

Mitchell frowned. "An escape door is made to escape through."

"We can put a double guard on it for now and close it later when the air has had time to clean up."

"Kind of concerned about them Yankees, aren't you?"

"I don't like to see anybody suffer if they don't have to."

Mitchell grunted. "Whatever you say, Davey. You're the officer."

"I thought that honor had been taken away from me."

"Just suspended awhile, you might say. You've got it back."

David thought it was probably unseemly to thank Mitchell for the restoration of something he had had no right to take away in the first place. But he said, "Thanks."

"Now, Davey," Mitchell suggested. "I think you better go get somethin' to eat, then sleep awhile. Tomorrow's a long day."

"That sounds like an order. I thought *I* was the officer here."

"On sufferance is all, Davey. Just on sufferance."

David didn't sleep much. He rolled his blanket on the ground just outside the circle of wagons where he could hear anything that happened. In short, fitful dreams he kept seeing the whole circle of wagons go up in one grand explosion, with himself in the center of it all. Betweentimes he thought he heard every stamp of a mule's hoof, every cry of the night birds, every yipping note from the coyotes which communicated their affections from the hills along the river. Sometime in the early-morning hours he heard a guard's sudden challenge out in the darkness. He sat up quickly, trying to fix the location.

The guard shouted, "You try to run and I'll shoot you."

A familiar voice came from the darkness. "That you, Homer? That really you?"

Gene Ivy had worked up the nerve to come in and try to discover what had happened to his friends. As David threw the blanket back and got to his feet he heard Homer Gilman laugh. "Come on in, kid. Everything's all right."

Ivy was still trembling when David got to him. The young soldier blurted, "I thought the Yankees had gotten all of you. When I seen them Yankee soldiers comin' toward the cave . . ."

David said, "Those Yankee soldiers were us. We forgot to send somebody to tell you." He explained about the capture of the wagons, about Luther Lusk putting out the powder blaze that Ivy had started.

Ivy looked at his feet. "I'm sorry. I guess I almost lost us the whole thing."

"It was our fault. You just followed the orders we gave you. Anyway, we all survived it."

Ivy was hungry and thirsty. Nothing had been left from supper. David decided it wouldn't be more than an hour or so before light began showing in the east, so there was no point in going back to bed; he wouldn't sleep anyway. He went into the house, opened the trap door and called for the Yankee cook to come up and start breakfast. Mitchell and the others saw to it that the mules were fed.

After everyone had had time to eat, and golden streaks were showing through the bank of clouds hanging low over the hills beyond the river, David went down into the cellar. He found himself looking first for Martha Townsend, though his business was not with her. She sat on the large wooden crate with Lieutenant Chancellor.

David took off his hat. "I hope you slept better than I did, Miss Townsend."

"I'd have no idea how you slept, Texas. I did not sleep worth a damn."

Back home he had been taught that good women did not use that sort of language, though he had found in recent years that his teaching had been somewhat exaggerated. "Maybe tonight will be better. We'll be gone from here."

She didn't answer, but her expression indicated she favored that change. David turned to Lieutenant Chancellor. "Lieutenant, I wish you would call up your wagon drivers, please."

Chancellor's eyes were brittle. "You intend to use our own men to take those wagons to your territory?"

"We had sort of figured on it."

Stiffly Chancellor asked, "What if I do not choose to call up the men?"

"You're a prisoner. I don't see where you've got any choice."

"I have a choice. I can sit here and refuse. If I so order my men, they'll refuse to obey you, too."

"This is no time for games."

"I'm not playing any." Chancellor spoke up so everybody in the cellar could hear him. "No man is to step forward. That is an order."

Anger warmed David's face. "I could have you shot."

"You could. I can only gamble that you won't."

David had never been a good poker player. He never could be sure when he was being bluffed. He started to draw his pistol but decided against it. He knew this would be purely bluff on his part. What could he do if Chancellor called that bluff, which he probably would? He stood awkwardly, his stomach churning from the frustration, complicated by the loss of sleep. He tried staring Chancellor down but saw that he couldn't; the man's defiant gaze was as steady as a rock.

David glanced at Martha Townsend and at the old army scout who was her father. Both glowed in triumph.

David turned to the Union soldiers. "You wagon drivers. I want you out here. Now!"

Most of the men were sitting on the dirt floor. They continued to sit there staring at David, challenging him to do anything about it. David tried to remember which men he had seen driving the wagons; he hadn't paid that much attention at the time. He recognized one a couple of paces from him. He stepped over, grabbed the young man by one arm and attempted to pull him to his feet. The soldier passively let himself be lifted, but when David eased, the man promptly sat down again.

David said sharply, "I'm orderin' you to get yourself up."

The soldier shook his head. "Wrong army . . . sir."

Chancellor said, "They're not going, Texas. And if they don't go, *you* don't go . . . not with the wagons."

David realized that his rising anger might cause him to make a fool of himself in front of the enemy. He climbed back up the ladder and found Noley Mitchell at the top, listening. "Sergeant," he said, "we have trouble."

Mitchell nodded. "I know. But maybe it's a blessin' in disguise. I been worryin' about how we'd keep all them Yankee teamsters under control. We've got men enough to drive the wagons ourselves."

"That doesn't leave us anybody, hardly, for point or outriders."

"We'll get along. We have to."

Jake Calvin had a suggestion. "Let's pull a couple of them Yankee soldiers out and shoot them. The rest would go."

David's eyes narrowed. "You know we couldn't do that."

"I could."

David called his Texans together and asked how many had had any experience as teamsters. It did not surprise him that Luther Lusk had; he appeared to have done a little of everything. And Fermin Hernandez had been a freighter on the San Antonio–to-the-border roads for years, though mostly using ox teams. Virtually everybody had had some experience handling teams, for they had come from a farming country. David put Lusk in charge of the wagon operation, with Hernandez to assist him. They began harnessing the mules.

They ran into one complication immediately. Lacking help from the Union teamsters, they didn't know the mules. Normally each mule had his own place. Some were naturally lead mules, some wheelers, others accustomed to other positions. Hitched out of their normal order and mixed indiscriminately with mules of other teams, they would not perform as easily as they should.

Fermin Hernandez had an idea. He cracked a whip a few times. It was a well-indoctrinated signal, for most of the mules moved into their individual harnessing positions. They found their places and stood there waiting for the harness.

Hernandez grinned. "Every day, Lieutenant, you learn something new."

David blinked. He had seen teamsters do this, but he would never have thought of trying it.

He went into the room where Pete Richey lay on the bed. Pete asked weakly, "We ready to go, Lieutenant?"

"About. How you feelin'?"

"Fine. I'm ready."

David doubted that. Even in the lamplight he could see that Pete was in worse condition than he had appeared yesterday.

"Pete, this is goin' to be a rough trip. We can make room for you in the provision wagon, but it'll jar the guts out of you. You'd be better off if you stayed here."

Pete almost shouted, "No! I don't want to be no Yankee prisoner. You promised you'd take me."

"And I will, if you want it. But it's goin' to be hell for you."

"I want to get back to Texas."

"All right. Somebody'll pick you up directly. Hope you ate some breakfast."

"Drank a little coffee, is all."

"That's not enough. You need your strength."

"I'll do better next time."

David frowned. He wished Pete were doing better *now*.

He needed a few words with Owen Townsend and Lieutenant Chancellor. He descended into the cellar. "I hate to leave you afoot in this Indian country, Mister Townsend. But I'll have to do it unless I have your word that you nor none of these soldiers will trail after us."

Townsend shook his head. "I can't make you a promise like that. It's their job to go after you."

David glanced at Chancellor, hoping the lieutenant would volunteer a promise for the good of them all. But Chancellor sat beside Martha Townsend and said nothing.

"Then," David said, "we'll have to shoot all the horses and mules we don't take with us."

Townsend's jaw dropped, but he regained his composure. "Do what you have to. We'll make you no promises that we don't intend to keep."

Leaving them afoot wouldn't be enough. Foot soldiers could be formidable. "We'll have to take all the guns, too."

Martha Townsend stood up, her eyes wide. "What if Indians come? What can we do without guns?"

"It's not the way I want it, but if I can't have a promise I've got to do it."

Townsend looked at Chancellor, asking with his eyes. Chancellor said, "You can't leave us defenseless, Texas, not in this country. And I can't promise not to come after you. But maybe I could promise to give you some time. How much time do you want?"

David made a quick mental calculation on the probable speed of the wagons. Men afoot could move faster, he knew. "I'll want thirty-six hours. Promise me none of you will start after us before noon tomorrow and I'll leave you your guns."

"Thirty-six hours?" Chancellor jumped to his feet. "I can't agree to that."

"Then we take all the guns, and I leave two men here to keep anybody from comin' up out of this cellar before at least the middle of the afternoon."

Chancellor wrestled with his conscience and grudgingly agreed. "All right. None of us moves against you till tomorrow noon."

Owen Townsend said brittlely, "It's Tom's decision to make, and he's made it. But I'll tell you this, Buckalew: the Army can't let you get those munitions to Confederate territory, to be used in killing our people. They'll be after you afoot if necessary, and I'll be with them. We'll take the wagons away from you if we can. If we can't, we'll blow them up with you in them. You know a bullet or two in the right place could send that whole mess halfway to the moon."

David looked into the old scout's angry eyes and felt ice in the pit of his stomach. Owen Townsend meant every word. And he would do it, for what did he have to lose?

David turned his gaze to Martha Townsend. A thought came unbidden, and at first unwelcome. But it persisted.

They wouldn't be so keen on destroying that wagon train if Townsend *did* have something to lose. He considered awhile and saw no alternative. He stepped back to the ladder and called up. "Sergeant Mitchell, would you come down here, please? And bring a man with you." Mitchell and Hufstedler came down the ladder. David directed them to hold their guns on the Union soldiers.

David told the men, "I want all of you to back up yonder." Puzzled, the soldiers complied. Some of Townsend's Mexican ranchhands moved to the old man's side, sensing that he was in trouble. "Back up," David told them. "Back with the soldiers. You too, Mister Townsend, and Lieutenant Chancellor."

Martha started to retreat with them. David caught her arm. "Not you, Miss Townsend. I want you to go up the ladder."

Her father took an angry step forward. Tom Chancellor took two. "Texas, you turn her loose!"

Noley Mitchell thrust his pistol toward them. They stopped.

"Go on up, Miss Townsend," David said, "before somebody gets shot."

She cast one fearful look back toward her father and Chancellor. Then she started up the ladder.

David waited until she was out of sight. "Mister Townsend, this is one thing I didn't want to do, but you've put me in a tight spot. Anything you do against that wagon train, you'll be doin' against *her.*"

He started up the ladder, looking back.

Chancellor stepped toward him until David drew his pistol. Chancellor said, "If you think you need a hostage, take me. Leave that girl here."

"She means that much to you, Lieutenant?"

Chancellor glanced back at Townsend. "Yes, she does."

"You think you mean as much to Mister Townsend as his daughter does? You think he would be as reluctant to blow up the wagons if you were with us as if *she* were?"

Chancellor didn't answer.

David shook his head. "You're a soldier. A soldier can always be sacrificed. A daughter can't. Sorry, gentlemen, but she goes with us and you stay here."

Chancellor took a couple more steps. "Texas, if you're any kind of *man*..."

David pointed his pistol and stopped him. "She'll be all right," he promised, "if you leave us alone."

Chancellor was coming up the ladder, still arguing, when David dropped the trap door into place, almost hitting the lieutenant's head. David was glad to be out of the cellar, out of the possibility of being forced to shoot the lieutenant. "He has nerve," he admitted.

The girl warned sternly, "And he'll kill you if he ever gets the chance." The look in her eyes indicated that she might try it herself.

For just a moment David indulged in the luxury of looking back on the peace he had left in Hopeful Valley. He found it difficult to comprehend just how he had gotten in a situation where he stirred up so much hatred. It had not been in his nature.

He said, "If there's anything you need to take with you—woman stuff or like that—you better gather it up." He turned to Hufstedler. "You'll drive the provision wagon. She'll be on it with you and Pete Richey."

The wagons were lined up and waiting to move. David asked Noley Mitchell, "How many extra horses are there that we can't take?"

"Just the ranch stock, and one Yankee mule that's lame."

"We'll have to shoot them, then."

Mitchell's face went into deep furrows. He turned regretfully toward the dozen or fifteen animals gathered in a pen. "We shot all those at Bearfield's tradin' post. I'm out of stomach for that job. What if we taken them with us a ways and turned them loose?"

"They'd come home."

Mitchell nodded darkly, seeing that it had to be. "I'll stay behind and do it, then. I'll also keep them folks in that cellar awhile. They won't know when I leave."

"Sorry to give you the meanest job, Noley."

David swung onto his brown horse and sought out Fermin Hernandez. He found the Mexican watching him, a vague resentment in his eyes. David did not understand the resentment.

"Hernandez, you can take the point."

Hernandez' jaw ridged grimly. "I am a good wagon driver, Lieutenant. But I have known you would put me on the point."

"That's been your position all along."

"Why *my* position? If anybody is to be killed, it will be the man out in front. He will be out there by himself. Always before, they put me there because I am a Mexican, and I am not worth as much as the others. You are like them; you do the same."

David was taken by surprise. "That's not true." But he realized it *was* true. He had done it subconsciously, but the reason had been there all along if he had taken time to analyze it.

He sat on the horse and stared uncertainly at the Mexican. A sense of shame washed over him.

"All right, Hernandez, you take a wagon. I'll put somebody else up there." He looked around and spotted Jake Calvin. "Calvin, you'll ride the point."

Calvin blanched. "Me? What for, Buckalew? Why me?"

"Because I'm tellin' you to."

Calvin began arguing that his eyesight was not good enough, that his horse was too slow for an emergency run, that he felt he could be of more use driving a wagon because he knew mules.

David told him impatiently to get the hell up there and follow orders. Calvin went, but he rode along looking back, talking to himself. David turned to Hernandez. "You satisfied now?"

Hernandez did not reply. David said, "I don't think he's one bit better than you."

Hernandez replied grimly, "He is not half as good." He climbed up onto the lead wagon and took a seat. David's jaw tightened. He gave Hernandez the signal to start. He heard the jingling of trace chains, the creak of leather, the crunch of wide-tired wheels turning under a heavy load. He sat on the horse and waited until all the wagons started,

the rising sun shining on their left flank. He looked to the east, study-
ing the hills, each range of them a darker blue than the one before it.
He rode down the line to the rear wagon, which was bringing along
the provisions. Martha Townsend sat on the seat beside Hufstedler.
Her eyes were almost hidden beneath the shadow of a slat bonnet, but
David saw them cut sharply at him as he reined up.

He asked about Pete Richey's condition. Hufstedler said, "He is not
good, *Leutnant*, but what can we do?"

David looked at Martha Townsend. "Anything you can do to help
him, I'd sure appreciate it."

She gave him a hard stare but said nothing.

They had traveled perhaps half a mile when David heard the slow,
methodical shooting begin behind them. Noley Mitchell was leaving
the ranch people and the Yankees afoot. David gritted his teeth. If he
ever got back to Hopeful Valley, he would never kill a horse again.

Because they were so short-handed, he kept moving from the front
of the train to the rear and back again, serving as a flexible outrider.
Homer Gilman rode behind as rear guard. They halted awhile at noon
to rest the mules and eat some bread and meat David had had the Yankee cook prepare along with breakfast. He put another man on point to
relieve Calvin. He had decided the only fair thing was to rotate the
point. Calvin was vastly relieved to be back from that exposed position.

A little after they set out on the trail again, Noley Mitchell caught
up with them. He took a long and careful look at the wagons as he
worked his way up the line to David.

David asked, "Did you leave everything in good shape back there?"

Mitchell said sadly, "I left it the way we had to. How's everything
with the wagons?"

"All right."

"I didn't have to push the horse too hard to catch you. Anybody
follows us afoot, he can outpace the wagons."

"They agreed not to come after us till noon tomorrow."

"That was before you took the woman." Mitchell looked behind
him apprehensively, as if expecting to see somebody trailing the wagons. "We'd better spend a short night."

David glanced quizzically at him. "Noley, you talked almighty confident yesterday. You don't look that confident now."

"Things always look easier when you're just talkin' about them."

"How much chance do you think we've really got?"

Mitchell shrugged.

David said, "You didn't show me that doubt yesterday."

"You're a horse trader, Davey. Do you ever tell a man all the bad points about a horse you want to sell him?"

"I never tried to sell a man a string of wagons loaded with gunpowder and ammunition, with Yankee soldiers and maybe Indians huntin' for them."

"That takes salesmanship."

"The kind of salesmanship you and Luther Lusk used on me, you could never use in a horse trade. They'd hang you."

"Don't fret over the risk, Davey; think of the benefits. We was comin' home failures, all of us. Now we got a chance to come home as heroes. Your old daddy will be proud of you, button. And them people of mine who voted me out of office, maybe they'll take a second look and decide old Noley Mitchell wasn't so wore out and useless after all."

David's eyes narrowed. "That why you're doin' this, Noley, to try and win an election?"

"Not just an election. I want to win back what I was in the eyes of those people before the rheumatism started, and the hair and the beard went to turnin' gray."

David didn't try to hide a measure of surprised realization. "You're usin' this war, Noley."

"Everybody's usin' this war someway. Them professional Yankee soldiers, it's their career. You came to try and win a reputation you never had. I came to win back one I had and lost."

"I came to fight for a cause."

"So did I. So did everybody here, on both sides. But as long as I'm fightin', I'd rather try somethin' big and lose than try somethin' small and settle for it."

In the middle of the afternoon David rode back to the last wagon.

Martha Townsend sat slumped and tired beside Hufstedler. Two nights of sleeping—or not sleeping—in that cellar had worn her down. The trailing wagon caught all the dust from the other ten, and she had a fair percentage of that dust on her face despite the slat bonnet.

David said, "Hufstedler, I'd appreciate it if you'd ride my horse a little while and let me take your place on the wagon. I'd like to talk to Miss Townsend."

She gave him no sign of welcome. "I don't believe we have anything to talk about."

Hufstedler pulled the team to a halt and got down. David handed him the reins and climbed up on the wagon. He set the mules to moving. David sat in silence awhile, her antipathy a wall between them. He glanced back beneath the tarp that covered the wagon bows. "How's Pete? You been lookin' in on him regular?"

"He is not doing well. He should have been left at the ranch."

"You know why we couldn't do that."

"I would have liked it much better if I could have stayed too."

"I know." David fumbled with the words, taking his time in bringing them out. "I don't guess it counts for much to tell you I'm sorry the way things came out. You wouldn't be here if it wasn't the only way I thought we could bring these wagons through. There was no other way your father would've backed off."

"He may still not back off. He's loyal to his country."

"But he's a father. I'm countin' on him bein' more loyal to you."

She was silent awhile. Her face was hidden behind the bonnet, so he had no idea what she was thinking. Finally she asked, "What do you intend to do with me, Texas?"

"You'll be treated like a lady. There's not a man in this outfit that would even think of doin' one thing . . ."

"I know that. That's not what I meant. Supposing you do get these wagons through to your own lines—which I doubt—what becomes of me then? Am I a prisoner of war? And if not, how do I get home?"

"I've studied on that. When we get these wagons safely to our side, you'll be free to go back to your own people."

"How? Through this Indian country, alone?"

"I've thought on that too. You'll have an escort home under a flag of truce. If it'll make you feel better, I'll lead that escort myself."

She turned and looked at him, her eyes incredulous. "I can't say it makes me feel better, but it *does* surprise me."

"We haven't always been enemies, Miss Townsend. Till a little while back we were part of the same country. I wouldn't of done you any harm then. I won't see any harm come to you now."

She pondered on that. He sensed the wall coming down a little. "Well," she said presently, her voice a bit less harsh, "I've heard of Texas chivalry. That may be carrying it to an extreme. Even if you ride back here under a flag of truce, you can't be sure our troops will recognize it after what you've done. They may take you prisoner."

That was a possibility he had recognized but had forced himself not to consider, lest it turn him back from what he saw now as a clear personal responsibility. "I'm a horse trader," he said, trying to make light of the risk. "Maybe I can talk them out of it."

"You may do well to talk them out of hanging you."

"Why? I just did what a soldier is supposed to do."

"You put on a Union uniform to carry out your plan. If I know anything about the military code—and I ought to—that makes you eligible to hang as a spy. Didn't you think of that?"

"I didn't even know about it. I never was a soldier before."

"That I can believe." She turned to study him, the hostility gone. "I don't quite figure you out, Texas. Why would you take that risk for me?"

"It's my responsibility. I'm the one takin' you away from home."

That didn't satisfy her, and he knew it. The real truth was that he didn't know why he had made up his mind to this. He suspected it might be because of a vague image that kept coming into his mind, unbidden and at odd times when he hadn't consciously meant for his thoughts to drift in that direction.

He frowned. "You sure you never seen me before, Miss Townsend?"

"I don't remember that I ever did."

"Think back. They said you did some nursin' work in the military hospital in Albuquerque for our side and them both. You sure you didn't help treat me, and put a cool wet cloth on my head when I was in fever?"

"I did that for a lot of men. I don't remember every particular one."

"I remember somebody . . . somebody doin' that for me."

"Do you remember her face?"

"I was too feverish to see clear."

She conceded, "It might've been me, or it could've been somebody else. A lot of women helped in the hospital. Old ones, young ones, all kinds. You don't remember anything about what she looked like?"

"I just remember that she looked like an angel."

"That ought to eliminate me. I've been accused of many things, but being an angel was never one of the charges."

"I *hope* it was you."

"We'll never know, though, will we?"

"If it was you, I owe you for it. If it wasn't you, I owe some other lady that I'll never see again. The only way I can ever repay the debt to her is by doin' somethin' for somebody else. If enough favors get passed around by enough people, maybe everybody comes out even in the end."

"You don't sound like a horse trader. You sound like a preacher."

"I been exposed to some of that, too."

She looked at him, but he found it impossible to read what was behind those blue eyes. At least she didn't seem angry anymore. She said, "It's too bad we couldn't have met under better circumstances, Texas. You might be a decent sort if you weren't a Confederate soldier."

"My mother always used to say I was a nice fellow. But of course she knew me before the war."

She laughed. Thinking back, he was sure it was the first time he had heard her do it. She said, "You even have a sense of humor."

"You've got to have a sense of humor down where I come from, else life will drive you crazy. It isn't always an easy country."

"That isn't the way I've heard most *Tejanos* tell it."

He warmed a little, sitting beside her with the hostility gone. He gripped the reins tightly to help fight down a strong impulse to reach over and touch her. To do that, he knew, would destroy whatever good feeling he might finally have attained from her.

He said, "You told me you wished we could've met at another time.

I wish we had, too. You suppose that if we had, there's any chance you might've looked at me the way you looked at Lieutenant Chancellor?"

She grew suddenly wary. "I didn't realize I looked any particular way at Tom Chancellor."

"You did."

"He's . . . well, he's part of the family."

"Seems like he thinks a right smart of you."

"He loved my sister. Maybe he sees something of her in me, that's all." She turned and looked him in the eyes, and he saw a wall of sorts come up again. "In any case, Mister Buckalew, that is a personal and private matter that doesn't concern you."

"No, ma'am. I guess I spoke out of my place."

"I believe you did."

Eventually Hufstedler came back and swapped places. David was more than ready. It had become awkward and uncomfortable to sit here beside Martha Townsend after she lapsed back into her stony silence. He had tried a couple of times to start a new conversation in some other direction but had not been able to break through that cool reserve.

David went back to working first one side of the train and then the other, watching for anything that might indicate trouble.

Late in the afternoon Homer Gilman loped up from his assigned position behind the train. David spurred back to meet him, knowing he wouldn't leave his place unless it were important. Gilman reined the horse to a stop, the dust swirling around him.

The tall miller looked agitated. "Lieutenant, I thought them Yankees wasn't to trail after us before tomorrow."

"That was the agreement."

"Well, they've busted it, I expect. There's a man walkin' behind us, gainin' on us from the way it looks."

David tried to see through the dust left hanging by the wagons, but it was hopeless. He frowned. "Just one man? You sure?"

"One is all I can see."

David hesitated, not wanting to leave the wagons but knowing he had to. "All right, let's go see about your Yankee."

Once they had dropped back a hundred yards or so where the dust had either settled or drifted off, he could see the man, possibly half a mile back on the trail. He was out in the midst of a broad, open flat. He was obviously alone. But David looked to the hills on either side, distrusting the obvious. He rode in an easy trot, not rushing into anything. Long before he and Gilman reached the man, David drew the rifle from its scabbard beneath his leg. He laid it across his lap, ready. Gilman watched his action, then did the same.

Even covered with gray dust, the man's clothes were plainly Union blue. David began to suspect the truth before he was near enough to see for sure. For the last two hundred yards, knowing nobody else could be hidden out of sight in this open flat, he touched spurs to the big horse. He held the rifle down to present no threat, but he did not put it away. He stopped just short of Lieutenant Chancellor.

Chancellor carried a rifle in his hand and wore a pistol on his hip. He made no threatening move with either.

David cleared the dust from his throat and spat on the ground. "You made an agreement, Chancellor. And you broke it."

"I made that agreement before you took Martha with you."

"You figured to take her away from us? One man?"

"No. I figured to come along and be with her."

"If I'd wanted you, Chancellor, I'd of taken you the first time you offered. Now you've got a long walk back."

"A long walk, maybe, but not back."

"What do you think you could do for her?"

"Protect her."

"She needs no protection from us, and we'll give her protection from anybody else that comes along. So go back, Chancellor."

"No. I've come a long way. I'm staying."

David stewed, uncertain what move to make next. "Gilman, take his guns."

Gilman stepped down. Chancellor gave up the rifle and pistol without resistance.

David said, "You'll need these for your own protection. We'll give them to you when you turn around and start back."

"I'm going to your wagon train, Buckalew. If you want to stop me, you'll have to shoot me." He waited a minute, watching David's eyes without evident fear. "See, I knew you wouldn't do that. So like it or not, Buckalew, you have another prisoner."

"You'll be one till the war is over."

"That can't amount to much, perhaps two or three months. When they see you Texans retreat from New Mexico they'll know it's hopeless all over the South."

Gilman said, "If you don't want to shoot him, Lieutenant, I expect Jake Calvin would do it for you. It's a specialty of his."

David shook his head. "I'll ask no man to do somethin' I wouldn't do myself."

Chancellor seemed not a bit surprised. "Now that we've settled that question, Buckalew, how about letting me ride double with one of you? It's been a long walk."

David grimaced. "You wasn't invited. I reckon you've *still* got a ways to walk." He turned and started riding away, Homer Gilman beside him. Chancellor seemed resigned. He started walking.

When they had ridden a hundred yards David told Gilman to go on. He turned and rode back, walking the horse, giving Chancellor plenty of time to look at him and wonder.

He reined up and let Chancellor walk the last thirty or forty yards. "You taken an awful chance," David said firmly. "What if Indians had come upon you out there, one man afoot and by himself?"

"Some chances a man has to take."

David was still distrustful. "Does the girl really mean so much to you, or are you thinkin' maybe you'll get lucky and do somethin' to our wagons?"

Chancellor looked him squarely in the eyes. "She means that much to me."

David studied him hard. The man's earnest look made him inclined to believe, but that graveling doubt still lingered. "I've seen prettier women. And she's strong-willed. She can stab you to death with her eyes."

"You, perhaps. Not me. There's another side to her, a side you haven't seen."

David wished he could remember that for certain. "You've taken an awful chance for nothin'. We won't let anything happen to her."

Pain came into Chancellor's eyes. "Someone promised me that once about her sister. I lost *her*."

David wanted to take him for what he appeared to be. "You promise you won't do anything against our wagons?"

Chancellor deliberated, then shook his head. "I'm still a soldier. No, I won't promise you that."

David cursed again, under his breath. It would be much easier to be tough on a man who wasn't so damned honest. He kicked his left foot out of the stirrup. "Step on up here. If you're bound and determined to get there anyway, I don't see any gain in makin' you walk."

As they approached the rear wagon David asked, "You bein' an officer and all, I suppose it would violate your dignity to drive a team of mules."

"I've done it before."

"Then you can drive the provision wagon. That's where Miss Townsend is at." He didn't feel he could trust Chancellor on one of the munitions wagons. And this, at least, would free Hufstedler to serve as an outrider.

He rode up beside the wagon and watched for Martha Townsend's expression as she saw Tom Chancellor. She cried out in surprise, "Tom!" For a moment her blue eyes lighted. Then her face changed as realization came that he was a prisoner, just as she was.

David said, "Hufstedler, stop the wagon. You've got a relief driver. You can saddle you a horse."

Hufstedler climbed down with a heavily accented expression of gratitude and stared curiously at the Union officer as Chancellor climbed up on the wheel.

David watched gravely as the two put their arms around one another. He felt a fleeting pang which he knew was jealousy, and realized he had no valid reason for it, or even any right. He started to pull away, for he felt like an intruder. But he had to have his say. "Chancellor, so you understand your place, don't ever forget you're a prisoner of war. You'll find no guns on that wagon, and you'll not go anywhere within reach of any other wagon. You'll stay at the end of the train and keep the same distance as the others. You won't turn off to the right or left, and you won't make any move to get away from here with Miss Townsend. Try any of those things and somebody'll just naturally have to shoot you."

Chancellor nodded. "We understand each other, Buckalew."

"I sure hope you understand *me*, because I think this good woman has already had trouble enough."

It took a long time for word to work its way along the wagons that the Union lieutenant was a prisoner. Most of the men up front had been in no position to see David bring him in. But somehow the word gradually spread, in that mysterious way that news always has in a military organization. One by one, the outriders dropped back to see for themselves.

As David rode by Jake Calvin's wagon, the skinhunter called him. "Hey there, Buckalew!"

David ignored the call the first time. The second time he rode over beside the wagon. "The name is *Lieutenant*."

Calvin spat low, streaking tobacco juice across the turning wheel. "Buckalew, I hear you brought that Yankee officer into the outfit."

"He's a prisoner."

"Dangerous, havin' a man like that around, with all this powder and stuff. If I was you, I'd play safe and shoot him."

David nodded. "But you're not me." For which he would ever be grateful to a merciful God. He rode on, leaving Calvin still talking, much dissatisfied.

A while before sundown David loped to the lead and halted the wagons in the center of a wide-open flat. Here, he thought, nobody could surprise them. As a precaution, nevertheless, he had the wagons start moving into a circle. He told each driver in succession that they would stop and fix a quick supper, then move on a few more miles before stopping for the night in a dry, fireless camp. The mules had been watered an hour earlier at a natural catch basin that fortuitously had had some water in it. They would be fed a little now while the men awaited supper.

He rode to the last wagon. "Miss Townsend, we're makin' a stop here for supper. There's no man in this outfit that's really much good at cookin'. I was wonderin' . . ."

He had looked back a few times and had seen Martha Townsend and Tom Chancellor in earnest conversation. The sight had always brought a flare of jealousy that he realized was needless. He meant no more to that girl than one of these Yankee mules.

She said, "I don't suppose being a prisoner carries any privileges?"

Chancellor told her, "You don't have to do anything you don't want to."

David said, "That's right, ma'am. You don't have to. But if you eat the men's cookin' a time or two, I think you'll *want* to cook." He made it a point to sound plaintive, and it seemed to work. She said she would see what she could do. Homer Gilman rode up and shoveled a firepit for her at some distance from the wagon circle. Gilman, Chancellor and David lifted from the provision wagon the things she needed for cooking. That done, David climbed back into the wagon for a close look at Pete Richey. At first he thought the young soldier was asleep, and he decided to leave him alone.

Richey opened his eyes. They looked more feverish than before. David felt his forehead and found it almost hot. Richey asked in a husky voice, just above a whisper, "Could I have some water?"

"You betcha." David brought it to him in a dipper and held the boy's head up to help him drink. Slowly Pete took most of the water. What was left, David poured onto a rag which Martha Townsend had been keeping wet and applying periodically to the boy's head.

"Pete," David said, "I'm sorry to be puttin' you through this."

"I could've stayed. Nothin's your fault."

Yesterday David had been hopeful about the boy. But Richey seemed to have lost ground. David lied, "You're goin' to be all right." His face would betray his doubt, he turned to leave.

Pete called weakly, "Lieutenant!" David stopped. Pete said, straining at it, "They done a lot of talkin' together, that Yankee and that girl."

"Talkin'?"

"Most of it they kept low to where I couldn't hear what they said. I think you better watch them."

David was not surprised. It was only natural that the two would try to figure a means to get away from here. "They'll be watched every minute. There's not much they can do."

"They argued a right smart over somethin'. I heard him say it would be too risky for her, and she said it was worth the gamble. I wish I could tell you what it is. They just wouldn't let me hear."

"I'll do the worryin' about it; you just lay easy and rest while the wagon is still."

He climbed down to the ground and walked out where the fire had been kindled in the shallow pit, downwind from the wagons so no spark would be carried to them. The coffeepot was already on. Martha Townsend was mixing up some water-and-flour bread. David was glad the Yankees had brought that provision wagon along. There was even cured ham in it, and potatoes, At least the men would have something decent to eat on this leg of the trip.

While supper was being prepared, David stood around worrying about the things Pete had told him. He tried to imagine what kind of plot the pair might have worked up. If they intended to run for horses, that was almost certainly doomed to failure. The horses were tied to wagons, and chances were that the Texans could catch the pair before they could ride away. They wouldn't shoot the girl, but they would probably not hesitate to shoot Chancellor out of the saddle, if he ever got that far. Surely Chancellor and the girl had figured this out for themselves.

Maybe they hoped to grab a gun and somehow gain an advantage. It would probably be futile, but they might feel it was worth the effort. David quietly passed the word to the men to hold their distance from the pair and give them no such opportunity.

Through supper he watched, puzzling. When Jake Calvin got too close, David stepped up to remind him of his earlier warning. Calvin said, "I was just hopin' he *would* grab for my gun. I'd be tickled to shoot him."

"I don't want any killin' here," David told him brittlely. "I don't want anybody causin' a reason for one."

Calvin glowered. "I thought killin' was what we went to war for."

Supper finished, the men walked by and dropped their plates, cups and utensils into a pot of water bubbling and boiling over the fire. Tom Chancellor, under David's watchful eye, had brought some fresh wood a few minutes earlier and placed it under the pot to bring the fire back up to a high level. The men began moving back, a few at a time, toward the wagons, ready to move on as soon as David gave the word.

He had just about made up his mind that Martha and Chancellor had either given up a plan for escape or intended to do it later, perhaps during the night. Suddenly, when he had stopped expecting anything, Martha Townsend began running out across the open flat. The move puzzled him for a moment; she had no possible chance of escape that way. A man on a horse could overtake her in a minute.

Nevertheless, she had his attention, and the attention of the men. David realized she was running alone. He turned quickly on his heel, looking for Tom Chancellor. The lieutenant was sprinting toward the wagons, carrying two blazing firebrands he had jerked from beneath the pot.

David had no time to give chase, or even to shout. Chancellor was already more than half the distance to the wagons. David pulled out his pistol, leveled it and started to fire. He let the muzzle dip, for he realized suddenly that a bullet which struck in the wrong place might set off a wagonload of powder. He leveled the pistol again, lower this time, and shot at Chancellor's legs.

The Union lieutenant went down, sprawling, the blazing wood sailing out in front of him. He tried to regain his feet but couldn't stand. He got to one knee, grabbed a brand and hurled it toward the nearest wagon. It fell short. He reached for the other, but Luther Lusk had reached him. Lusk kicked the burning stick away just as Chancellor's fingers had started to close on it.

Martha Townsend stopped running. Only one man, Homer Gilman, had started after her. He stopped too. The girl came back when she saw Chancellor down. She was crying, "Don't shoot him again! Please don't anybody shoot him again!"

She dropped to her knees at his side and threw her arms around him protectively. Her eyes sought out David Buckalew. "Please, Texas. Don't do it."

David realized then that he still had the pistol aimed at Chancellor. He lowered it, for the danger was past.

Not all of it. Jake Calvin had stood paralyzed in those few anxious seconds. Now he walked up with pistol in his hand. "Dammit, Buckalew, I tried to tell you. As long as he's alive there ain't a one of us safe."

He brought the pistol into line with Chancellor's head. Fear leaped into the lieutenant's eyes. The girl screamed.

David shouted, "Put it down, Calvin. You're not goin' to shoot him." As he spoke he brought his own pistol up again, pointing it now at Calvin.

Calvin said, "Girl, you step back or you'll get his blood splattered all over you."

David could see in Calvin's eyes that the hidehunter really intended to do it. "No!" David warned. "I'll kill you!"

Confidently Calvin said, "You wouldn't kill me over no damnyankee." He leaned down, bringing the muzzle of his pistol near Chancellor's head.

"Oh God," David whispered, and he squeezed the trigger. Flame belched from the heavy pistol. Jake Calvin lurched backward under the impact. His pistol went off by reflex, the slug lifting a spray of sand almost at David's feet. The Texan sank to his knees, dropping the pistol. He stared at David in a moment of agonized disbelief, then flopped face forward to the ground. He twitched, and that was all.

David's pistol was frozen in his hand. He could not bring himself to move, even to lower his arm. His nostrils burned from the bite of the black smoke. Tears rushed into his eyes. He found it in him to turn away, closing his eyes in pain at what he had done.

Noley Mitchell gripped his arm worriedly. "You all right, Davey? That bullet didn't ricochet and hit you?"

David found voice, though a broken one. "I'm all right."

Noley waited for David to say more. When David didn't, the sergeant put in, "That Calvin never did have any sense."

David knew, but he asked anyway. "You sure he's dead?"

"He's dead."

David shivered. He found his holster and put the pistol away. He didn't want to turn and look, but he felt compelled. Fortunately, Calvin's face was away from him. David didn't think he could have stood to look into those accusing dead eyes.

He heard Martha sobbing. She was still on her knees, her arms around Chancellor. David took a couple of slow steps toward the pair. "You can get up. Nobody's goin' to kill your man."

His own men were standing around, too numb to move. David tried not to look into their faces, for he was fearful of what he might see.

He brought himself to say, "Somebody better look at Chancellor. See how bad he's hurt."

Nobody seemed in a hurry about it, but Luther Lusk finally knelt and ripped the trousers leg open with his knife. A cupful of blood spilled out. Homer Gilman walked over to help him but didn't appear eager. Lusk gripped the leg and moved it a little. Chancellor's sharp breath reflected the pain. Lusk said, "I believe you missed the bone, Davey."

David looked regretfully at Calvin again. "Yeah, well, patch him up. Get him onto the wagon. We got to move."

Martha Townsend got to her feet. She faced David, the tears still brimming in her eyes.

David said accusingly, "I don't see that you've got anything to cry about. He's still alive. He's goin' to stay alive. That's more than I can say about Jake Calvin."

"We didn't intend it to end like this."

"You'd of blown up the whole train, and like as not yourselves along with the rest of us."

"But how many others would we have saved?"

"It didn't work like you figured. We've got a man dead, and I'm the one who had to kill him. I've got to live with that, if I can."

"I'm sorry."

"Sorry you tried, or sorry it didn't work?" He turned away, toward his horse, then stopped. His voice was cold. "It was for nothin' anyway. The wagon he tried to throw the fire into . . . there wasn't any powder in it."

He told Sergeant Mitchell to see that Calvin's body was placed in one of the wagons. They would bury him tonight, farther on. Right now they needed to make as many miles as they could. He turned in the saddle and watched from some distance as the wounded lieutenant was carried to the provision wagon. He stayed to one side while the train strung out again.

David watched the evening star come out and mentally calculated how many hours it would be until the Yankee troops at the Townsend ranch started after them, if indeed they hadn't broken the agreement and started already. He decided to keep rolling far into the night. There would be time enough to rest men and mules when they had reached other Texas units and safety.

He estimated they had traveled two to perhaps three hours in darkness when the lead wagon stopped. The others had to halt as each drew up close behind the next. David loped to the lead wagon and found Fermin Hernandez standing by his team, afoot. Just ahead, in the darkness, loomed a rough hill.

"What's the matter, Hernandez?"

The Mexican pointed. "Too rough for the dark, Lieutenant. I think maybe I hang the wagon or turn it over."

Reluctantly David had to agree. "Pull them back a little, then, and start a circle. We'll stop here." He stood by while the wagons began moving into position. As the last one made its move, he rode in beside it. He said to Martha Townsend, "You and Chanceller will get down easy and be placed under guard inside the circle. There'll be no fire here. We'll bury Calvin, then we'll get some rest while we can."

Sadly she said, "I'm sorry to tell you, but you'll need to dig two graves. Pete Richey died in his sleep."

David clenched his fist and turned quickly away. He drove the fist futilely at the pommel of the saddle until the pain made him stop.

CHAPTER 6

At first light the wagons were strung out again. It was not proper to call this a trail, for there was none. If any wagon had ever passed this way before, it had left no mark.

David hung back a little, his shoulders hunched. The two graves had been left unmarked because it was said that Indians sometimes dug them up and mutilated the bodies. He had no idea if this was true, but he had chosen not to run a risk. The wagons had deliberately been driven over the spot to obscure it. When the Texans left, no one would ever know that two of their number had remained here, forever. David doubted that he could find the exact place again himself, once he rode away from it.

He took off his hat. "We tried, Pete. We tried hard to get you back to Texas."

He rode on after the others. He imagined he could feel Martha Townsend's eyes upon him as he passed the trail wagon, but he made it a point not to look. He rode with his head down, leaving something of himself back there in those graves.

He rode up on a hill where he could see a long way in three directions. In particular he looked behind him. He saw nothing. But he could feel it gnawing at him; back there, somewhere, those Yankees were coming. He could feel them.

He took a position about even with the middle of the train and held it except for occasionally riding out to a prominence for a long look. Sometime about midmorning Noley Mitchell fell in beside him. The sergeant moved along in silence awhile, framing with care the thing he wanted to say.

"It's tough enough to kill an enemy," he said quietly. "It's tougher to kill your own kind. But Jake Calvin wasn't really ever one of us. He was just along."

"I keep askin' myself if I should've done it. I traded his life for a Yankee. If I had to do it over . . ."

"You'd have to do the same. Hell, Davey, there's not a man in the outfit that thinks you done wrong. It took guts to try what Chancellor did. If he'd managed to hit powder like he hoped, he wouldn't have had one chance in ten of gettin' away fast enough. He knew that. If he is a Yankee, he's a man. Jake Calvin never was."

David took a long time to digest that. He didn't say anything.

Mitchell made a lengthy study and came up with no answers. "I hope you're feelin' better," he said, probing.

"No, but I thank you for comin' and tellin' me, just the same."

They halted briefly at noon to fix coffee, eat a little leftover bread, fry up some ham and give the mules time to "blow." David saw to the men and the wagons before he took time to go in and get something to eat. He walked to the fire and poured some coffee. As he looked up, he found Martha Townsend staring at him. Their eyes met; he could not avoid her.

He asked, "How's Chancellor?"

"A lot better than he would be if you were a good shot."

"I *am* a good shot. Otherwise I'd of killed him."

"You mean you weren't trying to?"

"I wouldn't of shot Jake Calvin if I had wanted to kill your man."

She frowned. "He's not *my man*, the way you say it." She looked down. "I've said some hard things to you, Texas. I won't say that I didn't mean every one of them at the time. But I wish I could take them back."

"I wish I could bring back Jake Calvin, too. But I can't."

Her eyes commanded attention. "We had a duty, Texas, just as you have. We had to make a try. It's still a war, and we're still on opposite sides."

David could understand that. He had pleaded the same reasons just yesterday. Some of the bitterness lifted. "I hope you won't try again."

"Tom is in no condition to."

"But *you* are. It's bad enough havin' Jake on my conscience. For God's sake don't make me go through life rememberin' that I had to shoot a woman too."

She considered. "I won't. We've made our try."

The first sign of the trouble came an hour or so later. He saw a horseman at some distance on the left flank, toward the river. He halted, extended the spyglass and took a look. The rider was an Indian, moving at an easy walk paralleling the train. David's throat tightened. He scanned the hills as far as he could see, looking for more. He saw only the one.

Homer Gilman came loping up shortly, pointing in the same direction. David nodded. "I've already seen him. It's an Indian."

"What kind?"

"I don't know. All I know about Indians is that none of them seem to like us."

An hour or so later, one of the Texans on a wagon began gesturing at David, trying to get his attention. From his wagon seat he pointed off to the right. A quarter mile to the west, or a little more, was another Indian.

Noley Mitchell rode back to fall in beside David. "You've put the glass on them, I suppose?"

About that time the Indian to the west rode up on a hill and dismounted. David could see a mirror flashing.

Mitchell growled. "If it was a telegraph wire, we could cut it."

"Maybe we could anyway. A few of us could rush him and kill him."

Mitchell shook his head. "Too late. Killin' one now might be like killin' one ant out of a whole anthill. Anyway, there might be a bunch of them waitin' in ambush out yonder, hopin' we'll try that very thing."

David decided it was a good time to make use of Mitchell's experience in fighting Indians, an experience David himself had never had. "What do we do, then?"

"Keep on doin' what we're doin' now, just travel. There may not be many of them after all. If not, they're probably just hangin' on, hopin' for a chance to grab a few horses or mules. We'd best keep the wagons tight together."

The men were already taking care of that. The gap between the wagons had narrowed almost to nothing. Everybody on the train had seen the Indians.

David dropped back to the last wagon, where Martha Townsend rode beside Hufstedler. A grim-faced Tom Chancellor watched out the back. "Buckalew," he said, "under the circumstances, don't you think we ought to have some guns on this wagon?"

"They haven't made any hostile move yet. *You* have. You feel strong enough to be drivin' this wagon?"

"I guess so."

"Good. We can use Hufstedler on horseback."

Martha Townsend's lips were tight. "Those Indians, Texas . . . what do you think they're going to do?"

"They're *your* Indians, Miss Townsend. I expect you know more about them than I do."

There was no question of moving these wagons after dark. David had heard somewhere that Indians would not attack at night, but he had no faith in that story. He reasoned that if he were an Indian he would fight anytime and anywhere that he had a strong advantage, and darkness would certainly be an advantage to those out yonder if they intended to hit moving wagons.

At sundown, reaching a reasonably flat and open stretch of country where the bushes were scattered and short, David ordered the wagons drawn into a tight circle. The mules were unharnessed. They and the horses were turned loose for feed and water inside the formation. From the standpoint of Indian danger, he thought, it would have been safer to build the cookfire inside, too. But that would be too risky from the standpoint of the gunpowder. They dug the firepit away from the wagons but near enough that they could retreat in a hurry. Nobody lost any motion in getting supper started; Martha Townsend had more help than she needed.

David had never yet seen more than the two Indians. These had continued to ride along at a respectful distance, out of effective range, keeping up with the wagons but making no threatening move toward them. David wished he could tell himself that these two were all. But he sensed that they had company, somewhere yonder out of sight.

By dusk everybody had finished eating. The firepit had been covered with dirt to prevent flying sparks. With the night came a chill. David hunched his shoulders and wished the tattered gray coat were heavier. He had half the men out on guard duty. The other half, theoretically, were to sleep so they could stand guard later in the night. He doubted that anyone would shut his eyes.

He walked to the place where Martha Townsend and Tom Chancellor huddled together, each wrapped in a blanket. David looked at the girl, but he asked Chancellor, "How's the leg?"

"It hurts." He hadn't been able to walk on it. Somebody had had to support him and help him hop along. Well, he wouldn't be trying to run away, or running to destroy a wagon.

Chancellor said, "If it comes to a fight, you *will* give us guns, won't you?"

"Only if you give me a promise."

"You have it."

Well, that was a change for the better, anyway. David turned to the girl. "Miss Townsend, I'm sorry we've brought you to this. But if you hadn't been with us I expect we'd be surrounded by Yankees now instead of by Indians."

"Would that make any difference?"

"Not from our standpoint, I suppose. We don't seem to have any friends in this country, red or white."

Out in the night, a small fire began to flicker. David watched it and shivered from the chill. Well, some Indian was getting warm. In a few minutes another fire started, and another and another. In a little while a dozen or fifteen small fires burned at intervals all the way around the train.

Noley Mitchell walked around the circle, checking the guard. He stopped where David leaned against a big wagon wheel, watching.

David asked, "You figure they'll come against us tonight?"

"They might, but more likely they'll wait for daylight, to where they can see what they're doin'."

"They probably don't know what's on the wagons. If they've got guns, and they come in shootin', a bullet is apt to send this whole thing up in one big puff of smoke."

Mitchell grunted. "That's been my thinkin' too."

"The main danger is the powder, Noley. What if we take everybody we can spare and put them onto shovels? We can bury it."

"Good idea, button. I wisht I'd thought of it."

Nobody was sleeping anyway, or likely to sleep much tonight. They got onto the shovels. The men would work awhile, then swap places with the guards. The digging went on all night. Before daybreak they had dug a long trench. They began unloading the powder wagons, putting the kegs into the hole. When they had done with it, they threw a goodly amount of dirt over the kegs, packing it down tightly as they went. They piled cases of rifles and bar lead on top of and around the hole, setting up an additional barrier to stop bullets or turn them.

David worked with the rest of the men, so long as his bad arm let him. Those Indians wouldn't give a damn whether he was an officer or not. When the job was done he leaned against a wheel and looked out into the night, cold now from the sweat in his clothes. He could see color starting to break in the east. He saw fires beginning to flare up at intervals around the wagons.

The fires had worried him all night. For lack of any personal experience he tried to put himself in the Indians' place. If he intended to attack somebody, he doubted that he would make a big show of his presence for hours beforehand. He would be more likely to try to move in secrecy. The Indians had seemed to be making a show of their numbers, as if trying to scare the wagon people.

It occurred to David that they might be hoping the Texans, in their fear, would saddle up and ride off in the night, leaving the wagons behind. There might be more fires out there than Indians. Many a fight had been won on bluff.

But as daylight came that hope drifted away. The red sun lifted over the mountains and shone down full upon a rough circle of horsemen scattered all around the train, most of them two to three hundred yards away, waiting. David held his breath until his lungs started to ache, and then he took a rushing gasp.

Somebody—he thought it was Lusk—demanded, "My God—did you ever see so damned many Indians?"

David tried to count, but he could not see all those on the opposite side of the train. He guessed there were seventy or eighty, maybe as many as a hundred.

"What do you suppose they are?" he asked Noley Mitchell, not that it made any particular difference.

Martha Townsend gave the answer in a tight, unnatural voice. "Comanches. Maybe some Kiowa. They range into this country sometimes."

Luther Lusk called from his post. "If they rush us, Noley, what's our chances?"

Mitchell shook his head. "Damned poor."

The men had all armed themselves with rifles from the Yankee wagons, and each had plenty of extra cartridges within arm's length. David pointed to a broken case of rifles. "Miss Townsend, you'd better grab you one, and get one for Chancellor. Take ammunition, too. This time we're all on one side."

He shivered from the morning chill as he watched the Indians, wondering when they were going to come. His mind drifted back to another morning not long ago, when he and his men had waited behind hastily piled rocks on a mountain farther north, expecting any minute to be overrun. He felt that same cold knot of dread in his stomach, that same cold sweat making the rifle slippery in his hands.

He looked longingly toward the south and wondered at the treachery of fate. They had come a long way, but now it appeared this was to be the end of it. They would never get back to Texas.

Otto Hufstedler called, *"Leutnant!"* He pointed to the northwest. David spun, raising the rifle instinctively to his shoulder, expecting to see the Indians moving against them. He lowered the rifle and blinked, trying to clear the haze that his anxiety had put in the way. He saw a single rider coming toward him, carrying a big piece of white cloth tied to the muzzle of a rifle. He kept waving the rifle so the cloth would not be overlooked.

Quartering in, the man was hard to see in any detail at first. The nearer he came, the more evident it was that he was not an Indian.

Somehow David knew who he would be before he saw the face.

Floyd Bearfield stopped his horse fifty yards short of the wagons. He called out, "Is Buckalew in charge of the train?"

David hesitated, then answered, "I am. State your business."

"The rifle is empty. I have no cartridges with me. I want to come and parley with you."

"I don't see what we've got to parley over."

"You don't? Then you must be blind. Take another look at all my friends out here."

Martha Townsend's voice came from behind David. It was edged with hate. "Call him in, Buckalew. Call him in closer and I'll kill him!"

He saw the hatred in her eyes. He had no doubt whatever that she would do it. "Noley, you'd best relieve Miss Townsend of that rifle."

She said incredulously, "You're not actually going to talk to him? He'll lie to you. He'll make any promise to get what he wants, and then he'll kill you."

"He's in a good shape to kill us anyway. I'd as soon talk first." He turned to Mitchell. "Noley, I'll walk out a little ways and meet him. I don't want him gettin' close enough to see that we buried the powder."

"He's liable to get you out yonder and kill you."

"He's in easy rifle range. I doubt he'll try anything that would get him killed."

As David walked out to meet him, Bearfield moved cautiously closer. David had left his rifle behind, but he wore his pistol. Bearfield saw it. "I see you're armed, Buckalew. I've already told you I'm not."

"I know you *told* me. Now, what is it that you want?"

Bearfield's bewhiskered face was grim. He hadn't shaved in days. He looked as if he hadn't slept, either. "Well sir, Buckalew, the situation is somewhat changed from the last time we talked. This time I have a few good cards in my hand."

"You don't have the whole deck, though."

For some reason David felt a strange confidence now that he stood face to face with this man. He found his voice coming through with a strength he couldn't have explained. Perhaps it was the knowledge that at this moment he still had the upper hand over Bearfield on a personal level. Regardless of the eventual consequences, it was in his power to kill Bearfield anytime he took the notion.

It was a struggle to beat down that notion.

Bearfield said, "I think it would be to the advantage of both of us to make a trade."

"What have you got to offer?"

"Life, instead of death."

"In return for what?"

"You know I know what you have in the wagons."

"And you know what it's for. Our troops need it."

"I'm not greedy, Buckalew. I realize you're a patriot, and I respect that. All I'm asking for is a division. Give me half the wagons and you can go on your way. You'll still have the other half, and surely you Texans can wage a good fight with just half of what is in that train."

"What happens to the half that you take? Who will *you* use it against?"

"That needn't concern you. Your enemies are my enemies too."

"But some of your enemies are my friends, my own people. You'll trade that stuff to *your* friends out there, and they'll use it on raids down into *my* country to bring back stolen goods to trade to you. I'd rather blow it all up right here."

Bearfield's brow knitted. "And kill all your own men, and yourself in the process? Surely patriotism doesn't have to carry you that far. Nobody has to die. I am trying to reach an accommodation with you so that everybody can live."

David saw that he had one strong point of leverage, Bearfield's craving for the goods on those wagons, and his fear that they could all be lost in one suicidal gesture by the Texans. "You can't afford to attack us, Bearfield. One misplaced bullet from your people and it all goes up. Or, if I see we're about to be overrun, *I'll* blow it up. Either way, you lose what you've come for."

Bearfield's sharp eyes cut into David's; he tried to determine if David was bluffing. That unexpected strength let David stand his ground and meet Bearfield's steady gaze without flinching. Bearfield broke first. He looked away a minute, clenching his teeth so that his cheekbones seemed to push out.

"You may not be totally aware of your predicament, Buckalew. You have more than just my friends and me to worry about." He pointed north. "Just a little way from here is a force of Union troops with Owen Townsend. They're afoot, or they would already be upon you. They went into camp last night about three miles back. By now they're on the move again."

David tried not to let his surprise show. Assuming Bearfield was telling the truth, the Yankees had not abided by their original agreement. He could easily understand why they might feel that his taking Martha Townsend would negate all promises. After Chancellor had left, they had probably talked it over among themselves and decided to move.

Bearfield said, "So you see, Buckalew, if you do not give the wagons to me, the Union troops will be on you before long. Even if my friends and I pulled back, you couldn't get much farther. At least we offer to let you keep half the wagons. The Union will make no such offer."

David said nothing.

Bearfield started again. "You wouldn't have to worry about the soldiers at all. Make a deal with us and we'll take that problem off of your hands. You'll have a clear path all the way back to Texas."

"You'd kill those Yankees?"

"They're my enemies as well as yours."

A picture came to him, bringing back the chill of the night just past. David saw those Union troops he had found strung out in death through that canyon to the north. He shuddered. "I don't know as I'd want them to die that way."

"What difference does it make to you how they die? You Texans have been killing them for months, and being killed by them."

"But that was war."

"What do you think *this* is? It's been war here for two hundred years. Those people out there started first against the Spanish, and then against the Mexicans, and later against the Americans. This is their kind of war. Let them fight it for you."

David was tempted, but only for a minute. That bloody picture kept coming back, that scene in the canyon. He wondered how many more such bloody scenes would result in other places, including Texas, if he gave up even half of this wagon train.

He said, "I reckon we'll take our chances with the Yankees, and we'll take our chances with you. Don't you forget that it'll take just one shot to blow the whole thing plumb across the river. Now you'd better go back out yonder to your friends."

Bearfield instinctively brought his rifle around at David, then caught himself and looked with concern toward the wagons. He said tightly, "Buckalew, I'm offering you a chance to live. You're a fool."

"Not a blind fool, Bearfield. If we gave you half the wagons, how long would it be before you came after us to get the other half? You're too greedy a dog to settle for half a bone."

Bearfield seemed disposed to argue. David drew his pistol. "Maybe you're unarmed and maybe you're not. But I *am* armed, and I'm tellin' you to move."

Cursing, Bearfield rode away. David walked hurriedly back toward the wagons, looking over his shoulder most of the way.

Noley Mitchell met him, rifle in his arm. "He wanted the wagons?"

"Half of them. He said if we'd give him half the wagons he'd let us go."

Martha Townsend's eyes were anxious. "You didn't deal with him?"

"No. He wants them all. You can bet he wouldn't let us get far without givin' up the others."

Mitchell said, "There ain't much we can do, surrounded like we are. We can't move."

"They don't know we've buried the powder. Bearfield's afraid to rush us because he doesn't want the wagons blown up."

Martha Townsend said, "You had the advantage over him. Why didn't you make him a prisoner? We could have used him as a hostage against the Indians."

"He was under a flag of truce."

Her temper flared. "At a time like this, you worry about formalities?"

It hadn't even occurred to David to do it. Such a move would have been against his instincts.

"So now we just wait here," she said, exasperated. "For what?"

"For a break."

Mitchell said soberly, "I don't know what."

David pointed north. "If Bearfield wasn't lyin', those Yankee soldiers aren't far behind us, afoot." He looked at the girl.

Hope flared in her eyes, until a grim realization set in. "How many men?"

"However many we left in that cellar, I expect."

"Against this many Indians? They'll be killed."

He hadn't seen real fear in Martha Townsend's eyes until now. She demanded, "Did he say anything about my father? Is he with them?"

David hadn't intended to tell her, but he couldn't lie. "Bearfield said he was."

Martha Townsend turned away. She sank to her knees beside Tom Chancellor. He reached out and pulled her to him, letting her cry against his shoulder. Chancellor looked up at David. "You should have killed Bearfield when you had the chance, Buckalew. He's destroyed half of the Townsend family already. Now I suppose he'll get the rest of it."

David knew the Townsends' hatred of Bearfield was too deep to be based on general principles. "It's time somebody told me what he's done to the Townsends."

The telling was painful to Chancellor. His face twisted as he talked. "I was stationed in Albuquerque. My wife—Martha's sister—was going to have our baby. Her mother came up from the ranch and persuaded me to let her take Patience back home to have it. There was sickness in Albuquerque then, and I was afraid for Patience and the baby. Owen Townsend had sent wagons for supplies, and a force of men for guards. Mrs. Townsend assured me Patience would be safe. And I thought she would be, too, safer than in Albuquerque.

"But on the way home, Indians hit the wagons. They came so fast, and so many of them, that nobody had a chance. My wife . . . Mrs.

Townsend . . . everybody was killed except a couple of men on the trail wagon. They got cut off and made it to shelter in some rocks. The Indians didn't seem to feel it was worthwhile rooting them out. When it was over, Bearfield and some of his Comanchero traders came and drove the wagons away. They were in league with the Indians."

That cold chill came back to David. He looked at Chancellor, and he looked at the girl. He understood much now.

They had a scare once. Fifteen to twenty Indians gathered, parleyed awhile, then suddenly came riding. As they neared the wagons they dropped down behind their horses, only a little of a leg and an arm showing. For a moment David thought Bearfield was risking the wagons. The Indians let fly a volley of arrows. Most of them fell short. No shots were fired except by the Texans. One horse went down, and then another. The two Indians were on their feet instantly to be picked up and carried off. So far as David could see, none were hurt.

Mitchell said, "Just lettin' us know their intentions are serious."

David nodded. "And lettin' us know they think they can take us without usin' guns."

He thought about it a little and ordered one keg of powder dug up. He used an ax to chop a hole in one end. To nobody in particular he said, "I told him we'd blow up the whole thing rather than let it fall into his hands. It's time to show him *our* intentions are serious."

He carried the keg beyond the wagons, looked around to be sure no Indians were near enough to overrun him, then started in a straight line in the direction where he considered Bearfield to be. He let the powder string out thinly as he walked. Fifty yards from the circle he stopped and set the keg down. A couple of Indians were riding toward him, but they were a long way off. Even in a walk, he could beat them to the wagons.

He did not intend for them to see him run. He walked, though briskly. Where he had started stringing powder, he stopped, knelt and fired his pistol into it. The powder sputtered into flame. It flared, the flame racing outward in a trail of black smoke. He glanced at the Indians. They were still coming. He took the last three strides that put him inside the wagon circle.

When the flame reached the half-empty keg it exploded, sending fragments of wood flying high beneath a cloud of black smoke. One of the Indians' horses broke into frenzied pitching. He threw his rider, who sailed through the air with arms and legs flailing. David turned his face away instinctively to avoid being hit by any falling debris. It was too far out; none of it reached the wagons.

"That," he said, "will give him somethin' to worry about. He wants these goods worse than he wants us."

He watched the Indian horse run away, the Indian chasing after it in total futility.

No more Indians came against the wagons, but they remained out there, spread in a rough circle.

It occurred to David that he was hungry. They had never even made coffee this morning. "We'd just as well fix breakfast. I doubt as anybody is goin' anywhere for a while."

They did their cooking much nearer the wagon circle this time, for the powder seemed safe enough. Martha Townsend went about her work tight-lipped and shaken. David told her, "They ain't got us, ma'am. Not by a long ways."

"We have a trump card," she said. "But my father's out there somewhere without anything. They'll kill him, Buckalew. You know they'll likely kill them all."

He wanted to say something to comfort her. "There's quite a few soldiers with him. Good soldiers, I'd expect."

"They're afoot."

"Don't the Army sometimes send infantry out against the Indians?"

"They do, but the man on horseback has all the advantage."

He gave up the effort and moved away from her. But he kept watching her from the corner of his eye, feeling guilt for having brought her into this trap, no matter how good his reasons had seemed.

Mentally he began figuring distances and walking times, wondering just where Owen Townsend and those Yankees would be by now.

Presently he began to see movement among the Indians. He tensed, bringing up his rifle. But the movement was lateral, not toward the wagons. He saw that a major number of the Indians were heading north, taking their time.

"They ain't leavin' us?" Luther Lusk exclaimed, incredulous.

Noley Mitchell shook his head. "Don't get your hopes up." He walked to David, took a quick glance toward the girl, and said in a voice she couldn't hear, "I expect Bearfield was tellin' you the truth about them Yankees."

David nodded. "Bearfield figures they'd blow us all up rather than let us get back to our lines with the powder. He can't afford to have them do that."

"They wouldn't do it with *her* here."

"Bearfield probably doesn't know she's with us." He went for his spyglass, pulling it open. He studied the departing Indians, then tried to get some idea how many were remaining behind. These were only a scattered few, a token remnant, probably staying to be sure the wagons didn't move.

Mitchell said, "They'll wipe them Yankees out. It may take them a while, but they'll do it."

"The thought pleasure you any, Noley?"

"I can't say as it does. And I can't see where it'll help us in the long run. The Indians'll be back for us in due time."

"But the Yankees will thin them some. And while the big bunch is gone, maybe we can thin these others ourselves."

Mitchell stared at him, his mouth open.

David said, "Ask for volunteers. Half of us will saddle up horses and get ready. The rest will stay to guard the wagons."

"Which half am I with?"

"The half that stays here."

"It'd be a real favor to me, Davey, if you'd let me go. It'd mean a lot to me when I get back home."

"But it's my place to go. You're second in command. You've got to stay and take over in case I don't get back."

Most of the Texans wanted to volunteer, so David handpicked them, trying to leave as strong and dependable a group with the wagons as he took with him. They saddled their horses quietly, hoping not to get any particular attention from the Indians who waited out there, one small group on the east, another four hundred yards to the west.

The main body of Indians left a trail of dust as they moved north. The seven men were ready and waiting impatiently for David to give the word. He steadied the spyglass on a wagon and watched the half-dozen Indians to the west. The riders would be coming at them out of the sun.

Luther Lusk said, "What we waitin' for, Davey?"

"For distraction. The closer we get to them before they see us, the better chance we'll have." He waited, looking up from the glass to rest his eye, then going back to it to be sure nothing had changed.

Gunfire erupted somewhere to the north. He saw the waiting Indians turn away from the wagons, listening. Most of them were afoot, their horses quietly grazing nearby. The warriors were wanting in on the fight. *Well*, David thought, *here's a good time to give them one of their own.*

"All right. Let's go."

They led their horses out between the wagons and swung up with rifles in their hands. David didn't bother to look behind him. He knew the others were coming. He spurred the big brown horse into a hard lope across the flat, down into a shallow ravine and up again. So far as he could tell, the Indians were so intent on what was going on over the rise they hadn't noticed the Texans yet.

One of them saw. He loosed an arrow so quickly David hardly saw him draw it out of the quiver. The range was too long. The Indian sprang for his horse. The rest followed his example.

David fired a quick, poorly aimed shot toward the Indian horses. He knew he was unlikely to hit one, but he hoped to startle them and make them run. Luther Lusk did likewise. The Indian horses began throwing their heads and tails up and running, frightened. Two of the Indians grabbed theirs and swung onto their backs, but the others were left afoot.

"Get low!" David shouted.

He needn't have said it, for the men were already as low across their horses' necks as they could get. The rifles began firing. David saw one

Indian go down, and another. He saw the arrows flying at him. He felt the brown horse break stride as one glanced off of his chest, opening a shallow wound.

In moments they overran the foot Indians. The fire was murderous for a few seconds, until not an Indian remained on his feet. The two on horseback had slowed to try to defend their friends, but they were too late. Luther Lusk slid his horse to a stop, jumped to the ground, took careful aim and brought one of the horsemen down. The other rode off.

David didn't have to say anything. He gave a signal and all the men wheeled, spurring back toward the wagons. He looked around to be sure that no one had faltered, no one was hit. Fermin Hernandez' horse stumbled and went down. David reined around. He kicked his left foot out of the stirrup so Hernandez could use it and mount behind him. Hernandez dropped off when they reached safety. He stared at David with surprise and wonder. The Texans paused only a minute at the wagons while David stepped down to check the brown horses's wound. He found it was superficial. He looked through the glass at the Indians to the east. They had moved in closer, confused, unable to tell just what was happening. They couldn't be surprised like the others, but at least they were nearer.

"All right." David said, "let's get them." Hernandez had to stay behind, for there was no time to catch a fresh horse.

David spurred out and heard the rest of the men pounding along beside and directly behind him. The seven or eight Indians came riding to meet them, stringing their bows. This time the Texans' tactics were different. Taking a cue from Luther Lusk on the other run, David stopped the brown horse suddenly, jumped to the ground, dropped to one knee and took aim. Through the billow of black smoke he saw an Indian fall.

The other Texans did as David had done. They brought down two horses and three more Indians. The other Indians came on, two more falling in the next volley. The rest, seeing they were almost alone, reined their horses around and went running. The Texans fired after them. They brought down one more horse, but the remaining Indians got away.

David looked on either side to be sure none of his men were hurt. This time they had never allowed the Indians within effective arrow range. "All right, we've ripped them some. Let's get back to the wagons."

Lusk said regretfully, "I wisht Bearfield had been amongst them."

They took their time riding back, for there was no immediate danger that David could see. He kept looking toward the north, wondering if the sound of the shooting might bring reinforcements. But he saw nothing. They were too busy down there to have heard or seen what happened here.

From the north came a ragged pattern of fire, heavy at intervals, stretching out and almost stopping at others.

Noley Mitchell walked out to meet them. "Looks like you done right good."

"We whittled the odds a little." David looked around him with a pride he hadn't felt in this outfit before.

"Sounds like them Yankees down there are puttin' up a good fight. You been listenin' any?"

"Been kind of busy, Noley."

"Sounds to me like they're movin' closer. Probably tryin' to get to some kind of cover and form a redoubt."

Afoot, David led the hard-breathing horse in between the wagons. He saw Martha Townsend looking anxiously northward, listening to the firing. She gave the Texans little notice as they came back from their skirmishing.

He said to his men, "Keep the horses saddled. Any chance we get, we'll do it again."

She heard his voice and turned. "Do you hear that?" she demanded, tilting her head back toward the sound of the guns.

"I hear it. They're makin' a good account of themselves."

"But they can't win."

He knew that. He wouldn't tell her so.

Her voice was struggling not to break. "My father's out there."

"I'm sorry, ma'am."

He loosened the girth to let the horse breathe easier, and he tied the brown to a wheel. He checked the wound again; it didn't amount to much. He took out the spyglass and made a long study of the ground to the east, south and west.

It occurred to him that they could reload the powder wagons and move out of here while the Indians were busy elsewhere. The sudden sortie had left them no effective opposition out there. But he considered a little and gave up the idea. They would only face it somewhere else a few miles farther on. This was as good a place as any to see the thing through.

The men stood around in silence, their faces grave as they listened to the sporadic firing. David wished he did not keep thinking of that other time, back north, but the awful image kept flashing across his mind. He decided Mitchell had been right about the shooting moving nearer; the Yankees hadn't yet let themselves be nailed down.

Martha Townsend shouted, "Look!"

The urgency in her voice made David turn quickly on his heel. He thought he could see movement again, up where the main mass of Indians had disappeared. He moved to the north end of the wagon circle and braced his spyglass across an endgate. He thought at first he was having trouble bringing the image into focus, but he realized that what he saw was dust. Some Indians were riding back and forth. Then, to his surprise, he glimpsed men on the ground, moving.

"Those Yankees!" he exclaimed. "They're still a-walkin', fightin' their way along."

Noley Mitchell rushed to his side, squinting but unable to make out much with his naked eyes. David handed him the glass. Mitchell grunted. "By George, they're a gamey bunch. They just keep on a-comin'."

Tom Chancellor had dragged himself along across the ground. He pulled up on a wagon wheel and shouted, "Let me see! Let me see!"

Mitchell handed him the glass. Chancellor found the action and swore under his breath.

David demanded, "How many do you see?"

"It's hard to tell. A dozen at least, maybe more. They're keeping the Indians at a distance. They're putting up a good fight."

David frowned. They couldn't have much ammunition left, judging by the shooting, and remembering the amount he had left them at the ranch.

Martha Townsend moved close to Chancellor. "Tom, is my father among them? Can you see him?"

"I can't tell. There's so much dust . . ." He lowered the glass, his face grave. "They're trying so hard . . . but you know they can't make it. There's no way they can do it."

Martha Townsend turned to David. Desperation was in her eyes. "Texas, you could help them."

"Ma'am, they're the enemy."

"Right now there's only one enemy."

"They've come here to stop us from gettin' through with these wagons."

"Bearfield has stopped you already. You're going nowhere with these wagons anymore, don't you know that?"

David turned away, his face twisting bitterly. "They didn't have to come after us. It's their fight, not ours."

"It'll be yours again, once they've been beaten. Bearfield isn't going to let you move out of here with these wagons. He'll be back for you. You'll need all the help you can get." She grabbed his shoulder and tried to turn him around to face her. "Buckalew, you can help them, and then they'll help you!"

He didn't answer. She cried, "Buckalew, for God's sake . . ." Her voice lifted at the end, and broke.

David still hadn't looked at her. But he looked at Noley Mitchell, at Luther Lusk, at Homer Gilman and Otto Hufstedler.

"What do you all think?"

Mitchell nodded grimly. "I think we could do it."

David looked at Lusk. If Mitchell and Lusk were for it, the rest would follow. "Luther?"

Lusk was torn. He looked regretfully at the wagons, as if mentally giving them up. "Hell yes, let's go."

They saddled the rest of the horses, as far as the saddles would go. They put bridles on some of the mules and tied the reins to ropes so they could be led. The extra horses were also tied to ropes. David quickly picked three men to lead the horses and mules. The rest would form around them in a protective wedge.

Five men would stay here. This time Noley Mitchell insisted that he get to go. Luther Lusk was left in charge at the wagons. The rest of the men led their horses outside and mounted up. David made sure everybody was ready. The animals fidgeted and stomped, sensing the excitement.

David said to all the men, "We may be lucky. Busy as they are, the Indians may not see us at first. We'll do like we did last time . . . we'll ride in fast, pick up the men and ride out again as fast as we can. Anybody falls, it may be impossible to pick him up. We've got to save as many as we can and get the hell away. Everybody set?"

Noley Mitchell nodded. David didn't wait for the rest. He spurred out, hitting a hard lope.

The Yankees were half a mile out now, he judged. He leaned over the brown's neck, trying for all the speed he could get, hoping the men weren't strung out badly behind him. He took no time to look. Ahead he could see the Indians riding in wide circles around the beleaguered Union men. If they had seen the Texans coming they gave no sign of it; their attention was devoted to the men on foot.

For the first time it occurred to David that the Yankees might mistake the Texans for more Indians and start shooting at them. That, he thought, would be a hell of a thing to happen after all the risk his men were taking. It was too late now to reconsider, or to change anything.

The ground flew beneath him. The big brown's long strides reached out and gathered it in. The morning wind bit his face and burned his eyes until they watered, making it more difficult to see what lay ahead of him.

The Indians had seen them. The nearest were rushing out to meet them. David shouted, "Don't let them get close." He fired his rifle before he was in good range, hoping he might hit near enough to slow them down. He couldn't take any real aim from the back of a running horse, no matter how close he might have been.

The Texans all started firing except the ones in the center of the broad wedge, leading the extra horses and mules. David saw one Indian horse go down, but he didn't know if it was wounded or if it had stumbled. Any shot that hit under these conditions had to be purely accidental.

Ahead of them the Indian circle wavered, then broke. Inside it, the Yankees knelt, firing rapidly. The Union men were a hundred yards away, then fifty. Then the Texans were among them, swinging the horses and mules around. David's blood was racing. He didn't try for any kind of count. He thought he glimpsed Owen Townsend, but there was no time for making sure.

"Up quick!" he shouted. "Everybody onto a horse or a mule!"

He didn't have to repeat it. A couple of men, wounded, were helped on. Others jumped up behind them.

A wave of a dozen or so Indians made a desperate charge. Arrows started coming in. David heard the scream of a mule. "Cut it loose," he shouted, "and let's get out of here!"

He fired the rifle at the nearest of the Indians and spurred back into a run again, south toward the wagons. This time he looked back once. He saw the Yankees all up except one, who lay on the ground. They wouldn't have time to help him. They had to move fast, to save as many as they could.

Now, closing on both sides, came the main body of the Indians, fully alarmed, fully aware that the Yankees they thought they had trapped were about to be swept away from them. David fired as rapidly as he could poke cartridges into the rifle. When an Indian came close and he missed him, he whipped out his pistol and fired that, so near he thought the warrior must certainly be powder-burned. The Indian veered away, lurching to one side.

The wind bit David's eyes again. He spurred, listening to the hoofs pounding beside and behind him.

Just ahead now were the wagons. Luther Lusk had pushed one of them out of line to make an opening the men could ride through. David reined off to one side and began pulling up, letting the main body of men pass him by. Back in the heavy dust he saw two men and a horse on the ground. The horse was kicking. David could not tell who had fallen, Texan or Yankee, and knew there was no time to go back. A dozen Indians swept by the fallen men, swinging their warclubs. A couple jumped down. Whoever the men were, they were beyond help.

Arrows whispered past David. He marveled that he had not been struck. Then, suddenly, he was. He felt a jarring impact. Fire cut through his hip. He grabbed at the pommel to keep from falling. He cried out and held on. He had to stay in the saddle; nobody could help if he fell. He dropped the rifle. He saw the men gallop through the opening between the wagons. The brown carried him in that direction, sweeping past two Indians who tried to club David. David leaned over the horse's neck and knew he had entered the circle. He was dimly aware of men hurriedly pushing the wagon back into place, plugging the hole.

The brown carried him into the other horses in a blind rush and lost his footing. He went down on his side, kicking. Instinctively, the breath half knocked out of him, David crawled away. He narrowly missed being trampled by other horses and mules. Someone grabbed him beneath the arms and dragged him. Blinking away the haze, he saw Fermin Hernandez.

Hernandez brought him up against the wheel of a wagon. David could hear the firing as the men, Yankee and Texan, hurried together to hurl back the Indian rush. Somebody fetched a blanket and spread it. Hernandez eased David onto it.

David wheezed, "Much obliged, Fermin." He had never called the Mexican by his first name.

Hernandez said, "It is all even again, Lieutenant."

David tried to sit up, but the strain made the arrowhead cut deeper. He gasped and dropped back onto his side. He could see that the shaft had been broken when he fell, but part of it was still in his hip. He reached to touch it and found his hand warm and sticky with blood.

The firing let up. David kept closing his eyes, then opening them, trying to clear the blur. He saw Luther Lusk standing over him, looking down anxiously. "Luther, did we lose anybody?"

Reluctantly Lusk said, "One, Davey."

David kept looking around. "Where's Noley Mitchell? I want to see Noley Mitchell."

Grimly Lusk said, "He's the one, Davey."

David groaned.

He heard Lusk call, "Somebody help me. We got to take care of the lieutenant before he bleeds to death."

Lusk slit David's trousers from the waistband down past the arrow. Martha Townsend said, "Here, I'll do the rest of it." He could feel her careful hands stanching the flow of blood with a cloth, then she was pouring something over the wound that burned like the fires of hell.

Someone said, "We ought to be able to pull that arrow straight out." Martha Townsend replied, "The head of it might stay in. Be patient. We'll get it out, all in one piece."

Men held David while Martha cut around the arrowhead with a sharp blade. He tried to hold still, but the blade was agony. He could not help himself.

Then the arrow was out. He felt the blood flowing warm, cleansing the wound. Martha let it flow a moment, then dropped a handful of flour to clot and stop it.

The worst was over. David watched through a reddish haze of pain as she applied a folded cloth to the wound, held it a little, let up, then pressed again.

His voice sounded unnatural to him. "Just like it was in Albuquerque."

He could see a faint hint of a smile cross her face. "You never could remember for sure whether that was me or not."

"I want to believe that it was. And I'll always remember that it was you this time." He tried to look around but couldn't make out any faces. "Did your father . . ."

She nodded. "He's here. He's all right."

"How many of your people did we get back with?"

"Ten, I think. I haven't had time to really count."

"Ten. Well, at least we've got you outnumbered."

"It doesn't make any difference. Right now, everybody here is the same."

He became aware that the firing had stopped. He tried to turn his head to see beyond the wagon, but the wheel and a corner of the blanket were in his way. Martha said, "They've pulled back. Talking it over, I suppose. They've suffered a lot."

Someone was standing just beyond David's feet, throwing a shadow over him. David blinked and recognized Owen Townsend. Townsend said, "Buckalew, I see my daughter has finally gotten to use a knife on you. If she had done it any earlier she would probably have used it a lot higher up."

David supposed that was meant in a humorous vein, but he was not capable of appreciating humor now.

Townsend said, "I can't forget that we wouldn't be out here at all if it hadn't been for you. But I thank you for pulling us out of the untenable position they had us in."

David considered his answer before he made it. "I can't apologize for what we did. We had a job to do."

Townsend nodded, gripping his bad arm, which seemed to be paining him. "Each of us does his duty as he sees it."

Another man stopped beside Townsend. He was the burly sergeant David had hoodwinked to get control of the wagons. He frowned down at David, taking his measure. "Texas, I had made up my mind that if I ever caught up with you, I was going to challenge you to a duel. Would you be interested now?"

"I don't believe so," David said.

"I thought not. Since I owe you my hair, I guess it would be a little awkward anyway. But I will admit that you look good there, on your back."

David wasn't sure whether to take the sergeant seriously or not. He decided this was probably the nearest the man could come to saying thanks. He replied, "You're welcome," and hoped it fit. If it didn't, the hell with it. He wasn't feeling up to worrying about it anyway.

Some of the Texas men began gathering around to see about him, now that the Indians had eased their pressure. David tried to sit up. Martha warned, "You've just now quit bleeding. You'll start it again if you don't hold still."

It hurt so much that he quit trying for the time being. He said, "I reckon I'll do my travelin' in a wagon for a while."

Martha replied, "Those people out yonder . . . they're not going to let you leave here in *any* wagon. As long as they want these munitions, and you have them, none of us are going anyplace."

He heard a curse from the end of the wagon. He knew Luther Lusk's voice.

"That son of a bitch! He's comin' in again with another white flag."

David asked, "Bearfield?"

"Yes, him and some Indian. They're comin' in together, wavin' that flag. I'll get some of the boys, and when he gets in range . . ."

David knew the temptation. He had felt it before. But he said, "No, Luther, it's still a flag of truce. We'd just as well hear him out."

"You know what he wants."

"I know, and he's not goin' to get it."

"Then let's just kill him and see what happens."

He heard the voice call from beyond the wagons. "Buckalew!"

David pondered about it. When the voice called again, he said, "Luther, Fermin . . . would you-all help me up?"

Martha protested. David said, "I reckon I've got to get up sometime." He had to choke down a cry of pain when they got hold of his arms and pulled him onto his feet. He tried to put weight on the leg but couldn't. He was nauseous for a moment. If they hadn't been holding him he would have fallen on his face.

But his head cleared in a minute. The pain subsided to a level he decided he would have to tolerate. "Take me out there a little ways."

He put his arms around the two men's shoulders. He couldn't help much; they simply had to lift him enough that his feet cleared the ground and they could carry him.

He had them take him out twenty yards. He didn't want Bearfield any nearer the wagons, where he might see that they had the powder buried and protected. That would invite rifle fire against the wagons. He felt Bearfield's eyes burning at him as the Comanchero rode cautiously forward, not trusting the men who aimed their rifles at him from behind the wagon beds and the heavy wheels. If he made one treacherous move, they would cut him to pieces, and he knew it.

Bearfield said with some satisfaction, "Well, Buckalew, you don't look quite as healthy as you did when I last talked with you."

"I'm still here, though."

"Even assuming you live to get back to Texas, you'll be lucky if they don't shoot you for treason, rescuing a detail of Union soldiers. You have aided and abetted an enemy."

"Enemies is one thing I've had a-plenty of out here."

"You're a fool, Buckalew. You don't think those Yankees will ever allow you to take that ammunition train to Texas now, do you?"

David didn't answer. Bearfield said, "I offered you a good deal. I was going to take care of your *real* enemies for you, and leave you with half the wagons besides. Now you've cost us a great deal, and so my price has gone up."

"Your price?"

"You can't go anywhere so long as we don't want you to. You're in a trap. Give us your wagons, and we'll give you your lives."

"That's no kind of a trade."

"It's *my* trade. Leave now and you can all leave here alive. We'll get the wagons. Stay, and none of you will leave alive. We'll *still* get the wagons."

Luther Lusk gritted, "Say the word, Davey, and I'll shoot the son of a bitch."

Bearfield was plainly apprehensive, but he did not give ground. David shook his head. "No, we won't kill him. Not yet."

Bearfield appraised the wagons. "I know what you're thinking; you believe you're safe because we can't afford to shoot into the wagons and risk blowing them up. But I'll bet you've never seen a real rain of arrows, have you, Buckalew? If I turned these people loose to do it their way, there wouldn't be a man, a horse or a mule left alive." He jabbed his finger at David. "One way or another, we'll have those wagons. The only difference is whether we do it with you alive, or all of you dead. For my part, I can't say I really care very much." He began backing the horse slowly. "Talk it over with the rest of them. Make up your minds. I'll give you an hour to draw back from the wagons. After that, you're dead!"

He pulled his horse around and began riding away in a walk, giving everybody a good view of his back, almost as if daring someone to shoot him. David imagined the man was probably in a cold sweat, dreading that somebody actually would. But he was also making a show of his bravery for the benefit of the Indians.

Lusk said, "It'd sure be easy to do it right now." He had one hand on the butt of his pistol.

David said, "Get me back to the wagons. Call everybody over for a conference. We're goin' to talk this out."

They gathered around him . . . Lusk, Hernandez, Hufstedler, Gilman, Gene Ivy and the rest. In a quiet, strained voice David told them of Bearfield's ultimatum.

Lusk said heatedly, "I'd rather give it back to the Yankees than to him." The others nodded agreement.

David said, "But we can't afford to give it to the Yankees, even if *they* could get away from here with it. We can't give it away, and we can't move it. So what do we do with it?"

Lusk looked at the others, then back to David. A heavy sadness was in his face. "I guess we'll have to do what you wanted to do in the first place, Davey, what me and Noley wouldn't let you do. We'll have to blow it up. Then nobody gets it."

Gene Ivy's eyes widened. "But how do we do that? We'll blow ourselves up with it."

David felt Luther Lusk's sadness. He said, "Good men have died for what's in these wagons. If we blow it up, they died for nothin'."

Lusk shook his head, then raised it a little in a show of pride. "Not for nothin'. They *tried*, Noley and the rest of them. We *all* tried. We can look the whole world in the eye and tell them we gave it the best we had."

David looked them over thoughtfully, each in his own turn. He had realized for some time now that it might come to this, in the end. "Is everybody agreed, then? If not, this is the time to speak."

Gene Ivy asked again, more anxiously this time, "But how can we do it without blowin' ourselves up too?"

"Easy," David told him. "We won't be here."

Ivy nodded, then realized he didn't understand a bit of it. But David let his questions go. "Luther, Fermin . . . you-all reckon you can lift me onto my horse and tie me onto the saddle?"

Lusk frowned. "It'll be hell on you."

"It's hell anyway, lyin', standin' or a-horseback. First, help me over to those Yankees. We'll tell them what we've decided."

As Lusk and Hernandez carried him, the Union people began gathering. Martha Townsend began telling him he had better lie down, but he told her he probably wouldn't be lying down again for a right smart of a spell. He told them all, "We're goin' to leave the wagons."

Owen Townsend immediately protested, "You can't leave these goods to that butcher!"

David grimaced, the hip throbbing as if someone were driving a red-hot spike into it. "He's not goin' to get them. Neither are you, and neither are we. Ain't *nobody* gettin' these wagons."

Martha said tightly, "You're going to blow them up?"

When he nodded, he thought he saw her smile. She said huskily, "Thank God."

Somebody had helped Tom Chancellor hobble to join the group. When the Union sergeant protested that the wagons were government property, Chancellor said, "Let it go, Sergeant. Too many people have died already."

Martha said, "And more would die, no matter who got the wagons . . . the Union, the Texans or the Indians. It's time to end it, and this is as good a place as any."

David saw no argument, except perhaps in the eyes of the Union sergeant. He was muttering something about those "stupid incompetents back at headquarters," and how they would never understand or condone this. "They won't even believe what's happened here. I hope you don't leave it up to me to write the report, Lieutenant. I'll lie, that's what I'll do."

"I'll make the report," Chancellor promised.

David ordered the powder kegs dug up and at least one placed in every wagon, with a hole knocked in it. The men knocked holes in other kegs and strung powder around and through all the wagons. After that, each one caught a horse or a mule. They used the saddles as far as they would go, and the rest would have to ride bareback. They took all the provisions they could carry, tying them behind the saddles.

Several of the Texans lifted David onto his brown horse. He hovered on the brink of unconsciousness for a moment. He knew he was bleeding afresh. Perhaps there would be an opportunity later to stop it and make a new bandage. If not, it probably wouldn't matter anyway, for chances were he would be dead. Luther Lusk looked up anxiously at him. "Goin' to make it, Davey?"

"What choice have I got?"

Lusk and some of the others took up the remaining few kegs of powder and stove in the ends. One of the wagons was pushed a few feet so they would all have room to pass out of the wagon circle. Martha Townsend, Tom Chancellor and a few others were riding. Most of the rest walked, leading their horses and mules, making a shield so no one watching from afar could see what Lusk was up to.

They began moving out in a walk, in single and double file at first, then grouping just beyond the wagons to make a tight company. David held to the pommel of the saddle as the brown walked. Every step brought a stab of pain. He turned to look back. Lusk was walking along, spilling a thin trail of powder. When Lusk's keg was empty, Homer Gilman took up where he had left off. When Gilman's was gone, one of the Yankee wagon men continued the job.

David tried to watch the Indians, but his vision was blurred. He couldn't bring them into focus. His heart was beating like a hammer. He had little faith in Bearfield's promise that they would be freed. If Bearfield had any inkling of what they were doing, he would set the Indians loose on them instantly.

David remembered the ravine he had ridden across on the first sortie. *That*, he thought, *would be a good place to stop.* If they had to make a stand, it would provide at least some cover.

They reached the ravine. David made a signal for the others to ride into it. It was not as deep as he had thought. Standing in it, afoot, Owen Townsend showed from his chest upward. The Union sergeant and a couple of his men stepped forward to help David down, but he demurred.

"It hurts more to get up and down than it does to stay up."

He watched Otto Hufstedler empty the last powder from the last keg, twenty yards out from the ravine. They were now a hundred yards or a little more from the circle of wagons.

Luther Lusk pointed. "Looky yonder, Davey. They're startin' in."

David's teeth clenched tightly. He tried to make out Bearfield but couldn't be sure. He took the spyglass from its case and extended it, but he was too weak to hold it steady. "Here, Luther, take this thing."

Lusk held it to his eye a minute. "Yep, yonder's Bearfield, lopin' in. He's more eager than the rest of them, looks like."

David could see a blurry movement, though he could tell little about the man. "Luther," he said, "this is somethin' I'd rather do myself. But since I can't, I'm goin' to ask you to do it. Anytime you think it's right."

Lusk reached up and grasped David's hand. "This ain't just for me. This is for Noley Mitchell, and Pete Richey." He glanced at Hufstedler. "It's for Pat O'Shea and all them others. It's for you too, Davey."

He walked out to the point where Hufstedler had poured the last of the powder. David heard somebody saying, "Wait till he gets in amongst the wagons." Somebody else said, "Don't wait, Texas. Get it done."

Lusk kept his own counsel. He waited, while David's lips went dry and his heart pounded. David found himself whispering, "Do it, Lusk. Do it."

Lusk could have used a pistol, but this might have alerted Bearfield too soon. He knelt over the powder and began striking a flint. In a moment David saw the blaze. He saw the black smoke rise as the flame raced along the snakelike trail the men had left.

Lusk came trotting back. "Everybody into the ravine! And everybody hold on to your horses, or by God you'll lose them!"

Someone took the brown's reins and led him down the steep bank. Lusk said, "Hold tight, Davey, because he'll jump when them wagons go up."

David knew he ought to get down and try to protect himself from the blast, but he sat transfixed, watching through blurry eyes for the tremendous explosion that was about to come.

And he watched. And he waited.

But it didn't happen.

He heard Gene Ivy shout, "It went out, Luther. Looky yonder . . . it went out."

Luther Lusk was crying, "Oh my God. We can't let them get it. We've got to blow it." He clambered up out of the ravine and went running, rifle in his hands.

David shouted, "Luther, they'll kill you out there!"

But Lusk kept running. Thirty yards out he dropped onto one knee and began firing at the wagons.

The others realized what he was trying to do. Fermin Hernandez rushed out, and Gene Ivy and Homer Gilman and some of the Yankees. They formed a line on either side of Luther Lusk, and all of them set in to firing.

Martha Townsend cried, "There goes Bearfield! He's getting away!"

Someone placed a bullet where it was wanted. David saw a flash and felt the ground tremble before he heard the thunder. He could see the chain of flashes and feel the heavy reverberations as the blasts raced from one wagon to the next. A great billow of black smoke rose up from the wagon circle, its underbelly red as it reflected the secondary explosions that followed the first great convulsions.

The brown horse panicked, jumping, squealing in terror. It was beyond David's ability to control him; he did well to hang on to the saddle. Someone grabbed the reins and threw arms around the horse's neck and held him, talking to him as he transferred his hold to the animal's ears.

The brown settled down. As the explosions stopped, David could hear someone a long way off, screaming. He could see a point of flame, moving erratically across the open ground.

"It's Bearfield," he heard Martha cry. "He's afire."

The screaming went on until Luther Lusk and a couple of the others began firing again. The flame stopped moving. It went to the ground.

"Well," said the Yankee sergeant after a minute, "he got what he came for. He just didn't expect to get it all at one time."

David looked around. He saw Martha and her father and Tom Chancellor huddled, holding onto one another.

An old debt had been paid.

The men retreated to the ravine and began making preparations to defend themselves. David thought surely the Indians would attack out of rage and frustration. Gradually they began pulling into little groups, then finally all in one large council.

They'll be coming now, he thought.

Instead, they strung out into a line and began riding off to the east. In a little while they were gone in the direction of the open plains.

A long quiet fell over the people in the ravine. They stood watching the remnants of the wagons burning in that rough circle, the smoke still drifting thick and heavy over them, obscuring the sun.

At last Luther Lusk said, "Davey, I think we've all seen enough of this place. We could make a few miles before dark catches us, if you think you're able."

David turned in the saddle, looking for Martha Townsend. He stared at her for a minute. He did not see what he had hoped he might. She and Tom Chancellor leaned together, their arms around each other. David turned again until he found Owen Townsend and the Yankee sergeant. He said, "We're thinkin' we'll ride on a ways south while the light is with us, if you folks don't have it in mind to try and stop us."

Townsend glanced at the sergeant. "I believe they have us outnumbered."

"That," the sergeant replied flatly, "is also my belief."

The Texans began swinging onto their horses. David looked again at Martha Townsend. She walked to him, leaving Chancellor. David moved the brown horse out away from the people. Martha followed him.

David reached down, and Martha took his hand. He said, "I wish I could ask you to go with us."

She nodded. "But you can't. And I couldn't go with you, even if you could ask."

His gaze drifted to the burned wagons. "I put you through hell, and it was all for nothin'. I'm sorry."

"Don't be sorry you tried. You never had a chance from the beginning. You Texans had lost New Mexico long before you ever got to our place. Nothing you could have done would have changed that. What you did, trying to get to Texas with this wagon train, was just a gallant gesture, nothing more. What you did just now, blowing it all up, was the most gallant thing of all. I am proud now that I got to know you."

David's throat was tight. "Martha, I wish we could've met some other time, some other place. I wish there didn't have to be this war between us." He frowned. "I thought once it was goin' to be a short one. But what I've seen of your people here, and what I know of ours, it's apt to run on for a long time."

Tears came into her eyes. "Yes, I'm afraid it will."

"But it'll be over someday. I was wonderin' . . . when it does, I might just find my way back over into this country . . ."

She shook her head. "You won't, Texas. Even if you did, it wouldn't be of any use." She glanced back toward Tom Chancellor. "You've seen how it is."

If he hadn't already, he could see it now, in her eyes. He folded both his hands over her hand. "Then, all I can say is, be happy." He leaned to kiss the tips of her fingers, and he let her go.

He turned, looking for Lusk. Fermin Hernandez was there. Hernandez said, "I take the point, Lieutenant."

David shook his head. "You don't have to. I'll get somebody else."

Hernandez smiled. "It is all right. I like it there. Up front, I don't have to listen to foolish talk." He touched spurs lightly to his horse.

David looked around again for Lusk. This time he found him. "We all ready?"

"Ready."

David grimaced as he put his hand to the burning hip, wishing he could ease the throbbing. It would be hell, but damned if it was going to stop him. He glanced back once at Martha and the others and brought his hand up in a small salute. He said, "Let's go. It's still a long ways back to Texas."

EYES

OF

THE

HAWK

CHAPTER 1

No one wants you to tamper with a legend, especially by telling the truth. Over the years I have often been asked what I know of the Texas legend of Stonehill town, and of the man the Mexicans came to call the Hawk, the man who killed that town in vengeance.

I have found it convenient to live with the legend, for that is what people want to hear. The legend is mostly true, as far as it goes. But recently, feeling the growing weight of my years and knowing I may soon be learning the answers to other great mysteries, I have felt some need to set down the rest of the story as I know it. The truth will do no great injury to the legend, for the legend has a life of its own and will outlive both the truth and the teller.

Though I have lived out my graying years near what little remains of old Stonehill town, I do not often go there. Walking in the grass where her streets used to be, I can hear the wind whisper secrets through the sagging buildings that time has not yet crushed, and I imagine I hear ghosts of the years long gone rustling through her ruins. A chill comes upon me yet when I stand at the spot where he sat on his horse, looking down upon a boy who lay there in silence. I can see him shaking his fist in a black anger and shouting to all who could hear him that he would kill Stonehill town as mercilessly as it had murdered his son.

I prefer to remember Stonehill as I first saw it, the great freight wagons and the lumbering Mexican oxcarts challenging one another for space in the narrow streets, the busy clamor of a vital people searching for glory and riches that existed only in their dreams. They lived in hardship and squalor, and sometimes they died in a hostile wilderness, alone and afraid. But the leaders of the country told them this was necessary to the fulfillment of their manifest destiny. They accepted it, most of them, and never turned back. Good men, bad men, and those in between, they differed in many ways. But in one respect they were mostly much alike. They were people of ambition and nerve, and hunger.

I well remember my first meeting with Thomas Canfield in the old port town of Indianola. You won't find the place on a map; it was destroyed in later years by one of those killer hurricanes that occasionally roars in from the Gulf of Mexico to erase all trace of man and his works.

It was only a small town with perhaps one or two permanent stone buildings when I landed there off of the merchant vessel *James Callahan* in the winter of 1854–55. I was the youngest of several sons on a small cotton farm along the Mississippi delta in Louisiana. My parents were too poor to have slaves, so they had children instead. My limited schooling gave me enough skill with ciphers to understand that my share of the family holdings would not long shield me from starvation once I left the protective roof. At seventeen I put all my personal belongings upon my back, hired as a crewman on a boat hauling a load of cotton, and shortly found myself exploring the wonders of New Orleans. I found much there to interest and no little to tempt a boy whose pockets are empty, as mine soon were. I further discovered that few people would hire even a strong and willing white boy for wages when they had slaves to do the heavy lifting without pay. I also found people in general agreement that Texas was a wondrous land where money lay in the streets, just waiting for someone to pick it up. At first opportunity I hired as a laborer on the *James Callahan*, which was hauling manufactured goods to Texas and would be bringing cotton back.

It did not take me long to decide that a seaman's life was not cut to my frame, for I spent more time at the rail than at my work. The captain probably would have fired me had we not already passed over the bar and were well out to sea. Once the sickness passed, he saw to it that I made up for the lost time. It was, all in all, a miserable passage. We ran into one major winter storm that brought me fear of a type I had never known; I was certain I would soon drown in that cold, terrible water. But I was not so lucky, for all I did was become deathly ill from an attack of the grippe, brought on by working on deck soaked to the skin. I wished mightily that I could die and end the misery. But my protecting angel had remained in New Orleans.

Even at the beginning I had intended to remain a sailor only long enough to reach Texas, and my experiences on shipboard only served to deepen my resolve in this direction. I felt duty-bound to remain with the crew long enough to see the cargo unloaded, but I felt no such duty toward seeing the waiting cotton bales carried aboard. I took my pay from the captain's reluctant hands and quickly found how meager it was when I tried to convert it into the necessities of life ashore. It took much less time to spend than to earn.

Indianola offered no employment to such as I, and no money was lying in the streets. If there had ever been, the constant stream of humanity passing through had picked it up and made off with it long before I had my chance. I decided the fortune, if there was one, must lie somewhere inland.

I ate little and slept beneath a wharf while awaiting my chance. Even for a boy whose main concern was a hungry belly, there was much to marvel over. It was my first time to see the big Mexican oxcarts, their wooden wheels as high as a man's shoulder. The axles were crude and squealed in pain when not well greased, so that the carts' coming was known before they broke into view. The Mexicans themselves were a curiosity to me—little men, most of them, rattling away in a foreign tongue that made no sense in my ear. I had heard Cajun French, but I could find no similarity between that and the quick-fire Spanish these people spoke. I was fascinated by their wide *sombreros*, by the great jingling spurs worn by the horsemen.

I had heard, of course, about the two wars the Texans had fought against Mexico, and I had assumed those were long since over. They were not, except in name. The Texas freight wagons came lumbering into town, many hauling bales of cotton and general farm produce to be shipped back to the other states for money. I sensed the enmity which flared between these people and the little men of the brown-leather skin. Around the wharf I heard casual talk about a "cart war," a rivalry between the Mexican cartmen and the *gringo* wagoners over the freight business between the ports and inland markets such as San Antonio. I heard it said that many men had died or disappeared on those long, dusty trails that wound through the brush country, men of both persuasions.

On my second day I saw a Mexican and a Texan meet with knives in hand after a wagon and a cart hung wheels on an Indianola street. Nobody in the crowd moved to stop the fight until it became clear the Mexican was about to win. Then a broad-shouldered Texan with a red beard and long rusty-colored hair swung a singletree and clubbed the Mexican to the ground. I was satisfied the cart driver was dead, but friends carried him away. Later I saw the little man sitting up beside a campfire, his head swathed in dirty bandages. I decided they were a hardy lot, these Texas people, whether light-skinned or dark.

On inquiry I found that the red-bearded man was named Branch Isom. He bossed a string of wagons that was loading goods I had helped carry off of the *James Callahan*. It was said he would be taking them to San Antonio by way of Stonehill. I had never heard of Stonehill, and San Antonio sounded considerably more romantic. Perhaps it was there that money lay in the streets. I went to his camp and found him sitting on a bedroll, leaning his back against the huge rear wheel of a freight wagon. He held a cup of coffee in one hand and an open whiskey bottle in the other, taking a sip of each in its own turn. A coldness in his eyes made me hesitate in my last steps.

I said, "Mister Isom, I am Reed Sawyer."

No change came in his eyes. He studied me in cold silence, then asked, "Is there any reason that should be of interest to me?"

"I would like a job with your wagons to San Antonio."

He scowled. "I suppose you'd expect to be paid for it."

"Only what is customary. I was paid fifty cents a day, meals and a bunk on the ship. With your wagons there would be only the meals."

His voice was as cold as his eyes. "You don't look healthy to me. You've probably got some disease you'd spread to everybody in the crew."

"I had the grippe on board. I am over that now. I am strong. I can do my share of the work."

He laughed, but it was not the kind of warm, friendly laugh you like to hear. "There are people in this port who would pay *me* to take them along, and they'd work for nothing. Why should I pay *you?* Get away from here, boy, before I sic my dogs on you."

I saw the dogs, big ugly gray brutes of uncertain ancestry. They looked as if they would chew a man's legs off on command. A chill ran up my back. I turned without saying more and walked away from Isom's camp. The smell of the coffee and the cooking food went with me, for I had not eaten all day. I bought a fish from a man on the beach, roasted it over an open fire, then slept in my accustomed damp place beneath the wharf.

It was the next morning that the Polanders arrived. They came up the trail from Galveston. I learned later that they had been with a larger group of mixed Europeans who had landed there but had been delayed in Galveston by fever, so that the main body went ahead without them. Now, after having buried one or two of their party they had come on, bound for a settlement already laid out for them many days' journey inland.

They seemed as strange to me in their own way as the Mexicans. Having had little time for the study of geography, I had only the vaguest knowledge of the various European countries' names, much less their locations. For all I knew, Poland was a part of Africa. Mostly I looked at the women, particularly the young ones. At seventeen, I found it particularly interesting that they wore the shortest skirts I had seen except in the drinking halls of New Orleans. The skirts ended above the ankles, a scandalous sight. The better people of Indianola were quick to decide that these were loose women, for only that sort would flaunt themselves so. Some of the immigrant women wore wooden shoes, and most had black felt hats with wide brims.

People were laughing and pointing, but somehow I was stirred to pity, not laughter. These immigrants looked as hungry and poor as I was myself. At least I had the advantage of being able to speak with the people around me. These Polanders talked in a tongue that no one in Indianola seemed able to understand. They tried making signs but had scant success even with that. I could only imagine how they had made themselves understood well enough in Galveston that they hired Mexican cartmen to haul their belongings. In four big two-wheeled carts were piled trunks and a few feather-beds and some wooden farm implements they had brought from the old country.

Branch Isom came along to watch the show, he and some of his wagon men. It was obvious he had little regard for the foreigners. He had even less when he saw they were using Mexican cartmen. "Birds of a feather," he grumbled. "Dumb heathens, there's not one of them that understands English."

A man at his side said, "I wonder if they understand *dog*."

Those ugly gray curs had followed. The man sicced them onto the oxen that pulled the lead cart. Trapped in crude and heavy wooden yokes, the poor brutes kicked at the dogs and then tried to run. They only succeeded in dragging the cart into a ditch. It tipped over, spilling trunks and wooden plows and bedding onto the ground. The strange-looking foreigners went running after, trying to spare their goods further damage. They chunked rocks at the dogs and whipped them with sticks until the pair gave up and retreated to their master.

It was then that Thomas Canfield rode up. He seemed to appear from nowhere, sitting on a long-legged, beautifully built sorrel horse in the middle of the street. He was a tall man, not blocky and stout like Isom but well built just the same. He was then only in his early twenties but already mature in features, his bearing proud. He was clearly a man sure where he was going and unwilling to waste time along the way.

He said sternly, "Isom, do you want to talk some business, or had you rather bedevil a bunch of poor foreigners who have already had hell enough?"

Isom turned. His manner showed that this man on horseback was one he respected, though I also got the idea he did not particularly like him. "Hello, Canfield. What business could I possibly have with you?"

"That depends on how willing you are to talk price. Some goods came for me on that last ship out of New Orleans. I want them hauled to Stonehill."

The dogs stood by Isom's legs, their tongues hanging out. They still looked toward the ditched cart, considering the peril of renewed assault. One of them decided to try and started back toward the cart. Isom said sharply, "Here, dogs! Stay here." They obeyed. Isom had a voice that commanded obedience of man or beast. "What kind of goods?" he asked.

Canfield said, "Farm implements."

The foreigners did not understand the talk. It came to me later, when I took time to think about it, that they thought Thomas Canfield had come to their rescue and had ordered Isom to halt the harassment. One of the young women—just a girl, really—looked at Canfield with open admiration. In a minute Canfield caught the look, and he stared back at the girl.

Isom said, "Farm implements are heavy. I'll have to look at the load before we can figure."

Canfield didn't hear him; he was distracted by the girl. So was I. It was her ankles which got my attention at first. Growing up, I had had to take it on faith that girls even had ankles. But she had a pleasant face, too, and soft brown eyes that reminded me of a doe. Her full attention was devoted to Canfield, and his to her.

Isom repeated himself. Canfield nodded. They started together toward the wharf, Canfield still riding that big sorrel, Isom walking with the dogs behind him.

None of the American people helped the foreigners get the cart out of the ditch. Most simply went on about their business. In a few minutes some Mexican cartmen came along, and the Mexicans who were with the Polanders called on them for help. They had to finish unloading the heavy goods out of the cart. In a bit they manuevered the oxen up and got the big wooden wheels back on flat ground. Then all of the Polanders, women as well as the men, set in to loading their goods back into place. I stayed out of it at first because I didn't figure it was any of my business, but then I started thinking that if I helped I might be invited to share a meal with somebody. I didn't know what kind of food Mexicans or Polanders ate, but anything was better than fish roasted on a stick over an open fire, which was all I had had for three days. I pitched in and helped lift the heavy trunks and the wooden plows. Not until later did I realize I wouldn't recognize an invitation to supper if they gave me one. I never knew there were so many strange languages in one place.

One thing most people don't realize is that Texas was a mixed lot of humanity in those days. There seems to be a mistaken impression that early Texas had just two kinds of people: leftover Mexicans and Bible-reading, whiskey-drinking, rifle-shooting, English-speaking immigrants from Tennessee. In truth, it wasn't like that at all. Texas drew people from all over the world because it was so big, and it had so much land to offer. It was considered a place for starting anew, no matter what fate had dealt to each person before. All kinds of people moved to Texas. Wherever you went, you found settlements of Germans, Swedes, Irish, French, Czechs. It was a Babel without a tower. It was a melting pot that never quite melted.

I didn't find a soul in the party that I could talk with, so I stood off to one side, looking hungry and waiting to see what might happen. In a little while Thomas Canfield rode back from the wharf with a grim look on his face. I assumed Isom had asked him more than he had expected to haul his goods. Canfield headed directly up to the Polanders and spoke to the Mexican cartmen who had come along and helped reload the cart. I could tell he was struggling with the language. In later years he could talk Spanish like a native. But even when I first saw him, he was able to understand and make himself understood.

In a little he was accompanied back toward the wharf by a couple of Mexicans. Branch Isom stood in front of a dramshop watching, his face clouded and angry. When Canfield returned he was followed by two smiling Mexican freighters. Isom turned and went into the dramshop, slamming the door against the wintry chill blowing in off the water.

Canfield rode by the Polanders, tipped his low-crowned hat and said, "Good morning." The voice was slow and Southern. The people didn't know what he said, but he spoke in a kindly way, so they smiled. Especially the girl.

I decided if he was feeling so good, it was time for me to present myself and hope for better than I had received at the hands of Branch Isom. I said, "Mister, could I talk to you?"

He glanced at me in surprise. I realized he thought I was one of the Polanders. "You speak English?" he asked.

"That's *all* I talk," I told him. "These aren't my people."

"I didn't mean to offend you. They look like a decent sort. It isn't their fault they were born somewhere else."

In those days nearly everybody in Texas except the Mexicans had been born somewhere else, but most of them not quite so far away as the Polanders.

I said, "I take it you're going inland. I was wondering if I could travel with you? I'll work at anything."

He looked me over carefully. "You have kin that you're going to?"

"I've got nobody here. I'm looking for work to do, and a place to go to away from this coast. This is a feverish country, and poor."

"Anyplace is a poor country when you've got no money. I judge you have none?"

"Very little," I admitted. "But I have a good back and willing hands."

He wanted to know where my gun was, and I told him I owned none. I couldn't tell whether that pleased him or worried him. It was a little of both, I think.

"Well," he said finally, "I can't guarantee that you'll find any work where I'm going, but you're welcome to come with me. I don't suppose you have a horse?"

I barely owned a pair of shoes.

As he rode up the street, I followed him afoot. Branch Isom stepped out of the dramshop with a bottle in his hand. His face was half as red as his hair and his beard. "Hold up, Canfield," he said.

Thomas Canfield pulled the sorrel to a stop. His manner was that of a man doing something because he chose to, not because he had been ordered to. "I don't believe we have any business, Isom."

"Yes, we do. You've hired those Mexican cartmen."

"They bid the haul for half what you asked me."

"They're Mexicans. I'm white."

"My freight has no eyes to tell the difference. But my wallet knows when I take only half as much out of it."

"You can't expect a white man to work that cheap."

I was tempted to remind Isom that he had expected me not only to work for nothing but to pay for the privilege. I held my tongue, confident that Thomas Canfield could maintain his side of the conversation. Canfield said, "The deal has been made. Next time you want to do business with me, Isom, don't try to get rich all at one time."

Isom took the advice as a challenge. "If you shipped with me, I'd guarantee protection for your goods. You ship with those Mexicans at your own risk."

"That sounds like a threat."

"No threat. I am only pointing out to you that there has been trouble on the trails: Mexican cart trains have been burned, and the shippers took a loss."

"White men's wagons have been burned too."

"Not mine. And mine are not going to be."

"Neither are my goods, Isom." His voice dropped a little, so that I strained to hear him. "I'll kill the man who tries."

He and Isom stared at each other with a look that was near hatred. Without anybody framing it in words, a challenge had been flung, and answered. Isom shrugged. "You're twenty-one."

Canfield nodded. "And a few years more."

Isom went back into the dramshop, the bottle in his hand. Canfield stared after him a moment, then turned to me as I walked up even with his horse. "You heard all that, Reed Sawyer?"

I told him I had. He said, "You may want to reconsider going with me."

"He didn't *say* he was going to do anything."

"Yes, he did. You were only listening to his words."

"I still want to go," I said. "I've been in this town long enough."

"Do you know how to use a gun?"

In truth, my poor marksmanship had been a source of shame to my father, for to most farm boys in Louisiana handling a rifle was second nature; it was a boy's job to keep meat in the house. I did not admit to my shortcoming. I said, "I grew up with a rifle in my hand."

"Then I'll provide you one."

I followed him to his camp, such as it was. He had staked a pack-horse on grass at the edge of the little town. In camp waited a Mexican man several years older than Canfield. "Meet Amadeo Fernandez," Canfield said to me. I shook hands with the Mexican and said I was pleased to know him. He answered in Spanish. He smiled, so I knew at least that he was not cursing me. That was the only way I could have known the difference.

I made some comment to the effect that if I had known few people in Texas spoke English I might have chosen to go elsewhere. It was the first time I saw Canfield smile. Smiling was not a thing he did often, then or later in his life. He said, "The truth is the truth no matter what language it is spoken in. And a lie is a lie."

In the pack, spread out on the ground, was some flour for bread, some coffee beans, grease, and smoked pork. I hungered for the pork, but to my chagrin Canfield did not touch it. He said, "I had Amadeo buy us some fish. It has been a long time since I have had fresh salt-water fish."

Having contributed nothing toward the meal, I could ill afford to be critical. But I ate rather more of the bread than of the fish.

I felt it was not politic to ask questions about his business. He volunteered a little information, however, as we ate. He said he owned land north and east of Stonehill. He was farming part of it, raising cattle on the rest. His parents had moved to that region soon after the Mexican War and had broken out one of the first fields. Thomas was a good farmer, but his preference lay in other directions. He had gone west into Indian country with a party of horse hunters, capturing wild mustangs to bring back to the settlements for sale and trade. With his share of the profits he had bought the first land of his own. Later he went back into the Comanche hunting grounds with hired Mexicans and took more wild horses. This time the profit was his. He added more land to his holdings.

"All kinds of people are coming into this country," he said. "You saw those Polanders. A San Antonio priest bought property for them to break out and work, over past Stonehill. Some of them haven't brought any equipment. There's no one to buy it from where they're going, no one but me. I've been ordering farm implements shipped from New Orleans and reselling them to new farmers. Whatever I can make, I'll put into more land."

I ventured, "You must be a big man up there."

"Not yet. But I will be."

By next morning the Mexican cartmen had enough freight to fill out their loads. One of those big carts, drawn by two yokes of oxen, could haul up to five thousand pounds. The four Mexicans who had been carrying goods for the Polanders joined at the end of the line. Canfield talked worriedly in Spanish to Amadeo Fernandez. Together they rode back to where the foreigners waited. I followed at a respectful distance and listened to the arguments. I knew none of the language but surmised from the hand motions that the Polanders and their Mexican freighters intended to go along. Canfield was trying to tell them this cart train carried special danger, but he did not convince the four Mexicans. The Polanders listened in worried silence, understanding neither English nor Spanish. Finally a man came out of a warehouse and began speaking to them in still another language, which I learned was German. A couple of the Polanders understood that fairly well. So Spanish was translated into English through Canfield, then into German and finally, for the good of all the group, into the Silesian dialect spoken by the Polanders.

I could only imagine how much was lost or distorted through all the translations.

I began to think I should give Texas just a little more of my time, and if conditions did not improve I would move on to a more promising locale where everyone spoke my language.

At the time I thought the immigrants simply did not understand the seriousness of the situation. Later I learned they had already been through so much hell that the prospect of a little more caused no terror for them.

Canfield was looking at the girl. Talking to her was hopeless, but he tried. "I wish I could make you understand. You ought not to be on this trip."

She only smiled. It was not for the women to make the decisions anyway, not in those times or among the European immigrants. Canfield had no authority over the cart train; he was simply a shipper. But he would see his goods protected. I was to learn that when he felt something belonged to him, whether people or land or cattle, he would fly into the face of the devil to protect it.

Branch Isom and his wagons were still in Indianola when the cart train pulled out onto the well-beaten road. The wagoners had not yet gotten a full load, but a merchant vessel had docked late the night before and they would probably receive enough freight from it to finish out.

Isom stood in front of the dramshop with three of his teamsters as the last of the Mexican cartmen goaded his oxen into movement with the Polanders' goods. I was still afoot, of course, but so were the other people. Even the cart drivers walked most of the time. Thomas Canfield and Fernandez were on horseback, the Mexican leading the packhorse.

I looked back at Isom and said to Canfield, "At least they will be well behind us."

Canfield shook his head. "They have mule teams, not oxen. They will catch up."

It took most of that first day to get up out of the low-lying, swampy coastal lands and onto higher, drier ground. Though it was winter, the sun was strong and the air muggy. I found myself sweating, and I feared lapsing back into the fever that had plagued me on the ship. But as we worked our way up into a drier elevation I began to feel better and take more interest in the life I saw around me. We were passing through a country already partially settled, much of the better land broken for cultivation. This was the fallow time for most of it. The farmers we saw were mostly breaking out new land to go into crops the following spring. Though the great high-wheeled carts were still a curiosity to me, I noted that the people we passed paid little or no attention to them. But the Polanders were another matter. People stared and whispered as the strange procession of immigrants passed. I knew most people were fascinated as I had been by their clothes, particularly those of the women. A boy of ten or twelve, riding bareback on a shaggy mule in the direction opposite our line of travel, watched with open mouth as the Polanders passed. He turned the mule around and whipped it into a lope back the way he had come. A mile or so down the road we passed a couple of crude farmhouses built of logs. At least a dozen people stood in front, the boy among them. They looked at the immigrants as if they had been a circus parade.

I was bringing up the rear afoot. Canfield and Fernandez had ridden up front somewhere. A couple of the farmers edged closer and closer and looked me over carefully. Finally deciding I was of another breed than the Polanders, they fell in beside me.

"What kind of queer varmints are those?" the older one asked me.

I told him I understood they were Polanders but added that I didn't rightly know what a Polander was. All I knew for certain was that they had come from the other side of the big water.

"What are they good for?" he wanted to know.

I told him I supposed they were farmers inasmuch as I had seen some wooden plows. But I hadn't been able to talk to them, so I didn't really know.

"Foreigners," he said with a snort. "Every time we look up there's another kind of foreigners passing by. Germans, Frenchies, Sweders— God knows what all. We no sooner taken this land away from those Indians and Mexicans than all these foreigners start coming in. You watch, they'll be taking it away from *us* one of these days."

From what I had heard Texas still had more than enough land for everybody, but I judged he didn't care to hear that.

Through the day we passed other freight outfits coming from the interior, headed down to Indianola and Galveston. When they were Mexican oxcart trains there was a great deal of laughing and yelling between their men and ours. When they were American wagons, the hatred that passed from one side to the other was so thick and heavy you could almost reach out and touch it. I had never realized how long it took to get over a war, even after the battles had stopped.

Canfield said the hatred had come first, before the wars, and it would last a long time yet because people on both sides kept studying on the differences between themselves. They didn't pay much attention to the ways they were alike. Each one was convinced the other was inferior. They all talked to the same God, but they saw Him differently and were sure He was on their side alone.

All the Mexicans I had seen up to then were the ones on this train and a few in Indianola. To me they were still as strange as the Polanders. The difference in languages stood like a stone wall between us. I asked Canfield how he got along with them to the extent that he even rode with one, that he let them freight his goods for him when white men were available to do it.

"I learned a lot from Amadeo," he said. "He worked for my father, and now he works for me. Sure, some Mexicans will lie to you. So will Branch Isom. Some of them will cheat you. So will Branch Isom. Some of them will even kill you if there's a profit in it. So will Branch Isom. So where's the big difference?"

Late that evening the Mexicans reached a place they wanted to camp. They found another cart train there ahead of them, coming down toward the coast. Both trains camped together to double their defense. I could tell there was a considerable amount of excited talk between the Mexicans of the two outfits, but of course I couldn't understand a word of it. As we fixed ourselves a little supper out of the goods in Canfield's pack he told me there was talk of a cart train being raided a couple of days' journey ahead. The attack had been driven off, but there had been some loss of life and a couple of carts burned.

Attempted robbery was the reason which went down in official records, but the cartmen knew robbery was no issue. This was part of a sustained warfare between Mexican and American freighters for supremacy on the trail. Many San Antonio merchants favored the Mexicans because they charged less for making the haul. The Mexicans had less investment in equipment and were willing to live by lower standards. Americans needed more money because of their higher investments and their higher expectations. The issues were simple. Only the solution was difficult. Canfield said he expected the outcome would be decided more on the basis of force than of equity.

In the long run, he added, most conflicts are.

We were under no obligation to help the cartmen stand guard, and it was clear that those of the coast-bound train did not trust Canfield or me. One of the first Mexican words I learned to recognize was *gringo*, spoken like a curse. But Canfield and I each took a turn anyway, with Amadeo filling out the last part of the night. Nothing happened except a fight between Canfield's horse and one of the others. The sorrel quickly established dominance.

We were on the trail soon after sunup, the great carts creaking and squealing. A couple of the Polanders seemed to have trouble getting started. A woman of middle age was supported by younger women until a teamster made motions for her to be placed in a cart, where she could ride. I gathered that she had survived the fever—a common complaint along the coast—and she had not yet regained her strength. Canfield rode to the cart and helped lift the woman into it. He received a smile from the pretty girl for his efforts. I suspected that had been his object in the first place.

One of the cartmen had a lean brown dog. As the day wore on, the dog spent most of its time with the Polanders, who talked to him in their strange language and patted him on the head. He wagged his tail and seemed to understand them perfectly well.

I brought up the rear, carrying a long-barreled muzzle-loading rifle Canfield had lent me. Toward noon I began hearing a racket behind us and saw a wagon train gradually catching up. A horseman rode well out in front of it. As he neared I recognized Branch Isom's red beard, and the two bad dogs trailing along on either side of him. We pulled off the trail for nooning, and Isom brought his wagons past. He looked us over with hard eyes and said nothing. Not a word was spoken by anyone on either his train or ours. The only communication was between Isom's two dogs and the brown one which belonged to our train. They had a snarling match that led to a moment of tooth-snapping conflict. Isom rode back and popped a whip over the dogs' heads. His two pulled out of the fight and followed him, though they looked back and continued the quarrel so long as they were within range.

One of the cartmen patted the brown dog and spoke approvingly for his bravery in battle. He would have lost if the fight had been allowed to go on much longer, but it would have been to superior numbers, not to superior gallantry. The pretty immigrant girl got something out of a cart and smeared it on the dog's wounds, talking softly in words the dog seemed to understand even though I did not.

While we rested, one of the immigrant men came to me and began talking. He pointed to my rifle and made motions I could not decipher until finally he mimed the act of pulling a bow-string. I realized he was asking if there was a chance we might encounter Indians. I didn't know.

Canfield said, "No Indians. They're a long way west." Evidently his meaning was understood, for the Polander seemed relieved.

I said, "These people are in for a lot of trouble if they've got to go through this every time they want to talk to anybody."

Canfield said, "They'll get with their own and stay with their own. There'll be a few who will learn enough English to get by, and those will take care of the rest. I've sold plows to some Germans, and that's the way they've done it. These immigrants don't scatter amongst us much; they stay close together and lean on one another. They'll make it."

Watching these people, the language difference a barrier between us, I could only guess at what they had left behind them, what they had been through to get here. Later, when the barriers began to break down, I would learn that the Polanders were something like the Israelites of the Bible, made slaves in their own country and finally driven out. They had been conquered and divided up by the Prussians and others and their lands had been taken away from them until they faced the proposition of leaving or starving. There had been a few Polanders in Texas at the time of the revolution from Mexico, and some had been executed on Santa Anna's orders after the fight at Goliad. A few were with Sam Houston when he won the battle of San Jacinto. These wrote letters home, and so over the next few years they kept drawing in friends and family until they had several small communities spread across the country. The stories about money lying in the streets had probably reached Silesia too, just as they had reached Louisiana.

I doubted they were any more disappointed than I was to find out how little money existed in Texas, and none of it lying in the streets. They had chosen a hard time to come. Actually, it was always hard times in Texas. The rich you could count on one hand. The poor you found in multitudes.

Late in the day the Mexicans began stepping out on the trail and looking forward. The *capitán* rode back and visited with Amadeo, then the two spurred their horses and rode far out ahead, beyond sight. A while before dark they were back, disappointed. Canfield said they had hoped to meet another cart train coming down the trail so they could camp together for mutual protection, but they had found none. Now they could not put off camping any longer; it would soon be night.

The Polanders would probably have helped with guard duty if they had been asked, but no one knew how to ask them. So far as we could tell, they had not a single weapon with them. They had not been accustomed to owning or using them in the old country; the Prussians would not have allowed it. We two *gringos* and the Mexicans divided the guard duty between us. I had not thought about it until Canfield mentioned it, for I was not used to having to consider such things, but the *capitán* had camped the train in a broad, open area. If the moon was again bright and cold as the night before, we would have good visibility.

Because I could talk to no one else, I took Canfield as my example and copied whatever he did. He was concerned but not really fearful. I could not say the same for myself. I had never held a gun in my hands for possible use against another human. I asked, "Do you have to do this all the time?" It crossed my mind that I was still only two days' walk from the coast.

Canfield said, "When I was a boy we saw a few Indians, but they've all been pushed west. Once we're home nobody will bother us. But the trail is always a place to be watchful. Especially as long as this cart war goes on."

It seemed to me it would have been the better part of valor to have shipped his goods with Isom or some other wagon man no matter what the rate had been. I said as much.

Canfield told me sternly, "In this country you must never show a feather. Give up to them once and you're beaten." Through the years to come I was to learn just how deeply he believed that. Once challenged, cost was no factor to him. He never showed a feather.

The night chill closed upon us as soon as the sun dropped out of sight. When the people spread their blankets to sleep, one of the immigrants threw fresh wood upon their campfire. Canfield quickly dragged it back out of the flames. He tried to explain that for safety's sake it was better to keep a dark camp. I don't think he quite conveyed the message, but he had such a commanding way about him that no one presented any challenge.

I took the first watch. I doubted I could have slept anyway. Thomas Canfield seemed able to command himself even in the matter of sleeping, for within a few minutes after he rolled up in his blankets he was gone. It took Amadeo Fernandez a bit longer. I sat hunched with my coat on and my blanket wrapped around my shoulders, my bare hands stiff and cold on the steel barrel of the rifle. There was no danger of my falling asleep on duty. I was chilled to the bone.

I had no way of telling time and had not learned to follow the stars. I listened for the Mexicans who stood watch farther up the line of carts. When at last I heard them changing guard, I got up, trembling from the cold, and carefully awakened Canfield. He wasted no time yawning. He seemed to know where he was and what he had to do from the moment he opened his eyes. He got up and went about it in a quiet, businesslike manner. I lay down on the spot he had vacated, hoping he had warmed the ground. He had not. I shivered a long time before I dropped off to sleep.

When I awakened it was suddenly and to the sound of shots. I flung the blanket away and fumbled in panic for the rifle. I saw flashes of fire and vague movements out in the night. I heard men shouting and horses running. I had never realized how quickly a man could fire and then recharge a muzzle-loading rifle until I saw Thomas Canfield do it.

My heart pounded and skipped. I shouted, "What do I shoot at?"

He replied, "Anything that moves out there. We've got no friends past the cart line."

Some riders carried torches. Though they held them high, the flickering light showed the horses a little. Somewhere up the line I heard a man scream, and I saw a torch thrown into one of the carts. Behind me the immigrant women were crying, huddling together.

From out of the night a shape lunged at me, and I raised my rifle. It was close range, but I missed. Canfield was busy reloading. The horseman spurred into me, knocking me down and making me lose my hold on the rifle. The rider hurled a blazing torch into the nearest cart, one which held immigrant goods. A Polander jumped onto the cart and grabbed the torch, flinging it back into the horseman's face as the man fired a pistol. The horse squealed in panic at the blaze and whirled around while the man cursed. Canfield finished loading his rifle, brought it to his shoulder and fired. The man was driven back in his saddle. The horse broke into a run. The rider slid over its rump and landed roughly on the ground. Instantly Canfield was kneeling over him, a long hunting knife in his hand, the point pressing against the man's throat.

"You move," he said, "and I'll kill you."

The man groaned. The rifle ball had taken him hard.

Canfield glared at me as he reloaded his rifle. "I thought you said you could shoot."

I had no answer for that and did not try one.

"Watch him, then," Canfield said tersely, and turned his attention back to the men out there in the moonlight. He called a time or two for Amadeo. Both of us had lost sight of the Mexican.

The shooting died. The raiders pulled back, for they had flung their torches and had found the defense too strong. Down the line, one cart blazed. Despairing of putting out the fire, several Mexicans grabbed the tongue and pulled the vehicle away from the others to prevent its fire from spreading. Canfield said with concern, "I'm going to see if that's one of the carts carrying my goods."

The wounded raider kept groaning. I did not know what to do about him, so I did nothing except watch.

One of the Polanders touched my shoulder and pointed to the other side of the carts. He said something I did not understand except that the word *Mexican* somehow came out of it. I handed another Polander my rifle and pointed to the wounded man, hoping he understood that I meant for him to stand guard. He took the weapon nervously. Following the older man's repeated beckoning, I found two of the immigrant women kneeling over a fallen Amadeo. They spoke softly, trying to comfort him. He probably did not hear them. As little experience as I had had with that sort of thing, I sensed he was dying. I touched him and felt the stickiness of warm blood and came near being sick. I brought my hand quickly away, as if I had stuck it into fire. In the excitement I had forgotten about the cold, but suddenly it came back to me, and I was trembling all over.

Canfield called me. I responded with what voice I could muster. He came around the cart, knelt quickly and called Amadeo's name. The Mexican's breathing was spaced in ragged patches, and in a few moments it stopped. Canfield talked softly in Spanish, gently shaking the man as if he thought he could force breath back into the body. Finally he pushed to his feet and walked back to where the wounded raider lay. Canfield towered over him with fury in his face.

The man pleaded, "Help me."

Canfield looked at me. "Go relight one of those torches at that cart fire and bring it here so I can see."

I did. He held the torch over the man's face. "I know you," he said accusingly. "I've seen you in Stonehill. You're with Isom's train, aren't you?"

The man cried, "I'm bleeding to death. Help me."

"Tell me first," Canfield insisted. "It was Isom who led this raid, wasn't it?"

One of the Mexican cartmen dropped to one knee to tear the clothing away from the wound deep in the raider's shoulder. Canfield pushed the man to one side. He said something in Spanish, then said for my benefit and the prisoner's, "We'll treat you when you've told me what I want to know. Till then, nobody touches you."

"I'll die," the man cried weakly.

"Then die," Canfield said. His voice was as cold as the night. "It's up to you."

He stood over the man, a terrible look on his face. I saw a ferocity I had never seen anywhere before. Slowly the Mexicans began gathering around. They talked quietly among themselves, and I heard a word that I later learned described the look they saw in his eyes: *gavilán*. The hawk.

At that moment I think Thomas Canfield might have killed anyone who had stepped in to thwart what he was doing. I suddenly found that I was a little afraid of him, a feeling I never quite lost. There was a look about him then—and I saw it again at times through the years—that turned my blood cold.

It was, for a little while, a contest of wills between Canfield and the wounded *gringo*. Finally, as it would always be, it was the other man who gave up first. He lifted his hand a little way, pleadingly, and whispered, "I'll tell. Help me."

"Tell first," Canfield said.

The man tried, but he had waited too long. The strength was gone from him, and his voice. His lips moved, but no discernible words came. Canfield knelt and grabbed the man's collar. He shook him. "Louder! Tell me! Was it Isom?"

He had won the contest, but the victory cost him a price he had not intended to pay. The man died without telling him what he wanted to know. Canfield stood over the dead raider and cursed him for taking the life of a better man.

CHAPTER 2

awn came and we buried the dead, but not together. Canfield would not have that. It was a custom of the time that Americans and Mexicans not be buried side by side, but this was not Canfield's reason. He said bitterly that Amadeo Fernandez was a God-fearing man too good to keep company with an outlaw throughout eternity. We buried them on opposite sides of the trail. Canfield quoted Scripture by memory. The Mexicans worried that Amadeo needed the services of a priest to keep him safe from the devil, but many a good man had been buried along this road without the benefit of clergy. The immigrants bowed their heads and offered up a prayer. I did not know if it was for Amadeo or for their own deliverance. None of them had been hurt during the shooting, and their possessions were but little damaged.

The dead *gringo* had carried little worth salvaging except for a knife and pistol, unused, and his rifle. Canfield gave me these in recognition of the fact that I owned no weapons and that henceforth I might have need for them as a result of having been in the cartmen's company. A little silver was found in the man's pockets. Canfield took this for Amadeo's widow.

I tried the accuracy of the rifle by resting its barrel in the fork of a tree and aiming at a dried cowchip forty yards away. The bullet kicked up dust short of the chip. I was satisfied that the rifle was more accurate than the man who fired it. Canfield seemed to agree, though he did not say so. The pistol was one of the cap-and-ball style of the time, heavy as a sack of lead bars. It took a while to accustom myself to wearing it, for I developed a strong list in its direction.

The outlaw's horse had gotten away, but I probably would not have had more than temporary possession had we managed to capture it. There was always somebody around to claim a horse if there seemed any doubt about its true ownership.

I was set to walk, but Canfield pointed his chin toward Amadeo's horse. "You'd just as well ride. I don't care to lead him."

The stirrups were longer than was comfortable, but I put up with the inconvenience because refitting them would take time. I had no wish to be left alone now, even for a little while. I felt nervous about riding a dead man's saddle. I asked, "Did he have a family?"

Canfield was grim. "A wife and two boys."

"What happens to them now?"

"They'll stay on my place as long as I have one, and as long as they want to." His jaw ridged. I could see vengeance in his eyes, but there was frustration too. Though he was convinced Branch Isom had been at the foot of this, he had no legal recourse. One thing I learned about Thomas Canfield as time went by was that he had two characteristics in abundance: determination and a long memory. He had also a third: an inability to forgive. Somewhere, sometime, his chance would come. He was always ready. Meantime, he could wait.

A change came over the people on the cart train. Quietly, without anyone saying anything or making a show of it, leadership shifted to Canfield. The Mexicans showed him respect rather than general indifference. The *capitán* came to ask Canfield's opinion before he stopped for nooning or to make camp. The immigrants gave way each time he rode back to the rear of the train. They were fascinated, yet they feared him.

The Mexicans had a name for him now, though they did not use it in his hearing. They called him the Hawk.

I had seen larger towns than Stonehill but none more alive for its size. Its streets were crowded by great tarpaulin-covered freight wagons drawn by as many as sixteen mules or horses; by the creaking Mexican carts with their many spans of muscled oxen. Between the wagons, often seeming in some jeopardy of being crushed by the huge wheels, walked or ran people of all descriptions, a variety I thought would rival New Orleans. They all seemed to have someplace to go or something important to do.

Here, Canfield told me, two busy trails came together, one from Galveston and Indianola on the coast, the other from Mexico and the Rio Grande, joining here for the journey on to San Antonio, and north and west. This town was still new enough that the unpainted lumber had not yet darkened on some of its buildings. The courthouse, a simple two-story affair built like a square wooden box, stood in the center of the activity and told one and all that this was the seat of a newly organized county which destiny had marked for greatness.

It seemed to me that an inordinate percentage of the business houses were dramshops of some kind. The word *saloon* had not come into common usage as it would later on.

Canfield said, "One can become poor dealing in the necessities of life, but only a bad choice of location can make a pauper of a whiskey merchant. For that purpose, there is not a bad location in Stonehill."

A newly-painted sign over the door of a general store and post office declared: "Stonehill, the Jewel of Texas—Brightest Point in the Lone Star."

"A pesthole," Canfield countered.

I was too impressed by the busy, bustling aspect of the town to accept that judgment at face value. I said, "It must have a place."

"It does. If it were in my power, that is where I would send it."

I was in no position to argue the point, for he had been here before the town. I said, "I'll wager I can find employment."

"Perhaps. But you came in with a Mexican cart train, and that will go against you. A lot of local money is tied up in freight wagons and the wagoner trade."

Once he had broached this matter I began to pay attention to the people who watched us. I saw hostility in some faces, now that I began looking for it. The experience shook me. I had never had reason to encounter hostility back home. On the delta I had only friends. In Texas barely a week, I already had enemies. I was unprepared for so much progress.

As we passed a dramshop a young man strode out to meet us. Perhaps the word *strode* is too bold, for he weaved a bit. He had a broad and easy smile, and he waved at Thomas Canfield. "Hello, big brother," he shouted.

Thomas' eyes crackled. His voice was sharp. "Kirby! What are you doing in town?"

"I came to help you unload your goods."

"You were needed more at home."

Kirby Canfield had not shaved in days, but his beard was still soft and boyish. So was his manner. Thomas' harsh rebuke seemed not to touch him at all. He kept his grin.

"You're late," he said. "I thought you would be here yesterday."

"I suppose," Thomas said severely, "that you came the day before that, just to be sure?"

"I try to do my part."

"And so you've been drinking and gambling in this town for two days?"

"Not gambling." Kirby Canfield smiled. "You only gamble when you lose." He stuck his hands into his pockets and jingled a collection of coins. "You have your talents, brother, but you've never seen fit to acknowledge mine."

Thomas gave him no ground. "Since you came to work, I'll see that you do."

"Give me a stirrup," Kirby said, "and I'll swing up behind you."

"You'll walk, and burn the whiskey out of your blood."

We had kept moving all this time. Thomas rode up beside the Mexican teamster on his lead cart and pointed leftward at the next corner. His two carts pulled out of the train. The other carts lumbered along, filling the gap we had left.

The immigrants at the rear of the train attracted considerable attention from the townspeople. As they came up even with us the patriarch of the group nodded gravely and acknowledged Thomas Canfield, thanking him with a gesture and a few strange words. Thomas nodded back, but his eyes searched through the immigrants until they found the girl. I saw a long, silent look pass between them. Thomas turned his head and watched a minute or two after they had gone past us.

"Good luck," he said, too quietly for her or the others to have heard if they had been able to understand him.

We proceeded down the heavily rutted street to a small frame storage building set apart from the principal business district. It was not properly a store, for Thomas kept no store hours. I found when I got to know him better that such a thing was against his nature. This was simply a spartan little warehouse where he could meet a prospective implement customer at their mutual convenience for an exchange of goods and coin of the realm. He went there only on arrangement and stayed only so long as was necessary. Most Stonehill business was strictly for cash. Credit was hard for the borrower to find and for the lender to enforce, because this was a horseback society, always moving.

I helped unload the carts, but Thomas saw to it that his brother did the heaviest lifting. I had not entirely recovered from the effects of the sea trip and was soon tired. Nor was I an employee of Thomas Canfield; my only obligation was gratitude. During the last part of the unloading process I sat on a rough bench with Thomas while Kirby and the Mexicans finished the work. Kirby sweated so much that he appeared to have been caught in a rainshower. Thomas showed him no sympathy, though Kirby expressed a certain good-natured sympathy for himself.

A carriage approached, drawn by a pair of matched bays. On the seat hunched a thin man of middle age, dressed rather well by the standards of the time and place, though he would have been considered threadbare in the better delta towns. Beside him sat a young woman who quickly took my attention. About my age, she was brown-eyed and brown-haired and had a smile like sunshine. That smile was for Thomas Canfield, however, not for me.

Thomas stood up as the carriage came to a stop. In his eyes was a respect I had not seen him give to anyone else in the few days I had known him. "Good morning, Laura. Good morning, Mister Hines."

I remembered seeing the Hines name on the general store and post office back on the main street. "Good morning, Thomas," the man answered. He touched the brim of a dusty Eastern hat. He returned Thomas' respect in kind. "I see you have brought in another shipment. If ever I were to give thought to selling farm implements, you would probably undersell me." No malice or resentment was detectable in his voice.

Thomas came dangerously near smiling. "I would if I could, sir."

"That is as it should be. A bit of competition helps hold greed in check and keep us honest."

The girl had never taken her eyes from Thomas. I had just as well not been standing there for all she saw of me. I wished she were more observant. She said, "I hope you will come someday for Sunday dinner, Thomas."

"I hardly know when Sunday comes," he replied. I could tell that he liked her, but I did not see the same look in his eyes that he had given the Polander girl.

She said, "I'll have to send you a calendar."

"That would be nice," he said. By the tone of his voice, though, I knew he would not be waiting in suspense.

Hines said to Thomas, "My best regards to your good mother." He fingered his gray-tinged muttonchop whiskers as he briefly appraised first Kirby and then me, showing us no ill will, at least. He flipped the reins and set the team moving. Laura Hines turned and looked back over her shoulder, but only at Thomas, not at the rest of us.

Thomas stared after them. "Even Sodom and Gomorrah had a few good people. Linden Hines started this town. He's like a father with a wild son he can't control." He glanced at Kirby. "Or a man with a brother."

He paid the cartmen in silver. There was considerable bowing and beaming and wishing of happy times. At least, that seemed the gist of the talk. The only Spanish I had learned was a few words of profanity that had seemed effective upon the oxen.

Once the Mexicans had taken their leave, I decided it was time I did the same. Unless I found a source of income shortly, I would have to learn to live without eating. I told Kirby Canfield it had been a pleasure to make his acquaintance. I shook Thomas Canfield's hand and thanked him for his courtesies.

He frowned. "I've already told you to expect nothing from this town."

I assured him I intended to stay only long enough to replenish my thin purse, then proceed to San Antonio or farther into the interior. He thanked me for my help in fighting the raiders, though I had only fired some wild shots. I hoisted my little roll of blankets across my shoulder on a short rope and picked up the rifle Thomas had said I was entitled to. I started up the street, looking hopefully at each business house, trying to decide which might offer employment befitting the talents of a delta farm boy. This place was a long way from the cotton fields, both in miles and in character.

I tried six or seven places and met the same cold response at every one. Some mentioned that they had seen me in bad company. Others implied it or showed it with their eyes. I still had a little money but resolved to preserve it at all costs. I found a small place which advertised itself as a restaurant and volunteered to chop wood in return for a meal. The proprietor expressed some reservations about my strength for the work but said as an act of kindness he would feed me. All I had to do in return was to chop about half a cord of mesquite wood piled in the back. I accepted with proper gratitude. I was inclined to eat first and work afterward, but he expressed the opinion that a laborer performed best on an empty stomach.

It might have been cheaper for him had he allowed me to eat first. By the time I had chopped the wood I had a ruinous appetite. With no shame whatever, I filled my plate to its edges and sat down to the task. I was well into my second helping when a rough-looking teamster came in. Almost immediately his attention went to my rifle, leaning in the corner. He whispered to the proprietor, who had been morosely studying my progress with his foodstuffs.

The proprietor did not give me a chance to fill my plate a third time. He picked it up as I finished the last bite, and he stood waiting for my coffee cup. I complimented him on his skill in the kitchen, picked up my rifle and bedroll and went outside.

There I was confronted by the teamster who had been in the restaurant. With him were Branch Isom and ten or a dozen more. Had I known more about the character of Stonehill I would have brought up the rifle to a strong defensive posture then and there. It would have been all bluff, however. The rifle was not loaded.

Isom's eyes were narrowed and cold. "You're the boy that wanted to be paid to come up from Indianola."

I bristled a little. "And you are the gentleman who offered to let me pay for the privilege of working."

Isom's gaze fell to the rifle. "Where did you get that?"

I realized he knew very well. I said, "Some raiders attacked the cart train I was with. One of them left it there."

I doubted that these men knew for certain that the raider had been killed. Looking from one hostile face to another. I decided my life would not be worth a secondhand chew of tobacco if I told them.

Isom said, "I believe you stole it."

"I picked it up on the field of battle." I had read somewhere about the spoils of war belonging to the victors, but this did not seem an appropriate time to go into history.

A teamster said, "It's Fitz's rifle, all right. Got his initials carved on the stock."

Isom took a step toward me and stopped. I could see little of his eyes because of the heavy red brows. "What happened to the man who carried it?"

I suspected they had guessed but were not quite certain. It was not my place to bear ill tidings to strangers. I said, "You should know better than I do. You were with him."

I did not see Isom's fist coming, but a sledgehammer could not have struck me harder. I staggered backward with lights flashing in my eyes. He hit me again and I landed on my back, on top of my rolled-up blankets. The rifle fell. I acted by instinct, though not very well. I got to my feet, took a couple of hard swings at him and missed, then was knocked down again for my trouble. I scrambled at him from hands and knees and managed to get both arms around his legs, tripping him. We rolled in the dirt. I hit him three or four times, but never as hard as he hit me. From the first it was clear I was going to lose.

Toward the end I was seeing through a painful blur. Thomas and Kirby Canfield had walked up. Kirby seemed about to come to my aid, but Thomas held him back. It was my fight.

It came to me later, when I knew him better, that Thomas Canfield was not a crusader. He did not go rushing about looking for other people's fights. He would have taken no part in the Mexicans' fight against the raiders had he not had a shipment of freight on their carts. He took no part in my fight. Had it been over something or someone who belonged to him, he would have.

At last I was lying beaten, hardly able to move. Branch Isom had his knee on my chest. "Now, boy, you tell me what happened to Fitz."

Thomas Canfield said evenly, "Let him up, Isom."

Isom glanced at him with uncertainty. "This is not your affair."

"I believe it is. *I* killed your man Fitz."

Isom pushed to his feet. "He wasn't my man, Canfield. He quit me on the trail."

Canfield's voice was as cold as January. "Only after I shot him. He was your man, Isom. You led him, and you killed a man of mine who was worth more than a dozen of you and the scoundrels who hang around you in this scabby town."

It came to me suddenly that they were about to try to kill one another, and I was lying on the ground between them. But I could not move. I lay there trembling, not able even to breathe.

Isom said, "You're wrong, Canfield."

Canfield's voice dropped lower. "You're a liar."

Fury flashed in Isom's eyes, and his hand went to the pistol. As I watched, he drew it from the holster, then stopped, the muzzle pointed more or less at me. The fury in his eyes melted to something else, to uncertainty, to fear.

I turned my head toward Canfield and saw that his pistol was up and aimed straight at Isom. His finger was tight on the trigger. In his eyes was a cold hatred far removed from the quick fury that had drained from Isom's. I could see his finger turning white. I lay paralyzed with fear of my own, knowing that if he fired, Isom's last convulsive act might be to kill me.

Isom tried to bring up the muzzle of his pistol but could not. He seemed frozen, staring into the face of death. After what seemed an age, he let his pistol slip back into its holster.

Weakly he said, "I see no reason to kill you, Canfield."

For another heartbeat, Canfield seemed still determined to fire, but the moment had slipped away from him. Isom's hand lifted clear, showing he was no longer a threat.

If Canfield had intended to shoot him, he had waited too long. For a moment he had had all the excuse he needed. No one could have blamed him. Now that moment was gone.

Isom swallowed. His eyes cut away from Canfield, betraying his fear. From where I lay, I could see his legs tremble even if others could not.

Canfield lowered his pistol reluctantly. Regret was in his eyes, regret that he had not followed through when the moment was right. I could not know, then, how he would grieve in later years over that missed opportunity.

Isom backed slowly away, trying to recover the lost bravado, to deny he had shown the feather. He reached for strength but never quite found it. His shaky voice gave him away. "You watch what you say about me, Canfield. I won't stand still for your slander."

Canfield said nothing. There was no need, for he had made his point and had shown himself the stronger man.

Isom watched narrowly until the rancher's pistol finally returned to its holster. Only then did Isom turn away, walking unsteadily into the nearest dramshop. Some of the dozen or so men followed him. Others simply pulled back to some distance and kept watching. Isom's defeat had been their own, for now at least. The sense of humiliation clung to them.

Kirby Canfield was the first to speak. The tension drained away, and he laughed uneasily. "You beat him, big brother, in front of everybody. That should be the last trouble we'll ever have from Branch Isom."

Thomas' rejoinder was severe. "If you believe that, then you're a fool. He'll have to get back at us now or leave here for good." He turned to me, catching me under the arms and helping me to wobbly feet. "You put up a good fight, Sawyer, for a boy in your condition. I should have stopped it sooner. In a way it was my fight, not yours."

The two Canfields helped me away. It would have been easy for the remaining Isom crowd to have shot any or all of us in the back, for the Canfields did not deign to look behind them, and I could not. After a little while they sat me down on the edge of a wooden porch at the Hines store. "Go fetch the wagon here," Thomas ordered.

When Kirby went to obey, Thomas said to me, "I told you you'd find no friends in this town."

Weakly I acknowledged his perception.

He went on, "I can't pay you much because I have little cash money. But there's room for you at our place if you want to work and are in no hurry to run up a fortune."

I told him I would consider staying at least awhile. It was becoming plain to me that I should learn a lot more about this country before setting myself loose upon it, alone. In truth, I felt as if I were crawling beneath a sheltering arm.

I rested the first couple of days in and about the old double cabin and gorged myself upon the simple but good cooking done by Thomas Canfield's mother. She was a small, spare woman bent at the shoulders by a life of hard work. She said a thing or two that indicated Mr. Canfield—Thomas' father—had been dead several years. She said nothing about how he had come to die, and I did not ask. I was gradually coming around to the notion that when Texas people wanted to talk to you about something, *they* would introduce the subject.

After those first days of shameful indolence I went to work clearing mesquite and other brush from a flat, deep-soil pasture Thomas was preparing to break for the plow. He was resolved to increase his cultivated acreage in the coming spring. It soon became apparent to me why he had so little money. Every bit of cash which came his way—above what went for immediate necessities—was converted almost immediately into land, wherever he could find any for sale within riding distance of the home place. His properties were scattered like the squares on a checkerboard, and he was constantly striving to solidify them.

He gave me the first of many lectures I was to hear from him about the importance of owning land. I suspected he had inherited the hunger from his father, who had taken up the original ground in the Canfield name.

"Land is where the real wealth lies. Businesses come and go. Towns grow and then die. But the land is constant. Whenever you have the chance, Sawyer, grab onto the land and hold it. Everything else is just rainbow."

Over the next month or so he sold most of the implements stored in Stonehill and ordered more out of New Orleans. The profit went to buy a parcel of unbroken rangeland from absentee survivors of a San Jacinto battle veteran who had received the property as a reward from the Republic of Texas, before statehood, but had never lived on or worked it.

All winter he talked of making up another expedition into the Indian country farther west, so he could bring in another stock of mustang ponies to break and sell. The wild horses, subsisting on winter range, would be at their weakest and could not so easily outrun those helped along with grain. But we remained so busy that spring planting time caught us, and we could not go.

Some people like Thomas Canfield seem born to lead, to accumulate and build. Others, like Kirby, seem content enough to follow and to work for someone else. Kirby lacked his brother's passion for acquisition. He tended toward observation of the lilies in the field, toward savoring the full flavor of each day which came to him. He seldom deferred today's pleasures in the hope of accumulating interest for a greater payment at some vague future time. He worked hard and carried his share of the load, for to do less was considered a poor show of one's manhood in those days. But in the evenings when Thomas busied himself with ledgers and survey records and maps, when Mrs. Canfield spun yarn on an old wheel so they wouldn't have to buy cloth, Kirby was likely to be playing an old fiddle or proving the dexterity of his fingers with a deck of cards. He even taught me how to play.

Back home it had been given to me as holy writ that cards were a device invented by the devil to aid him in stealing men's souls. Kirby never took advantage of me by playing for money. We played only for pleasure. Still, the old preachments plagued me every time my fingers closed upon the cards.

Kirby would laugh. "Anything is made a bit more pleasant for being just a little wicked."

Occasionally he liked to slip away to Stonehill. Although he was a grown man and Thomas had no authority to prevent him, Kirby usually waited until Thomas was away from home for a day or two. He tried to get me to go with him, but I declined the first couple of times. I had vivid recollections of my rough experience in that town. Finally, however, I succumbed to temptation, for the town with its bustle and great activity was always an object of curiosity. Most of the people who had frowned before had forgotten my past associations. They seemed to remember only that I was connected with the Canfields. This threw a thin protective cloak over me.

I found that Thomas Canfield was not the only ambitious person in the Stonehill region. Branch Isom, the freighter, had bought out a dramshop and operated it in addition to his line of wagons. He had built an extension onto the back and set it up with gaming tables. These drew Kirby Canfield as a bin of oats draws a frisky young horse. He tried his luck there and more often than not found it good. I was glad I had never played him for money.

Had he chosen to do so, I think he might have sustained himself by his proficiency with cards. But when I suggested the possibility, he said, "I play for diversion. If I ever depended on it for a living it would be pleasant no longer."

On our way home we rode by the little fenced cemetery on the slope above the ranch headquarters. Kirby dismounted and took off his hat while he stared at a headstone. "Papa was the only one who understood about me," he said, the fun suddenly gone from him. "I think he had a little of that streak in him too. If he hadn't, he might still be alive."

It was the first good chance I had had to ask, "What happened to him?"

"When things got too thick around here for him, he would occasionally ride over to Stonehill for a few drinks. It was a harmless thing, or should have been; he never did it very often. One night he just happened to get caught in the middle when a couple of teamsters started shooting at one another. Papa was the first man killed."

"The teamsters . . . did they die too?"

Kirby nodded. "One of them went down in the fight."

"And the other one?"

Kirby looked away. "Thomas found him."

<hr />

We were struggling with our work oxen, breaking the hard ground for spring planting, the day the San Antonio priest came to us. His face was grave. He spoke good English, though his accent was heavy and I had to listen with care to understand him. He nodded to Kirby and me, but he seemed to sense on sight that Thomas was the man in charge.

"Are you aware," he asked Thomas, "of the desperate situation in New Silesia?"

I knew that was the name of the village the immigrants had built for themselves. Though it lay only about ten miles north, my work had never taken me there.

Thomas said, "I didn't know there *was* a situation."

"If you care for your fellow man," the priest told him, "you should go and see for yourself. Surely you can do something to help those poor people in their misery."

Thomas' face clouded. "Have you been to other places around here for help?"

"I just came from Stonehill. I find the town well named. The merchant Hines has pledged some help, but most of the others say let those people go back where they came from."

Thomas frowned. "Perhaps they should."

"They cannot. Nothing is left for them in the old country. They have not the means to move ten miles. They must stay."

I had seen slaves living in little more than chicken coops on some delta farms where owners took insufficient care of their property. But at their worst most of them fared better than the people we found as we rode into the immigrant village. The newest arrivals had come in the dead of winter and for shelter had been able to do little more than dig into the cold ground, covering the holes with a matting of thatched grass for a roof to try to see them through to spring. Some who had been there longer had built picket houses, copied after the style of Mexican *jacales*, but these with their mud chinking and brush roofs had been poor shelter against the elements.

Ragged children bunched before the miserable hovels, watching with wide and hungry eyes as we passed. It occurred to me that there were few dogs. Children without dogs were like coffee without sugar, or meat without salt. These families had nothing to feed to a dog. Adults crossed themselves as the priest passed them. Both men and women still wore the same odd clothing I had seen among the immigrants who had accompanied us from Indianola to Stonehill.

It was as if I had been picked up suddenly and transported to some strange land beyond the seas. I found it little wonder that people in Stonehill had nothing complimentary to say about this alien settlement. What we do not understand, we reject.

Thomas Canfield's face became like stone, grim and brooding. He looked carefully at each person he saw on the street. At length he asked the priest, "Where are the ones who came in last?"

"You have seen most of them. A few are out breaking their fields."

"There was one family . . . I don't know their names. They had a girl, sixteen or seventeen."

The priest considered. "The Brozeks, perhaps. They have a girl named Maria."

"Show me."

We rode almost to the end of the village. Thomas saw the girl before the rest of us did, and he straightened. She was sweeping the bare ground clean in front of a crude dugout, using a rough broom fashioned out of dried weeds tied to a mesquite branch. It seemed a futile thing to be sweeping bare ground, but it was at least an effort at cleanliness. It was an act of defiance.

Her eyes went right to Thomas and held there. The two stared at each other a minute, and Thomas took off his hat. "Hello" was all he said. She responded in words I did not know, in a voice almost too soft to hear. It struck me that she was thinner than on the trip from Indianola, and even then she had been barely large enough to cast a decent shadow.

Thomas said to the priest, "Tell her we are going to help. We don't have much except cattle, but we'll bring some of those. They'll have milk and meat."

The priest translated. The girl never took her eyes from Thomas more than a moment. She said something which the priest told us was simply "thank you."

As we rode away, Thomas turned in the saddle and looked back.

We gathered some of his cattle, which he had scattered widely on the land he owned and upon unused land which lay between his tracts. He picked some recently calved cows which had udders swollen with milk. "They are wild, and they'll have to be tied, but they'll give milk for the children," he said. He picked some fleshy long-aged calves and yearlings, though after a hard winter none were really fat. It was a sacrifice of some dimensions, but he did not grieve over it. We drove about twenty beeves and as many cows into the stricken village.

There we found Linden Hines and his daughter Laura distributing flour and coffee, and some woolen bolt goods out of his mercantile store. Thomas tipped his hat to Laura, whose face glowed at the sight of him. Gravely he shook hands with Hines. "It's good to see you, sir. I knew you would be the only man in Stonehill with enough Christian charity to bring anything here."

Hines shook his gray head. "This isn't all mine. Branch Isom wouldn't want it talked about, but he contributed part of it."

Thomas blinked. He seemed somehow angered, somehow affronted. "Isom? What can he ever expect to get out of *this* place?"

The priest walked from the small crude building which passed for a church. He smiled as he came and thanked Thomas for being a man of his word. "You may have saved some poor children from dying, and others from becoming orphans."

Thomas looked for a place to pen the cattle. A couple of the Polander men hurried ahead of us, pointing and talking in their language until they reached a rough enclosure built of mesquite. They let down the crooked bars that served as a gate and helped haze the cattle in.

Most of the village people had gathered, all trying to talk to us at once. Laura Hines had followed along and stood at the edge of the crowd, saying nothing but watching Thomas with admiration. To me the talk was a babble, though the priest did not have to translate the gratitude, the smiles on haggard faces. He went through a ceremony which I surmised was some form of blessing on the gift of cattle.

The girl Maria was there with some younger brothers and sisters and her parents. I remembered them from the trip. She smiled at Thomas, and he smiled back.

I glanced at Laura Hines. She looked puzzled, her smile gone.

Thomas beckoned the priest. "Father, I want you to talk to this girl for me, please. Tell her that if it is all right with her, and with her father, I'd like to come here and call on her."

The priest showed misgivings. Clearly he thought Thomas was asking a price for the cattle. "These are a moral people," he said.

"If I had not thought so I would not have helped them. There are already more than enough of the other sort in this country."

"But you cannot even talk to her."

"We'll talk. You just ask her."

The priest spoke. The girl turned excitedly to her parents. I could see the question in the eyes of the older couple as they stared at Thomas. Perhaps they remembered the coldness they had seen in him as he waited for the wounded raider to talk or to die. But that had to be weighed against his sacrifice in bringing cattle here to feed the hungry. If this was the judgment they were making, the cattle won.

I suppose girls where she came from were trained to be reserved, and she tried. But her eyes, brown and big and pretty, sparkled with delight.

Thomas said to the priest, "I lose track of time when I am busy. What day is this?"

"Friday."

Thomas nodded. "Tell her I will be here Sunday."

I looked around for Laura Hines, but she was gone.

CHAPTER 3

He was there that Sunday and almost every other for a long time. His one suit was tight on him because it had been made several years earlier, before hard work and maturity had muscled him. But few people there in those days kept up with styles. A tight suit or a threadbare one was better than no suit at all. Many people had none at all.

Thomas did not allow romance to spoil his penchant for hard work or for business. He did not *send* Kirby and me out to work, he *led* us, and usually he did more than either of us. Even with all his other responsibilities he managed to sell some farming implements, to keep the cash turning. Sometimes he willingly allowed profit opportunities to escape him, however. He distributed a number of plows and other tools among the Silesians with the understanding that they would pay when they were able. I was convinced he would never realize a dollar and would have to mark these in his blue-backed ledger as a gift, along with the cattle. I did not know at the time how dedicated these immigrants were both to hard work and to their own good word.

When the planting was done and the new calves branded and worked, we had a while when the home duties could be allowed to slacken. True, the fields would need to be cultivated to keep the emerging crops free of weeds, but Amadeo Fernandez's widow and two sons still lived on the place. The boys were big enough that together they did a man's work. Thomas said we could leave the cropland to them for a while. It was time to ride west and gather mustangs.

The thought set my heart to pounding. It had seemed adventure-some, far out in the future. But suddenly confronted with the fact of going, I realized with a chill that we would be venturing into Indian country. Kirby assured me with card-player confidence that the chances were two to one we would never see an Indian. I found myself looking with trepidation at the third chance.

Thomas told Kirby he was to stay to look after their mother and su-pervise the place. Kirby's face flushed with a touch of anger, but he said nothing. The Fernandez boys begged to go, but Thomas told them gently that they might do so the next time.

Mrs. Canfield cooked us a good breakfast before daylight of a Sun-day morning, and we set out at daylight, each riding a good horse and leading another. We rode by New Silesia, for Maria would be expect-ing Thomas. She did not expect him so early, however, and he had to wait restlessly for her to come out of mass at the little church. I had not seen her since the day we had delivered the cattle. She had fleshed out a little, with color in her cheeks and a warm smile in her eyes. The smile was not for me, of course.

She had learned some random words of English. Thomas even spoke some words of Polish. At least I assumed that was what they were, because they did not have the sound of Spanish. It occurred to me, though I was inexperienced in that field, that romance can be an educational endeavor.

I tried to find something else to occupy my interest and give the couple privacy, but Thomas called me back before I strayed far. It does not take long to see all one wants of poverty.

In the limited vocabulary they had established between them, Thomas had made Maria understand he was going away for a while. She was tearful, but it was the way of her people that the man made the decisions and the woman quietly agreed; at least that was the way they made it appear. When we left, Thomas kept looking back so long as the village was in sight. The girl stood there by herself, watching as long as there was anything to see.

We rode by a Mexican settlement somewhat farther west and picked up three Mexicans Thomas had known for years. They were good, dependable hands, he said, though given to extortion when it came to wages. They wanted fifty cents a day. He got them to agree to forty, and to furnish two horses apiece for the work.

Only two of them actually rode away with us. The third disappeared into the brush. Thomas seemed to have no concern, so I decided not to worry about it. That night, when we camped, that Mexican came into camp with a fourth man, a tall, bewhiskered countryman with one eye gone and the other fierce as a panther's. He shook hands with Thomas, stared at me with silent suspicion, ate a little supper and disappeared back into the brush.

Thomas let me simmer on my unasked questions awhile before he told me, "That's Bustamante. The law is interested in his whereabouts."

I did not doubt that. "What for?"

"Murder."

"And you'd take him with us?"

"He's one of the best mustang runners you'll ever see. Out yonder, there is no law."

That was a point which worried me.

Whatever preconceived notions I had had about adventure quickly faded in the bright sunlight of reality. Catching mustangs was mostly hard work and very little adventure. Thomas at one point remarked that the Indians did not often bother with the mustangs except to shoot them for meat. It was much easier to take broken horses from the settlements than to catch and break mustangs for themselves. After a few days I could see why.

A set of traps and corrals Thomas had built on previous excursions was still standing but in need of repair to be able to hold wild horses. The task involved more digging, lifting and cutting than riding. An Indian battle would have seemed a welcome relief from all that manual labor. Once we finished repairing and extending the corrals, we started hunting mustangs. My first reaction upon the initial sighting was disappointment. They were small animals, ungainly in appearance, their manes long and shaggy, their tails bristling with burrs and almost dragging the ground. But they were deceptively swift of movement, elusive as jackrabbits. The chase had its moments of thrill and hard spurring as we brought the wily horses down to the wings and traps, but those moments were quickly over and gone. Then the hard work started again.

I did not sleep much the first couple of nights, worrying about Indians murdering us in our blankets. I did not like Bustamante's looks either. I was glad we had no money with us, for I was convinced he would have murdered us all for a dollar and a half. At times, the look in his single eye hinted he might even do it for nothing more than the pleasure. I quit worrying about the Indians before I quit worrying about Bustamante. I became convinced that if any Comanches had come upon us and had seen what we were doing, they would have left us alone. Thomas had said Indians did not bother the insane.

Once we had caught a band of horses, Thomas would pick out those he thought might have market value in the settlements. We let the others go. For seed, he said. We then set in to rough-break the good ones so we could take them home without undue trouble. This involved, more than anything, teaching them respect for rope and halter. It was with the *reata*, a leather rope, that Bustamante showed his greatest skill; I marveled at how he could judge distance so well with one eye. He would catch a horse by its forefeet and trip it, let it up and trip it again until it became educated to the power of the rope. After the horses had been through enough of this bruising exercise, we placed makeshift hackamores on them, tied them firmly to posts or trees, and scared them into running against the end of the tie rope, jerking them back or jerking them down until the hackamores had rubbed their heads raw. It seemed brutal, but it was a traditional Mexican system for teaching them that the rope was master, always to be obeyed.

We even rode some of them, or attempted to. The Mexicans were good at this, especially the fearless Bustamante, but I invariably hit the ground faster than I had left it. Thomas commented that I could ride little better than I could shoot and suggested that I quit trying. He did not want to take me home with a broken leg and lose my services altogether. I conceded the wisdom of his advice.

Exhaustion made me sleep well at night, but I remained watchful during the day. An Indian could not have gotten closer than a quarter mile without my seeing him. I gradually put aside most of my dread of the dark Bustamante, too, though I contrived whenever possible to keep Thomas between him and me. When we finally haltered our catch and tied each animal to a long lead rope for the trip home, I felt an odd mixture of both relief and regret that we had not seen a single Comanche. I thought how disappointing it would someday be to my grandchildren—if I ever had any. I decided I would do like most other garrulous old liars and make up a story to please them.

The Mexicans left us for their own homes. Bustamante disappeared into the brush as quietly as he had first come.

I expected Thomas to go first by New Silesia to see Maria, but he fooled me. He rode by the fields to see if they had been properly cultivated during our lengthy absence. He expressed pleasure in the hoe work done by the Fernandez boys, Juan and Marco. That pleasure faded when he found out Kirby was in Stonehill and had been for three days.

The little Mrs. Canfield rocked restlessly and knitted on some kind of black shawl on the breezy dog run of the double cabin. She said, "I tried to tell him he'd better stay away from town. Been a right smart of trouble."

Thomas stiffened. "What kind of trouble?"

"Fights between the wagon people and the cart people. Been some men killed on the trail and one or two in town. Government's got soldiers patrolling the trails now, guarding carts and wagons. A patrol was by here just yesterday, trailing some raiders who got away. They had burned up a good part of a cart train headed for San Antonio."

Thomas said, "That doesn't concern us."

"Might concern *you*," the old woman said, laying the knitting in her lap. "Didn't you send orders to Indianola for implements to be sent to Stonehill on Francisco Arroyo's carts?"

Thomas blinked in sudden concern. "I did."

"We heard Francisco got hit two days short of Stonehill. Lost three men and four carts. That's how come Kirby went to town, to find out how much of a loss you taken."

Thomas Canfield seldom wasted anything, including profanity. He employed a few choice words suited to the occasion and started toward town. He shouted back at me to take care of our mustangs.

Next morning I was in a corral with the horses we had captured when I saw two men coming in something of a hurry. I thought at first they were Thomas and Kirby, but they were strangers, or almost so. I had seen both in the Isom dramshop when I had been there with Kirby. They were rough fellows, the kind you do not normally associate with hard labor and honest endeavor. They stopped to water their horses, and they eyed our mustangs as if contemplating a trade. It occurred to me that they could make any trade they might decide upon, for my rifle was at the house. But they seemed to agree after some consultation that the horses they rode were more dependable than the wild ones in our corral. They proceeded in a northeasterly direction at a strong trot that could carry a man many a league between sunup and sundown.

Perhaps an hour later a number of horsemen approached from the same direction where I had first espied the two. This time, for precaution, I hurried down to the cabin and fetched my rifle.

They were blue-uniformed government troops, with Thomas and Kirby riding at the lead. They came directly to the place where I stood, halfway between the log house and the pens. Thomas did the talking, what little was done.

"We are following two men."

I pointed out where they had gone.

An officer said, "We can take the trail from here, Mister Canfield. You have been of more than enough service to us."

"I'll stay with you until the job is done," Thomas said sternly. His sharp eyes were on Kirby. "You'll stay here."

Kirby did not argue. His beard was four or five days long, and his eyes showed he had traveled in considerable discomfort. Kirby was ordinarily a jovial sort, but he watched darkly as Thomas led the soldiers northeastward.

He complained, "Thomas doesn't give me credit for anything."

I had no inclination to insert myself into an argument between the brothers, so I did not ask him what his trouble was. He told me anyway. "Thomas lost a good part of his shipment. I hung around town, drinking a lot less than I made out. I figured sooner or later I would hear something, and I did. If it hadn't been for me they wouldn't have known who to go after."

"Then those two raided the cart train?"

"They were in the bunch. A couple more put up a fight in town. The troopers blew their lights out for good."

Long shadows fell behind the soldiers and their mounts as they returned shortly before sundown. They led two very tired horses. Across the saddles, two men were tied belly down on the last horseback trip they would ever make.

Thomas watched somberly as the soldiers watered their weary animals. He said to the officer, "You and your men are more than welcome to camp anywhere that suits you. We'll slaughter a fresh beef for you. You've done a hard day's work."

The lieutenant's shoulders were sagging. "I'd appreciate it, Mister Canfield. There will be bad feelings in town. I had rather we face it in the daylight, when we can see everybody."

The two bodies were laid out in a shed. Thomas looked at them with no more compassion than if they had been wolves caught chasing calves. A fierceness was in his eyes.

In the morning he lent the soldiers a wagon, for the bodies had stiffened. The officer suggested that it might be just as well to bury them then and there. Thomas said coldly, "Let Stonehill bury its own. This place is for ours."

He had lost about half of his shipment. Losing those implements meant losing land he might have bought with the profits. By the time he forgave these men, if he ever did, the headboards on their graves would probably have rotted away.

Kirby suggested, "I'll follow the soldiers into Stonehill and see what happens."

Thomas' eyes were grim. "No. We'll all stay out of Stonehill. A town which caters to people like that can do without our patronage."

Kirby argued, "We have to have supplies of one kind and another. Stonehill's the only place to buy them."

Thomas nodded. "It doesn't have to be that way. New Silesia is no farther than Stonehill."

"It doesn't even have a store."

"It can have one. There are enough farmers and cattle people in the vicinity to make a store work if someone will finance it. I can get credit in San Antonio. I'll finance it."

That took me by surprise. I remembered his many lectures about the permanence of the land, about the vagaries of towns and retail business. But I realized the store in New Silesia would not be undertaken as a business venture; it was an instrument of revenge.

He rode to New Silesia that afternoon, telling me he might not be back for a few days; he was going from there to San Antonio. He left orders for Kirby and me to keep working with the mustangs, gentling them for sale. It was a week before we saw him again.

The old storekeeper, Linden Hines, was there before Thomas returned. His daughter Laura was driving. I helped her down from the carriage, warming to the quick smile she gave me and the momentary chance to hold her hand. Her father said nothing beyond the fact that he wanted to talk to Thomas, but we could see in his pale eyes that he was troubled. He sat on the dog run, gossiping idly with Thomas' mother, who seemed joyed by the company. They talked of the hardships and the spiritual rewards of earlier times, but his gaze was always to the north, watching for Thomas. I tried to engage Laura in conversation, but her mind was not on me. She was helping her father watch.

When Thomas finally appeared, it was hard to tell whether the old man was cheered or depressed. In an odd way, he seemed both. There was no question, however, about Laura's reaction.

Thomas howdied and shook with Laura and her father. They talked in general circles before the gray-haired storekeeper came down to cases. "I heard you're going to open a store in New Silesia."

Thomas blinked in surprise. "News travels fast."

"I have friends in San Antonio." Hines frowned, looking off across the prairie. "It will hurt my store, of course. I had always regarded us as friends, Thomas."

Thomas studied him in regret. "This is not done with any malice

toward you, Mister Hines. We are friends. But we Canfields have no
other friends in Stonehill. I would not grieve if I knew I would never
have to set foot in that town again."

The old man nodded. "Then this is done against Stonehill, and not
against me?"

"I have never had any wish to hurt you. Or Laura." He glanced at
the girl. There was nothing in his eyes to match what I saw in hers.

The old man asked, "What do you know of the store business, beyond selling farm implements?"

"Nothing." An idea seemed to strike Thomas, and he appeared in
some danger of smiling. "I could use a partner who *does* know the business."

"Me?" The old man seemed intrigued by the notion for a moment.
But he shook his head. "It would be disloyal to Stonehill. That town is
like my own child."

"My parents had two children," Thomas pointed out.

"I could not divide my loyalties. I gave the first breath of life to that
town. It has grown away from me, like an unruly son sowing wild
oats, but it will outlast that. The wildness will pass."

"I doubt that, sir. There is a malady in it that has rooted too deep. It
will never be yours again."

The storekeeper mused, looking at Thomas' mother. "Do you believe you or Kirby could ever do anything so bad that your mother
could never forgive you, could never take you back and love you?" He
shook his head. "Stonehill is my town."

"It will break your heart, Mister Hines. Or kill you."

"Not Stonehill. It is my child." He dismissed further argument with
a small wave of his hand. "You'll not want to spend your own time
running your store, Thomas. I have a young man named Smithers;
you've surely met him. There is not always enough for him to do in my
place, and I have dreaded having to let him go."

"I would be pleased to have him."

So it was that Thomas Canfield branched out into yet another enterprise. For the next few weeks he spent the larger part of his time in
New Silesia, supervising carpenters who put up a frame store building

for him. Not all of his time was spent on business, evidently, for when the carpenters had finished the job in town he brought them to the ranch. He set them to building a new house. Thomas was not in the habit of volunteering much information, but in this case it was not necessary. We all knew who the house was for.

Kirby and I kept busy cultivating the crops or peddling mustangs to prospective buyers sent or brought by Thomas. When we had sold what he wanted to sell, Thomas surprised Kirby and me by giving us a bonus. I was not sure what to do with mine.

"Land, Mister Sawyer," Thomas advised. "Whatever you save, put it into land."

I did. I bought a small piece of unimproved rangeland to the west of New Silesia, paying part in cash—all the cash I had—and signing a note for the rest. Because I had no cattle to turn loose on it, Thomas leased it from me and paid me enough that I was able to make payments to the San Antonio bank which carried the paper.

The night after becoming a landowner, I sewed a new patch atop an old patch on my britches and pondered the glories of wealth in land.

Mrs. Canfield had never met Maria. One Sunday morning Thomas took a wagon to New Silesia and brought Maria back to show her how well the carpenters were doing. He made official what we had known for a long time, that he and Maria would marry when the house was finished. I had worried over what Mrs. Canfield would think of Maria in view of the fact that they could not talk much to each other. The two women fell into each other's arms, and my worry evaporated like spilled water in the summer sun. I was amazed by how much English Maria had learned since the last time I had seen her.

Though we had much work to do, Kirby became restless. We played cards some nights, for matches rather than for money, and he usually won though his heart was not in the game. In his hands a card seemed to turn magically into whatever he wanted it to be. I was little challenge. He tried to teach the Fernandez boys, but they were too young and no challenge at all. He would even have played against Mrs. Canfield, if she would have stood for it, but like my own parents she remained convinced that playing cards were the antithesis of holy

Scripture. Whenever she found a deck of cards they went into the blazing cookstove. Fire, she declared, was the proper element for Satan and
his instruments.

The wedding was performed in the little church in New Silesia.
Most of the Polander people were there. Not all of them could get into
the church, but those who couldn't stood outside and listened through
the open windows. I was inside but had just as well have been outside
for all I understood of the service. The only part I was sure of was
when the priest said Thomas and Maria were man and wife.

The only people who came over from Stonehill were Linden Hines
and his daughter Laura. She tried hard to keep smiling, but this was
more like a funeral to her than an occasion of joy. Kirby stood beside
her and held her arm, which I wanted to do but lacked the nerve. That
didn't help her.

A broad grin was spread across Thomas' face as he walked out of
the church with his new bride on his arm. I had never seen that look
on him before, and I never saw it again.

Times had improved some for the Polanders. A wedding was a fes-
tive occasion, celebrated by everybody in town, with more food than
an army could eat, and more than a little of spirituous liquors, these
mostly furnished by Thomas, who ordinarily would not have approved
much more than his mother would. A big dance was set for the wedding night. I looked forward to it because I thought finally I would
have a suitable opportunity to put my arms around Laura Hines. But
when the music started and I looked around for her, she was gone.

Thomas never did anything haphazardly. He even timed the wedding so he would not miss anything important at home while he took
Maria for her first trip to San Antonio. The crops were fairly well laid
by, and it was too early to brand the new calves; screwworms would
have eaten them alive. It should have been the best possible time to
have taken a long trip. It would have been, except for Kirby.

I figured out very soon that he had been waiting for Thomas to get
so far out of reach that Kirby could do whatever he wanted. He stayed
just long enough to wave the newlywed couple on their way, then saddled his horse.

"You take Mother home, Reed," he told me. "I'm going to go find some card players who can keep me from going to sleep in the middle of a game."

I tried to argue him out of it. I told him Thomas wouldn't like it, a point I probably should have kept to myself. It seemed only to urge him on. He didn't say he was going to Stonehill, but that was obvious. He rode off in Stonehill's direction, new suit and fresh shave and all, while I walked along after him, futilely throwing out every argument I could think of. He spurred into an easy lope and left me talking to myself.

His mother wanted to know where he was going. I evaded any direct answer, but she knew anyway; I could tell by the set of her jaw. As we rode along in the wagon together I saw tears come into her eyes. She said, "I used to look forward to the day when my sons were grown, so I would never have to worry about them anymore."

That night I sat down by lamplight and wrote a letter to my own mother in Louisiana, the first one in many months.

I thought Kirby might come back that night, but he was not there for breakfast. Mrs. Canfield said nothing, not about Kirby or anything else. She was normally a fair to middling talker, and I expected her to relive the whole wedding over the breakfast table, but the only time she spoke was to ask me if I wanted more coffee. I didn't; I wanted to get out of that cabin as quickly as I could.

I rode among the cattle all day, looking for screwworm cases. Marco, the older of the Fernandez boys, was with me so we could rope and throw cattle as a team and doctor them where we found them. Juan, the younger, remained in the fields, hoeing out the careless weeds. When I rode up to the shed late in the afternoon, I saw that Kirby's saddle was still not on its rack.

Mrs. Canfield met me at the door, her face uneasy. "Reed, I hate to ask you to ride into Stonehill alone, but I wish you'd go see if you can fetch Kirby home. The devil has many allies in that place."

I ate a hurried supper, then saddled a fresh horse, a young bay named Stepper that Thomas had kept out of that set of mustangs. Almost as an afterthought I shoved a big pistol into my boottop. It was a useless gesture; I probably would never have pulled it. But it gave me a feeling of some security, rubbing a blister on my leg.

Just before dark I began to make out a movement on the town road ahead of me. It was a carriage of some kind, flanked by a couple of riders. For no good reason I could think of, my uneasiness increased. I put the bay mustang into a long trot, which it resisted, almost pitching me.

Linden Hines and his daughter Laura were in the carriage, a couple of Mexicans riding horseback beside them. A wagon followed fifty yards or so behind.

One look at the Hineses' solemn faces told me my uneasiness had been fully justified. Laura began to weep. Her father said evenly, "We are bringing Kirby Canfield home."

I looked back at the wagon, the heart dropping out of me.

The old man's voice went lower. "He was shot down in a gaming place in Stonehill."

I took a grip on the big horn of the Mexican saddle I rode. When the shock had passed a little I asked him who did it.

"A tough named Johnroe. I am told there was some disagreement over cards."

I knew before I asked him. "The gaming place . . . was it Branch Isom's?"

He nodded, seeming a little surprised at my guess. "But Isom had nothing to do with it," he said. "In fact, he was in my store when we heard the shots. Laura can tell you. She was there."

The girl nodded, but she did not look at me.

Convenient, I thought. How could Isom better take out his revenge on Thomas Canfield—a man he was afraid of—than to have someone kill his brother, with Branch Isom himself in the clear?

I had gone out into Indian country and helped hunt mustangs, but I knew this thing was beyond my courage. "You-all going to tell Kirby's mother?"

Hines nodded sorrowfully. "All the way from town I have been trying to decide what to say. The Canfields have been among the best friends I ever had. But my town has cost them dearly."

Laura Hines looked up. "I'll tell her."

I think Mrs. Canfield sensed it before we quite got there. She stood in the dog run, watching the carriage and the wagon. The fact that I was with them told her Kirby was too. Without a word, she just looked at us, and died a little. She never shed a tear, at least where I could see it. Whatever crying she did, she held until Laura had gone into the cabin with her.

Laura came back outside, looking for me. She had been crying, whether Mrs. Canfield had nor not. "Reed, you'll have to go to San Antonio. Thomas has to know."

The trail to San Antonio was an old one, cut by wagons and carts past any counting. I had no trouble staying with it through the long, dark night. My horse gave out toward daylight. I stopped at a stagecoach stand and talked the people into lending me a fresh one. They weren't going to do it until I mentioned Thomas Canfield. They seemed more than willing then, and genuinely distressed when I explained my mission.

Thomas and Maria had a room in the Menger Hotel, Mrs. Canfield had told Laura. Though I had never been in San Antonio, it was no trouble to find the place. As was the custom in old Mexican towns, all roads led to the center like a wagon spoke leads to the hub. The Menger stood with a squared-off German elegance next to the ruins of the Alamo. Commerce moved up and down that street as if nothing had ever happened there. Hardly anybody seemed to look at that shell-marked old mission except me, and for a minute or two I could look at nothing else, remembering the stories I had heard of the good men who had died fighting there. It seemed somehow sacrilegious that the U.S. Army was using the blood-bought building for a quartermaster depot. But I turned away from the Alamo, for that trouble had been more than twenty years in the past, and my problem was *now*. I made my way around several spans of Mexican burros that struggled to pull a wagonload of heavy freight, and I tied the borrowed horse at the rail in front of the hotel. I dusted myself the best I could with my hat, for the Menger was a place that bespoke gentility. I entered the little lobby, pausing to look up in awe at the balconies that towered high above the ground floor. Even New Orleans could have nothing better or taller than this.

The man at the desk betrayed a touch of German accent when he asked what service he could render me. I told him I had to see Thomas Canfield.

"Mister Canfield and his lady, they went upon the city out."

"I have to see him," I said. "I have a death message for him."

That got the clerk's full attention, but it did not help me find Thomas. "I wish to help, sir," he apologized, "but I know not where to tell you to seek. Best perhaps you sit here and wait."

The smell of food from the kitchen reminded me I had not eaten. It was coming on noon, but I went into the dining room and asked for breakfast. I sat so I could watch the front door. I put away some ham and three or four eggs, then went back into the lobby and took a soft chair where I could see who came and went. My intentions were good, but the flesh was weak after a night's ride. I drifted off to sleep within minutes after I sat down.

A strong hand shook my shoulder and startled me awake. "Reed Sawyer! What is wrong at home?"

It took me a moment to realize where I was. I stared up into the worried eyes of Thomas Canfield, and beyond him, Maria. There was no easy way to tell him. "Kirby was shot in Stonehill. He's dead."

Maria choked off a cry. Thomas made no sound. I don't think he even blinked. His eyes went fierce, like the night he watched the raider die. "Was it Branch Isom?" he demanded.

"No," I told him quickly, trying to head off that line of thought because I feared he would ride straight to Stonehill and kill Isom, or try. "Mister Hines said Isom wasn't there. It was somebody named Johnroe."

Thomas seemed to stare right through me. "I know Johnroe. His hand moves as Isom directs it. I suppose the law has done nothing."

"I don't know. I came straight to you." But I knew within reason, just as Thomas did. The law had done nothing and would not.

Thomas gritted, "Something *will* be done." He turned to Maria, softening a little. He gently rubbed away a tear that ran down her cheek. "I am sorry, little girl. We have to go."

She put her head against his chest. "I am sorry also."

Thomas looked back at me. "Is anyone with my mother?"

"Laura Hines. She and her father brought Kirby home."

He nodded. "Laura. Whenever help is needed, she's always there."

It was almost on my tongue to ask him if he did not know why. I caught myself.

It was a fast but silent trip, and I slept a good part of it. Thomas wore out several teams, changing them along the way with people he knew, like those at the stage stop. I don't believe he spoke twenty words beyond what was necessary. Maria sat beside him, but as he had always been and always would be in times of stress, Thomas seemed somehow completely alone, drawn up within himself like some brooding, secret spirit out of another time and another life. That Maria accepted this without protest was a source of wonder to me, but I supposed all things here seemed mysterious to her compared to that far-off country she had come from.

Thomas' determined pace brought us to the Canfield place in the early hours of the night, the last set of horses dripping sweat. He pulled up in front of the double cabin. Linden Hines arose from a rocking chair on the dog run and walked out to meet us. He gave Maria a hand down from the carriage.

Thomas demanded, "How is my mother?"

"Laura finally got her to bed. It has been a long day."

Thomas put a hand on the old storekeeper's shoulder. "For all of us." We quietly went inside, where Laura arose from her chair beside Mrs. Canfield's bed. She tiptoed to us, putting a finger on her lips, but it did no good. Mrs. Canfield called, "Is that you, Thomas?"

"I'm here," he told her.

The rest of us went back outside, leaving them alone. Maria stood uncertainly in the doorway, trying to decide if she belonged in there with her husband, finally coming out with us. She and Laura stood on the dog run, looking at one another. It was an awkward moment for me, knowing how both women felt about that man beyond the door, knowing both had cause to hate each other. But Maria reached out and touched Laura's hand.

"You do good thing, Laura. You are good friend."

Laura's voice broke. "I have always been a friend to the Canfields, all the Canfields. You're a Canfield now."

"Always, you be *my* friend."

If I had any doubts, the funeral at the ranch showed me how many friends the Canfields really had. Ranchers and farmers from a wide area came out, along with a goodly part of the Polander community, many of them afoot. I saw few people from Stonehill, other than Linden and Laura Hines, and quite a few of the Mexican oxcart freighters the Canfields had done business with. It struck me as never before how many of the Mexican people were friends of Thomas Canfield. The mustang hunters were there, except Bustamante, and many others I could not remember seeing before. It came to me that the Canfield family had settled here when most of the other people *were* Mexicans. Somehow they had avoided the enmity that beset so many later settlers.

One official representative of Stonehill *was* on hand. The county sheriff and one of his deputies stood at the edge of the crowd, saying nothing but watching everybody, most of all watching Thomas. Thomas was aware of them, but he made no move in their direction or they in his until the services were over, the coffin had been lowered and earth was being shoveled into the grave. Maria was saying something about it was wrong to bury people here; this was not consecrated ground. But Thomas seemed not to hear her. He stood with his mother and Maria, solemnly accepting the condolences of the visitors as they filed by. When all were finished and most had started home, I noticed that many of the Mexicans were staying, huddling to one side. It came to me that every one of them was armed.

Instinctively I knew they were waiting for a signal from Thomas. To them this was another incident in the cart war. True, it had happened to a *gringo*, but the *gringo* had been their friend. Indirectly, in their view, he had died for them.

The sheriff sensed it too. His face was taut; he dreaded having to talk with Thomas. But he could delay it no longer. With hat in hand he spoke his condolences to Mrs. Canfield, then to Thomas. He jerked his head sideways. "Thomas, I wish you'd step out here a ways. We got some talking to do."

Thomas looked at his wife. "Maria, would you please take Mother back to the house?"

Both women looked apprehensively at Thomas, but he assured them there was no trouble. They started reluctantly, Laura Hines moving in supportively to take Mrs. Canfield's right arm. Thomas watched them go, then turned to the sheriff and the deputy.

"My brother was killed the day before yesterday, Sheriff. What has been done?"

"I've investigated the incident thoroughly. I've talked to all the witnesses."

"Do you have Johnroe in jail?"

"No, the gentleman left the county immediately after the shooting."

"Then you should be after him."

"There is no case against him. All the witnesses told me your brother accused him of cheating at cards, then drew a pistol. They told me Johnroe fired in self-defense."

"Did my brother fire at him?"

The sheriff hesitated. "There was only one shot. Your brother had been drinking. He was slow."

"Not that slow. Your witnesses lie, Sheriff. You know that."

"I do *not* know that."

"You know the whole thing was deliberately planned. You know Branch Isom was behind it."

"Mister Isom was not even present. Your friend Linden Hines will tell you that, if he hasn't already."

"He told me. Isom used him. He knows it, and I know it, and you know it."

"Mister Isom is as upset over this as any of us. He wants no trouble, and I want no trouble."

"If you don't do something about Johnroe, I will."

"You'll not find him in Stonehill. I don't want you coming there looking for him, and perhaps getting someone else killed in the process.

I don't want trouble with you"—he looked past Thomas at the cluster of waiting Mexicans—"and I don't want trouble with your friends."

"Do I have your word that Johnroe is not in Stonehill?"

"You have. And if he ever shows up there again I'll arrest him. For his own safekeeping."

Thomas had that look in his eyes. "Then you had better find him before I do."

The sheriff blustered, but he could not hold his ground against that hard stare. When he looked down, Thomas turned his back on him. The sheriff appeared to have something more to say but saw the futility of it. He nodded at his deputy, and they mounted their horses. Thomas did not look in the men's direction, but he was listening to the fading sound of the hoofs. After a bit he walked slowly toward the Mexicans. He addressed them in Spanish. I had learned enough to follow a little of it. He thanked them for their sympathy. Past that, the conversation turned from difficult to impossible for me. I heard the name "Johnroe" two or three times, and "Bustamante" once. At first I thought Thomas might be planning to lead them into Stonehill and take the town apart; he was capable of it. But presently the Mexicans dispersed, riding off in the several directions from which they had come.

Life on the ranch settled down to something of routine again, somewhat quieter and grimmer. Thomas was living in his new house with Maria, so I saw less of him than before. When I did see him, he had little to say beyond whatever was necessary to the work at hand. His face had seldom been host to a smile even before Kirby's death. He probably smiled when he and Maria were alone in that house, but I never saw it. His eyes had a steely look that indicated his mind was elsewhere. We took care of the fields and worked the cattle and did what we could to doctor the screwworm cases, but all the time in his mind he was killing Johnroe.

As winter came on, Maria showed signs of gaining weight. She had been so thin that I thought the weight became her. It took a while for me to realize there was more to it than just having food enough. Thomas was busier than ever, partly because of the store in New Silesia. At first he took Maria with him when he had to make a trip to San

Antonio, but as she became heavier and nearer to her term, she stayed at home. After supper, when he was away, she would come down to the old cabin and sit in a rocking chair beside Mrs. Canfield on the dog run, the two women waiting together for Thomas to come home. Nights when he didn't, Mrs. Canfield would go up to the new house and sleep where she could be near Maria. A couple of times she sent for Mrs. Fernandez with considerable agitation, but nothing happened.

After the second time, Thomas decided to defer all other business trips until the baby was safely "on the ground." He would ride out during the day, but always he was home before dark. Nobody told me anything, but I sensed that the time of delivery was at hand.

The mesquites were putting on their first new leaves, pale green and so thin they seemed transparent. The nights were still cool, but the days were warming enough that it would not be long until time to put corn and cotton into the ground. Maria was so heavy I wondered if she might not be going beyond her normal term.

One morning before daylight I went out to rustle horses and saw a blanket-wrapped form on the ground, near a mesquite-pole corral. As I approached the blanket was suddenly flung aside, and I was looking into the muzzle of a huge pistol. My heart leaped as I recognized the evil eye staring at me over the barrel.

Bustamante.

He recognized me and lowered the pistol. *"El patrón,"* he said. He had come to see Thomas.

I indicated that Thomas was up at the new house, but Bustamante insisted that I bring him down to the corrals.

Thomas came irritably to the door when I knocked, asking me if I didn't know Maria needed her sleep. But his attitude changed to excitement when I told him Bustamante was waiting. He disappeared for only a moment, coming back fully dressed, pulling the long ears of his left boot. He strode briskly ahead of me. I did not see Bustamante until the tall Mexican stepped out from the shadow of a fence. The sight of him was like ice pressed against my chest.

Thomas motioned for me to stop, not to come any closer. I watched them from twenty or thirty paces, catching the tone of an intense conversation but none of the words. At last Bustamante reached inside his shirt and brought forth a leather pouch, hanging around his neck on a string. Thomas loosened the puckerstring and looked into the pouch. He nodded in satisfaction and dropped the pouch on the ground. He brought a handful of coins from his pocket and placed them in Bustamante's outstretched hand.

The men silently shook. Bustamante mounted a long-legged black horse that bore Thomas' brand and loped away, disappearing quickly into the brush.

Thomas leaned down and recovered the pouch from the ground. When he turned I saw a smile, a cold one and mean. He seemed to have forgotten about me, for he was startled to see me standing there.

"Go on about your business, Reed," he said.

I caught up my horse and set out to bring in the mounts for the day's work. As I rode away I saw Thomas at some distance beyond the barn, a shovel in his hand. While I watched, he dug a hole and dropped the pouch into it.

A week later, word drifted down to us from San Antonio that the gambler Johnroe had been killed there. Four days after his arrival, a tall, ugly, one-eyed Mexican had suddenly confronted him on a sidewalk and plunged a knife into him to the hilt. While the man lay dying, the Mexican coldly cut off both of his ears, mounted a black horse and rode away.

Very mysterious, people said. It was probably over a gambling loss.

The news seemed to affect Thomas not at all. Maria had just presented him a son.

He named the boy Kirby.

CHAPTER 4

Because we lived and worked a long way from the largest towns, we let the war slip up on us. We knew, of course, that sectional bitterness had built for years, but mostly we looked on it as a quarrel between the Southern people who owned slaves and the Northern people who wished they did but couldn't. Not many folks down in our part of South Texas had slaves, either; they were too poor for that kind of luxury. So long as the Yankees stayed out of our country and left us alone, we didn't do much except clench our fists a little when we read an occasional angry newspaper editorial. We went right back to our own personal concerns as to whether it would rain, and whether the corn was going to make, and what kind of calf crop would hit the ground. All else was talk, and talk was a surplus commodity without a market.

But war did come, and a lot of us let ourselves get swept up in the emotion of it. We did foolish things, like volunteer for the Texas companies that were joining the Confederate Army.

Thomas seemed immune to that kind of emotion. His was reserved for whoever and whatever belonged to him. A war way off in Virginia was too far from his land to be of deep concern to him. He grieved over the thought of all the suffering, all the wreckage that came out of the first fighting, but he did not anger. He told me it was a long way from Texas, and he saw no reason it should ever affect us.

Even Thomas Canfield could be wrong.

Peace, of a sort, had settled over us. The cart war had ground itself to a standstill. The Texas Rangers and the federal troops—before the bigger war pulled them away—stomped hard on some participants. A few of the worst men on both sides found themselves invited to a quick, quiet hanging, which got everybody else's attention. Most people involved in the feud decided they did not hate each other enough to risk that kind of rough justice.

I half expected the Rangers to fall on Thomas for what had happened to Johnroe. Talk spread around Stonehill that he was somehow responsible. But the lawmen seemed to figure that the killing of Johnroe by some unknown Mexican probably saved them the trouble of a hanging, sooner or later. Or, perhaps they were simply afraid of Thomas. A lot of people were, by then.

I thought Branch Isom might find some way to continue the trouble at no danger to himself, but he did not. Though I took pains to stay out of Stonehill, I heard enough talk to keep up with what went on there. Some of the Mexicans said Isom had fetched himself a bride from San Antonio. He was building a house in Stonehill larger than the one Thomas had built on the ranch for Maria. I figured this was a show of rivalry, but I never mentioned it to Thomas. Nothing brought anger to his eyes like hearing the name of Branch Isom.

The anger came often enough to its own bidding; I did not like to be the one who drew it forth. I much preferred Thomas' company when he sat on the edge of his porch, watching his son take his first faltering steps in the yard, falling over an affectionate pup one of the Fernandez boys had brought to him. Thomas rarely laughed, even with the baby, but the deepening lines in his face would seem to ease, and he would look—for a little while—as young as he really was. He would sit in silence with Maria's loving arm around him and watch that little boy with a feeling akin to worship.

Thomas had stayed out of the cart war except when his own property was involved, and he was determined to remain out of the Confederacy's war too. He said little about it, but he leaned toward the views of old Sam Houston, who tried desperately to keep Texas from seceding and, when it did anyway, retired to his home down in Huntsville to live out his days without ever endorsing the Confederacy.

I tried to see it Thomas' way, but too many things kept pulling at

me. I received a letter from home telling me a couple of my brothers
had marched out to fight for Jeff Davis. I saw quite a few younger men
from around Stonehill and New Silesia do the same thing, laughing
and hollering and promising to be home in six months. They could
not all be wrong, no matter what Thomas said.

The Polanders avoided being caught up in the war much. They had
been in the country too short a time to understand what the fighting
was about—if any of us did—and most of them did not know much
English. The army recruiters quickly decided they were too dumb to be
of much use. The Confederates were so confident about whipping the
Yankees in a hurry that they did not want to share the glory with a
bunch of foreigners anyway. They saved that honor for the true Southern boys.

My conscience nagged me as more and more men went to war while
I stayed home on the ranch. Finally I received a letter telling me one of
my brothers had taken down with the fever and died on the way to the
fighting. Though he had not reached the battle, my mother considered
him a patriot, a martyr to his country. She said nothing about me picking up my brother's sword. I got that idea all by myself. When a cowboy named Bill Eskew announced that he was going to San Antonio to
join the war, I decided to go with him.

Thomas took the news with a deep frown. "It's not our fight."

"It's mine," I told him. "I've lost a brother."

"You never could shoot straight. What use will you be?"

But he dropped the argument when he saw I had made up my mind.
He shook my hand and told me I would always have a place with him
when I came back. Maria—by now beginning to push out in front
again—kissed me on the cheek. The old lady Canfield hugged my neck
and wet the side of my face with her tears. I tried not to look back as I
rode away, but I couldn't help it. Until we passed over the hill, Bill and
me, I spent most of my time twisted around in the saddle, trying to fix
it all in my mind as if I might not ever see it again.

I almost didn't.

We halfway expected to be wined and dined and have a lot of fuss
made over us in San Antonio, but the "new" had worn off by that

time. They had already seen a lot of men march away, some west to invade New Mexico and Arizona, the rest east to join up with the main Confederate forces off in Virginia and such. Nobody paid much attention to us or bought us any drinks, and the officers didn't treat us as respectfully as the recruiters had led us to believe. They handled us a lot like we used to treat fresh-caught broncs in teaching them to respect the rope and follow directions. I was considerably disappointed with the war before I ever saw any of it.

I was even more disappointed when I *did* see it. I had seen blood spilled in Texas, but this was not the same. We didn't hear the bands play much. Bill Eskew got shot in the stomach the second battle we got into, and I had to watch him take two days in dying.

There is no point in going on with a lot of detail about my years in the army. Like Thomas had kept saying, it was a long way from Texas and had nothing to do with the Canfields. I got nicked a couple of times, but never anything serious until the last year of the war. A rifle ball struck me in the hip and knocked me off of my horse. When I came back to consciousness I found Yankee soldiers running around me afoot, going the way I had come from. They were too busy to stop either to finish me off or to patch my wound. First time I got the chance I dragged myself into some bushes on my belly and hid. I soaked up most of my coat trying to get the blood stopped. I lay there until almost dark before the Yankees passed me again going the other way, and some good Reb boys came along in pursuit.

My hip was a long time healing. They furloughed me home to Louisiana. That way I was a burden to my family instead of to the Confederacy, which already had more burden than it could carry. The war was over before the healing was. Hobbling around on crutches, not able to do any respectable work except patch harness and such, I watched the straggling remnants of a beaten army come limping home a few men at a time. I watched the grief of families who finally had to admit that some of their own had simply disappeared and would never come home. Another of my brothers was one of these. My mother went to her grave wondering what had become of him. None of us ever knew.

There came a time when I could ride a horse. It wasn't easy, not like before, and it never would be quite the same again, but I knew I could at least take care of myself and put up a showing of respectable work. I had been thinking of Texas for a long time. After the many years away, the delta was no longer my home. When my grieving old mother breathed her last and we put her under the deep black soil, nothing was left to hold me. I made my way downriver to New Orleans like before and found a freighter about to set sail for the Texas coast. The captain had seen more than enough of crippled, hungry ex-soldiers, but he decided I could earn a bunk helping the cook. I spent most of that voyage in a hot, steaming galley. But it was worth it all to see old Indianola materialize through the early-morning fog. The town had grown since I had seen it that other time, but I had no difficulty finding the place where I had slept beneath the wharf while awaiting passage inland.

The wharves were sagging beneath the weight of cotton bales consigned to hungry mills back East, and the ships were unloading machinery and other goods for which Texas had starved during the long war and the blockade that had strangled its ports. Nobody in Texas had much solid Union coin, but they bartered cotton and tobacco and corn.

As before, I was dependent upon the generosity of people I had never seen before. Like most Confederate soldiers I had been paid little, and that in a currency no longer worth the paper it was printed on. The ship's captain gave me a few dollars for my labor, barely enough to buy a few days' meals and lodging ashore. My heavy limp and the cane I leaned upon made me a poor candidate for employment in a place where many able-bodied men hunted desperately for work. But I owned a little land near New Silesia, and I had Thomas Canfield's old promise of a job.

As before, I began looking for a freight outfit that might take me inland. I saw a line of big, heavy freight wagons near a wharf and made my way hopefully in their direction. I walked up to a man who appeared to be in charge of loading and asked where his wagons were bound. He looked me over carefully before answering. He probably guessed my situation without being told; a lot of others like me were making their way to an old home or looking for a new one.

"San Antonio," he said.

"By way of Stonehill or New Silesia?" I asked hopefully.

He frowned. "I don't remember you from Stonehill, and you don't talk none like them damned Polanders."

"I've been gone a long time," I told him.

A heavy voice spoke behind me. "I heard you mention Stonehill."

I turned and almost fell. There, staring me in the face, was Branch Isom. He carried more weight than when I had last seen him, the red beard was gone, and the lines were cut deeper into that ruddy face. But there was no mistaking the man. My hand tightened instinctively on the cane, and my first thought was that I would have to fight in another minute.

Recognition came much slower to him. I had aged a lot, thinned a lot. But after a long moment he said, "You're Reed Sawyer."

I could only nod, waiting for the trouble to come. An angry thought flashed through my mind, that I had outlived the war only to come back here and, more than likely, end my days on the wharf at Indianola.

To my surprise he showed no enmity, no grudge over old battles. If anything, he betrayed a touch of regret. He said, "The war was not kind to you."

"Kinder than to some," I told him. "At least I'm here."

"And looking for a ride home?"

If he had forgotten our first meeting, I had not. My first treatment at his hands was something I would remember to my last day. I said, "You needn't bother about me. I'll find one." I started to turn away.

He touched my shoulder and stopped me. "We'll be rolling in a couple of hours. I'll be glad to have the company of an old friend."

"We never were friends, Branch Isom," I said.

"That was a long time ago. Things have changed. You're a soldier home from the war. I've tried to bury old enmities."

You've buried a lot of old enemies, too, I thought, but I had the judgment not to say it.

I had no wish to travel with Branch Isom, so I made a couple of excuses and worked my way down into the town, hoping I might find someone else going my way. Luck was not with me. In a couple of hours I saw the wagons moving out in a line and resigned myself to a long stay in the coast town. But a light carriage drawn by a couple of nicely matched bays came down the street. Branch Isom waved to me and pulled the horses to a stop. "Ready to travel, Sawyer?"

I had no more excuses. I had been prepared to argue that a long ride on a heavy freight wagon would probably jolt my knitting hip too much, but I could see he meant for me to ride in the carriage with him. I put old hatreds behind me in the stresses of the moment and joined the devil.

He put the bays out in front of the wagons so we would not have to eat the dust, then slowed them to a walk that would not outpace the train behind us. He wore a good suit, better than any I had seen during my short stay in Indianola. The carriage, though not new, was a symbol of some prosperity. Prosperity, I knew, had long been a stranger to most people in Texas. My first thought, a natural one in view of past history, was that he had stolen it. But again I had the judgment not to ask.

He did most of the talking. He inquired about my war experiences, and I told him in a sketchy way. I had a hundred questions I desperately wanted to ask him, but most were about the Canfields. I could not believe enough time had passed that they would be a welcome subject for him. Perhaps sensing my curiosity about his relative well-being, he volunteered to me that freighting had made him a lot of money during the war. The Union blockade had closed the Texas ports within the first months. Cotton, always one of Texas' most important money crops, had stacked up by the thousands of bales, shut out of its traditional markets. But Texan ingenuity had not allowed this condition to become permanent. Soon the bales were on their way to the Mexican border in long, dust-raising wagon trains. Carried across the border, they were sold to European buyers for gold coin or traded outright for munitions and other Confederate needs. Union ships had no authority to prevent the shipment of merchandise in and out of Mexican ports. The great wagon trains wore deep ruts into the trail to Brownsville and Mata-moros. Not only had Branch Isom joined his wagons into this trade, but he had bought many more and expanded.

Isom told me, "We put a lot of cotton across that river and brought back a lot of guns and powder and equipment for you boys fighting the war. We did all we could, but I guess it wasn't enough."

It appeared to me it had been enough for *him*. Indirectly he told me as much. "I always took my payment on the Mexican side, in gold. I never did trust that paper money. People who did, like old Linden Hines, they're broke now."

"Linden Hines, broke?" That news hit me hard. Stonehill had been his town; he had started it.

"Lost his store, the freight wagons that used to haul goods for him, everything. Had a barrelful of that Richmond money when the war was over. It's not fit for wallpaper."

That hurt. I had always had a good feeling about that old man. "What does he do now?"

"Lives in the past, mostly. His daughter keeps books for me. I try to find the old man some things to do. Isn't much he *can* do, though. His health broke toward the end of the war, when he saw he was going to lose everything."

Suspiciously I asked, "Who got it?"

"First one and then another. San Antonio banks, mostly. He borrowed to keep the wagon outfits supplied, trying to help with the war. They lent paper but wanted gold back. I finally bought his store from him, but the money went to satisfy the banks."

"It's not fair if he did it all to help his country."

"Nothing is fair in this life. A man takes care of himself. Like your friend Thomas Canfield. He pulled into his hole like a badger and didn't give anything away."

That gave me the chance to ask what I had wanted to.

"He's all right? His family's all right?" I had received a few letters from Thomas' mother, early. Mail had a hard time finding me later on.

Isom's voice hardened. "Sure he's all right. Anything he ever owned, he still owns. Land-poor, maybe, without a dollar of real money to his name, but he'd eat jackrabbits before he'd borrow a dollar on one foot of that land." Isom grunted. "He can keep his land as far as I'm concerned. Give me a going business anytime, like mine . . . the town, the freight line. That's where the money is."

"Last I heard, a long time ago, Thomas and Maria had a baby girl."

Isom nodded. "She'd be three now, or maybe four. She was born after my little boy came."

I don't know why I should have been surprised at the thought of Branch Isom having children. The meanest dog can sire a litter of pups. But the thought of him bouncing a child on his knee didn't fit the image I had always carried in my mind. It was even more of a surprise, then, that he set in to telling me all about his boy. His name was James, and he was four. He could ride horseback by himself, and he could name most of the horses and mules in half of Isom's many freight teams. Once started, Isom seemed unable to stop talking about him. Somewhere in the conversation he told me Mrs. Isom had never been able to have another child. I suppose that was why Isom seemed to put so much store in this one, because there would not be another.

I kept expecting, sooner or later, that old grudges would surface in Isom's conversation, that he would turn his anger against me on the trail where nobody but his own men would see or know. But he never did. It was as though the old differences had never existed. In the few words he spoke of Thomas, I knew the angers of the past had not died, but for me personally he betrayed no resentment. Perhaps he took my army service into account, or my crippled hip, and he wiped the slate clean. All the way to Stonehill I remained uneasy, expecting trouble. It never came.

The town looked little different. Some new houses had been built. The streets were moderately busy, mostly with freight wagons engaged in the gradual renewal of normal commerce. I noticed a fair number of Mexican carts, holding their own against the *gringo* freighters. Isom seemed not even to see them. He pulled the carriage to a halt at his open double gates and watched his freight wagons enter a huge corral, all but the last one in the line. He signaled for the driver to follow him. "That one," he said, "is for my wife. Things for the house, ordered all the way from England. Even a piano."

Coming into Stonehill had increased my uneasiness. It had seemed a forbidding town, especially since the death of Kirby Canfield. Even after the many years, I still had that feeling about it.

I said, "I'd better get down here. I'll find a way to get out to the ranch."

Isom nodded. "You know I can't take you. Thomas Canfield and I have not set eyes on one another in years. It is best we keep it that way. I'd be glad to lend you a horse."

I did not want to arrive at the Canfield ranch riding a horse that belonged to Branch Isom. I thanked him for his generosity and assured him I would find a way. He asked me to come up to his house and meet his wife and see his boy, James. I told him I would, another time. He pulled away and left me in the trailing dust, much relieved to see the last of him even though he had shown me nothing but friendliness since Indianola. Old suspicions die hard.

I had no idea, at first, what my next move should be. I was not sure who I might still know here. It was in my mind that I could seek out some of the Mexicans who had worked for or dealt with Thomas years ago, if any still lived in Stonehill. I started up the dusty street, one hand holding the carpetbag containing nearly everything I owned, the other holding the cane for support. I looked vainly for a familiar face.

Reading the signs, I learned that Branch Isom had his roots sunk deeply into this town. A dramshop bore the names "Smith & Isom" in small letters beneath the title "Texas Lady." A blacksmith shop and livery barn proclaimed "A. Dandridge & B. Isom." I came in a while to the big general store that had been built by Linden Hines. The sign declared, "General Mercantile. Branch Isom, Prop."

I felt a little as I supposed the Europeans must have felt when a usurper took the throne.

Laura Hines had remained on my mind during the long war years. I had more or less reconciled myself to the idea that there would never be anything between us except friendship, but I knew no other face that appealed to me quite so much, so I let hers be the player in many a fanciful daydream, some of a high order, some I would never have wanted her to know about. Futile or not, the dreams had been a means of lifting me out of intolerable reality and, perhaps, keeping me from losing my mind.

Isom had said she was keeping books for him. I stood in front of the store a minute, bracing up my courage, wondering how far I had let my dreams stray from truth. I had long suspected that I had made over her face to suit myself, so that the one in the dreams was probably at considerable variance with reality.

I made my way past barrels and boxes on the wooden porch and stood in the open double door, trying to accustom my eyes to the dim interior. I heard Laura before I saw her.

"Reed? Reed Sawyer?" She came out from behind a tall counter in the rear of the store. I could not see her clearly because it was dark in there, and my eyes were filling up, too. "It's me," I said.

She threw her arms around me, putting me off balance and almost causing me to fall. My hip shot through with pain, but I tried to hide it. She stood back a little to stare at me, her hands keeping a strong grip on my shoulders.

"We were afraid you were dead," she declared.

"I wrote."

"The mail service broke down, toward the last."

She made a good deal of fuss over me, which I enjoyed, but I sensed that it was friendship, nothing more. All those daydreams had served a purpose at the time, but they were dead now. I felt like crying.

She had changed a lot, or perhaps my creative memory had been at fault. She was mature, a woman well past twenty, face still pretty but eyes sad from the unhappiness she had seen. I realized we were both ten years older than when we had first met.

"You look wonderful," I said. That was true. She did, to me.

She brought herself to ask about my cane, about my thinness. I admitted that I looked as if I had barely escaped the grave, but I was sure I would get much better now that I was home.

"First thing you need is a good meal," she said. "I have the books in good shape. I'm going to take you home with me and cook you a real dinner."

I protested, but weakly. Nothing could have pleased me more.

She said, "It will do Papa good to see you. He hasn't seen much in a long time to make him smile."

I thought I knew what to expect, but seeing Linden Hines was like a blow to the stomach. He was an old man, a shell. He smiled at the sight of me, but the smile lived only a minute. He had given up the will and surrendered to infirmities that he normally might have stood off for many more years.

"I am glad you came back, Reed," he said. "So many didn't. It cost us so much . . ."

The casualties of the war had reached far beyond the battlefields.

I remembered that the old gentleman had been partial to a good toddy. While Laura was busy fixing dinner I thought I might cheer him a little. I said, "It has been a long, hard trip, and I think a drink would do me good. I would be obliged, sir, if you would go with me."

That faint smile returned. "I would be honored, sir."

Neither of us moved very fast, me burdened by my bad hip and my cane, he by his health. We went into the place called Lucky Lady, which Mr. Hines indicated was as good as any in town. Business seemed slack, but it was a time of day when most respectable people were working, if most people in Stonehill could be considered respectable. Thomas Canfield had always regarded the Hineses as something akin to Lot's family, two good people in a town of arch sinners.

We had our drinks, and I laid the coins on the bar. A voice came from the back of the room. "Keep your money, Sawyer. The drinks are on the house."

Branch Isom had entered the back door. I told him it was not necessary, but he protested that it was an occasion when a soldier came home, especially the friend of an old friend like Linden Hines. He went behind the bar, opened a door somewhere and fetched out a bottle. "This is the best I can buy, too good to sell across the bar." He poured our glasses full, and one for himself. He held up his glass in a toast: "To the soldiers of Texas, wherever they fought."

I looked closely at Mr. Hines, expecting him to betray resentment toward this man who now owned all that used to belong to him. But I saw no such emotion there. He nodded at the toast and downed the whiskey and said something about its being good.

Isom said, "And now, gentlemen, I must leave you. I have pressing business all over town. Come in again, Sawyer. Mister Hines, my compliments."

Hines thanked him for the whiskey, which prompted me to do the same. I had been so surprised by Isom's generosity that I stood off balance. I could not escape a feeling that I was a calf being fattened for slaughter, though I could not imagine how.

I was not used to whiskey and never held it well. It glowed like a comfortable fire in my stomach, though. Mr. Hines seemed ready to go home, so we started. He took the lead, picking his way among a group of teamsters who had just come in. They did not move aside for him. They would have, a few years earlier. My cane brought me no particular respect either. They were used to crippled ex-soldiers coming home.

From the porch down to the street was a fair distance, and I was a little slow negotiating the three steps. Mr. Hines was ahead of me, looking back to be sure I didn't slip. I heard a rumbling and a loud shout and glanced up the street. A big freight wagon was bearing down on Mr. Hines.

"Look out!" I shouted to him and tried to hurry. I caught one foot on my cane and fell down the steps. I could hear the wagon driver cursing and shouting at his mules. Through the dust and the blur of movement I sensed that Mr. Hines had stepped back quickly enough to be in the clear.

"Why don't you watch what you're doing, old man?" the driver shouted back, once the danger was past. "Damned old relics, ought not to be allowed on the street without a guardian."

I got up angry enough to do battle, even in my condition. I shouted after the driver that an old pioneer like Linden Hines was due respect, but the words were lost in the air. Nobody cared what he had been in the past. They saw only what he was now, a worn-out old man existing on others' generosity. The generosity of Branch Isom.

My conscience began nagging me. I knew all my indignation had not been over the general lack of gratitude to Linden Hines. Some was for myself. My being a wounded soldier seemed to have little meaning either; few people exhibited any gratitude. I supposed it was because we had lost the war. I had just as well have stayed home.

Laura put more steak on the table than we could eat, even with the appetite I had saved up through a long lean time. Beef was cheap, she said, even free for those who had a horse and could go get it. The war had blocked most outside markets for years. So many men had gone into Confederate service that herds went untended, unbranded. Cattle had multiplied to a point that South Texas ranges were badly overstocked, the grass short. The unbranded ran wild and free for the taking, with no one to object.

Before the war, cattle had represented wealth. Now, if anything, they were a liability.

"Eat some more," she said. "You're doing some rancher a favor."

I made the sacrifice, to my later discomfort. My thoughts returned then to the Canfield ranch. If I dallied much longer I would be obliged to stay the night. That would be an imposition on the Hineses. Their house was small and had no real place for me. I began making my excuses to leave.

Laura said, "I'll take you out there. I'll get a wagon from the company barn."

I told her I did not want to be any more burden than I had already been. Also, I had let myself become more beholden to Branch Isom than I would ever have imagined in olden times. I felt uncomfortable, owing a debt to a man like that, and I told her so.

She frowned. "That's Thomas talking, not you. Branch Isom has many faults, but he's not a completely forsaken sinner."

I figured she felt obliged to loyalty because she worked for him, and he occasionally extended cheap courtesies to her father. It struck me as unfair that Isom had enriched himself from the long conflict while soldiers like myself had paid a hard price.

Laura would not accept my refusal. I said my good-byes to her father, then walked with her to the big barn where empty freight wagons stood in a neat line and dozens of horses and mules milled in dusty corrals, pulling hay from crude racks built of mesquite. I looked around uneasily for Branch Isom, hoping not to have to belittle myself by thanking him once again. The stable men never questioned Laura's request for a light spring wagon. I could tell she carried weight around here. One of the men confided to me, out of her hearing, that she officiated at the monthly pay table. Bought loyalty was effective, if sometimes shallow.

We rode in silence much of the time. After several years of absence I was busy taking in the country, remembering. It was drier than when I had left it, the grass poor. I could see cattle in every direction, thick as fleas on a butcher's dog.

When Laura talked it was mostly about Stonehill, which seemed to have prospered more than the average Texas town during the war because of its importance on the freighting roads. I asked about New Silesia, well remembering how nearly it had come to starvation in the beginning. She said it had suffered some harassment early because so many of the people were opposed to the war. It had not grown much but had solidified its position. Unlike Stonehill, it had been largely self-sufficient. What the Polish immigrants could not raise or make for themselves, they managed to do without. For this reason they had not suffered unduly from the collapse of the Confederate currency; they had little of it in the first place. Laura said they had broken out more fields and strengthened their hold on the little they owned. Like Thomas Canfield, they drew their strength from the land and regarded it as the only thing solid in life. Money was but sterile paper or metal. The land was alive.

When I asked about Mrs. Canfield or Maria or the two children, Laura talked easily. When she spoke of Thomas she was slower and more thoughtful, and she did not look at me. Earlier I had been tempted to ask why she had not found another good man and married him. Before we reached the ranch, I knew without asking.

Approaching the headquarters, I could see little change. There were still four houses of varying size, the double cabin for the old Mrs. Canfield, another for the Fernandez family, a small one for single hired hands, and the big frame house Thomas had built on the slope for Maria. From a distance I could see it needed paint. That, in itself, told me much about financial circumstances.

Two men were in the round bronc-breaking corral, one riding a crow-hopping young horse, the other throwing a sack under its feet to try to make it pitch. I was astounded when Laura told me these were the Fernandez boys. In my mind they should still be as young as when I had left. Now they would pass—at a distance—for grown men. But this was a country that did not tolerate childhood very long. The boys quickly tied the bronc and scaled the fence, then ran to meet us, hollering at me all the way.

It was getting to be a grim joke, everybody saying first off that they had assumed I was dead. I told them I hated to be such a disappointment. They ran ahead of us up to the big house, shouting for the Canfields to come out. The old lady was the first onto the porch. She threw up her hands and came running to meet me. She had grayed more in the nearly four years I had been gone, and the lines had cut deeper into her face, but I thought she had fared far better than Linden Hines.

Maria came out then, her brown eyes shining and beautiful. Like Laura, she had matured into a fine-looking woman. Her face was still pretty and fleshed out better than I remembered it. Her waist was fuller, the result of bearing two children, but if anything that was an improvement. Before, she had looked as if a strong wind might carry her away.

A small girl, who had to be past three now, peered shyly out from behind her, keeping one hand full of her mother's skirt, pulling it out to cover all but one big brown eye, very curious.

The two women both hugged me at the same time, while the little girl ran and threw her arms around Laura's neck, then clung to her while she looked at me with both curiosity and a little fear. Youngsters like this, growing up far out in the country, were not used to strangers. I heard the girl saying, "Aunt Laura." I saw the gentle way Laura and Maria looked at each other, and it occurred to me how unusual a friendship theirs really was.

It was a while before I knew the little girl's name. The old lady called her "child," and Maria called her something I never quite understood, then or later. It was in Polish. Eventually Laura spoke of her as Katrina when the girl led her off into another room to show some doll clothes her mother had sewed from scraps.

Maria's English had improved, though she still spoke with an accent. She looked at me with pity. "We must make for you much food.

We must get you fat again." I never had been given much to weight, but I realized I must look like starvation now.

Not until near dark did Thomas come home. I saw Maria's eyes light at the sound of the wagon. If I had ever doubted that he had chosen well, that look dispelled all question. The boy Kirby sat beside him on the wagon. The original spring seat was gone, replaced by a flat board that jolted the innards. The two had been shoveling stock salt into troughs at some of the watering places. The boy's rough clothing was crusted with it. He was six now, or near it, and as shy of me as the girl had been. Thomas tied off the reins and came up into the yard with a tired but happy step. The boy remained a full pace behind him and eyed me with dark suspicion. I had bounced him on my knee, but he had been too small to remember that.

Thomas stared at me a long moment without a word. He had aged more than the years alone would account for. He was not original with his first words. "Reed, I thought they had killed you," he said.

I didn't care what he said so long as there was welcome in it. He gripped my arms in the Mexican style of *abrazo*; much of his manner had come to him from the Mexicans.

I managed to say, "You told me I would always have a home here." I wondered, for by the looks of things an extra mouth might be a burden.

"I hope you never doubted that," he said.

"I probably won't be much help for a while."

He glanced at my cane but only shrugged. "You've already been a help, just coming back. Now I know things have got to get better."

One of the Fernandez boys came up, and Thomas asked him to take care of the team and wagon. He put his arm around Maria, and they walked into the house. Laura watched them, then took the girl's hand and followed.

Only the boy and I were left. I asked, "How about it, Kirby?"

He just stood on the ground and stared in silent distrust.

I turned and went into the house alone, figuring he would open up to me after a while.

But he never did, not completely.

CHAPTER 5

The first days on the ranch produced many satisfactions, but they also held frustrations. My hip punished me for my ambition in trying to ride horseback. I went three or four miles with the Fernandez boys, thinking the pain would stop sooner or later. Instead it became so bad I had to dismount and could not climb back into the saddle. I waited in humiliation while Marco returned to headquarters and brought a wagon to fetch me home.

"You're trying too hard," Thomas admonished. "Take your time."

I said, "I was brought up to work for what I get."

Thomas' face was sad. "You're not getting much here. I haven't the money to pay you anything."

"You feed me. You give me a place to lay my head down. I owe you for that."

I owed for much more. I was not simply a hired hand, and I was not treated as one. Maria and the old Mrs. Canfield competed with each other to see who could fix the best meals for me. The little girl, Katy—Thomas would never call her Katrina—toddled after me as if I were some good uncle, even if the boy never warmed to me.

"There is a lot of work you can do in a wagon," Thomas said. "You can carry salt. You can haul supplies from New Silesia." He tried to keep my mind and my hands occupied, to make me feel useful rather than a burden, even when I knew it was not true.

I would watch him ride his favorite horse, this spirited mustang bay he called Stepper, which had never completely given up the fight and occasionally challenged Thomas' right to mastery. Thomas always won, but not without a contest. I envied him that ability and wondered how long it would be before I was a whole man again.

He asked me to go with him to San Antonio to buy goods for his struggling store in New Silesia. That store, since the collapse of Confederate currency, had become a financial tribulation to him. I sat in the lobby of a San Antonio bank and watched from a distance as Thomas humbled himself to a well-dressed Yankee banker, something I knew hurt him worse in its way than my wound had ever hurt me. He finally got most of what he had asked for, but the cost in pride was high. On the long trip home in the rough wagon, he was silent, withdrawn into a heavy shell.

When he finally spoke the suddenness of it startled me. He said, "You haven't seen your own place since you came home."

I had, one day when I was hauling salt. I had made several extra miles in an empty wagon to look upon the little piece of land I had bought with my saved wages before the war. It wasn't much, a fraction of Thomas' holdings, and it had not so much as a dugout on it for habitation. There was no point in my building one; it was too small a place to yield a living. But I felt a glow from the sense of ownership.

Thomas stopped the wagon on a knoll and gazed in silence. I could see cattle scattered across a wide, sun-baked flat and knew most of them were strays, not mine. The few cows I had owned before the war would be old mossyhorns now, the ones that might have survived.

Thomas said, "We kept up your brand for you while you were gone. We branded the increase every year."

I thanked him, though it seemed to me the work had been largely for nothing. Those cattle were worth no more than their hides and tallow would fetch, which wasn't much. And the land wasn't worth the lumber it would take to build a good house on it.

He seemed to sense what I was thinking. "Hold on to it, Reed. It will be worth a fortune to you someday. Land is the only thing that is real."

"Gold is real," I said. "This whole thing, today, wouldn't bring enough gold to plate a watch."

"Gold doesn't grow food. It doesn't keep the rain off of your head."

I spoke rashly, and immediately wished I had kept my mouth shut. "It seems to be doing very well for Branch Isom."

He shook from the impact of the name. "It will betray him someday. Through the war, when others were working for patriotism, he worked for gold. Now he puts it all back into Stonehill. He has no feeling for land; all it means to him is the roads to carry his freight wagons. That town will blow away someday, like tumbleweeds. The freight business will die with it. All his gold will be gone, and his sins will be visited on him like a plague. He will sit there with ruin all about him, but we'll have our land, Reed. The land will always be here."

We circled back by New Silesia, where he spent some time in the store with the manager Smithers, going over the ledgers. The store was like a stone weight around their necks; they had extended credit to too many people unlikely ever to pay.

While they talked about their business problems I looked over the little immigrant town. Thomas felt strong ties to it, mostly because of Maria and her people, but I was never at home there. I never had learned the language, not even enough to ask for coffee. The customs remained strange to me. Many of the Polanders had put up solid if unfancy houses—mostly of stone—in the years I had been away. I could not quite accept their way of building house and barn together, their milk stock staying in one end while the people lived in the other. I understood this was the way of the old country, but I never felt that friendly toward a cow.

Thomas was not much at going to church. Maria was faithful about it. Every Sunday she put the two children in a wagon and drove over to New Silesia. Sometimes Thomas went with her but found other things to do while she and her family and the children attended mass in the Catholic church. Other times he sent one of the Fernandez boys to make sure she had no trouble along the way. There were still people in the country who enjoyed harassing the Polanders. A couple of times, I went. The church service was alien to me, like most other things in the town. New Silesia seemed like something that had been lifted up from Europe and set down in Texas with few modifications.

We heard about the fever when it first moved up from the coast with one of Branch Isom's freighting outfits and struck in Stonehill. A Mexican wrangler told us several people in town had come down with it. Branch Isom sent his wife and young son to San Antonio to avoid their being exposed. There had been other epidemics, and none had ever touched the Canfield ranch. I remembered several times before the war that sickness had traveled inland with the freighting crews or immigrants. It would always run its course in a little while. Here and there somebody died of the fever, but people died of many other things too. Folks talk about the dangers we used to face from Indians and outlaws, but more died during epidemics in those days than ever died of arrow or bullet. Being isolated, far out in the country, was sometimes an asset. We probably missed more hazards than we realized.

One day a boy came out from town with a message from Laura Hines. The fever had struck her father suddenly, and in his weakened and spiritless condition he had died the second night.

Thomas struggled with his conscience. Not since his brother's death had he set foot in Stonehill. But the funeral of an old friend, and the bereavement of Laura, overcame his reluctance. He gave the two children into the care of Mrs. Fernandez, then four of us went to town in the wagon. Thomas hardly looked to right or left as we moved down the main street; his jaw was set in contempt for the place. Forgetting at first that Laura and her father had moved, he pulled the wagon up to the front of the large house that had long been their home. I had to tell him how to find the smaller one where they had lived since the war.

Laura was better reconciled to her loss than I expected. Maria hurried to embrace her. Laura accepted our condolences but said death had come to her father as a friend; life had lost its flavor to him.

The fever had people fearful about congregating indoors. The funeral was conducted entirely at the cemetery, a dry south wind blowing a skim of fresh earth into the open, waiting grave while the minister gave the eulogy. Maria stood on one side of Laura, Mrs. Canfield on the other, but she was strong enough; she did not need bracing up.

Branch Isom came to the funeral alone; his family was still in the comparative safety of San Antonio. He and Thomas did not speak, but their eyes met. Thomas' hatred flashed with the crackling reality of St. Elmo's fire. Isom quickly looked away. The uneasy truce of recent times had not overcome the open hostility of other years.

When the service was over Isom made his obligatory comments to Laura about the loss of a good man, the father of the town. Thomas watched him resentfully as he walked away.

"By rights he should not have come here," he said. "He robbed Mister Hines of all he owned, even the will to live."

Laura shook her head, her voice quiet but firm. "Branch Isom did not cause our trouble. That came because Papa gave everything he had to the cause he believed in. Isom just picked up the pieces."

"He could afford to. He hadn't given anything away."

Thomas seemed to realize the subject was painful to Laura, so he fell silent. But he watched Isom while the man's buggy was in sight.

Maria tried to persuade Laura to go to the ranch a few days, to get away from the unhappy town and the sorrow it had caused her. Laura shook her head. "I've fallen behind on the books. What I need most right now is work to keep my mind busy."

We followed her home but found a goodly number of sympathetic women there. She would not lack for company. Thomas made excuses, and we left. He was relieved to put the town behind him. On the way home, nobody talked much. Mrs. Canfield finally began to comment upon the fever, and how fortunate we were to live in the open country where God kept the air clean.

Her words were ironic, for Thomas' mother was struck down a few days later. No one knew much about the fever or its causes. We could only guess that she had caught it somehow at the funeral. Thomas immediately asked me to take the children to Maria's people in New Silesia. So far the fever had not struck that town. Little Katy did not mind; I had already seen how much she loved her grandparents. But the boy Kirby was silent during the wagon trip to the Polish town. His eyes were resentful when I turned him over to the old couple. He understood what they said to him in their language, but he stubbornly refused to answer them except in English. I sensed that I had been introduced to a shameful secret. Even as the Brozeks fawned over the children, it was easy to see they were covering up their hurt. Kirby came to the door of the stone house and watched me as I left for the ranch. He said not a word, but I felt his eyes following me.

Unlike Linden Hines, Mrs. Canfield had a strong wish to live. She put up a battle that she seemed for a time to be winning. But it was not enough. The doctor managed to see her only once, for he had more than enough suffering patients in Stonehill. Maria stayed beside the old lady constantly during the three days and nights she struggled. She was still on her feet, but barely, when the fever carried Mrs. Canfield away. Thomas just sat in his mother's rocking chair at the foot of the bed and stared. He did not talk; he did not weep. He just sat there, rocking.

Maria cried a little, then put that behind her and tried to comfort her husband. She seemed unable to reach him, and her silent eyes pleaded to me for help.

I said to Thomas, "I'll go to the preacher. Your mother was a believing woman. She'd want the words read over her."

A quick nod was the only sign that he had heard.

I knew without asking that he would want to bury her up on the slope, alongside his father and brother. Backing away, I said, "I'd better fetch the children home. They ought to see her laid to rest."

He stopped rocking. "No, there's fever here." That was all he said. He started rocking again.

Maria followed me to the porch, tears shining in her eyes. "He does not let me help him," she said.

I told her, "He's not a man who leans on people. He stands by himself." It struck me how thin and haggard she looked. She had slept little the last several days. "You'd better help yourself," I said. "You'd better get some rest."

She nodded, but she would not do it, not so long as she thought Thomas might need her.

The minister was almost as busy as the doctor. There had been other deaths since that of Linden Hines. He promised to come out to the ranch as soon as he could, but all preparations had to be made ahead, for he could not stay long. I tried to think of any people in town who should be notified. The only friend Mrs. Canfield had there, so far as I knew, was Laura Hines. Laura put a few clothes together and rode back to the ranch with me in the wagon.

Scarcely a dozen people stood at the graveside to hear the brief services. Thomas said little. He stood alone. When Maria reached once for his hand, he pulled it away and folded his arms.

I glanced at Laura. She frowned.

Laura did not like the tired, drawn look on Maria's face, and she offered to stay a day or two. Maria insisted she was all right; a good night's sleep was all she needed. Thomas took no part in the conversation. He seemed not even to hear it, though he was only an arm's length away. He responded to nothing until Laura said, "If you will then, Reed, please take me back to Stonehill."

The word *Stonehill* seemed to bring Thomas around. "You should get away from that place, Laura. It brings nothing but misfortune and death."

She gave him a look of surprise, as if not quite believing he cared that much for her welfare. "I have nowhere else to go."

It was in my mind—I had not given up—that someday *I* might provide her a place to go, when I was able to build my land holdings and my cattle herd some more, and after I put up a house of my own. But the thought passed when we sat in the wagon together. She glanced back, and what I saw in her eyes for Thomas, I feared I would never see there for me.

Maria started to climb the steps as we pulled away. She never made it to the top. I saw her sway, then fall. Laura cried at me to stop. She was down from the wagon and running before I could bring the team to a halt. I saw fear strike Thomas. He called Maria's name as he knelt and tried to lift her to her feet.

By the time I got the team still and the reins wrapped around a spoke, Thomas had Maria in his arms and was rushing into the house with her. Laura was directly behind him. I followed them into the bedroom, where Thomas gently placed Maria on their big hand-carved wooden bed.

"She's just tired out," he said desperately, more to himself than to the rest of us. He was trying to believe it, but it was obvious he did not.

Laura felt of Maria's hand and then her forehead. "It's more than that." Fear came into her face. She immediately took over, for Thomas seemed helpless, as he had been helpless when his mother was burning with fever. This was an enemy he did not know how to fight.

"Reed," she commanded, "run down and fetch Mrs. Fernandez. Then hurry to town and drag that doctor out here; bring him with a gun if you have to. Thomas, you help me get these clothes off of Maria."

Thomas had braced his feet, and he stood like an ox struck behind the horns with the flat side of an ax. Laura saw he was stunned. She gripped his shoulders and shook him savagely. "Thomas!" I waited in the door until he began to respond, then I ran down to the little Fernandez house.

What Laura said about bringing the doctor with a gun if necessary was not much of an exaggeration. He still had about all he could do without leaving town. I thought I would have to wrestle his hefty wife, who protested that *he* would be the next to die if he didn't get some rest. I sympathized with both of them, but I had to sympathize with Maria more. I took him to the ranch.

Nobody had to tell me the situation was grave. The hard-set look in Thomas' eyes said that, and the quiet desperation of Laura. Maria was talking irrationally, crying out in words I could not understand about things that had happened long before, or perhaps never happened at all.

I looked to Thomas to see if I could do anything for him. He seemed unaware of me, even when I spoke to him. Laura touched my arm and beckoned me into the parlor. Quietly, her voice trembling, she said, "You'd better hurry to New Silesia and bring her parents here. You'd best not lose any time."

"They have the children. I shouldn't bring the children to this fever."

"There's other family to leave the children with. But bring her parents, and hurry."

I never had been able to converse with the Brozeks very well because of the language problem. I went directly to the church and found the priest hunched over a giant Bible. I explained the situation. He went with me to the Brozeks'. Katy was playing in the front yard of the rock house with some other children, chattering happily in Polish. Kirby was off to himself, chunking rocks at some chickens. The girl recognized me and came running, shouting my name. Kirby walked only partway to meet me, then stopped, saying nothing. I could tell he hoped I had come to take him home, but he was too proud to ask, or to seem eager. He had much of Thomas in him.

Anguish came into the old couple's faces as the priest told them of my message. Kirby listened in silence. I could tell he understood it all. Katy cried and begged to be taken to her mother. The old grandmother picked her up and smothered her in her arms and hurried outside to call to a neighbor. In a few minutes she had the children placed with others of the family. The priest had a buggy, more comfortable than the ranch wagon, so he took the old folks in it while I followed close behind, one of Maria's brothers riding with me. The long miles I had made, first to Stonehill and then to New Silesia, began to tell on me, and the brother took over the reins. I tried to nap sitting up, but the wagon was too rough. I sat with my eyes shut and kept seeing all those anguished faces.

We arrived almost too late. Maria opened her eyes at the sound of voices. She recognized her parents and called their names and cried out for her children. Laura tried to explain that they had stayed behind to protect them from the fever, but I don't think Maria understood. She sank back into the fever. When the priest leaned over her with his beads and began to give her absolution, I knew the ordeal was nearly done. She cried out once and was gone.

The old couple crossed themselves and leaned into each other's arms. Mrs. Fernandez made the same sign and turned her face into a corner. I looked into Laura's tired, stricken face, then to Thomas, frozen, unseeing. His mind had carried him far away, denying reality, rejecting recognition of death. For several minutes he did not move. Then he gripped Maria's shoulders and tried to shake her awake.

"Maria! Maria!" he cried.

Laura gently touched his arm. "She can't hear you, Thomas," she whispered.

He shook Maria harder and kept calling to her. When realization finally reached him he pushed to his feet and stared down at that silent face now without pain. A terrible look came into his eyes, the look that had always frightened me a little. Instinctively I glanced at his hip, though I realized he was not carrying a gun. The dark thought came to me that if he had, he might use it on himself.

He spoke to no one, looked at no one, but turned and strode out of the room. The fear still pressed on me, so I followed him, keeping my distance. I thought it unnatural that a man could go through so much and never cry. I had not seen him cry when he buried his brother Kirby, or his mother. I saw not one tear in his eyes now. He walked carefully down the steps and toward the barn. Quietly I followed fifteen or twenty steps behind him, not sure what he might do or what I *could* do. He stopped at the horse corral.

His bay mustang Stepper was in there, pulling hay from a rack. He turned his head to watch Thomas, and he made a nervous, rolling noise in that long, ugly nose. Thomas walked in, shutting the gate behind him. I kept my distance, moving up quietly and looking between the poles. Thomas walked slowly toward the horse, his hand extended. The bay watched him suspiciously, little ears flicking in nervousness. Once he started to turn and run away, but something in Thomas' manner seemed to hold him. The bay flinched as Thomas reached out and touched his neck. Thomas slipped his left arm under the neck and up the off side. He patted the horse awhile. If he said anything, it was in a whisper I could not hear. Then he had both arms around the horse's strong neck, his face buried in the dark mane, and Thomas did something I had never seen him do. He cried.

The horse, normally nervous as a cat, stood quiet and still, as if it understood, and let Thomas spill out all his grief.

I walked back to the house. The best help I could give Thomas was simply to leave him alone.

Thomas Canfield had long seemed a man the world could not touch, a man too strong to bend before the wind. Now, for a while, the fight was gone out of him. He held his ground on just one thing. Maria's parents wanted to take her to New Silesia for burial in consecrated ground. Thomas insisted she would be buried in the family cemetery up on the slope. That, too, he said, was consecrated ground, hallowed by so many he had loved. The priest blessed the place, and it was all right.

Beyond that one issue, he had no strength left. If the denizens of Stonehill had come then to drive off every head of cattle and to post a confiscation notice on his land, I do not believe he would have resisted. He drew into a shell where nothing from outside could reach him.

The girl Katy was too young to realize fully the meaning of death. Kirby knew. I never saw him cry, but I could see the pain and the helpless anger in his eyes. He did not know who to blame, so he blamed everyone. Some of the anger was directed toward his father for sending him away and some toward me for taking him. During the services I saw him resist attempts of Maria's parents to hold his hand. He stood alone, as his father stood alone.

The worst part of all was in returning to that big house, which must have seemed empty to the children. Thomas brought Mrs. Fernandez up from her own little place to live in the house and be a guardian of sorts. Her own sons were doing man's work if not drawing a man's pay. They slept in the little house where they had grown up, though they went to the big house to take their meals, cooked by their mother for them and for what was left of the Canfields. Much of the time they were not at headquarters anyway; they were often camped on one part of the ranch or another, looking after the cattle, batching. So, for that matter, was I. My hip had healed to the point that riding horseback no longer hurt me much, unless I let the work carry me too far into the night. I still had a limit.

I saw more of Kirby than of his sister because Thomas made it a point to keep the boy with him as much as he could. Where he went, Kirby usually rode by his side, on horseback or in the wagon. They talked little to each other. At least, Kirby talked little. His father volunteered points to him about the cattle or the horses, about the wild animals they encountered, about the land itself. Kirby absorbed this teaching without much comment. The long months went by, but he remained as distant as the day his mother was buried.

Despite our isolation, we heard things. Business began picking itself up from the floor where the lost war had left it. Union dollars, though still scarce, began to sift into the channels of commerce. Thomas had stubbornly held on to his ailing little store in New Silesia, not so much for its own sake as for the irritating competition it could give to Stonehill and to Branch Isom. Somehow he managed to pay off some loans and get himself back into reasonably good graces with the bankers in San Antonio, themselves hard put to find much real U.S. specie in circulation. An awful lot of scrip and plain old-fashioned barter were used in those days.

I had a horse in my string called Stomper, a name well given. He had a way of walking and trotting that jarred a rider's innards. Every time I rode him my hip would ache, but I could ill afford *not* to ride him, for a horse unused tends to forget his teaching and backslide into outlawry. I could have turned him over to one of the Fernandez boys, but they had not done anything to me that justified so sorry a treatment. I kept the horse as penance for whatever shortcomings I might have in the sight of the Lord.

One afternoon the pain was so sharp that I quit early and rode back toward the house while the sun was still an hour or so high. I cut into the Stonehill road and heard somebody hail me. I stopped Stomper and turned him around, welcoming a chance to shift my weight in the saddle and perhaps ease the aching hip.

The rider who trotted to catch up to me was one I would recognize from a mile away. Branch Isom.

Thinking back, I could not remember ever seeing him on the Canfield ranch. I saw no pistol on his hip, though he carried a rifle in a scabbard beneath his leg. Everybody did; that was no sign of war.

He reined up and offered a few pleasantries. His manner was cordial enough that my initial suspicions were suspended, if not dismissed. He seemed no longer the unrepentant sinner that he had appeared years before, when we had first made our acquaintance. Perhaps it was the graying with the red in his hair, or the deeper lines in a ruddy face growing heavy with the weight of years and relative prosperity. He seemed to have mellowed. Or perhaps I had seen so much brutality in the war that he paled by contrast.

He spoke of regret for the sorrows that had befallen the Canfields. He said, "I'll admit I never felt any love for Thomas, and it's certain he's had none for me. But I've had only the kindest thoughts for his womenfolks, even that Polander girl he married."

That surprised me a little. I felt honor-bound to ask about his own family. He said they were fine; his wife and son had waited in San Antonio for the fever to run its course. "Boy's getting to be a goer. I'd like to have brought him, but I didn't know what kind of reception I might get from Canfield. Some things a boy shouldn't see or hear."

It wasn't any of my business, but I felt compelled to ask anyway. "What have you come to see Thomas for?"

"Business. A mutual profit for both him and me, I hope."

My suspicions revived, though not so strong as before. It had been a long time since much good had come to this place from Stonehill, Laura Hines being the exception. She had visited occasionally on Sundays to look in on the children, or so she said.

I rode into headquarters with him. He told me much I had not heard about the Union occupation army and Indian troubles farther west, and of business trends and hopes and fears. As we approached the barn I saw Thomas' wagon in front of the salt house. He was shoveling salt to carry to the watering places. Kirby stood in the wagon bed, evening out the load with a shovel whose handle was longer than he was tall.

"Thomas," I called, "you have company."

His jaw dropped and his face darkened as he recognized Branch Isom. He cut his eyes reproachfully to me as if Isom's visit had been my doing. *"Isom,"* he said. Not *welcome* or anything like that. Just *Isom*. Recognition, but not approval.

Isom studied him a long moment before he said a word. Then he laid most of it right out on the table. "Thomas Canfield, you've never liked me, and I've never liked you. Men have been killed over differences smaller than we've had. But that's all in the past."

Thomas said nothing.

Isom said, "I have a business proposition. It could be profitable to both of us."

Thomas let his suspicions come bitterly to the surface. "More profitable for you than for me, I would warrant."

"Quite possibly," Isom admitted. "But I would carry considerable risk. Your profit would be guaranteed."

Thomas noticed his son watching Isom with unusual interest. Curtly he said, "Kirby, you go to the house."

Kirby was hesitant, and Thomas told him again, his voice brooking no question. "Go!" Kirby went reluctantly.

Thomas never invited Isom to step down from the saddle, so Isom sat there. He said, "Thomas, they're building a railroad west into Kansas."

Thomas pondered that fact a moment and failed to see significance in it. "You should not have to worry about that. They can't hurt you until they build one west from Indianola to San Antonio. Then you may be selling your freight wagons cheap."

Isom passed over the sarcasm and explained that the new railroad was opening up a market for beef in the East. "Cattle can be sold at the railheads to be shipped back there."

"We're a long way from Kansas. What good does that do us?"

"Cattle have legs. They can be walked to Kansas. I have started putting together a herd to take north. I'll buy cattle from you here and take all the responsibility and all the gamble. I'll pay you two-and-a-half a head for whatever cattle I can use. You won't have to go anywhere or take any risk. It's cash money, Union silver, placed into your hands right here at your corrals."

Thomas looked down, hiding his eyes. "What will you get for them, up in Kansas?"

"I won't lie to you. There is every indication they could bring fifteen dollars, perhaps more. But it's a long way and a risky trip. I'll lose some on the way. I *could* lose them all. If I make it, I'll earn a good profit. If I don't, I'll stand a loss. In either case, you'll have your money before the cattle ever leave this place."

Thomas said, "You've never handled cattle."

"I've handled horses and mules for years." He paused. "It's cash money. I'll bet you haven't seen two hundred dollars in Union specie since the war."

Thomas stared off into the distance, toward the slope where he had buried so many Canfields. When he turned I could tell from his expression pretty much what he was going to say. He would have dealt with Lucifer before he would deal with Branch Isom.

Coldly he said, "Isom, you were right when you rode up here. You never liked me, and I never liked you. What's between us is not forgotten. It never will be. I would not do business with you for a hundred thousand in Yankee gold."

Isom's face flashed to anger. I saw at least a little of the hostile Isom I remembered. "That's your final say?"

Thomas nodded grimly.

Isom had as much pride, in his way, as Thomas. He would not argue or plead. He said only, "I had hoped we could bury the past."

Thomas grunted. "Not until they bury *me*."

Isom's shoulders were stiff as he rode away. Thomas watched him as if half expecting him to turn and come back shooting. There had been a time, once, when that might have happened.

I could contain myself no longer. "If he offered you two-and-a-half outright, you could probably have carried him up to three. Maybe even three-and-a-half."

Thomas turned his back on me.

Next morning, without any word to me of what he planned, he left for San Antonio. Late the second evening he returned with two men following him in a buggy. One was a San Antonio businessman wearing a light duster over a good suit. The other was obviously a cowman by his clothes, his boots, his Mexican-style hat. He had the look of a man who had spent his life in the sun. Thomas introduced them as Mr. Jensen and Mr. Hayes.

"I have agreed to sell these gentlemen two hundred cattle at two dollars a head," he said.

I shook their hands and tried to look pleasant, though I quickly calculated that this represented a clear loss of one hundred dollars from Isom's offer.

Hatred could be expensive.

Branch Isom was by no means the only person putting cattle together for the trail to Kansas. These men had the same notion, Jensen putting up the money and Hayes the ability. Before the war Hayes had trailed cattle all the way to Missouri, and during the war he had taken some over into Louisiana to feed the Confederate soldiers. He had the look of a man who knew what the cow was about to think before she had time to think it. Those old cowmen bore a mark hard to explain but easy to recognize.

Thomas had us round up cattle from the end of the ranch nearest to Stonehill. Many people in town had become accustomed to helping themselves to Canfield beef. Thomas had done nothing about it because the cattle had been worth little anyway. Now times appeared to be changing. Thinning the cattle nearest to town might not stop the beef killing, but it made the thieves work harder. Hayes and Jensen were not interested in cows. A cow-calf herd was slow and difficult to trail. Anyway, the Yankees wanted beef, not breeding animals. The range was overstocked with long-aged steers and unbranded bulls born during the war years. They belonged to whoever caught them, if they bore no brand. As we gathered cattle, the two buyers were joined at headquarters by a crew of hungry-looking cowboys excited about the chance for a paying job that would put real silver in their pockets for the first time since the war.

Thomas had never been one to talk much, and he had said less in the time since Maria's death. He had shown little real interest in anything other than those two children. Now he spent a lot of time with Hayes, listening to all the old cowman volunteered to tell him about driving cattle. When the counting was over and the cowboys left with the herd, Thomas had a canvas sack that clanked with the heavy sound of silver.

"Sounds like more than it is," I remarked, remembering that he could have gotten better payment from Branch Isom.

"The devil always outbids the righteous," he replied, looking oddly satisfied as he watched the dust stirred by the departing cattle. "Reed, I want you to get an early start in the morning. Ride over west and see if the Ramirez boys want three or four months of work." They were among the men who used to go with us mustang hunting. "Get Abe Johnson and Farley Good and the Martinez brothers. We'll need a good crew who know cattle and horses."

"To do what?"

I could see something kindling in his eyes, a fire I hadn't seen there in a long time, a touch of excitement I had feared had died forever. "To put our own trail herd together and drive them to Kansas." He hefted the bag of silver. "This will be enough to outfit us."

I stood there with my mouth hanging open, thinking of a dozen good objections but undecided which to voice first. I didn't want to dim that light growing in his eyes.

Thomas said, "If their cattle can walk that far, so can ours. If they can get fifteen dollars at the railroad, so can we."

I said, "Branch Isom will throw a fit."

That, I realized, was one of the factors which put that new spirit in Thomas' face; that thought had come to him days ago.

"Yes," he said with satisfaction. "He will."

CHAPTER 6

My circle took me two days. I brought some of the men with me. Others were to follow when they could put personal business in order. Seeing some of those faces again made me remember old mustang-running days, and I felt a chill as the dark face of Bustamante came into my mind. It was said he had gone down into Mexico and had been killed fighting on the side of the *Juaristas.* Yet, there were among the Mexicans some who swore they had come across him in the brush country, in one secret camp or another. Somehow, people never wanted to let any of the old outlaws die; they kept seeing them whether they were dead or not.

I took the Fernandez boys and the crew that had come with me and started putting cattle together. Following Hayes's advice and example, we sorted out steers and bulls and hazed them toward headquarters, pushing cows and calves back out of the way. We had no fenced pastures, so we kept a couple of riders circling the outside, preventing the gathered cattle from drifting far.

Thomas arrived with a couple of extra *gringo* cowboys and a Mexican cook he had come across in San Antonio. They brought two well-used wagons, one with high sides built for hauling freight, the other an old canvas-covered army ambulance, wrecked and partially rebuilt. The words *U.S. Army* had been painted over but still showed. The heavy wagon was full of food and supplies. The ambulance was empty.

I watched little Katy rush out of the house and down the steps to throw her arms around her father's neck. Kirby kept his reserve.

Thomas took for granted what had been done in his absence; he had expected no less. I watched the youngsters go reluctantly back up the steps as Mrs. Fernandez called them to supper. Thomas lagged behind.

I said, "It's going to be tough on them, you being gone three or four months."

"They'll go with us," he replied. "We'll fix bunks in the old ambulance for them and Mrs. Fernandez."

I had never been inclined to give Thomas advice, but I could not accept this without argument. "We can't take those kids."

He didn't even look at me. "I wasn't much older than Kirby when we left Tennessee."

"That was another time. They'd be better off here at home with Mrs. Fernandez. Or with Maria's folks over in New Silesia."

"They're *my* children. I won't leave them with anybody." His eyes cut at me, telling me the argument was finished.

Laura Hines came out the next Sunday to see the children. Her reaction was the same as mine. Thomas' decision remained as stern. "I know of no one I'd leave them with."

She thought on it a little. "Leave them with me."

He wavered, for a moment. That idea had not occurred to him. "You couldn't stay with them and work too."

"I can keep books anywhere. I can do it at home."

"At home in Stonehill?" He spoke the name with bitterness. The moment of wavering was past. "That town has brought grief to this family ever since it began."

"This trip could bring a lot more." She looked accusingly at me. "Why haven't you talked him out of this?"

"I tried." Nothing more needed to be said.

Laura spent longer than usual with her Sunday afternoon good-byes. She held to the girl, her eyes begging Thomas. "Katy, at least."

"They're my children," he said, ungiving. "They're my responsibility."

Thomas avoided a similar argument with Maria's parents by simply not letting them know of his plan until too late. The first day's drive carried us to New Silesia and a little beyond. Thomas departed the drive long enough to take the ambulance and Mrs. Fernandez and the children into the little Polish town. He left me in charge of the herd, so I did not see or hear whatever challenge they gave him. But when we camped on water at dark, Thomas rode up with the ambulance. The look on his face spoke of victory hard won.

Those were the earliest days of trail driving north. Trailing was still an instinct, not a science. The first drives had no clear pattern to follow, so each outfit felt its way along. Later, old drovers would look back and laugh at the mistakes we made and the time we occasionally wasted. What most of us did, at first, was simply to use what we knew of handling cattle on the open range. We knew little of lead steers, of proper pace, of avoiding stray cattle, of always being sure where the water was, of crossing strange and unfriendly rivers. We did not even have a proper chuck wagon. That was a refinement yet to come, credited to cowman Charles Goodnight and copied and altered to fit the fancy of every trail boss and herd owner who pointed their cattle north. We simply carried grub and cooking utensils in the bed of the old freight wagon Thomas had brought from San Antonio. A certain amount of it had to be unpacked and then repacked at every meal, which soon had us wishing for a better way. The invention of the chuck-box was inevitable, with its drop-down lid that became a work table for the cook. But we didn't have it on that trip. We did the best we could with what we had, hoping for better the next time. If there was to be a next time.

We pushed the cattle hard the first few days to keep them tired, less likely to spook and run, or to try to turn back south toward home. The cattle were half wild, many of the bulls dragged out of the brush and handled by men and horses for the first time in their lives. They were always looking for something to booger at, and they often found it. Those first three or four days they must have run at least twice a day. Usually it was in the wrong direction, so the distance they made was wasted. I never could understand why cattle had such an adverse way of stampeding every direction except north.

The wildest of the early runs was on the third day, not long after we had strung them out in the morning. A black cloud had been hanging low in the north since long before daylight. We had watched a distant flashing and knew the cloud was coming at us. After sunrise, thunder rolled from west to east like the sound of cattle running. A sharp clap put the herd into a panic, running past the swing men on the east. We spurred as hard as we could push our horses, for the ambulance with the kids and Mrs. Fernandez was in the path of those cattle.

Mrs. Fernandez was not one to lose her head in a crisis; she had seen a fair number in her time. She swung the team to put the vehicle into an easterly direction, same as the cattle were running. This would keep it from being struck broadside. The cattle broke and went around either side of the ambulance. A few bumped it going by, but no real damage was done. The worst that happened was that one of the mules got its forelegs over the wagon tongue and hung up in the harness. Kirby was hanging out over the front, watching, and the jolt bounced him off of the wagon. He jumped to his feet, waving his hat and shouting. The last of the cattle swung away from him.

Thomas had been on the far side of the herd, so he was one of the last to reach the ambulance. I saw that everything was all right with Mrs. Fernandez and the kids, so I waved the rest of the riders after the cattle. Thomas spurred up, slid his horse to a stop and hit the ground running. His face almost white, he grabbed Kirby into his arms and hugged him. I thought the boy was in more danger of being crushed by his father than he had been from those running cattle.

Mrs. Fernandez's face was pinched. Katy tried hard not to burst into tears. I turned to Thomas. "I can keep the herd moving. Why don't you take the kids back to New Silesia? You can catch up to us in a couple or three days."

He just gave me that look. "You never give up, do you?" he asked.

I saw in his eyes that he would not change his mind. "I do when I can see there's no use fighting it anymore."

If Thomas did not change, little Kirby began to. Looking back on it afterward, I suspected it might have begun when he managed to wave the last running cattle around and escaped unhurt from a bad situation. He began to develop an attitude that nothing could hurt him if he stood his ground, an attitude to which he had been amply exposed at home. Thomas could not watch him all the time. When his father was not nearby, Kirby would saddle a horse and leave the ambulance to ride with the herd. Thomas soon gave up forbidding him. He ordered Kirby to stay with the drags at the rear of the herd where nothing was likely to happen to him. In no time Kirby would move up to the swing position and often to the lead, where one of the older, more responsible men was riding point. He accepted no authority except his father's, and that only when Thomas was nearby. No one else could send the boy back where he belonged. If one of the hands became insistent, Kirby would tell him in either English or Spanish to mind his own business.

He took to sleeping on the ground at night with the rest of the crew. A wagon, he declared, was for women and girls. Only on rainy nights would he compromise his pride and go into the covered ambulance. As the days wore into weeks he settled into a position with or near the Fernandez boys during days, and he rolled his blankets near theirs at night. The other men had started the drive mostly as strangers to him, and grown men at that. He never warmed to them much.

Kirby seemed to avoid Thomas as much as he could, pulling away on his horse when Thomas approached. I took it as a natural thing, a youngster's desire to escape his father's critical eye and reprimands for his shortcomings. But Thomas took it for something more. Nights, sometimes, I would see him staring at his son across the campfire, his eyes troubled.

One day we came to a small creek that under normal circumstances would be no challenge. Rain had fallen during the night. It must have been heavier upstream, because the creek was rushing along at a goodly clip. Thomas motioned me up to the point, where we sat with Farley Good and studied the brownish water, colored by the soil the rain had carried into it. We quickly decided it didn't present much danger to the herd. I could have thrown a rock across it with a sore arm.

"Put them into the water at a run," Thomas said, "and they'll be over before they know they're wet." He looked back, seeking out the Fernandez boys. Wherever they were, there Kirby would be also. "I'm putting Kirby in the ambulance."

I became too busy rushing cattle across to pay attention to what was happening behind me. By and by I heard a boyish whoop and saw Kirby spur his pony into the stream. I yelled at him to come back, but the order was lost in the noise of the cattle splashing into the swollen creek. Halfway across, the pony lost its footing and turned under. Juan Fernandez hit the water before I had time even to move. I went in behind him.

Kirby came up threshing. Almost as he surfaced, Juan grabbed him, pinning him against his leg as he carried him out of the creek and onto the far bank. I was beside him the last few feet, ready to grab if Juan showed sign of losing his hold.

I was too scared to talk, and Juan looked as if all the blood had drained from his face. But Kirby was laughing.

I struggled to say something. Juan gave Kirby a strong shaking. "Your papa say you don't come on your pony. He say you ride the ambulance."

"I didn't get hurt," Kirby said defensively. "And neither did my pony. Looky yonder, he's coming out of the water. Go get him for me, Juanito."

"I get a *belt* for you," Juan said angrily.

Thomas rode up, his eyes afire. "Go catch his pony, Juan. I've got the belt for him." He stepped from his saddle and caught Kirby as Juan let him slide to the ground. Thomas unbuckled his belt and pulled it from his trousers, then held it at half swing. Kirby drew himself up to take the blow, jutting his jaw but not quite closing his eyes. He stared defiantly at his father. I sat on my horse, watching the conflict play itself out in Thomas' face. Slowly he lowered the belt without using it on his son.

In later years he *would* strike him. By then it was too late.

Sharply he said, "Next time I tell you something, you listen."

Kirby did not reply. He stood braced, still half expecting the belt to strike, but he yielded nothing.

"Damn it, boy . . ." Thomas said slowly, not finishing what was on his mind. Juan brought up the dripping pony. "Get on him," Thomas commanded Kirby, "and then you stay on this side of the creek. Don't you go back into that water for anything."

It was an empty order. There was no reason for Kirby or anybody else to cross that creek twice. But Thomas had to assert his authority, even if he had lost it.

Most trail drives were a long, slow stretch of boredom, with a few minutes of excitement now and again to take the place of the sleep there never was enough time for. Crossing rivers was one of the few times we had any reason to let our blood pump fast, once the herd wore the "run" out of its system. A few cattle naturally took the leadership, rising up off of the bedgrounds at daylight and setting out to graze. About all we did was point their direction, north. Most of the other cattle would gradually get up and fall into the positions their natures best suited them to. Like people, cattle developed a standing in the social order. The ones highest up protected their places with all the jealousy of a San Antonio matron. The ones which took the lead in the first days of the drive held it the rest of the way. The one which fell back early stayed back. After a time you would get to know the individual cattle and just where they belonged on the drive. Unless one went lame or sick, he would not vary his position much.

After the first days, when the cattle were used to walking and Thomas was sure Branch Isom hadn't started his drive yet, we let the Longhorns graze along and set a pace that suited them. Thomas occasionally dropped back a few miles to be sure nobody was catching up to us with another herd. He became touchy about our front position; he would not stand for pressure from behind. One day we saw dust way to the rear, and I went with Thomas to see about it. Another herd was pushing along at a pace faster than ours. I thought for a while it might come to a fight. Thomas held on to that lead like it was a gift from the Almighty, and anybody who challenged us was on the devil's string. Hot words passed, but the trail boss of that other outfit shrank back from the look in Thomas' eyes. He decided his herd needed a day of rest to make up for the hard pace it had traveled.

The nearest we came to a genuine scare was with the Indians. They had been in the back of my mind from the beginning because there was no way to get to Kansas from South Texas without crossing Indian land. I had always felt we were overdue for trouble in the old days when we ran mustangs in the wild country far to the west of Stonehill, but somehow we had never run into them. Now we were pushing through country the government had granted to them, and a herd of cattle was a hard thing to hide. The people who had been north ahead of us said the Indians wouldn't usually bother an outfit that let them have a few cattle, but this was never a sure thing. A lot of them hadn't settled yet and hadn't agreed to any reservation. You couldn't tell by looking whether they were treaty Indians or the wild bunch. If they took a disliking to you it didn't make much difference anyway, people said.

I was riding point the afternoon they came on us, out of the sun. In the first excited moment I thought there must be fifty, but later I re-counted and found only seventeen. I guess it was always that way with Indians; there were seldom as many as there seemed to be. They made no warlike signs against us, but they all carried armament—bows, lances, a few old muskets worn out before they traded for or stole them. They stopped in a ragged line. One who made it clear he was the leader came toward me, walking his horse. He held up one hand to show he was peaceful, but I watched the other hand more; it held a rifle with a barrel four feet long. He started talking and making signs with his hands. I decided he had rather talk to us than fight us, though he might fight if the talk ran thin.

Thomas loped up to me, some of the other men just behind him. The ambulance had stopped. The two Fernandez boys had moved beside it, ready to protect their mother and the kids.

My first thought was that Thomas' sign language would be no bet-ter than mine, but I didn't consider the fact that he had been married to a Polander woman and had talked to both her and her family with his hands. It didn't take him and the Indian but a minute or two to find enough common ground that they could parley.

Thomas' face was cold serious. He told me, "He says he's got a lot of hungry people. He wants a beef for every man he brought with him."

By this time I had made the count and told Thomas how many that was, in case he had not counted for himself. He agreed with me that this was a San Antonio fancy-house price. He bargained awhile and cut the number to ten. The Indian looked satisfied; I suspected he had been willing to settle for less.

We had been so taken up with the Indians that the sound of the wagon chains right behind us came as a shock. I turned in the saddle and saw that Mrs. Fernandez had brought up the ambulance. I suppose she didn't consider her boys protection enough; people instinctively looked to Thomas for that. Kirby had his horse up real close to the ambulance, and real close to Marco and Juan. Little Katy stood behind the wagon seat, beneath the tarp cover, but she looked out around Mrs. Fernandez, her eyes as big as brown saucers.

The Indian stared at her, and a smile spread across his face. That took me completely off balance; I had never featured Indians smiling at all. He edged his pony up closer to the ambulance. It shied at the wind-flapping canvas, but he held it with a tight rein. Katy faded back under the cover, where we could see little more than her eyes.

The Indian motioned for her to come back out. I suppose he was trying to tell her he intended her no harm, but Katy was not interested in getting better acquainted. The chief laughed and turned to Thomas. Thomas was trying not to show his uneasiness, but the effort strained him. His hand was on his gun butt. The Indian made some more sign talk. Thomas gradually eased, but he contrived to work his horse around between the Indian and the ambulance.

"Katy," he said, "he wants to trade for you. He says he'll give us six ponies."

In later years Katy would laugh over it, but at that moment she did not laugh. Her fear gave way to a flash of anger.

"You're not going to do it, are you, Papa?"

He said, "Six ponies is a lot."

She leaned out from under the canvas, a long steel pothook gripped in both of her little hands. "I'll hit him on the head!"

The Indian broke into laughter. He turned back to the men behind him, pointed and said something about the girl. I knew he was approving of the fight he saw in her. Several of the Indians laughed, which only deepened Katy's anger. Thomas held out his hand to calm her.

"It's all right, girl. He didn't mean it. Nobody meant it."

The chief turned away from the jesting and back to business. He signaled a few of his men forward. They rode into the herd with him and started picking some of the fleshier cattle. The deal had been ten. I decided Indians didn't count very well, because they took an even dozen. But Thomas didn't count, either. As soon as the Indians were on their way he climbed down from his horse and into the ambulance to hold the girl in his arms.

When it was over, Thomas was shaken more than Katy. Kirby didn't have much to say that night, but he had stood his ground too.

Backing down had been bred out of the Canfield line.

We saw Indians only a couple of times after that, and just once that they actually approached us. Mrs. Fernandez kept the ambulance way back—Thomas had a long parley with her about that. Katy crouched down behind the canvas with the pothook in her hand, out of sight until the Indians had taken a few steers and were gone beyond the hill. I kept watch on Kirby out of the corner of my eye. He stayed by the Fernandez boys, who stuck to the ambulance like burrs. That night Kirby had more to say. He was bolder, now that he had experienced Indians close up for a second time without coming to harm. He talked about what he would have done if the Indians had made any threat. The Fernandez boys pestered and hoorawed him about his bragging until he started hitting Marco. They were friends again, after a while, but Kirby could flare like a match.

We made all the river crossings with a certain nervousness, mostly because of the kids and Mrs. Fernandez. Rainstorms, hail, wind—all these things visited our drive and left us miserable, though they did not strike anywhere near the heart. We reached the railroad tired and thinner than when we had started in Texas, but we had lost no men and relatively few cattle.

The railroad was something new to most of the Texans, though I had seen a few in the war. That first train clanging and banging and smoking up a black cloud awed some of our crew. It came near stampeding the cattle. Both of Mrs. Fernandez's boys had to hold tight to the reins to keep the ambulance team from running away. The wagon team ran a little and bounced off some of the bedrolls.

Ours was one of the early herds. We were considerably ahead of the season's rush, when several herds might hit the shipping pens the same day. Most of our crew was primed to ride into town and paint it a bold shade of red, but Thomas stood tough. Nobody was to leave the herd until it was sold and delivered. I heard some grumbling, but Thomas did not.

Selling the cattle would have been easy except for Thomas. Three or four prospective buyers rode out to the herd where we held it on a flat above town. Each new one raised the bid a little. Thomas waited until he had a bid from every buyer, then told the high bidder he wanted payment in gold. That gentleman turned three shades of crimson and declared that his check was as solid as the U.S. mint. Thomas calmly told him he knew nothing about the mint, but he was familiar with the value of gold. Mr. High Bidder denounced him as an unreconstructed rebel and rode off talking to himself.

Thomas sold the cattle to a man who had bid him a dollar a head less, but he said it was better to lose a dollar than to risk it all to fraud. The buyer was friendly enough, a former Yankee major named Thorne, who had his beard cut in the style of Ulysses S. Grant and wore a black coat even though it was summertime. He chewed a foul black cigar that refused to stay lit. Unlike some other people we ran into in Kansas, he knew the war was over, and he didn't throw it in our faces that we had been on the losing side.

"I'll have to send to Chicago for the gold," he said.

Thomas told him, "We spent three months getting here. We can wait."

The buyer smiled. "I can't blame you for wanting gold. They've thrown out the honest men in Washington and turned the treasury over to blackguards. It would surprise me none at all one day to be able to buy their paper money at ten cents on the dollar."

Some of the men itched for a frolic, but Thomas was as ungiving as an army sergeant. We loose-herded the cattle, watering them a bunch at a time in a natural lake that held water from the spring rains. Not a man in the crew got to drink anything stronger than Mrs. Fernandez's coffee, which she boiled with sugar in it. The enforced sobriety didn't bother me; I had been in the army long enough to work that foolishness out of my system. But some of these younger fellows had never been out of Texas, so even the lamp-lit windows of a little Kansas prairie town looked like Chicago. They thought they had seen the elephant.

They never got a chance to test it. The gold arrived with the same engine that fetched a string of empty cattle cars to haul away the herd. We eased the cattle up to the stockpens and counted off a carload at a time. The engine chuffed and smoked, pulling the cars forward a notch each time we finished loading one and sealing its sliding doors.

I caught the distrust in Thomas' face as the train finally left, smoking slowly eastward up those shining tracks. But the Yankee major was an honest man. I accompanied Thomas inside the bank while the crew waited restlessly outside. Thomas and the major each counted out the gold coins on a table in a small side office while I stood at the door with a nervous deputy marshal who was sweating over his responsibility.

Thomas closed and strapped a pair of new saddlebags he had bought to carry the money. The major said, "I would suggest you lock it in the bank's safe until you are ready to leave town."

The deputy's jaw dropped. But Thomas relieved him of worry. He said, "We guarded the cattle. We'll guard the money." His fingers closed so tightly over the bags that his big knuckles showed dots of white. I saw something in his eyes not unlike the look men sometimes get from drinking too much. It was not the money itself which intoxicated him; it was the thought of the land he could buy with that Union gold. Money was a tool, like a pick or a shovel. *Land* was what counted.

The men still waited outside. Thomas told the major, "I promised the crew a drink when the business was all done. I would be pleased if you would join us."

"It would be my pleasure, if you will allow me to buy a round."

Thomas frowned at the men. "Just one. I need them sober."

The bartender pulled a pair of bottles up from beneath the plain bar as we walked in. He saw the major and put those bottles back, taking better ones from in front of the big mirror behind the bar. He started pouring the glasses full. Thomas stared dubiously at the two Fernandez boys, then held up a finger. "Just one," he told them. The first round was Thomas'. We were sipping the major's round and looking at our trail-beaten images in the long mirror when we heard several horses. In a minute boots were stamping off dust on the little porch. Three dusty, bearded Texans walked through the door. One of them took two steps and stopped.

Thomas pushed away from the bar and dropped the leather saddle-bags to the floor, freeing his hands. He made no move toward his pistol, but he was ready.

I stared a moment before I recognized Branch Isom, but Thomas had known him at a glance. Isom had the wearied look of a long, hard trail, his red-and-gray beard untended, his clothes hanging in ribbons, his boots crusted in dried mud. Resentment rose in his eyes, then he shoved it away.

"Congratulations, Thomas," he said evenly. "You got here ahead of me."

"That was my intention."

"I never regarded it as a contest."

"It has always been a contest between us, Isom."

"It seems so, but I can't remember anymore why it ever started."

"I remember."

The men with Isom were strangers. They appeared as bewildered as the major. Isom told them, "I believe we will be more comfortable elsewhere."

Everybody stood in silence until Isom and his men were gone. The major seemed disconcerted, being drawn into a situation he knew nothing about. In all likelihood he would be called upon to bid on Isom's herd after being made to appear in league with Isom's enemy.

Thomas said, "We have things to do. We'll take leave of this town in a little while."

The major shook Thomas' hand. It was clear he thought leaving was a good idea. The men in the crew, by and large, would not have agreed, but they had not been asked.

As we rode toward camp I moved close to Thomas. I said, "You owe these men a night free in town."

Thomas shook his head. "I owe them wages, nothing else."

He had an effective way of shutting off argument simply by not listening anymore. We brought the wagon up to a mercantile store and loaded it with supplies for the trip home. Thomas had sold the extra horses, leaving us just the ones we rode and a few to meet any happenstance. Thomas would not brook much in the way of happenstance.

We were able to travel only a couple of hours before evening. It seemed to me we could just as well have waited until morning, but we put that many miles between ourselves and the temptations of the town and camped with a crew dissatisfied but sober. I had thought Thomas would ease a little as we headed south, toward home. But he was just as tense carrying the money as he had been driving the cattle.

I said, "If it'll make you feel better, we can set a guard over the camp." The men had been used to night guard on the way up. Thomas shook his head. "I won't sleep much anyway."

I hadn't been asleep long when I was jarred out of it by somebody hollering, out in the night.

"Hello the camp," he called. "I'm coming in."

I threw back my blanket and grabbed first for my pistol, then for my boots, which was all I had taken off.

Thomas shouted, "Who's out there?"

"Major Thorne," came the answer. "Is that you, Canfield?"

"It's me. Come on in." Thomas held a rifle.

The major was alone. The fire had burned down so that it did not throw much light on him, but he was easily recognized by the military set of his shoulders. His voice was urgent. "You had better rouse your camp, Canfield. I am not the only company you are going to have tonight."

There was no handshaking or attempt at pleasantries.

Thomas demanded, "What is the trouble?"

"Word has reached me that a gang of toughs is going to raid you for your gold."

Thomas spat. "Branch Isom!"

"No, not Isom. Some of the riffraff that have been hanging around town to see what they can steal from better men's labor. The whole town knows I paid you in gold."

Thomas was silent a minute, staring at the old ambulance. "This is as good a place as any to defend ourselves. But we have to get those children out of here, and Mrs. Fernandez."

We had crossed a dry wash just before we stopped for the night. We had ridden up onto higher ground to make camp, a standard precaution in country where a quick rain somewhere else could bring a rush of water down on a place that hadn't seen a drop. I suggested we hide the woman and children somewhere in that wash, where no stray bullets would find them.

Thomas agonized over it. "I don't want to be separated from Kirby and Katy."

"They could be killed if they stay here," I told him.

He called the Fernandez boys to him. "I want you-all to take your mother and Kirby and Katy and hide out in the wash yonder. Go far enough to be out of the way."

Katy did not want to leave. Kirby kept his silence. Thomas hugged the girl and handed her to Mrs. Fernandez, saying, "Take her and go, quick." The Mexican woman carried Katy while Kirby walked behind her, looking back at us with regret. The Fernandez boys each carried a rifle.

Thomas turned to the major. "I thank you, sir, for coming to tell us. Now I believe it is time you leave this place."

"I would stay and help."

"You've helped already. You have no stake in this, and there is no need for you to risk your life. I have good men here, all sober."

The major was an honest man with a good heart, but he was not rash. Extending his hand, he said, "Good luck," and rode off, making a wide swing away from the trail to avoid an unpleasant midnight meeting.

I had had military experience, but Thomas did not ask me for advice. He ordered that the horses be moved into a little grove that was like a black patch in the moonlight, a couple of hundred yards away. We tied them there, hoping they would be far enough from gunfire not to hurt themselves surging against the ropes. That done, we pulled back a little way from camp, from the ambulance and the wagon, leaving our bedrolls. Thomas carried the saddlebags over his shoulder. He spread us in a semicircle, covering the camp from the southeast so that no fire would be directed toward the kids.

We were prepared for a long and nervous wait, but they did not give us that much time. Almost as soon as we were positioned, we heard the soft plodding of hoofs to the north. The riders were walking their mounts, trying to make no noise, but a horse is not by his nature the most silent of animals. He rolls his nose, his stomach sloshes of water, and the more contentious will squeal and bite if a strange horse gets too near. For a while we could only hear them, then we began to see them, a vague dark mass moving slowly toward us in the thin moonlight. They drew close together as they spotted the two vehicles, or perhaps the dying light of the campfire. Some of the horses stamped nervously, but the men were evidently talking in whispers.

Suddenly they came spurring, fanning out to hit the camp broad side. Gunfire flashed in the darkness, roaring and ringing in our ears as the riders fired into our blankets, into the wagon. When one of them put three quick shots into the ambulance, Thomas came up from the ground with a curse and began firing his rifle. In a second or two we were all shooting. The surprised raiders shouted and screamed and fired back, but all they had to shoot at was the flashing of our guns. That, in the night, was half blinding, working against our marksmanship as well as theirs. The black powder burned our noses and put us to choking, the way I remembered it from the war. It brought up all the old feelings I had known of fear and hate and exultation, mixed up together and confusing.

Amid the fire and smoke and milling of frightened horses, we could not see much, but neither could they. Two or three men rode over and past us. One of them fell, crying out to God for mercy. The thought struck me that God hadn't sent him on this errand.

As suddenly as they had come, they were gone, the ones still on horseback. As best I could tell, half a dozen rode away. A couple more escaped afoot, limping and carrying themselves hunched over in pain.

None of us left our places at first, each waiting for somebody else to move. The smoke still clung thick and heavy, catching in our throats, burning our eyes. I saw men on the ground where our camp had been. Some moved, some didn't. Three horses were down, kicking and fighting and squealing.

Thomas was the first to move in. He walked warily, hunched over to present less of a target. He stopped to shoot one of the wounded horses, and I thought for a bad moment he was going to shoot a wounded man who lay nearby. The raider pleaded for his life. Thomas picked up a pistol, then poked his way among the other fallen men, kicking weapons from their reach. A couple of the men were beyond using them. Thomas shot the other two horses, putting them out of their pain.

We counted two men dead, another far into his dying. Three more were wounded but not in immediate danger unless Thomas lost his head and shot them. I could see the temptation rising in him.

"You," he seethed to a man sitting on the ground, gripping a bleeding leg, "you fired into the ambulance. If my kids had been in there you'd have killed them!"

"I didn't," the man pleaded, feeling death's cold breath. "I didn't shoot in there. God as my witness."

Thomas couldn't really have told one man from another, dark as it was, the gunflashes blinding us. He just fastened onto that man because he was available and seemed a little less shot up than the others.

Thomas demanded, "Where's Branch Isom?"

The man sobbed, "I don't know no Branch Isom."

"You're a liar!" Thomas shoved the muzzle of his pistol against the bridge of the man's nose. "Branch Isom led you out here."

The man was crying so that he could not answer. Thomas took that for answer enough, but I didn't. I said, "We've got no solid reason to think Branch Isom was behind this. The major told you himself it was a bunch of the town trash."

"It has the smell of Branch Isom," Thomas insisted. "He would have killed my kids!"

I was convinced he was wrong, but it was a waste of time and breath to argue with him. He wanted so badly for it to be Isom that he would ignore any contrary evidence. If I had ever doubted how deeply his hatred had gripped him, I knew it that night.

A voice called from the darkness. "Hello the camp."

Thomas replied, "Come on in, Major."

Major Thorne dismounted. The smell of smoke and blood had his horse dancing in nervousness. The major made no idle comments and asked no empty questions. He could see the wounded and dead for himself. "How many hurt in your party?"

"None seriously," Thomas told him. "We have you to thank for that."

The major said, "I couldn't bring myself to ride far. I saw what was left of them tearing off for town. I knew you'd bloodied them."

Thomas stood beside the ambulance, poking his finger at the bullet holes in the canvas. His anger had not lessened. "If my children had been in there . . ." It seemed to strike him for the first time that the two youngsters and the Fernandez family were still in the wash, probably frantic to know what had happened.

"Reed," he said, "you and the men get up the horses and hitch the teams. We'll leave as soon as I fetch the kids." He started for the wash, trotting hard.

Thomas never had actually asked if any of us were hurt. He had seen everybody, and nobody was down. I did some quick checking and found one of the cowboys had taken a shallow bullet-burn along his hip. It did more damage to his clothes than to his body. We had the teams harnessed and the horses saddled by the time Thomas came back, carrying Katy. Kirby followed. Thomas turned the girl so she would not see the wounded and the dead. He quickly lifted her into the ambulance. Kirby stared at the carnage.

Thomas roared at him, "Boy, you get yourself into that ambulance." Kirby did not move fast enough to suit him, so Thomas grabbed him by one arm and the seat of his britches, hoisting him up.

The major said, "You're going back to town, aren't you? The law will want to know all about this."

Thomas' voice was bitter. "Where was the law tonight? If they want to talk to us they can come to Texas."

"What about these wounded men?" the major asked. "They could die if you just leave them here."

"Then let them die. Good-bye to you, Major." Thomas swung into his saddle and waved his arm. We pulled away from that unlucky camp, leaving three wounded men crying for us to help them. Thomas acted as if he never heard, but I did. I kept hearing them for years.

CHAPTER 7

We traveled fast and hard the first two or three days, pushing until the teams were plainly giving out. Thomas looked back often. I thought at first he was apprehensive over possible pursuit, but that was not it. Toward the end of the first day he told me, "I didn't want to leave that place, Reed. If we hadn't had the children with us I would have ridden back into that town and faced up to Branch Isom and had it out with him for once and for all."

I tried to tell him again that I did not believe Isom had anything to do with the raid on us. He just rode off and left me. He never wasted time on things he did not want to hear.

He was not given much to talk, and he talked even less than usual as we picked our way south the way we had come. We met many trail herds pushing north, but we stayed on the upwind side and visited little. I would catch him rough-counting the cattle and mumbling to himself as he figured up how much money they might bring at the railroad. It was unlikely many would receive as much per head as ours; the market would go down as the season went on and the numbers increased. The fact that we reached the market ahead of him probably cost Branch Isom a dollar or two per head.

We were bone-weary as we moved into the familiar rolling country that meant home was just ahead of us. The sight of those South Texas prairies and occasional tangles of thorny chaparral was as welcome as a mother's face. We skirted around New Silesia. Thomas did not offer to explain, but I supposed he did not want Maria's folks to see the kids so trail-gritty and tired. He would clean them up and feed them up, *then* show them to their grandparents.

We came in sight of the homeplace, the houses, the barns, the corrals and fields. I sighed in relief. "I don't think I will ever leave again. This is one trip I never want to repeat."

"You will," Thomas said matter-of-factly. "There is money to be made taking cattle to the railroad, money to be invested in land. You'll make the trip again, and so will I."

I could think of a dozen arguments. The best one was in the ambulance, tailing up the outfit. "But the kids . . ."

"I made a mistake, taking them. I realized it the day Kirby nearly drowned. It was too late then. I'll rectify that mistake now."

He did not explain himself, and I did not ask him.

I never could understand how news could carry so fast. The morning after we reached home, Laura Hines arrived in a buggy, pulling right up to the big house. Katy shouted and ran down the steps. The woman and the little girl embraced one another and cried. Thomas and I watched from the barn, then walked up to the house. Kirby stood on the porch, looking at Laura but not running to her as his sister had done. Laura had to go up the steps to him. She tried to hold him, but he struggled away.

Thomas stopped at the gate and studied the woman with his children. I could not be so calm. I still thought Laura Hines was the finest-looking woman I had ever seen. I wanted to take hold of her but could not bring myself to do it. I shoved my hand forward. She hugged me. I melted to a mixture of delight and despair.

"It's good to have you back, Reed." She looked past me toward Thomas. "All of you. I haven't had a night's sleep the whole time, worrying about these children." She stepped back from me and put her hands lovingly on Katy's shoulders. "I'll bet you have a lot of stories to tell me."

Katy said, "An Indian wanted to buy me, but Papa wanted too many ponies."

Laura looked reproachfully at me. "You took these children where there were Indians?"

Kirby could not let Katy's story go unchallenged.

"Aw, it was just a big joke. Those Indians were scared of us."

Laura turned toward Thomas, watching him as he slowly came up onto the porch. The reproach drained swiftly from her eyes.

"Welcome home, Thomas."

"Hello, Laura. I'm glad you came out. I was going to send for you."

They did not hug; they did not even shake hands. They just looked at one another. Thomas reached for the screen door and held it open. "Come in, Laura. We have things to talk about."

He closed the door behind them, leaving me with the two youngsters on the porch. Katy went inside, but I heard Thomas say something to her, and she came out again, disappointed.

I said, "You-all haven't seen the colts. You'll be surprised how much they've grown while we were away." They followed me to the barn, and I kept them busy.

After a long time Laura came out looking for us. Her face was flushed. She was trying to hold down excitement. "Children, your father wants you at the house."

Kirby was brushing one of the colts and did not want to leave. He paid no attention to Laura. I told him sternly, "You go up yonder and see what your daddy wants." Katy had not waited; she had gone on ahead.

Laura stayed, trembling a little. I could not tell whether she wanted to laugh or cry, but she was holding back one or the other. She blurted, "He asked me to marry him."

I felt as if I had been kicked in the stomach. I knew upon reflection that this should not have come as any surprise. Badly as I wanted her myself, she had never had eyes for any man except Thomas Canfield.

I asked a foolish question. "What did you tell him?"

"I told him I would."

It took me a while to work up the nerve to ask the next question. "Do you think he loves you?"

Tears edged into her eyes. "He was honest with me, Reed. He likes me. He respects me. But the only woman he ever loved lies on that hill yonder." She pointed her chin toward the family cemetery.

"Then why . . ." I started.

She cut me off. "He needs a mother for those children. The trail drive was a nightmare because of them. He wants to know they'll always be here safe, with somebody who cares for them."

"Katy cares for you, too. But I don't know about Kirby."

"I'll have to manage with Kirby. He'll learn. We'll both learn."

I was suddenly angry at Thomas, angry because it seemed to me he was buying Laura much the way he would buy cattle or horses or a block of land. "So Thomas gets a mother for his children. What do you get out of this?"

"A home. *His* home. I'll be near him from now on."

"Near him, but not really *with* him. Will that be enough for you?"

"It's more than I've had."

I slapped the palm of my hand against a post so hard that it hurt. "You can't be happy with half a marriage."

"Happier than I've been with none at all."

Over the years I had learned to tell from Thomas' eyes when an argument was over. I saw that look in Laura's. I took her hand and said, "I've never said anything to you, but I think you know how I've always felt."

"I know. Sometimes I've wished it could be otherwise for me, but it never will."

"Then, be happy, Laura."

"I will," she said. She kissed me and returned to the house.

The wedding was quiet, almost as if Thomas did not care to have it noticed. As usual he did not explain himself. Laura told me he felt that a show was inappropriate because it had not been so long since Maria had died. She did not have to tell me the rest, the fact that this was a marriage of convenience on his part, almost a business arrangement, done for the children rather than for himself. One did not throw a public celebration over the buying of property.

A handful of us, close friends all, watched the ceremony in the parlor of the house Thomas had built for Maria. He was solemn, almost regretful. Laura glowed. Kirby, young though he was, saw through it about as well as any of us. After the vows had been spoken he walked onto the porch by himself and stared darkly up the hill toward the cemetery. Katy went out after a minute. I followed them because I felt like a hypocrite, joining the other people in telling Thomas and Laura how fine a match they were, how everybody knew they would both be very happy.

Katy was puzzled by her brother's coldness. "Aren't you glad we've got a new mother?"

He turned on her in a flash of anger. "We don't have a new mother. She's just going to watch after us, is all. Mrs. Fernandez could have done that."

He walked out to the barn and proceeded to soil his new suit chunking rocks at the milkpen calves.

Looking back, it is hard to pinpoint just when Kirby started going wrong. At times I remember the river crossing on the drive to Kansas, but the seed may have been planted earlier. It might even have been there from birth, an inheritance of the wild anger which sometimes cropped out in Thomas. I was gone a lot of the time and did not fully realize the extent of Kirby's rebellion until later.

After the wedding I made up my mind I did not want to live at the headquarters anymore, so near Laura. Of course I could not give Thomas my real reason, so I told him I had decided it was time to put up a house on my own land and see after my own interests. If he saw through me he gave no indication of it. He said, "I have been making some plans, Reed, and I was counting on you to help me with them. We can make money supplying cattle to the railroad market."

"I don't want to go back up that trail, not this soon."

"You won't have to. I can hire other people to do that. I want you to travel around the country buying cattle for me and shaping up herds for the trail. You have a knack for that kind of thing. You have an easy way of dealing with people, something I never learned."

I couldn't deny that. Thomas had just one way of dealing with people, on his own terms. If they didn't like those terms, there was no compromise, no deal.

When I still hesitated, he said, "You'll be my full partner in the operation. Whatever we make, half of it is yours. You can buy a lot of land."

I found that I enjoyed traveling. Over the next several weeks I saw a great deal of South Texas, visited a lot of ranches and became acquainted with a large number of people. It was my observation then, and still is, that as a class the people who make their living directly off of the land are among the most honest there are, probably because the land itself does not compromise or accept excuses. A person can lie to his fellow man and even to himself, but he cannot lie to or cheat the land. If he does not irrigate her with the proper amount of sweat, she will not produce for him. She will not be short-changed.

We put together three more herds in time to go up the trail that season, using the money received for the first herd at the railroad. Not many people in South Texas had any clear idea what cattle were worth up north, so prices hadn't increased much. They were glad to get rid of some surplus and lay their hands on real Yankee gold. Most trades in the outlying parts of the state were still by barter, and these people had little to barter other than cattle. They would gladly trade several steers for a barrel of flour or a sack of coffee beans. Poverty lay like a curse across the land in those first years after the war. Nobody had much, and a lot of people had nothing.

Once I unexpectedly met head-on with Branch Isom at a salt-grass ranch not far from the steamy Gulf of Mexico. Usually I was ahead of him, offering better prices and getting the better cattle. He wound up having to take a lot of the aged steers and the staggy kinds castrated too late in their lives. These too would fetch a price at the railroad, but not like the three- and four-year-old steers that could gain weight on a slow drive and arrive at the railroad in flesh enough for slaughter.

Isom and I sort of circled each other, wary as town dogs encountering a stranger. We shook hands and then stood apart, awkward and both wishing we were somewhere else. He said, "You've been busy, Reed Sawyer. Most places I go, you've been there and left."

"I don't plan it that way," I said.

He half smiled. "It would please Thomas Canfield if you did."

I didn't try to deny that. Isom frowned. "I heard he was blaming me for that robbery attempt up in Kansas. I want you to know, Reed, I had nothing to do with that."

"I never thought you did."

"But *he's* convinced I did, so the hell with him. He's a little bit crazy, I think."

I had never considered Thomas in quite so extreme a light. I changed the subject. "How's your family?"

"Fine, just fine. Got my boy with me out in the buckboard. Bet you haven't seen him in a long time. Come on out and let him say howdy to you."

I really wasn't wanting all that much familiarity, but I couldn't with any kind of courtesy turn him down. I followed Isom to his buckboard in the shade of a big moss-hung liveoak tree. "James," he said to the boy, "I want you to shake hands with Mister Sawyer."

The boy was about Kirby's age, probably already taking some schooling. He had a bright, eager look about him, like a boy who would learn well because he wanted to. He looked me in the eye when he shook my hand; most youngsters won't do that without coaching. Kirby wouldn't; he never had. I glanced at Branch Isom and saw the strong pride in his round, reddish face. Whatever he might have been once, he was a father now. He did not have to tell me he was wrapped up in that boy; it showed all over him.

Isom said to his son, "Mister Sawyer has beaten us here, James. I expect we'll have to go somewhere else."

I could see partisanship rise in the boy's eyes. I could not help thinking of Kirby, if he and Thomas had been in the same situation. Kirby probably wouldn't have given a damn.

I found myself asking, "Son, you really want these cattle here?"

The boy said firmly, "My daddy does."

I said, "Then your daddy will get the chance to make the first bid on them." Later, when Isom made that bid, I didn't raise it. I rode away from there wondering what Thomas would say if he ever heard what I had done. I wasn't going to tell him. It would have been worth going through the storm, though, just for the pleased look I saw on that boy's face when his father got the cattle he wanted.

Thomas was always a man to keep his promises, but occasionally things worked out so that he could not. He was unable to find anybody he thought was suitable to boss that third and last set of cattle up the trail. I had to do it myself. The snow was starting to fly a little by the time I sold the cattle at the tail end of the season's market and turned south, carrying Thomas' saddlebags heavy with gold coin. The raw north wind helped hasten my trip home, that and the memory of the robbery attempt the spring before.

I never told Thomas that Branch Isom and I pooled our trail outfits and rode back to South Texas together for mutual protection. Because some of the Canfield crew as well as his came from Stonehill, I remained with him until I watched his arrival at home, his little boy James running out onto the porch, then down the tall steps and into the yard to throw his arms around his father. Isom carried the boy up onto the porch where his wife waited, and Isom hugged both of them.

He had not made nearly so much money out of the trail season as Thomas and I had, but it seemed to me he was rich in one respect that neither Thomas nor I would ever be.

I turned loose the last of the crew and rode to the ranch alone, reining up in front of the big house a while before dark. I tied my horse to the fence, unstrapped the heavy saddlebags and walked wearily up the steps, thinking surely someone must have seen me.

Katy had. She flung open the door and shouted, "Uncle Reed." I received, in a distant-relative sort of way, the kind of greeting Branch Isom had gotten in town. Laura came into the hallway at the sound of Katy's shout. To a tired and lonely man she looked beautiful. I wanted to crush her, but I reached out my hand and took off my dusty old hat.

She shook my hand. "It's good to have you back, Reed."

Kirby appeared at the end of the hall. He stared at me with no more emotion than if I had been some stranger come to sell his father a load of hay.

"Where's Thomas?" I asked her.

Sadness showed in her eyes before she covered it. "Mister Canfield is off looking at some land west of here. He had no clear idea when you'd be back."

Mister Canfield. "He's gone a lot, I suppose."

"He works awfully hard."

I slid the saddlebags from my shoulder. "I'd best put this in the safe." Thomas had bought one in San Antonio after the first trip. It was in the parlor, where some people would have placed a piano.

Laura watched me close the safe and give the knob a turn. "You must be starved."

I told her I would eat at the bunkhouse. We had a full-time Mexican cook there now for the growing number of cowhands. Mrs. Fernandez had been relieved of all responsibilities other than the care and feeding of her sons Marco and Juan. But Laura would not hear of my going. She insisted I needed and deserved a good woman-cooked meal, served on a table with real dishes instead of tinware. After all that time on the trail I could put up no good argument.

By this time I had the use of the old double log cabin where Thomas' mother had lived so long. I cleaned up and put on some fresh clothes and made my way back to the big house with mixed feelings. Being that close to Laura was both pleasure and pain.

Katy was helping Laura in the kitchen, happily fetching and carrying. There had always been this free and happy and loving relationship between them. I did not see the boy. In a bit the table was set and ready. Laura stepped into the hall and called for Kirby. He did not come. Katy kept her head down when Laura asked her if she knew where her brother was. Reluctantly the girl said, "He went to the barn."

"I told him not to. He knew supper was almost ready."

Katy flushed a little, clearly wanting to defend her brother but knowing he was in the wrong. I said, "I'll fetch him."

I found him sitting on a mesquite-rail fence, studying a mare and a newly-born colt. I said, "Your supper's ready."

He ignored me. I said, "Come on, son, before you get yourself in trouble. Your mother wants you."

He turned on me angrily. "She's not my mother. I don't have to do what she says."

Never having raised any kids of my own I didn't know how to answer that. I had a strong inclination to exercise my hand about six inches below the back of his belt. I just reached up and plucked him from the fence, took his hand and led him to the house. He pulled back on me all the way. He ate his supper in grim silence, pushed his chair away from the table and stomped off to his room. I tried not to look at Laura.

Katy said, "I'll tell Papa. He'll spank him."

Laura shook her head. "Don't tattle. We'll have to find a way to handle Kirby ourselves, you and I."

I asked her as gently as I could, "This happen much?"

She only nodded. I asked, "Does Thomas know?"

She nodded again. "He's done all he knows to do."

I thought I knew something but tried to keep the idea from showing. I guess she read my mind. She smiled uneasily. "He's tried that. He's tried love too. I guess the only thing that will work is time."

She was wrong about that. Time made him worse. He soon hit that period when he was growing rapidly, and all of it away from Laura and Thomas. By then Thomas had twenty-five or thirty cowhands scattered over the place, ranging from devout Christians to devout hellions. Kirby seemed, when he had the choice, to tag after the hellions.

When he was eight I caught him smoking tobacco swiped from somebody in the bunkhouse. When he was ten I found him slumped against a corral post in a stupor, an empty whiskey bottle on the ground. I never told Laura or Thomas; they had enough worries.

I didn't enter the big house oftener than was necessary anymore. Remembering the warmth and happiness there in Maria's time, I found the place cool. From the beginning, Thomas had formed the habit of addressing Laura as Mrs. Canfield, and he was Mr. Canfield to her. The relationship was one of formality and respect on his part. On hers there was always a holding back, a love suppressed out of fear that it would be rebuffed. Only with Katy did Laura let herself go. She lavished on the girl all the affection she wanted to give her husband and stepson.

Had she lived, Maria could hardly have been much closer to that flashing-eyed child.

That seemed only to widen the distance between Kirby and the rest of the family.

Katy was always eager to visit her grandparents in New Silesia, and Laura seemed happy to take her. Whatever reservations the old folks might have had about seeing their daughter's place in the house taken by someone else, they accepted Laura as a friend. The difference in language was always a problem, but Katy acted as interpreter; she spent enough time in New Silesia that she spoke Polish as well as she did English.

Kirby was another matter. He seemed always to have something he had rather do than visit his grandparents. At first I thought it might be simply that he did not want to ride in the buggy with his sister and stepmother, that he thought it unmanly. I offered to take him there myself. I had just as well suggest that he shovel out the corrals.

"They're just dumb old potato-eaters," he declared. "I don't want to see them."

If he had been mine I would have struck him across the mouth. Kirby glared, daring me. I might have done it had I not heard Thomas behind me, cold as December. He had been in the barn. He had a look in his eyes that usually meant blood to somebody. "Reed," he said very quietly, "I want to have some words with my son."

Badly as Kirby needed correction, I dreaded what that look bespoke.

"Thomas," I argued, "he doesn't know what he's saying. He's been listening to foolish talk from men who ought to be fired off of this place."

There had been more and more of those lately, men who laughed at the Polanders and condemned the Mexicans.

Thomas' voice took on an extra barb. "Go somewhere, Reed."

I went somewhere, but not so far that I didn't hear the crackle of heavy leather striking against cotton britches. Kirby did not cry.

His feeling against his grandparents seemed only to deepen; it was as if he blamed them for his punishment.

When he was about fourteen Kirby started running with the Hall-comb boys. Their father was a muleskinner by trade and had been fired by just about every freighting outfit from San Antonio to the Gulf. During one of his periods between jobs he was in the Alamo city help-ing create a boom in the saloon business when a prominent merchant was pistol-whipped one dark evening and the receipts of a busy Satur-day removed from his safe. The crime was never solved. Some people thought it strange that old Goodson Hallcomb showed up back in Stonehill soon afterward with enough money to buy a little stock farm. In those days you didn't throw accusations around unless you had the facts. Nowadays they'll sue you for slander. Back then they were more likely to come looking for you with a pistol.

Hallcomb was good at raising and training draft stock for the same freight outfits that had fired him, and the San Antonio merchant soon made back all he had lost in the robbery, so most people abided by the old adage and let a sleeping dog lie. They wished he did as well at rais-ing his boys as at raising and training mules, though. They were a salty pair, Bo about a year older than Kirby and Speck two years older. They were freckle-faced, tobacco-chewing, knot-fisted and knot-headed. Besides mules, old Goodson raised a crop of corn every year, part to feed and part to drink. Growing up, those boys of his put away more of the old man's corn whiskey than of milk.

Thomas warned Kirby to stay away from that unholy clan, which made him turn to them all the more. At first it was mostly harmless things like riding the old man's wild mules. That led to drunken sprees in which they turned over farm outhouses and let pigs out of their pens into people's gardens and bobbed off the tails of some choice buggy teams.

Thomas was inclined to severe lectures and now and then a strong application of razor strop while Kirby leaned over the washstand by the back porch of the big house. It was always a case of punishment but never of correction. In no time Kirby would be back with the Hall-comb boys, dreaming up some new form of devilment for the commu-nity.

One Sunday Kirby and the Hallcombs, well supplied with the old man's corn, rode into New Silesia and fired at the church bell while mass was in progress. Then they tried to ride their horses into the church itself, to the shame of Kirby's old grandparents. Katy happened to be with the Brozeks. She pulled her brother out of the saddle, no hard chore in view of his condition. She then pounded him over the head with her grandmother's old-country Bible, which weighed almost too much for Mrs. Brozek to carry.

Kirby was shamed more by his sister's publicly administered retribution than by the words of the priest, who led him outside and reviewed the sacraments to him, placing particular stress on those sections that had to do with sin, punishment and hellfire. The Hallcomb boys, who had never received instruction in any of these subjects, stayed on the other side of the dusty street, grinning.

Thomas was outraged when the news came home to him. He nailed Kirby against the wall with his eyes. "Those are your mother's people," he said. "She would be mortified to know what you've done."

Kirby defiantly shook his head, denying any contrition. "They're not *my* people. I wouldn't claim them if she was *here*."

Thomas slapped him across the mouth, drawing blood. But he was too late. Much too late.

Afterward Thomas sat with me on the front steps, staring sadly toward the family cemetery. "I gave him a bad name, Reed."

"No, Thomas," I said. "Kirby's a good name."

"He's wild, like the other Kirby was."

Wild yes, but there the similarity ended, I thought. The first Kirby had never hurt anyone except himself. The second Kirby hurt everybody around him. I didn't see that my saying so would do anybody any good, so I kept the feeling to myself.

Thomas made up his mind to put Kirby's excess energies to use. He sent him to Kansas with two thousand head of cattle and a toughminded trail boss who had the disposition of an old wildcat with one foot in a trap. The boss brooked no foolishness. He made no distinction between the owner's son and the poorest Mexican cowhand in the crowd. When Kirby came home three months later he was lean, tanned and sober. He bore a small scar high on his cheek to remind him of the folly of challenging authority that was a head taller and forty pounds heavier.

For a while he applied himself to business and the school Thomas helped finance for youngsters in that part of the county. Any sign of backsliding could be stopped by reference to the possibility of another trip with that hard-driving trail boss.

Katy had been a little chubby as a small girl, but around twelve or thirteen she started growing up instead of out, taking on some of the look of her mother. She had those same wide brown eyes, a shy, sideways smile that often made me remember early trips I had made with Thomas to New Silesia. She must have made Thomas remember, too, for sometimes I caught him watching her with a sadness that put a chill on me. He had never completely buried Maria. Her ghost walked his house and lay with him in that big wooden bed.

From things Laura occasionally told me, and more she did not, I knew she did not share Thomas' bed. I knew they seldom talked to each other anymore, not about the things that really mattered. They spoke of the weather and the crops and the cattle, and of news in the San Antonio paper. That was enough to carry them through the meals. Afterward, each had a place in the house apart from the other, a retreat from the responsibility of conversation.

As Katy grew older, Thomas became increasingly uncomfortable around her. He appeared confused, uncertain, and he kept a relationship almost as formal as his with Laura. When Katy was fourteen Thomas sent her to San Antonio to boarding school, over Laura's protests. Laura went with her to see her settled and secure and was a month in coming home. That seemed to suit Thomas all right; in seeing after Katy she was performing the duties he had married her for.

Thomas seldom felt obliged to explain anything, but one night as we ate supper in the bunkhouse—Laura was still gone—he said to me, "Katy's by way of growing up. She'll be a woman before we know it. We have too many young men around this place who have no attachments and no responsibility. She needs to be gotten to a better climate."

I could not argue with him about that. Even at fourteen she had begun to distract some of the young hands from their work. I never did tell Thomas about the boy who kissed her and then tried to take her behind the barn. I would have thrashed him, but that seemed unnecessary after Katy had blacked both of his eyes and split his lip. I just fired him and told him to leave before Thomas somehow found out.

By the time she was sixteen, there was no telling what the situation might be.

Somehow, neither of us considered that there were boys in San Antonio too. Not that Katy was one to let her head be turned, but you don't solve a problem just by moving it out of your sight. When she came home to spend that first summer she seemed to get an awful lot of mail and spend much time with a pen in her hand, answering it.

She was near sixteen when she came home for the second summer. Thomas was away on a land trip, for which I became thankful at the time. Laura had planned to take the buggy to San Antonio and fetch her, but all of a sudden and unannounced Katy showed up in front of the house in a buggy driven by a boy, or rather, a young man. He climbed down quickly and raised his hands to help her to the ground. Laura appeared on the porch, recognized Katy and hurried to the front gate with a smile I could see all the way from the corrals. The smile left her as she looked at the young man.

It was good to have the girl back on the place. I walked up from the corrals and hugged her like the uncle I was supposed to be. Katy pulled back and nodded toward the boy.

"Uncle Reed, I have somebody here I want you to meet."

The young man said, "We've met, Mister Sawyer, a long time ago. I'm James Isom."

I've knocked down many a slaughter steer with the back side of an ax, and I felt as if somebody had just done that to me. An Isom here, on *this* place . . . It hadn't happened since the time Branch Isom had come out to try to buy some cattle from Thomas.

I shook the boy's hand and tried to remember how he had looked long ago when I had let his father have the cattle I had intended to buy. Now that I knew who he was, I could see he still had the same general features, the same big eyes that didn't look as if they ever had anything to hide. "It's good to see you again, son," I lied, thinking how fortunate it was that Thomas had gone somewhere.

Katy said, "James is going to school in San Antonio too, Uncle Reed. His mother and father went up to get him, and they offered to bring me home."

I could hardly believe what I heard. "You've been to Stonehill?" Her father had not set foot in that town since before she was born, except for a funeral. He had forbidden his children ever to go there. Kirby had violated that order for years, but I had never featured Katy doing it. I glanced at Laura but saw no surprise. I suspected she had known the Isoms were sending their boy to school in San Antonio. I also knew that if she had ever told Thomas, he would have moved Katy to Galveston, or maybe as far away as St. Louis or Kansas City.

Good manners meant I had to say something. All I could do was ask him how his folks were. "Fine," he said. "Just fine." I already knew that. Branch Isom had given up the cattle trade, mainly because of competition from Thomas and me, and had concentrated on business in Stonehill and on his freighting trade, which still thrived. So long as the freight line stayed busy he would prosper, and he didn't have to do anything illegal. So would Stonehill, for it lived from the commerce that passed through it going to and from the Gulf and the interior of Texas.

Katy said, "James, I hope you'll stay for supper."

Laura became very flustered. I pointed out how far it was back to town. Even if he left now, James would have to make part of the trip in the dark. I guess he understood the situation better than Katy, because he agreed that he could not stay.

"I'll see you when school starts again," he told Katy.

She looked disappointed. "That's a long time."

"Not when you stay busy. I'll be helping my dad with the business all summer. We'll see each other again before you know it."

Katy watched him ride away on the old town road we didn't use much. "He's a nice boy," she told Laura.

Laura put her arm around the girl's shoulder. "Come on into the house. We have a lot to talk about before your father comes home."

I was at the barn when Thomas rode in just at good dark, looking weary. I could have unsaddled his horse for him, but that was something a man did for himself. Worriedly he asked, "Have you seen Kirby?"

"Yes, I sent him down to the south camp to help brand out those calves."

"Good. I was afraid he might be off someplace with those Hallcomb boys, hunting for trouble."

I told him, "Katy came in a while ago."

Some of the weariness seemed to slide off of him. He smiled. "It sure is nice to have *one* child I don't have to worry about."

CHAPTER 8

The railroad rumors had risen periodically ever since the war, about as regularly as the big crops of grasshoppers that plagued us now and again. They always seemed reasonable enough. Somebody, someday, was bound to decide there was a profit to be made hauling goods from the coast by rail instead of by trail. I figured this fear must sometimes have awakened Branch Isom in the middle of a long night. Now the rumors started again, but this time there was a difference. A surveying party moved through the country. They made no secret of the fact that the newly-organized Gulf Coast and San Antonio Railroad planned to build along the general route of the old cart and wagon trails.

I expected Thomas to be pleased, but as usual he was looking farther ahead than I did. That was why I was still a little landowner and he was a big one. He said, "Sure, it'll be the end of Isom's mainline freight outfit, but they'll still need smaller lines to serve towns away from the rails. And a railroad will mean more prosperity for Stonehill than the freight trails did. Isom can throw the freight line away and still be richer than he ever was. He owns half of that wretched, damnable town." His face clouded over, and I was sorry I had brought up the subject.

There was a lot I didn't know about railroads. I guess I was like the fellow who buys crackers out of a barrel and figures they just grew that way. I had assumed somebody with a lot of money just came along and built the line. The people in Stonehill must have thought as I did. It came as a shock to them when the builder of the road arrived one day and asked for a sixty-thousand-dollar bonus to put his tracks through town. Their first inclination was to treat him to tar and feathers. As I heard it later, Branch Isom had a better grip on reality and advised that they study the proposition. Lamps burned far into the night at the big Isom house. Sixty thousand dollars was not a sum you snapped your fingers and called up easily, not in those days.

Our interest in the matter was only one of curiosity, because the route the surveyors had marked lay a couple of miles south of Thomas' land at the nearest point and a good dozen from mine. Thomas paid no attention to it. He predicted that the deal would blow apart anyway, and the railroad would never be built. Some sharp Yankee lawyer would get away with a lot of money and never be heard of again; it had happened before.

But one day while Thomas and I were at the corrals watching one of the Fernandez boys—men now, really—sack out a new bronc, a nice black carriage drew up to the big house. It had a Negro driver. A portly gentleman climbed down from the back seat and dusted himself. He looked up at the many front steps with dread.

Thomas called to him and saved him the climb. I followed along with Thomas. I had no real business there, but I gave in to curiosity, my biggest vice. We seldom saw such a rig at the ranch. It, and the gentleman who had arrived in it, reeked of money and importance.

I am sure the gray-bearded man sensed who Thomas was but he went through the polite motions. "I have come to see Mister Thomas Canfield?" He put it like a question.

Thomas introduced himself. The gentleman wasted no time with me; he could probably tell at a glance that I had about as much authority over major business decisions as one of Laura's white chickens scratching about the yard. "I am Jefferson P. Ashcroft, sir, vice-president of the GC and SA Railroad."

I had known right off that he had not come to sell hay and that he was no horse trader. Well, maybe he was, but of a higher order than those of my previous acquaintance.

"I have come on a matter of urgent business, Mister Canfield," he said, fanning himself with his felt hat. Thomas led him to a bench Laura had placed beneath a big tree in the front yard. The man looked too tired to climb those front steps right now. He said, "You have perhaps heard of the impasse we have reached in our negotiations with the businessmen of Stonehill? We have asked what we feel is a reasonable bonus for placing a terminal in their city. They have not seen fit to meet our offer."

Thomas shrugged. "Stonehill's affairs are of no interest to me, Mr. Ashcroft. I have no interest in whether that town gets a railroad or not. For that matter, I do not care whether your railroad is ever built or not."

Ashcroft frowned. "I am given to understand that you are the largest landholder in this region. You ship thousands upon thousands of cattle each year."

"Drive, not ship. I have them driven."

"But sooner or later they are put upon a train. How much more beneficial would it be to you, sir, if you were able to ship them from right here on your property?"

"To where? Your railroad will go nowhere except to San Antonio and to the coast. My cattle go to Chicago and points east."

"Our railroad will someday connect with others."

"Someday! Someday I will be dead."

Ashcroft was a horse trader, all right. He recognized when he had a lame horse on his hands. "I shall lay my cards on the table, sir. As our route is surveyed it will cost us several miles of extra track to pass through Stonehill. We could cut our cost by building across your land."

There was not a trace of "give" in Thomas' eyes. "I am sure you could. And I suppose you would want me to pay you for the privilege."

Ashcroft seemed surprised at the thought. "No sir. We would buy your right-of-way at a fair price."

Thomas did not study the proposition long. "I buy land. I do not sell it. I would be happy to have you stay for supper, Mister Ashcroft, but our business talk has come to an end."

Ashcroft was inclined to argue the point, but that look came into Thomas' eyes, the one that always turned away argument.

Laura came onto the porch as Ashcroft's carriage rounded the barn. "Mister Canfield, wasn't your company staying for supper?"

Thomas shook his head. "No, Mrs. Canfield. His digestion seems poorly."

I have always sort of blamed the Hallcomb boys for what happened to Kirby, though I know the fault was not theirs alone. Kirby rode right into it himself. And I know you could blame Thomas, for not knowing how to give him a more righteous upbringing. I even blame myself, remembering the times I should have put him over my knee instead of leaving that for Thomas when I knew he would not do it either, unless sorely provoked. A strong rod can sometimes help a tree grow straight and tall. Kirby bent with the wind.

It started, in a way, when the sheriff threw Speck Hallcomb in jail for beating up a San Antonio teamster he outweighed by thirty pounds. This put Speck in a mood for retaliation, a task for which he would need help. Kirby had not been running with the Hallcomb boys for a while; they had gotten along well enough without him. But Speck could not get out of jail, and Bo became tired of hunting up deviltry by himself, so he came out to the ranch and fetched Kirby when he knew Thomas was away from home. When Thomas returned, Kirby had been on a double-rectified drunk with Bo Hallcomb in Stonehill for three days. He was nineteen then, going on twenty, and tall for his age. Buying whiskey was easy for him so long as he had the money. Thomas would not go to Stonehill himself to bring Kirby home; he sent the Fernandez brothers.

They brought Kirby home grimly, all three looking somewhat the worse for wear. The brothers would not talk about it, but I found out later that Kirby had fought them, saying some sorry things about their being nothing but a couple of dirty Mexicans who could not tell him what to do. Those were things they would not have heard from him had he been sober, for Marco and Juan had taught him most of what he knew about horse and cow work and most of the decent things he knew about life in general. But the things a man says when drunk are often those which have been on his mind when he was sober. The brothers did not have much to do with Kirby after that.

Thomas put Kirby to the dirtiest, meanest work he could find around the ranch. As usual, the reformation was shallow and short. Speck Hallcomb got out of jail in due time, nursing his grudges. He and Bo sneaked out to the south camp and took Kirby away with them. He did not need persuasion, just an opportunity.

The first any of us knew about it, the priest came hurrying down from the church in New Silesia, the buggy team lathered, his face furrowed with trouble. Thomas was gone, as usual. Laura sent for me. I knew when I looked at her and at the priest that something was badly wrong. Kirby and the Hallcomb boys had ridden into New Silesia roaring drunk and had shot up the place, running all the "potato-eaters" off of the street.

It was a merciful thing that both of the old Brozeks had gone to their reward and did not have to suffer through another humiliation at their grandson's hands, the priest lamented.

Laura cried softly. She looked older than she really was; part of it was Thomas, but a lot of it, I knew, was Kirby. "Reed, maybe you can talk to him. Please, bring him home," she said.

It had been a long time since Kirby had talked much to me, and longer since he had listened to me. I had to call on all the persuasive powers I had to convince Marco and Juan that they should go with me. They had not forgotten the last time, and probably they never would. I managed to convey to them my concern that Kirby might require stronger persuasion than I was physically able to give.

We arrived in New Silesia too late. Kirby and the Hallcombs had moved on to richer game, to Stonehill, where Speck still had a score he wanted to mark off. New Silesia normally was a quiet little place where you still heard more Polish spoken on the streets than English. The only local law was a little constable whose most strenuous normal duty was chasing schoolboys home at dark to study their books. Kirby and the Hallcombs had buffaloed him the first ten minutes they were in town; he had not come back outside again until they left.

He spent a minute or two telling me what he would do if they ever came back, then said darkly, "Stonehill is not New Silesia. They will kill somebody there, or be killed."

I did not want to take him all that seriously, but I got a cold feeling in my stomach. I glanced at Marco and Juan. Their eyes told me they had it too. We set our horses into a long trot for Stonehill. For the animals' sake I tried to hold the pace to that, but in a while I was loping, and the brothers were close beside me.

The New Silesia–Stonehill road led by the Goodson Hallcomb farm. As we passed it, Speck and Bo Hallcomb came riding out. I hailed them. They glanced at us but kept riding. I had to spur a tired horse to catch up to them. I rode past and turned around to face them before they would stop. They were cold sober, both of them, and scared.

"Where's Kirby?" I demanded. Neither would look at me. I asked them again. The Fernandez brothers pushed in behind them, adding to the pressure.

Speck still would not look at me, but he said, "It was Kirby done it, not us. We didn't figure on anything going that far."

I grabbed the front of his shirt and shook him. "Did what?"

"He shot and killed the sheriff. We tried to stop him, but he went and done it anyway. Now you got to let us go, Mister Sawyer. Them people'll be coming after us."

"What people?"

"The whole town, I expect. We turned and lit out when we seen the sheriff go down. Seemed like the whole town was shooting at Kirby, and at us too."

"You went off and left him there by himself?"

"Them was awful mad people."

I put spurs to my horse, cursing and praying at the same time. I could hear the Fernandez brothers pushing to stay close behind me. We were still in a lope as we hit the edge of town. I reined up to look for a minute. The chill came back, for the place was quiet, much too quiet. Not a wagon was rolling. I saw a few horsemen milling around, and people standing in clusters. Whatever had happened was over and done. I could not bring myself to look at the brothers, but I knew they must share the cold dread that came over me like a winter fog. We walked our hard-breathing horses down the street. The people turned to stare, and I felt anger and hostility rising against us. Everybody knew who we were.

A familiar figure walked out into the street and stood waiting. Branch Isom had put on weight the last few years. He was not exactly portly, but prosperity had made him comfortable and soft, a far cry from the muscular, driving man I remembered from my first acquaintance with him in old Indianola town. I noted that he was not armed, though nearly everyone else on the street was.

We stopped our horses a few feet from him. He seemed to be looking beyond us. "Is Thomas Canfield on his way?" he asked.

I sensed right off that the town was braced for invasion. They took us for the vanguard. I hoped they could see we were not carrying guns. "We haven't seen him," I said. "Where's Kirby?"

Isom did not answer me directly. "You know what he did? He killed the sheriff. Wounded a couple of other people, too."

"We just heard about the sheriff from the Hallcomb boys. We didn't know about anybody else. Where's Kirby?" I was afraid I knew better, but I added, "You have him in jail?"

Isom shook his head and turned, beckoning. The people had moved out into the street as if to block us, but they stepped back and made room as Isom led us fifty yards to the open livery barn. Beneath a brush arbor, on a pile of hay, lay an old gray blanket. I knew what was under it and did not want to look as Isom pulled it back, but I forced myself.

Kirby must have been shot twenty times.

Isom said, "I wouldn't have had it happen for the world. But the way things were, people didn't have a choice. He had to be stopped."

I supposed he was right, but the grief and the anger and the cold nausea all came up on me just the same. They did not have to shoot him to pieces.

"Who-all did it, Branch?" I asked.

He let the blanket down gently. "All I can tell you is that I was not among them. Don't ask me to tell you more."

"Thomas will ask you."

"I hoped you would head him off, Sawyer. If he comes in here boiling for trouble, he'll find it. This town is in a black mood. I'll have a wagon fetched around so you can take Kirby home. Try and keep Thomas away from here. Please!"

It was hard to realize this was the same Branch Isom I had known so long ago. There had been a time he would have stood in the middle of the street and dared Thomas to come. Now he was begging me for peace.

"I have worked hard to get this town a respectable name, to live down what it used to be," he continued. "Now we have a railroad coming in. We don't want any more trouble here."

I said, "Bring the wagon."

The hostility of the people was silent but as real as a pit of rattlesnakes. Juan and Marco and I lifted Kirby into the wagon and covered him with the blanket. Nobody offered to help. Juan climbed onto the wagon seat. Isom handed him the lines and looked back at me. "For God's sake, Sawyer, keep Thomas away from here!"

A shout lifted from the far end of the street. My heart came to my throat as I saw a group of riders coming, fanned out in a wedge. Townspeople pulled back to the porches and wooden sidewalks, making room.

"It's too late," I said. "He's here."

Thomas' face was gray as he rode up the street. He stopped before the wagon, his jaw set like a block of stone. He stared at the covered form. The voice did not sound like his.

"Pull back the blanket."

Juan started to obey. I reined my horse in close and caught the corner of the blanket. "No, Thomas. You don't want to, not here."

Thomas' eyes cut me like a knife. He bumped his horse's shoulder against mine and pushed me aside. He lifted the blanket for himself. His cheekbones seemed to bulge. His eyes glassed over. When he turned, he was in a wild rage. He fixed his gaze on Branch Isom.

"Who did it?"

Branch Isom had lost color, but he did not back away. "Your boy killed the sheriff, Thomas. He was shooting up the town."

"I want to know who-all did this to him!"

"Nobody wanted this. I know how you feel, Thomas; I've got a boy of my own. If there'd been any other way . . ."

"Damn you, Isom! I don't want to take on this whole town, but I'll do it if I don't see the men who did this to my boy. You call them out here!"

Thomas' hand was on the butt of his pistol. My throat went dry as I looked at the cowboys he had brought with him . . . *gringos*, Mexicans . . . he had never made much distinction so long as they did their work. They were scared, most of them, looking into the guns of half that town. But they also appeared determined. If Thomas said the word, war would explode then and there. Seeing those wild and ungiving eyes, I was sure Thomas was about to give that word. We were badly outnumbered, but not one man of Thomas' crew pulled back or showed any sign of the feather. No less was tolerated of a man in those days; he was expected to be loyal to the brand he worked for and die for it, if circumstances carried him to that. Marco and Juan and I were unarmed, but I knew we would be shot down with the rest.

I said, "Thomas, Kirby was in the wrong."

Thomas did not respond.

Cold sweat glistened on Branch Isom's round, reddish face. "For the love of God, Thomas, look around you. There's two men dead already. You pull that gun and there may be twenty."

"You'll be the first one."

Isom's shoulders slumped. I thought he had given up. Then he said something I would never have expected. "Shoot me, then, if it'll satisfy you. Shoot me and let my town alone."

Thomas seethed. "I should have shot you twenty years ago. I had the chance, once. I've always been sorry I didn't do it."

Fear was plain in Isom's eyes, but he did not back away.

Thomas said, "You're not armed."

"I haven't carried a gun in years."

"Get one."

Isom brought himself to look in Thomas' terrible eyes. "No. You'll have to shoot me as I am."

Thomas drew the pistol halfway out of the holster, and thirty men brought up their guns. Isom stood watching him, his face frozen. He did not plead. He did not move his feet.

Thomas seemed oblivious to the guns raised against him. He never took his eyes from Isom's face. "One last time, Isom, tell me who killed him."

Isom said nothing. He held his eyes to Thomas', and after a long moment it was Thomas who looked away.

"Whoever you are," he shouted to the town, "whoever shot my boy, come out here and face me!"

Nobody answered. Nobody came.

Thomas let the pistol slip back into the holster. His gaze ran the length of the street, touching on every man. His voice rose so that everybody on the street could hear. "Then you *all* killed him. This whole town killed him, the way it's killed almost everybody I ever cared about in my life. This town killed my father. It killed my brother, and my mother, and my wife. Now it's killed my son!"

He paused. I could not hear a sound except the nervous movement of horses, the squeak of saddle leather.

Thomas stood in his stirrups and raised his fist over his head. In a voice that must have carried out onto the prairie he shouted, "This town has killed the last of mine. I swear by Almighty God, I am going to kill this town!"

He reined his horse around and moved back down the street. The crowd melted aside as the Red Sea must have parted for Moses. The cowboys, much relieved, turned their horses and followed him. I felt weak enough to fall out of my saddle. I nodded at Juan, still on the wagon. "Let's go."

I tried not to look at the townspeople, though I had to give one more glance to Branch Isom. He looked drained and limp and incredibly sad. But he never moved.

We buried Kirby in the family plot on the slope, beside the uncle whose unlucky name he bore. Staring at the weathered stone with the first Kirby's name on it, I thought of the many ways in which the two young men had been alike, impetuous, even wild. But the first Kirby had sought nothing more than fun; there had never been anything little about him, or mean.

Mostly I watched Thomas during the ceremony. Laura held his arm at first, trying to give him comfort. But Thomas seemed to draw away, shutting her out. He stood alone. Laura put her arms around Katy, and the two women wept quietly together.

As the minister finished his final prayer, the little crowd dutifully came by in an informal line and expressed their condolences, the custom of the country, a burden the bereaved were expected to endure stoically. Thomas received them with a stony face and a mechanical manner. The last two men to come up were strangers, each wearing a circular badge with a star in its center. One of them asked, "Could we talk with you a minute, Mister Canfield? Somewhere in private?"

Thomas blinked, taken by surprise. His stony look returned. "This is private enough."

The Rangers were ill at ease. The spokesman said, "We've been sent from San Antonio to keep the peace."

"It's a little late, don't you think?"

"We were sent to be sure nothing more happens. Our orders are to do anything necessary to see that it doesn't. Anything."

Thomas' eyes narrowed. His gaze dropped to the pistols both men wore prominently on their hips. "If I were going to shoot up Stonehill, I would have done it yesterday."

"You made a threat about killing the town."

"I intend to," he said coldly. "And there won't be one thing you or anybody can do about it."

He turned from the Rangers as if they were not there. He drew me away from the crowd and asked, "Do you have any idea where that railroad man is, that Ashcroft?"

I thought he might be in Stonehill, but there was no way to know except by going and seeing for myself. I did not want to go to Stonehill.

Thomas said, "Please, Reed, go for *me*. Go for Kirby. Find him if you have to ride all the way to San Antonio. Fetch him here."

I began to sense some of what was in his mind. It made me feel sad. "Thomas, you don't really want to do this."

He looked me in the eyes, and I could not hold against his stare. "If you don't go, I will," he said.

It was ticklish, riding into Stonehill. My skin prickled at the sight of the town. Its streets seemed deserted. Most of the people were at the cemetery, showing the sheriff's family their support at the funeral. The Canfield ranch had few friends left in that place, but I sought out one of those few who might know something of the railroad man. He told me Ashcroft had departed Stonehill in anger the day before the shooting, bound for San Antonio.

I spent the night on the road, stopping for a few hours' sleep on the ground. I found Ashcroft in the Menger Hotel bar, where he had been paying homage to the state of Kentucky for most of three days. He was in little mood to talk to anyone from Stonehill or its environs. "Robbers and thieves, all of them," he grumbled, "hoping to enrich themselves at the expense of the railroad."

I explained that I had nothing to do with Stonehill but represented Thomas Canfield instead. His resentment survived intact.

"I suppose Mr. Canfield has decided to sell us a right-of-way and enrich himself at our expense also."

He had no intention of coming with me. I thought of force but rejected that because I knew San Antonio had a high ratio of policemen to citizens and would not tolerate that kind of behavior. I sat with him in the bar and plied him with bourbon until he went to sleep in his chair. Had he died then and there, the undertaker would have had nothing to do but place him in a box. I rented a carriage from a wagonyard, loaded him into it and started for the ranch. We had put many miles behind us before he rallied enough to realize he was on the road. He cursed me for twelve kinds of blackguard and threatened me with a lifetime in Huntsville penitentiary, but he had no wish to walk back to San Antonio. It was far past midnight when we reached the ranch, and he was cold sober.

Thomas dressed and met Ashcroft in the front parlor. He got right to the point.

"Mister Ashcroft, are you still interested in a right-of-way across my ranch?"

Ashcroft blustered, "Kidnapping me and dragging me out here is a poor way of doing business. If you think we are going to pay you some exorbitant price—"

Thomas did not let him finish. He leaned forward, into the man's face. His eyes had the look of a hawk at the kill. "I'll *give* you the land!"

He had Ashcroft's total attention, and mine. "Give it?"

"With conditions. I want you to route your rails as far from Stonehill as you can."

Ashcroft blinked a few times. "We need Stonehill."

"No you don't. If you need a town, build one. I'll give you the land for that too."

Ashcroft was momentarily shocked beyond speech. He stared at me as if he did not quite believe, as if he feared he might still be drunk and dreaming all this.

"I don't understand."

"You don't have to understand. All you have to do is agree."

Ashcroft mumbled, benumbed, "I am not certain I can speak for the board of directors . . ."

"To hell with the directors. Just say *yes.*"

Ashcroft was still looking for a catch but could not see one.

"Well, yes," he sputtered. "Of course, yes."

Not until that moment had I realized the full depth of Thomas' hatred, the sacrifice he was willing to make for revenge. I could not remember that he had ever sold a square foot of land; once he had gotten hold of it, he had held it fiercely. Now he was giving it away.

I stared at the fire in Thomas' eyes, and at the bewilderment in Ashcroft's.

I said, "There's a passage in the Bible, Thomas. 'Vengeance is mine, saith the Lord.'"

He shook his head.

"No. This time, it's *mine.*"

CHAPTER 9

The surveyors had been working their way across the ranch for several days before the people of Stonehill got their first inkling. Quickly Branch Isom consulted other community leaders and offered the railroad the bonus Ashcroft had originally asked. When he refused it, they raised thirty thousand more. It was too late. The railroad had signed the contracts with Thomas and saved itself thousands of dollars in right-of-way investment. This was at Thomas' expense, of course, but if he ever gave the cost a moment's notice he betrayed no sign.

Stonehill should have had a long, slow period of grace before its decline; railroads are not built overnight. But dry rot set in with the realization that the wheels were in motion and that there would be no reversal of plans for going around. Though freight lines still passed through the town, and would until the trains were running—and though wagon service would still be needed to the border and to towns that lay south and north of the railroad—the heart quickly was gone from Stonehill. One by one, businesses began to be boarded up or moved away.

Branch Isom tried desperately to hold the place together. He argued that branch lines serving the railroad would still bring commerce to Stonehill streets, that many ranchers and farmers would still choose Stonehill as their place to trade. He pointed out that it was the county seat and still had the courthouse. He even made rash guarantees of financial support in a desperate effort to keep his town alive.

The railroad platted a new town on its right-of-way. A few buildings were up even before the rails reached it, an evidence of more faith than I could have mustered. There was some question about a proper name. The railroad people first suggested it be called Canfield, but Thomas rejected that notion as self-advertisement. He wanted to name it Brozekville, for Maria's family. The railroad people thought that sounded too foreign. When Washington approved the post office, the chosen name turned out to be Ashcroft City. Thomas fumed over that a few days, but the cause was lost. One area always foreign to him was politics.

He still carried weight with the railroad, however, and the power of veto over who could buy property in Ashcroft City. At first he would allow no one from Stonehill to own property in his town. But soon he realized that the way to drain Stonehill and leave Branch Isom presiding over a dead town was to give people there another place to go. Once he made up his mind to that, and swallowed the fact that he would have to tolerate at least some of the Stonehill citizens in the new town, he saw to it that the lots in Ashcroft City were sold cheaply enough for anybody to buy one. He screened the buyers, turning away some of Stonehill's more notorious denizens. He put it down as an ironclad rule that no property would be sold to Branch Isom or any of his kin.

Once the tracks were laid through town and stretched westward toward San Antonio, the exodus from Stonehill turned into a stampede. Thomas financed several of his cowboys who had higher ambitions. They invested in teams and heavy timber-moving equipment, which they converted to the moving of frame buildings. It was no great engineering feat to jack up a small structure, put runners under it and move it the ten or twelve miles from Stonehill to Ashcroft City.

Thomas was getting what he wanted, but he never smiled. I sensed it was not enough.

One day while we were working cattle on the south part of the ranch, not far from Stonehill, one of the chuck-wagon mules became entangled in the traces, and the wagon fetched up in a gully with a broken wheel. I took the wheel to Stonehill to have a wheelwright fix it. The sight of the place hit me like a fist between the eyes. It looked as if half the houses were gone, jacked up and hauled away, leaving nothing but the cedar-post foundations on which they had stood standing like broken ribs of a wolf-eaten carcass. Most of the business still operating belonged to Branch Isom; the other storekeepers and artisans for the most part had left, bound for Ashcroft City or San Antonio or points west. Traffic was so slow that chickens scratched in the middle of the street.

The only smithy and wheelwright still operating worked in a shop which serviced the Isom freight wagons. He assured me he could get to my wheel right away; he had nothing else to do.

I walked down the street past empty stores, past empty lots where stores had stood. I stepped into a bar and had a drink. The bartender seemed glad to see me, though he knew full well who I was and who I represented. He and I were the only people in the place.

The drink seemed sour, and I did not tarry long. I walked on down to Isom's big mercantile store, where a lone farm wagon stood out front. I was tempted to go in but didn't know what, if anything, I could say to Branch Isom. Suddenly he was standing in the door, staring at me in surprise. I could not pretend I had not seen him. I said howdy, not knowing anything that seemed appropriate.

"You'd just as well come on in, Reed Sawyer," he said. "No use standing out in the sun."

I walked into the store and stood awkwardly, making small talk about the weather and how we needed a rain. I don't think Isom paid much attention to what I said, any more than I paid to his make-talk efforts. Finally I blurted out what was really on my mind. "Goddammit, Branch, I'm sorry."

Isom went silent awhile, then said, "I guess it would've been better if Thomas and I had shot it out with each other a long time ago. Whichever way it went, it would've saved a lot of people a lot of grief."

"Why don't you just leave here, Branch, and start over someplace else? You could do good in San Antonio."

"This is my town. Everything I own is tied up here. I have no choice but to ride it to the end of the line."

I was about to say it might be a short ride, but I kept that observation to myself. I said, "It's not much of a future for your boy."

"James will be all right. He has a good position in a bank in San Antonio. He's a smart boy, even if he *is* mine. You watch, he'll be a wealthy man someday. They'll put up a statue of him in a San Antonio park."

I caught that pride in his eyes, the kind of pride Thomas had never been able to have in Kirby. Strange, I thought, how the seed can sometimes produce a tree so much different than the one it came from.

I told Isom I had not seen his son in a long time. He said, "He's home for a visit." I heard a jingle of trace chains through the open back door. Isom turned an ear in that direction. "I'll bet that's him now."

In a moment a pair of shadows fell through the open door. A girl entered, followed by a slender young man. My mouth dropped open.

"Katy!"

Katy Canfield was so startled that she dropped her purse. James Isom stooped to pick it up and place it back in her hands. She stared at me with big, pretty brown eyes, disconcerted. "Uncle Reed, what're you doing here?"

"I'm a grown man; I can go where I want to. But you're not a grown woman yet, not quite. Your daddy have any idea where you are?"

She took a minute to answer. "Mother knows."

Somehow that did not surprise me. Kirby's raising, such as it was, had been mostly Thomas' doing. But the raising of Katy had been left mostly to Laura. Katy and Laura had always drawn together, two women combining their strength against a man's world of land and cattle and commerce.

Katy had much of the look of the mother she barely remembered. But I could not recall that I had ever seen so much trouble in Maria's eyes.

I said, "This is the last place in the world your daddy would want to see you."

"He's wrong; you know that."

"But he *is* your daddy."

James Isom touched Katy's arm, and she leaned to him for support. I had known they both went to school in San Antonio, and I remembered the time James had brought her home. But *this* . . . The idea had never entered my mind.

There was no pretending I had not seen. "How serious is it between you two?"

James said evenly, "It's serious, Mister Sawyer."

I could see Katy's answer in her eyes. She said, "Uncle Reed, do you have to tell him?"

I studied the pair, clinging together. James was a clean-looking young man, his face appearing honest and without guile. He said, "I love her, Mister Sawyer."

Branch Isom told me, "It's been none of my doing. I've tried to talk them out of it. But if you've ever been in love, Reed, I guess you know how little good it does to talk."

My stomach drew into a knot. I could remember.

Katy touched my arm. "Uncle Reed, if you think he has to know, let me be the one to tell him. Please, give me a little time. I'll have to find a way of my own."

I said, "You kids know he'll find out sooner or later . . . someday, some way. But it won't come from me."

They drew against one another, and Katy thanked me.

<hr>

Though much of Stonehill's population wound up in Ashcroft City, it would be a mistake to think of that place simply as Stonehill transplanted. The building of the railroad, a round-house and service facilities brought in a lot of new people, enough to give Ashcroft City a different political complexion. Even while Stonehill was still the county seat, Ashcroft City began electing most of the county officers. And it was not meant that Stonehill keep the county courthouse forever. In the Ashcroft City plat was a block in the center of town, reserved for a new county courthouse. When Ashcroft City had the political power firmly in its grip, an election was called, to decide whether to move the county seat. Branch Isom and his hangers-on tried hard, electioneering diligently among the country folk. But the issue was lost long before election day. Ashcroft City carried five to three. A bond issue was passed for a new stone courthouse, bigger and better than the old frame structure in Stonehill. In due course the building was completed. The only task remaining was the transfer of the county records.

This process, though it had the full backing of law, had caused bloodshed in several old Texas counties as they outgrew their original county seats and attempted a move. The ballot was one thing; possession was another.

The sheriff and one of his deputies, Ashcroft City men both, were met at the courthouse one day by a group of armed Stonehill men who blocked their entrance and served notice they did not intend to allow movement of the county records. They denied the lawmen access to their own office. The sheriff went directly to Thomas, who called in all his cowboys. I could see a grim satisfaction in Thomas' eyes as he stood on the steps of his house with the sheriff, the rest of us spread out on the ground. The sheriff swore all of us in as deputies. We rode together to Ashcroft City, where he swore in enough townsmen to give him a posse of sixty or seventy.

It was my bad luck to have been at the headquarters at all that day. I had begun trying to take care of my own business, my own cattle, and had even built a small frame house on my place. Personally I didn't much give a damn which town had the courthouse. I tried to tell Thomas so, but as always when he had his mind set on something he did not listen. He just nodded, taking it for granted that I was agreeing with him on everything.

I should simply have ridden away, but Thomas still had that power to pull people to him, and I was not immune from it.

We trooped down the wagon road to Stonehill like a ragged cavalry unit, guns bristling. A lot of the younger men were bragging about what they would do if it came to a fight, hoping it would. Pleasure showed in Thomas' face, too, which fed the uneasiness growing in me. Having been in that other war, I had already enjoyed about all this type of conflict that I ever wanted.

Behind us rumbled half a dozen empty freight wagons, enough to haul not only the county records but most of the courthouse furniture. Thomas and I rode up front, with the sheriff. Thomas said, "This is about what I expected from Branch Isom. If he puts up a fight, I want everybody to remember: he's mine."

I should have been angry at Stonehill for its resistance to the law, but I found myself angering at Thomas instead. I said, "The Texas Rangers could handle this, and nobody would get hurt."

Thomas declared solemnly, "We don't need the Rangers, or anybody else from outside. This is our business."

I let my exasperation rise into my voice. "You'll never rest easy till you've killed him!"

Thomas flashed me a look of surprise, which turned into doubt. His anger arose to meet mine. He said, "Reed, something has been gnawing at you lately. You've been partners with me for a long time, but if you've wanting to leave . . ."

I had not fully realized it, but suddenly I knew that I did. It was time to make a full break, as I had intended to years earlier when he married Laura.

I said, "I know Branch Isom a lot better than you do. At least let me go talk to him first. Maybe there won't be a need for anybody to get hurt."

His anger built. "You *don't* know Branch Isom. You never did."

"You just know him as he used to be. People change. He doesn't want to be your enemy; he hasn't wanted to in a long time. He's just old, and he's tired. Like us."

"I'm not tired." Thomas gave me a long, hard study. "If that's the way you feel, maybe you'd better ride on ahead and stand up with him."

"If the time comes that I feel like I should, I will."

I half expected him to explode, but instead he cooled. The look in his eyes was of hurt, of puzzlement.

After a time he said, "You don't mean that, Reed. We've been together too long."

"Like I said, people change. *You've* changed, and most of it hasn't been any improvement."

I watched him as we moved into Stonehill. I do not think he had seen the place since the day Kirby was killed. I do not believe he was fully prepared for the shell that Stonehill had become. It was as if a tornado had skipped through and had taken half the buildings away, damaging many of the rest.

"Good God!" he exclaimed.

I told him, "You *said* you'd kill this town. You've done it."

"I haven't killed *all* of it. *He's* still here."

We rode straight for the old courthouse. Its two stories had been built originally of green lumber so that the siding was beginning to twist and curl in places. The long comb along the roof had a gentle sag in the middle, like an old horse needing retirement to green pasture. But lined in front of it were fifteen or twenty men with pistols, rifles and shotguns in their hands. They were a pitiful remnant compared to the force Stonehill might once have offered; we had them badly outnumbered.

The sheriff made a wide motion with his hand, signaling his posse to spread out. He rode in front, his hands high against his chest and far from his weapons, reins in the left hand, a sheaf of papers in the right. He tried to pick out the leader of the Stonehill defense. Branch Isom was not among them.

I glanced at Thomas. His eyes betrayed disappointment. Then they lifted. I swung around to see what he had seen. Branch Isom was coming out onto the porch of his big house on the hill.

The sheriff was saying, "Gentlemen, you all know who I am. You know the authority I represent. I have here the official canvass of the vote, making Ashcroft City the county seat. I also have here an order from the district court that all county records be duly removed to Ashcroft City. I ask that you step aside and let the law peacefully take its course."

Half the men talked at once, or tried to. This group had no leader. That could be good, or it could be bad. A leaderless group of angry men was unpredictable.

The sheriff, still in his saddle, made a move toward the courthouse. Three men jumped forward and grabbed the reins and bit. He shouted, "In the name of the law . . ."

Thomas drew his pistol. Branch Isom was running down the hill toward us, waving his hands. The commotion around the sheriff was so loud I could not hear what Isom was shouting. I put my hand firmly over Thomas', pressing down against his pistol.

"Wait," I said. He struggled angrily to free his hand, but I held tight.

Isom's face was flushed. He breathed heavily from the exertion of the run. Age and soft living had sapped the strength and endurance of his youth. "Sheriff," he said urgently, "please hold off a minute. Let me talk to these men."

Through gritted teeth Thomas said, "We don't care to listen to you, Isom."

The sheriff turned in a fury that surprised me. "Mister Canfield," he said, "*I* am in charge here."

Thomas said, "The hell you are." He tried again to raise the pistol, but I pressed it hard against the horn of his saddle. He cursed me.

Isom turned his back on us and addressed the men who had chosen to defend Stonehill.

"Friends, I asked you before. I *plead* with you now. The law is with them. They have you outnumbered. Even if you beat them today they'll be back tomorrow with more. They'll bring the Rangers, or even the army. Give it up now, and let's not have anybody die. Too many have died already for lost causes."

Most of them seemed to be listening to him. Perhaps they were looking for an excuse to back away from a fight they could readily see they would lose. But it seemed to me they were listening to him with respect, the way men in this town once listened to old Linden Hines.

It came to me with a sudden jolt that Branch Isom, even in his wild younger days, had respected Linden Hines. He had respected him so much that—perhaps unconsciously—he had taken the old man's place.

Isom saw the men's hesitation, their doubt. He pounced on it.

"Tobe Haney, you have two good kids. You want to take a chance on dying now, when they need you the most? Bill, who's going to take care of your old mother? This courthouse means very little to her, but you mean all there is."

Thomas stared at Isom in disbelief and deep disappointment. He had wanted Isom to be the ringleader here, not the peacemaker. I let go of the pistol. Thomas burned me with a look of resentment.

He had watched Branch Isom so intently that he had not noticed James following his father down from the big house. Now James stood beside Branch, saying nothing but lending his silent support. Thomas studied him. I saw the sudden stiffness when recognition came. Thomas' jaw hardened.

He knew, I realized. Somehow, he knew.

The fuse still sputtered, but Branch Isom had pulled it from the powder. The Stonehill men began to draw aside, muttering grudgingly but without violence. The sheriff climbed the short steps and threw open the courthouse doors. He signaled for the wagons to be brought up. He was suddenly in a hurry, wanting to be done with this before someone fired the fuse again. The Ashcroft City men marched into the courthouse without fanfare, without cheering. A few were probably disappointed about the avoidance of a fight, but I think the majority were relieved whether they would ever admit it or not; the sight of the other side with guns in their hands had taken a lot of the romance out of the showdown.

Branch Isom moved closer to Thomas. "All right, you've won." Bitterness edged his voice, but resignation was there, too. "What little is left of my town, you'll be hauling away in those wagons."

Thomas seemed not to hear. His eyes were on young Isom. They were the hawk eyes I dreaded so much. He said, "You'd be Branch Isom, Jr., wouldn't you?"

"James Isom," the young man quietly corrected him.

"Well, Branch Isom, Jr., my quarrel with your father is an old one. My quarrel with you is new. You know what I'm talking about?"

James' eyes did not waver. "I guess I do."

"I intend it to stop, now! I'll send her to Europe, if I have to. And I'll send you to hell!"

Thomas cut his gaze back to Branch. "I had a son. You remember how I lost him. If you don't want to lose yours, you'd better talk to him!"

He pulled hard on the reins, turning his horse half around. He stopped and looked at me. "You have something to say?"

I did. "You'd have killed half the men here, just to settle your own private feud."

"Yes," he said flatly, "I would have. You coming?"

My stomach was cold. I said, "No."

"Stay here, then. Stay with Branch Isom."

I found myself giving voice to a notion that had been rising in me. "*He's* not Branch Isom, not anymore. *You* are!"

What I said never reached him, not to the point that he understood. He shrugged. "Suit yourself," he said, and left there in a long trot, his cowboys following him. I watched them until they were on the trail, then I turned and headed for the saloon.

I never had much luck solving my problems in a whiskey glass. When the glass was empty the problems were still there, as big as ever. I nursed a couple of slow drinks, however, trying to decide what to do next. I did not lack for a place to go. My ranch was nowhere nearly so large as Thomas', but it was mine. I had gone there often to see after my cattle, sometimes staying several days. But always I had gone "home" afterward. "Home" had always been Thomas' place.

I knew it never would be again.

I heard horses on the street occasionally but paid little attention, mulling over my own problems. I became aware of a man standing in the open doorway, blocking much of the light. "Reed?" he called. "Reed Sawyer?"

I was startled to see Branch Isom there, a rifle in his hand. My heart bumped with the thought that the rifle was for me, because I had ridden into town with Thomas' invading army.

Urgently Isom said, "Reed Sawyer, I need your help."

The whiskey had gone to my head a little. Whiskey always had a tendency to make me sullen, one reason I drank so little of it. At that moment I was mad at everybody. "The hell you say."

"Reed," he said, "you've got little cause to look on me as a friend, but at least I hope you don't see me as your enemy."

The whiskey's glow began to fade. "What's your trouble?"

He stepped closer. For the first time I saw a cut at the corner of his mouth, a bruise starting to purple. "It's James. That fool boy has gone to the Canfield ranch to get that girl. I tried to stop him."

I was cold sober. "Thomas'll kill him!"

"Not if I can get there first. You have any influence over Thomas?"

I shook my head. "*Nobody* has any influence over Thomas."

"I wish you'd come along and try. I don't want to kill him, but I'll do it to keep that crazy bastard from killing my boy."

In my haste to get up from the table I turned over the bottle. It fell to the floor and went rolling, spilling whiskey. In a few long strides I was out of the place and into the saddle, riding out of town in a hard lope. I had to spur to keep Isom from pulling far out in front of me.

At times we could glimpse James at some distance ahead. He had seen us and knew we would try to stop him, so he held his lead. When we speeded up, he speeded up. We could not run the horses long at a time, or they would not endure to take us to the ranch headquarters. We would lope awhile, then slow to a trot to let them catch their wind. I told Isom there was a chance Thomas would not be at home. But the tracks along the trail told me Thomas and the cowboys had come this way ahead of us.

James arrived at the Canfield house a few minutes before we did. That was more than time enough. As we rode through the open gate of the outer corral, I saw someone fighting on the broad porch.

Isom's face twisted in fear. He shouted vainly against the wind. "Wait! Wait!"

Someone fell backward off of the high steps. It had to be James, for Thomas stood on the porch, pistol in his hand. Katy struggled with him. As we spurred up I could hear her screaming, pleading with him. Laura was there too, trying to hold Thomas' arm. He gave her a rough push. Laura stumbled and fell backward over a chair. Thomas pulled free of his daughter and shoved her violently. She fell over Laura. Thomas started down the steps toward James, the pistol pointed.

"Canfield!" Branch Isom shouted. He jumped from his horse and sprinted defensively toward his son. James was on one knee. I knew at a glance that he was not armed. He had not come here to kill; he had probably realized that if he brought a gun he might be forced to use it.

Thomas swung the pistol toward Branch Isom. I was off my horse and running toward him. "Thomas, don't!"

Thomas fired. Branch Isom stumbled, his hat spinning from his head. He pitched to the ground. The rifle clattered from his hands. He had not had time to pull the trigger.

Thomas' face was a roaring fire. The pistol had leaped in recoil, and he lowered it to fire again. I managed to grab his arm.

"For God's sake, Thomas, come to your senses!"

I had never realized how powerful he was, especially with the fury pounding hot. He flung me backward, off balance. I saw the pistol swinging at me and tried vainly to throw myself out of its path. If my hat had not cushioned it, the heavy gun barrel would probably have broken my skull. I felt my face slam against the ground, and dirt was in my eyes. I raised up, trying to clear my throbbing head.

Now instead of Branch trying to protect his son, James rushed to his father.

"No, Mister Canfield! Please don't shoot him again!"

Red and white flashes went off like fireworks before my eyes, and my head pounded. In spite of that, I saw Katy run down the steps and across the yard. She picked up the fallen rifle as her father raised the muzzle of his pistol against James.

Cold dread crawled up my back. Katy was about to kill her father. I said something akin to prayer, rolled onto my side and drew my six-shooter. As Thomas half turned, steadying his pistol, I squeezed the trigger. The recoil wrenched it from my weak hand. Through the gray smoke I saw Thomas stagger, drop to his knees, then sink awkwardly onto one shoulder.

Katy stared at him in horror, the rifle unfired but pointed at him.

Laura cried out and ran down the steps, taking them two at a time. Katy lowered the rifle, her eyes wide in shock. I believe that for a moment she thought she had shot her father.

Legs shaky, James hurried to her and took her in his arms. The rifle slipped into the dust.

Laura dropped to her knees and threw her arms around Thomas, pulling him against her. "Thomas! Thomas!"

He groaned, so I knew he was not dead. I glanced at Branch Isom. He was trying to push himself to a sitting position. Blood ran down the side of his face from the crease Thomas' bullet had given him. James pulled away from Katy and went to his father's side, crying out in relief that Branch was not dead.

Katy stood alone, staring in disbelief at her fallen father.

Laura hugged Thomas and begged him not to die. I managed to get my feet under me and stagger to Thomas' side. I slumped to my knees and tore his shirt open. I had put a bullet into his shoulder.

"Branch Isom," Thomas mumbled. "Seems like I'll never kill him. He got me after all."

I did not want to tell him, but I knew I had to.

"It wasn't Isom. *I* shot you."

He seemed to have trouble seeing me clearly. He could not reconcile himself to what I had said. "You're lying. It was Isom."

"It was me. I had to, Thomas. You went crazy."

He shook his head weakly, not accepting.

I said, "If I hadn't, Katy would have. I couldn't let her do that."

Thomas turned his face from me, searching for his daughter. She had not moved. He blinked, trying to bring her to focus.

"Katy . . . you'd have shot me?"

Firmly she said, "I was about to, Papa."

Thomas closed his eyes. He made no sound, but he was weeping.

By this time a dozen cowboys had come running. It took some strong talking on my part and Katy's to keep them from killing the two Isoms on the spot. They listened to Katy more than they listened to me. They had to, for they saw her eyes, the fierce eyes of Thomas Canfield.

The Fernandez brothers fetched a team and wagon. We managed to clot the blood with flour and bind Thomas up enough to hold him. I was lying when I assured Laura that he was going to live. At the time, I did not really believe it. But after Marco and Juan lifted him onto the blankets in the wagon bed and we started for town with him, I began to hope. Laura knelt beside him, oblivious to the bouncing of the vehicle on the rough road. "Hold on, Thomas," she pleaded. "Please don't leave me."

I had not heard her call him anything but "Mister Canfield" in years.

Katy remained with James and his father. Branch was having trouble standing without support. The last thing I heard him say as we left was to his son and Katy: "You crazy kids. The whole world to choose from, and you had to pick one another."

The doctor said later that if it had taken us much longer to get Thomas to town, he would not have lived. Even as it was, he would suffer from a bad shoulder for however many more years the Lord saw fit to allow him.

I waited on the doctor's porch until Laura came out, weary and red-eyed, to tell me he was awake. She went in with me and sat in the cane-bottomed straight-chair where she had been from the first.

Thomas was pale and sick at his stomach from the chloroform, but his eyes locked on me with a challenge.

"I suppose you've come to apologize," he said.

"No," I told him.

He was disappointed. "You still think I was wrong."

"If I hadn't thought so, I wouldn't have shot you."

He chewed on that awhile, not liking it. "That wasn't a lie, about Katy fixing to shoot me?"

"She was about to. I couldn't let her do that, Thomas. I couldn't let her live the rest of her life knowing she had killed her own father."

"But *you* could live with it?"

"Yes. We used to be friends, Thomas. But I could have done it." I watched the hurt crowd into his eyes. I added, "Lucky for you I never was much of a shot."

He lay silent awhile. "Have you seen Katy?"

I hated to tell him. "She and James went over to New Silesia. They're talking to the priest about marrying them." I waited a minute before I told him the rest of it. "They asked me to stand up for them. I said I would."

Tears started in Thomas' eyes. "She didn't even come to see me."

"She was here. She stayed until she knew you were going to be all right. That's something, at least."

He closed his eyes. "The bitterest thing of all is to know she would have killed me for that boy . . . an *Isom*."

"He's a good boy, Thomas, better than you or me. You'll see that, someday."

"Isom." He spoke the name as if it were a curse. It *had* been, for much of his life. Acceptance would take time, a lot of time, for "give" was not in Thomas' nature. But ultimately he would have no choice. I suppose he realized that too, because somehow he seemed an old man, vulnerable, dependent.

He said with more despair than hope, "Katy'll come back to me, someday."

I told him, "She's got a Canfield stubbornness about her. You'll have to bend."

Dying would probably be easier. I could only hope he had it in him to bend.

I got up to go. He called for me to stay. I told him I had business of my own to look after.

He pleaded, "I wish you wouldn't, Reed. With Katy gone, and you gone, who have I got left?"

Laura sat staring at him, biting her lip to keep from speaking. A prayer was in her eyes. Up to that minute, I guess I had always hoped there might someday be a chance for me in her life.

I said, "Open your eyes, Thomas. God knows you don't deserve her—you never did—but you've always had somebody."

She reached out to him. He turned his head and looked at her a long time, then slowly raised his hand to hers.

I left them there together and walked out onto the porch, trying to blink away the blurring as the sun hit me in the eyes.